BLACK WATERS

Thank you
for the hospitality

Best Besuch

BLACK WATERS

BOOK I OF THE CARSON GRIFFIN SERIES

DAVID H. HANKS

www.mascotbooks.com

Black Waters

For more information, please contact:
Mascot Books
620 Herndon Parkway #320
Herndon, VA 20170
info@mascotbooks.com

Library of Congress Control Number: 2017916431

CPSIA Code: PBANG1117A
ISBN-13: 978-1-68401-440-8

Printed in the United States

I would like to acknowledge my mentor,
Ann K. Fisher, of Creative Editing Services.

I would like to dedicate this book to my wife, Wynne, and our children: H. Taylor, Bryan, and Laura Dee.

CHAPTER 1

Explanations exceeded sincerity when locals told stories about the caves and tunnels of Idrija, Slovenia. Residents of the small mining town described a murderous dwarf who waits for unsuspecting miners to pass his nest in the oldest mercury mine in the world.

An Idrijan tub maker first found quicksilver in the year 1490, flowing above ground near the main shaft, but this historical tidbit had little to do with Serif Muhammad Rezaabak's current plans. Lowering himself on a spelunking rig down into a dark hole, he moved closer to the deepest cavern of the nearly 400-mile maze of cinnabar-lined tunnels. He loved to climb through the multitude of tunnels – some left by years of mining. Others were natural voids, formed millions of years ago.

Serif was born in Turkey in a small village on the outskirts of Istanbul, along with his brother Reza. Now in their early thirties, the brothers were raised in a family atmosphere of hatred for the entire Western world – its politics and religion. International politics, long abandoned by the brothers, were now a hindrance to their goal of expanding the power of their home country.

Reza stood beneath Serif, guiding his older brother's descent to the smooth floor of a huge cavern, brightly illuminated with tall freestanding floodlights. The football-field-sized cavern was about fifty feet high and had digging-machined walls that were covered with small droplets of mercury, naturally seeping from the reddish tinted rock.

Roaring sounds from ten large ventilation exhaust fans could be heard above their heads, pulling the poisonous vapours of the mercury and radon gas away from the space. Six supply fans powered by a marine-sized gas turbine electric generator drew in air from the top of the mountain above them, their inlet screens camouflaged by a series of empty sheep barns. Beside one of the supply air ducts was a small elevator that Serif and Reza would use to return up to the surface.

Both men picked up a dosimeter from a rack and pinned it to the lab coats they donned after removing their climbing harnesses, then moved toward a controlled area buzzing with activity.

The brothers watched as three scientists manned the controls to a nuclear reactor submerged in a vast pool of clear blue underground water. Engrossed in the 100-megawatt reactor's operation, the scientists ignored their visitors.

"Good morning. How are you?" Serif called out to Dr Regina Kny (Nī). In her late twenties, smart and good-looking, she had earned her PhD in reactor physics from a Canadian university. Kny's specialty was in heavy-water-moderated reactors and plutonium yields from light-water-cooled tank reactors. She headed this clandestine project deep below the earth's surface, which would instantly make her a millionaire when it was completed.

Her two colleagues were both older men from the Yugoslavian nuclear weaponisation program, established by Marshal Tito himself: Drs Mrak and Broz. They once worked at a Serbian test reactor site near Belgrade, learning their plutonium separation skills from scientists brought in from Sweden by Tito's army generals during the 1970s.

Mrak earned his doctorate working with Broz in a think tank, common to some former Soviet countries. Groups of scientists generated theses and awarded each other a PhD in order to keep whatever research centre they happened to be working at supplied with enough money to survive.

"It's cold down here, Serif," Kny said.

Serif's deep voice was smooth and sinister. "Yes, I know, my dear." He smiled slightly.

"We have finished the preliminary testing of the reflector and are ready to take the reactor supercritical," Kny said in her no-nonsense style. "It should generate enough plutonium to produce at least two medium-sized nuclear weapons."

Serif walked to the edge of the pool and saw the bluish glow coming from a powerful uranium-fuelled core, currently producing enough heat energy to quickly vaporise the 400,000 litres of water in the pool, should the cooling system trip off line. Ingeniously, the cooling system used a spring-fed underground lake as a heat sink. It was impossible to trace using satellite imagery, and the cool lake water kept the secondary side of the reactor's support systems' heat exchangers at an efficient temperature.

Above the core, Serif could see a large uranium-impregnated graphite cylinder suspended by eight pneumatic pistons – a unique design that was acquired during a black market sell-off of information from Romania's nuclear weapons program in its last year of communist rule. The cylinder was open on both ends and fitted tightly around the core's circumference when it was forced downward by the pistons, creating a neutron reflector that would cause the reactor to go dangerously supercritical. Damage to the core structure would be tremendous, but the weapon's grade plutonium yield would be extremely high when the damaged fuel was recovered.

Serif walked toward Kny, who was standing near a control panel with a reactor and its supporting systems embossed on its protruding metallic shelf, known to the scientists as the panel's apron. The mock reactor's gauges showed withdrawn control rods locked in place and the reactor's thermal power at its maximum value.

"All right, I am ready," Serif said with a nod.

"Everyone to the alternative control room," Kny ordered.

The group took a small passageway, lit with dim yellow lights, that led into another room, far from the reactor hall. The Idrija mercury mine was rich in minerals, including high density lead, which made for a fantastic radiation shield from the reactor – its walls would protect the group during the reactor's power excursion event. They came to a slim panel in a small hole of a room, with droplets of mercury hanging from the ceiling, reflecting a reddish tint caused by the cinnabar ore.

Originally, cinnabar was mined for centuries by the Idrija people to make a high-quality red dye and was so sought after that its miners were sworn to secrecy. Brought to the surface using manpowered sleds, the poisonous resource was heated in clay pots over wood-burning furnaces to remove the mercury from the dye that was then sold all over the world. It brought great wealth to the area, which the local residents used to buy supplies from neighbouring communities. Surviving the harsh winters of the mountains was not easy for them, but their secret was safely guarded until the rise of communism in Yugoslavia.

Tito's gang of extremists brought in new machinery that was used to extract the precious mercury fairly efficiently, creating a market for the poisonous substance. Eventually weapons manufacturers designed a powerful jungle defoliant using the mercury called Agent Orange, utilised during the Vietnam War to clear miles of dense forests. Agent Orange could also be linked to some diseases contracted by US veterans and the indigenous population of the affected war zones in country.

Kny examined the panel to ensure it was now in control of the reflector and the reactor's control system. She looked over at a closed-circuit TV monitor that displayed a picture of the underground reactor hall.

"Dr Broz, drop the reflector," Kny instructed.

"Yes, I understand you want me to drop the reflector," Broz repeated back the orders, as if he was still working for the Yugoslavian military.

"That's correct," Kny said.

Broz pushed a backlit amber button, which turned red upon his release.

The group watched the TV monitor as the reflector dropped at lightning speed to a position encircling the reactor core; water splashed high into the air when the two-ton device entered the pool of heavy water.

Seconds after Broz released the reflector, water once cooling the reactor's internal parts and its nuclear fuel flashed to steam as the thermal power of the nuclear reactor promptly jumped to a catastrophic level.

"Release the boron," Kny ordered.

"Releasing boron injection," Broz replied.

A deafening roar arose from underneath the reactor pool. The small group stood speechless as they watched the closed-circuit TV monitors. Serif attributed the surging sound to four large pumps sending a neutron-capturing poison into the fissioning uranium core. He was confident of Dr Kny's expertise and felt safe. The core's chain reaction was abruptly interrupted as per the scientists' plan, stopping a complete meltdown of the reactor and damage to its containment pool.

"Deploy the reactor pool shields," Kny instructed, her voice calm but firm. "We need to contain the fission fragments inside the pool."

Mrak pulled down a small red lever on the side of the panel, releasing a pneumatic piston-driven set of lead- and polyethylene-coated doors that covered the pool. The water and the poly and lead shielding would now protect the team from a highly radioactive nuclear reactor's damaged core. The shield would allow them to use remote manipulators to process the fuel fragments through Kny's highly innovative plutonium recovery process.

Serif was pleased with the sequence of events, smiling toward Reza as he realised that their plan to generate plutonium from natural uranium fuel was successful. In fact, a great success. It took the terrorists years to gather the reactor-controlling circuits, machines, materials for the reactor, and then to obtain nuclear fuel from the Romanians after their revolution against communism in 1989.

Starving from impoverishment, a few Romanian workers at an established uranium fuel fabrication plant in the Carpathian Mountains sold several tons of uranium pellets to Turkish terrorists on the black market for a few million lei. Ceauşescu's loyalists, wanting to finance a future return to power, were eventually blamed for the stolen nuclear reactor fuel and sentenced to prison. Very few of the pellets were ever actually recovered by the police, who were more interested in feeding their families than locating a load of untraceable uranium pellets on a huge, illicit trafficking market.

Ceauşescu, Romania's former communist leader, had

also made several military equipment deals with Josip Tito before their eventual falling out dissolved the alliance. The old Yugoslavian guard never gave up their efforts to join the two communist entities toward a common goal: to destroy capitalism during the 1980s. Some suspected an old allegiance was rekindled just before the revolution of 1989, when Ceauşescu sent his Romanian liaison to a meeting in Zagreb with Tito's inside man. The equipment, consisting of heat exchangers, pipes, and pumps, was lost in the shuffle – until finding its way into Dr Kny's underground experimental reactor hall.

Radiation monitors in the makeshift reactor hall showed that it was safe to return to the main control panel once the sliding doors were fully interlocked. The team and the two brothers left the alternative control room and made their way back through the dimly lit tunnel to the main reactor hall.

When they arrived in the large cave where the experiment had taken place, they saw that the pool was completely covered with the two thick plates of lead and poly; cooling pumps were still rumbling beneath them and the exhaust ventilation was running at high speed.

"Reza, pick up our gear," Serif said. "We must go."

"I want to stay. It is very interesting, this experiment," Reza replied with a heavy Turkish accent.

Serif's annoyance was obvious, but he quickly realised he could probably travel faster alone. Reza's right leg had been damaged by a land mine when they were young boys, leaving him with a pronounced limp. Jena, their eight-year-old cousin, had stepped onto an Iraqi mine near the south eastern Turkish border. The landmine killed her instantly – sending shrapnel through her tiny body and one molten slug into Reza's thigh.

"Fine, my brother," Serif said. "Dr Kny, we shall be anxiously waiting for your report and the final product."

Looking away from the main panel briefly, Kny nodded to Serif. "We see a positive result in our instrumentation. I will finalise my assessment and bring it to you myself when it is done."

Satisfied, Serif walked back to where he and Reza had descended through the mineshafts and natural tunnels. Strapping on his spelunking harness, he turned on a high-intensity light fastened to his helmet and began his climb back out of the mercury mine – leaving the small elevator for the others.

Serif reached the surface and came out of the mine feeling certain that his master plan would soon be fulfilled. But he also knew he had his work cut out for him. It would take enormous scientific skill, effort, and patience to separate the damaged nuclear material and fashion it into an extraordinarily uncommon fissionable component.

CHAPTER 2

Carson Griffin walked into the Red Lion Café wearing a navy blazer, jeans, and sporting a new pair of climbing boots that he recently wore on a mission for INWA, the International Nuclear Weapons Agency based in Vienna. He located a table near the stage and ordered a cognac in German from a pretty waitress who nodded at him in recognition. Carson smiled back.

The café was established in 1876 and had been frequented by so many smokers over the years that the ceiling and walls had been darkened by a constant deposit of cigarette tar. A baroque melody played softly over an old German sound system, Bach or Beethoven – no, it was Mozart, Carson realised.

Carson felt comfortable in the room full of international travellers. He noticed some sitting at a table near the rear of the espresso bar who were probably Turkish. He was accustomed to distinguishing different nationalities in this particular café, especially patrons who spoke their native language within earshot. Moreover, it was a typical hangout for the Turks, who were in Vienna from time to time on oil-trading business with OPEC. Their home office was located in a five-storey glass and metallic building just across a canal from the Stephansplatz Cathedral.

Carson nodded toward the youngest of a group of three men.

The young man got up and walked over to Carson.

"Long time no see, my friend," the young man said.

Carson smiled and nodded. "Yes, you look as whipped as the first time we met, Haddie."

Hadier Erim scanned the room and quickly turned back to Carson. "I have something that may be of interest."

Politically tied to the reigning government in Turkey by marriage, Hadier was no doubt ready to leak some underhanded transactions that his government wanted to accuse their weaker rivals of committing. Hadier's backers had opponents that were being supported by a terrorist cell, which the INWA had not yet identified. Carson slowly raised his arm and removed his jacket, then laid it over one corner of the rectangular, dark oak table that had a glossy shellac finish.

Hadier slipped a large manila envelope underneath Carson's jacket and left the table. Carson noticed that Hadier looked relieved to have just passed off what he claimed to be important information to an international nuclear inspector.

Carson picked up his jacket, taking the envelope from the table and slipping it into the back of his jeans as he put on his blazer. Leaving the Red Lion Café without touching his drink, Carson made his way to a crowded taxi stand, about a block away. The late model Mercedes smelled of shoe polish and stale cheese.

Carson was always careful to be aware of his surroundings. Wherever he travelled, he continuously scanned the area for a tail or camera – all part of the Agency's special training. Ten blocks from his pick up, Carson got out of his taxi and made his way to the underground subway. It was near midnight, and very few people were riding one of the last trains of the night.

Carson found a seat in the rear of the fourth subway car. German graffiti was sloppily drawn on the wall below a neon sign that flickered brightly "U-1 Leopoldau." One of Vienna's six underground U-bahns, the U-1 was deserted, except for one drunken passenger sitting near the front end of Carson's car. Carson opened the envelope and began to study eight sheets of A4 paper – copies of some kind of blueprint. A moment later, Carson understood what he was looking at – Hadier had turned over a diagram of a medium-sized research reactor that was positioned inside some kind of makeshift deep water cooling pool. The nuclear reactor was too small to produce electrical power and was definitely not going to be used for any gamma or neutron irradiation experiments. Its design was more for producing a lot of nuclear power, quickly – resulting in the production of a mass quantity of weapons-grade plutonium.

The train stopped and a man and a woman, both in their early thirties, got on board. The man sat two rows behind Carson and the woman directly across from him in a pair of facing seats. Putting the document slowly back into its brownish sleeve, Carson stood up, ready to get off at the next stop.

The woman got up from her seat and stood too close to him. "*Guten Abend.*" (Good evening) She smiled provocatively at Carson, who had no interest in talking to her. His mind was filled with thoughts of a clandestine plutonium-generating nuclear reactor that may or may not be real. The reactor could be used to make enough weapons-grade plutonium for at least one bomb, should the right scientist get his or her hands on the drawings. He held the envelope high underneath his right arm, gripping it tightly.

"*Guten Abend,*" Carson replied politely.

"Do you speak English?" the woman asked.

"I do," Carson said, glancing down at his wedding ring. "But my wife doesn't like me talking to strange women."

"We don't have to be strangers," the woman said.

The train began to slow down, preparing to stop at the next station. Carson moved to the door as the man came close enough to step in front of him should he make a move toward the pneumatically operated sliding doors. Carson was now certain that his newly discovered documents were in danger of being pinched.

Grabbing Carson's rear end with her right hand in order to distract him from her accomplice, the woman stepped forward. The man also reached out to grab Carson, but, re-alising what was happening, Carson began to spin away. Ig-noring the woman's tight grip on his right buttock, he spun to his right and backwards far enough to be out of the man's reach. He'd learned the spin-off-and-hit move while playing football in college. It was his favourite one to get from his defensive end position into the backfield and maybe sack a preoccupied quarterback.

Lunging forward while crouched down, Carson ploughed into the man's kidneys with his left shoulder, putting him down on the ground with one quick tackle. Then with his boot, he held the man's neck to the floor of the U-bahn car while twisting his arm into a position of great pain. The train came to a stop before Carson could finish his assault, and the woman pulled out a small pistol from her black leather trousers pocket.

"I thought that we would be friends," the woman said. "Now, let my friend go."

"You win, take it," Carson said, releasing his grip and picking up the envelope from the sticky train floor behind him. "Will you send me a postcard?"

"I'm not gonna kill you tonight, Mr. Griffin," the woman said. "Just make sure you know that I could have."

She reached out and took the envelope from Carson's extended left hand. Keeping one eye on Carson, she looked inside the envelope to make sure it actually held the documents she was sent to recover. The woman then opened the pneumatic doors with a quick bump of her left hand on one of its handles.

"Let's go," she ordered her cohort.

The man stood up, clutching his back in pain as he and the woman stepped off the train. The doors closed, and Carson watched as the two got onto an escalator that would take them up to ground level, away from any chance of Carson finding them in the future. He sat back down in the red padded seat, wondering who might want to use the information in that envelope. Carson had taken a mental picture of the drawing, but it had not been assigned a primer or legend to identify its place of origin. As a matter of fact, it looked much like a researcher's conceptual drawing and not really a reactor that anyone had ever built.

Carson drove his 1988 Mercedes 560SL into the Vienna International Centre's underground car park the next morning, still mulling over the previous night's unfortunate incident. Carson's office at INWA was on the twentieth floor of the Alpha building, and he took one of the building's elevators to his floor.

As Carson walked toward his office, Todd Sinclair, his section head, intercepted him. "How did it go last night?"

Carson followed Todd into his extremely modern office, thanks to an overzealous Austrian decorator. Carson closed the door. Todd had worked his way up through the Agency for twenty-three years, but still had problems adjusting to formal Austrian décor – he preferred his native Australian comfort.

"Todd, the Turks are looking to build some sort of pool-type nuclear reactor," Carson said. "Its core would be rather small but powerful enough to produce a butt load of plutonium once started up."

"Did Hadier give you the evidence?"

Pouring himself a cup of coffee from Todd's old-fashioned percolator coffee pot, Carson hesitated for a moment. "Yeah, Haddie came through all right. I took a rushed look through the documents on the subway, until my ride was interrupted by a pair of Turks. Even though I was able to pin the guy, the woman had me cold – her cocked pistol pointed at my head. The pair took the envelope and left the train at the Karlsplatz station.

"I got a good enough look at the documents to decipher the drawings, and I can tell you that it was an impressively innovative design. Possibly one of the most advanced I've seen for a onetime plutonium producing, pulse heavy-water-moderated core."

Todd trusted Carson's instincts. "Who do you think is gonna be building this plutonium generator?"

"I'm not sure," Carson said. "I believe it was a modified design of one of the Yugoslavian research reactors. One that Tito's scientists wanted to build before he pulled the rug out from under their funding."

"We can't bring your suspicions to the UN Security Council without validation. They're gonna want hard evidence," Todd said. "I want you to retrace your steps and see if you can find something more on this reactor design that we can use to establish what these guys are up to."

"I'll see what I can do." Carson took a last gulp of coffee, threw the paper cup in a wastebasket, and turned to leave.

"Say hello to Christy for me," Todd said.

"Will do, thanks."

Carson left Todd's office wondering in what part of the world he would have to look to find more information on the reactor design in Hadier's stolen documents. Its controlling circuits seemed to be very similar to a research reactor he had seen at an inspection just outside of Ljubljana, Slovenia, but it was not really the same. The differences were readily apparent to someone who had operated reactors for many years, as Carson had done before joining INWA.

Walking down the corridor and into one of eight elevators to the Agency's enormous library, Carson settled down to begin his research. If he could find something similar, it would give him at least one possible lead. At six o'clock he called Christy to tell her that he'd have to stay late to finish some important work. The evening turned to night, and before Carson finished reading his last theoretical nuclear reactor design, the summer sun's light broke over the mountains east of the Vienna International Centre.

Driving along Seyringer Strasse that morning to his home on the outskirts of Vienna to grab a shower, shave, and change his clothes, Carson knew he wasn't any closer to finding out where the reactor design had originated. He needed to find Hadier and question him, but that was virtually impossible – his informant had many retreats to hide in besides the Red Lion Café.

The trail turned very cold over the next few weeks. Then came even worse news: Carson saw on a Romanian news magazine's website that Hadier had been killed in a horrific car accident near the Black Sea. But the truth about his death was that an order of assassination by the Turkish underground had been put out. Serif had learned that there had been leaks to the Agency by one of the opposition party informants and was given Hadier's name as one of four possibilities. All were proficiently killed by a man Serif called "the Hunter."

CHAPTER 3

Serif's planned exploitation of the young female scientist from Canada would not be interrupted by anyone. He had worked too hard to acquire Dr Regina Kny's reactor design – once a hot commodity on the terrorist black market. The design and its creator were now totally under the control of the Rezaabak brothers. Serif especially wanted to make sure the Yenilikçiler, Turkey's ruling party, would not prevent him from carrying out his plans to construct a clandestine nuclear reactor that would produce weapons-grade plutonium.

Serif spent the next few days, after leaving the tunnels of Idrija, using his wireless modem and satellite phone to get into a remote Internet connection that Reza had set up back at his headquarters in Mamaia, Romania. Mamaia was a Black Sea beach resort, once only visited by Romania's privileged communist leaders before the people's revolution. It was now a popular place for anyone to spend time off, relaxing from their poorly paid jobs in Bucharest and other surrounding small towns. Every country bordering the Black Sea watched the Romanian coast economy grow exponentially since the anti-communist revolt yielded open capitalism.

Serif stayed at a small hotel in Idrija which was partially built on stilts, backed up to the Idrijca river, and run by a

Slovenian couple trying to make a living catering to travellers who passed through the small mining town.

Idrija was kept alive by a city-owned tourist company, which brought money into the economy by showing its castle, now a museum, and part of the mercury mine's upper tunnels. The city's only other significant income came from manufacturing small, high-speed commutators and electromagnets, which were shipped all over Europe and the Americas. Commutators proudly displayed in the Miner's Museum showed a post-World War II industry that allowed the isolated little town to survive when traversing the surrounding mountains was virtually impossible. Some of the men and boys would work in factory jobs throughout the snowy months in their self-imposed captivity in the deep valley, while their wives and daughters delicately crocheted beautiful doilies and made embroidered clothing.

Guests in the small Idrijan hotel that Serif had selected for his satellite headquarters had a choice of eight rooms, each with its own bath and satellite-fed TV. Breakfast was included and very European, except for a mulberry jam that the Slovenian couple made from a silkworm tree behind their wood pile. They called it murve fruit, a local derivative for the tree berry.

Using a 128-bit encryption on his laptop Serif sat at a table, his back to a wall, and wrote an email to his mentor:

Though we have experienced too many failures in the past, recently I have made an extraordinary step forward for both our causes. We are brothers in our origin and desire to eliminate the capitalistic and Jewish domination of the Western States by creating an uninhabitable land west of the Black Sea. Our revolution will meet at the broken iron curtain.

The encrypted message was delivered and Serif received

a confirmation that the intended party opened his message somewhere in cyberspace. Serif's mentor had kept his identity hidden from everyone in the JTS organisation except by secure email, all personal accessibility prevented by his closest guards.

Serif nodded with satisfaction, packed up his laptop, and went for a run in the late afternoon sun. It was July and usually too hot for most people to go jogging between ten in the morning and five in the afternoon, and this day was no exception. The thermometer nailed to a hotel porch column registered 28°C (83°F) when Serif began his ten-mile jog.

His run took him along the Idrijca river – mountains on both sides of the crystal-clear rushing water – a little lower in its banks than usual that day due to a dry summer. Rainbow trout skirmishing through its currents could be seen by anyone taking time to enjoy the fantastic view of one of Slovenia's cherished resources. Serif's pace along the small winding road that followed the river's meandering kept his breathing rhythmical and a little laboured. He enjoyed running through the scenic environment and felt completely invigorated by the fresh air and dogwood blossoms still lingering on some of the younger trees. The temperature had dropped some from when he started his trek by the time he finished at 7:00 p.m.

Serif spent the rest of the summer and autumn observing Kny, Broz, and Mrak working together in the depths of the underground research centre. When the winter winds began to blow over the mountains and whitecaps appeared on the higher peaks of the range, Serif felt compelled to go home.

On a mild November day, Serif had one last afternoon run, then met with Reza over dinner that night in the hotel's small dining room. Warmed by a blazing fireplace in one corner, the two brothers sat together as if they were still in their family's hovel of a home in Turkey.

Occasionally, a squat little man would enter the room with an armload of aged oak firewood that he'd lay carefully onto the hearth's apron before placing each split piece on the burning pile of hot ash and orange flames. The tables and chairs in the dining room were all of simple wood construction, pinned together with dowels instead of nails.

"What do you think of our scientists' progress, Reza?" Serif asked as he began eating his dinner of a pan-fried chicken breast, mixed sautéed vegetables, and a few potato wedges.

Reza was tired and his right leg ached from working in the chilly secret underground reactor hall. "I believe that we will complete the plutonium separation within twenty months, as planned. Dr Kny is a genius; her new methods of chemical isotope separation are extraordinary. Her technique will be able to remove the weapons-grade plutonium from the other spent fuel much quicker than the Russians."

Isotope separation was the most difficult activity involved in safely recovering the weapons-grade plutonium from the spent nuclear fuel. Complex chemical processes for plutonium isolation and subsequent gathering had to be performed with great care to get the proper purity and desired explosive yield.

"I'm leaving for our headquarters in Mamaia tonight, my brother," Serif said, referring to his home on the Black Sea coast.

"I will stay in touch, Serif," Reza said, while eating a bowl of borscht with homemade bread. "Just do as I ask and upgrade your encryption codes. Our mail may be read, even now, by the Americans."

"Yes, I will take care of that as soon as I return home," Serif promised.

The two brothers finished their meal reminiscing about

their father's date farm in Turkey – its fruit was always plump and tasted like sweet candy. Their farmhouse was located near Ankara on a plateau surrounded by low-lying hills, south toward the salt lake. They could see two of Turkey's volcanoes from a high hill on the border of their father's farm. They laughed and joked as they relived the good times of their childhood. But they were both careful not to mention the hardships and painful beatings each had suffered at the hand of their father.

At evening's end, Reza went back to his room for a few hours' sleep and Serif ordered one of his bodyguards to put his suitcase into the four-wheel-drive jeep parked in the rear of the hotel. Serif jumped with easy agility into the jeep and motioned for his man to begin driving to a flat field near the hotel. There he got onto a waiting helicopter and flew east toward Romania.

———

Arriving at a small airport just north of Mamaia, Serif got into his waiting jet-black Humvee. He liked the feel of the powerful American-made machine – its ride was very smooth when driving over Romania's pothole-filled roads. The extra comfort of his top-of-the-line interior was an expensive addition, but he loved its feel.

Serif's driver took him to his beachfront house, overlooking the Black Sea's cold, dark waters. A recent snowfall sent the last of the locals inside early, away from a frigid northern wind blowing over the brownish sand. Serif's house was well insulated from the chilly weather, unlike most of the distant surrounding structures. He could see the poverty the

Romanian people were still suffering, but couldn't care less about how they were getting on with what he considered their meaningless lives. Some evenings he could see dim lights across the bay, coming from old housing left over from a terribly failed economy. Rundown block apartments remained from an unfulfilled promise, which gave way to Ceauşescu's egomaniacal ambitions to leave a legacy of enormous government buildings in Romania's capital. His great palace in Bucharest was built using communist forced labour, and even today, is still second only to the Pentagon in size and stature, while his people starved in the streets of the country's lesser cities, including Mamaia.

Serif entered his whitewashed, thick cement walled home through solid oak double doors. The floors on the main deck were tiled with Romanian ceramic, polished to a blinding shine by two of his five house servants the morning of his arrival. He handed his hat and coat to Radu, his butler, and then went into his study for a Brancoveanu cognac. He was a drinking Muslim on certain occasions, such as a moderate sunset or an inspiring trip across the Carpathians. Catching up on all the news he could absorb before midnight, Serif retired alone to one of his bedrooms.

The next day at four in the afternoon, he stood at the window of his elegantly decorated study and brushed back the lace curtains made in Idrija by daughters of mercury miners, who had learned their craft from generations of widowed mothers. Serif's binoculars zoomed in on a Romanian yacht-building plant where his new boat was being constructed. It would carry him from Romania's Black Sea coast to the port of Izola, Slovenia, in a few months.

"Sir, Ms Ianescu to see you," the butler said.

Serif had another vice that he greatly enjoyed – his Romanian girlfriend Viviana Ianescu. "Send her in, Radu."

Viviana came into his study wearing leather trousers and a black lace top; her hair was shoulder length and black as coal. She looked at him with penetrating eyes that glowed like a yellowish-brown fire smouldering underneath a crystal-clear pool of cool water.

"I've got what you need for your little game," Viviana said.

Her voice was unusually smooth and powerful for a woman in her mid-twenties. Viviana started her career after spending her life savings and as much borrowed money as she could find to attend engineering school in Bucharest. Eighteen months after graduation, Cernavodă (tjer-na-'vō-da) finally hired Viviana at a miserably low monthly salary, but she had no choice.

Viviana worked as an electrical engineer in Cernavodă's nuclear power plant support department, which gave her access to all the plant's confidential system diagrams. This was the ultimate position for someone who wanted an integrated knowledge of the overall plant's operational capabilities. All the piping and instrumentation diagrams were labelled with a primer that could be used to tie each of thousands of components together into one huge machine – a machine that was used to transform energy released from nuclear fission into electricity. A person with some *real* nuclear power plant operations experience could use them in many ways, including a scenario that could inflict a dangerous breach in Cernavodă's protective containment.

Viviana stayed after work every day for several weeks, gathering all the schematics from the plant's security, civil, mechanical, instrumentation/electrical, and operations departments. Information Serif would need to plan an abduction of the plant's control systems, and maybe even access to its highly radioactive spent fuel which was stored inside the power plant.

Cernavodă's large reactor was refuelled every eighteen months with low enriched fuel assemblies, brought in from the United States and installed in its large boiling water nuclear reactor core. All of the spent fuel assemblies were removed from the core when their usable fissionable material was partially expended, then placed in a cooling pool, stacked vertically in a horizontal matrix of 250 rows. Currently there were 3,750 spent fuel bundles being kept cool by three large heat exchangers one deck below the pool. It was a huge store of highly radioactive uranium enriched to about five percent U235.

When Serif offered Viviana five thousand Euros to steal the schematics, she jumped at the chance. She was also passionately attracted to him.

"Thank you, my dear," Serif replied. "You are always on time; promises fulfilled – paid in full. Your money is in the top drawer."

She moved closer to Serif. "It's what I like to do."

Viviana's father had emigrated to Romania from Turkey and died an agonising death from blood poisoning when she was fifteen years old, but not before leaving his daughter with a deep hatred for capitalism and the West.

"I want people to remember us, Serif. I want them to remember the Turkish empire that my father yearned for," Viviana said. "What we will do in Cernavodă could resonate throughout civilisation for many years to come. It is our destiny to return the land to its previous powerful reign – it is ours!"

Serif put his arms around her and brought her into him, caressing her small waist. "Yes, you are right. Our task is but unrelenting providence. We will bring the Ottoman Empire to its former glory – a true world power again."

He took the thumb drive from her, put it into his computer with one hand, and checked its contents.Then, smiling, he slid it into his trousers pocket.

"Shall we retire for the evening?" Serif asked as he kissed her neck.

"It's still daylight outside," Viviana teased, and returned his kisses.

"The better to see each other," Serif said, caressing her hair.

Serif and Viviana spent their night together in his bed. The next morning, as she slept, Serif put a .22 calibre slug into the top of her skull with his favourite handgun. He felt no remorse or emotion of any kind. He was only doing what had to be done. Viviana was expendable.

"Radu, bring my Mondeo around," Serif ordered. "Then grind that meat in the bedroom and feed it to the deep-water fish."

"Yes, sir," Radu replied.

It was a heartless end to a life of striving for success.

Serif left his waterfront home and drove down the crowded boulevard along the hotel strip on his way to meet with a formerly discharged senior reactor operator from Cernavodă's nuclear power station. Viviana had recommended Bogdan to Serif, in the hope that she would eventually secure her future with her lover. But Bogdan and Serif quickly forgot about how they had been introduced, basing their arrangement exclusively on money.

Bogdan Saliba was fired when Western security standards were introduced at Cernavodă. He failed a random drug test for marijuana after fifteen years of service, leaving him to offer the use of his rusty tub of a fishing boat for about one hundred Euros a month to other more successful entrepreneurs. He was almost forty years old and needed the money Serif was offering to start up his own fishing business. He'd always wanted to fish the waters of the North Sea and live in Latvia – his father's home country. Fishing the Black Sea for someone else's seaworthy flotilla was something that Bogdan never intended.

After meeting Serif and getting a little up-front money, Bogdan put together a fairly efficient reactor-operating crew made up of men that he had previously worked with at Cernavodă's nuke plant. His team consisted of two reactor operators and two equipment operators with experience and reasons why they needed money.

Serif parked three streets down from Bogdan's house and walked along the shore for a short distance – preoccupied with trying to memorise every detail of what he needed for the operation's success. He spotted Bogdan sitting in a small dinghy tied to a ragged short pier behind his house.

"Hello my good friend, Bogdan!" Serif shouted from the shoreline.

Bogdan stopped bailing the water from his dinghy. "Hello, what's the latest news?"

Without answering, Serif motioned for Bogdan to follow him up a small incline to Bogdan's back porch, which overlooked the bay. When they arrived at the greenish-tinted house, paint peeling from the effects of salty air, Bogdan poured them both a small glass of Vlad Tuica Extra fina – plum vodka made in Cluj-Napoca, an ancient city that was once Transylvania's capital and played a significant role in Hungarian history.

"Here's to our successful business partnership, *noroc*!" Bogdan toasted.

"*Noroc*," Serif replied, meaning, *Good life!*

The Tuica washed into Serif's sinuses, causing his eyes to water a little as he sipped the powerful clear liquid. It came from a distillery that had earned the right to put a picture of Vlad the Impaler, better known as Count Dracula, on the label.

"Have you the drawings we requested?" Bogdan asked.

"Yes, here they are." Serif handed Bogdan the thumb drive that Viviana had given him the night before.

"Aye, we will need a few months to put together our plan to melt the reactor's nuclear core," Bogdan said.

"Remember, my friend, we must not release the radioactivity until it has reached its most deadly density," Serif warned.

Bogdan plugged the thumb drive into a fairly new Fujitsu laptop he had stolen from a visiting tourist's Mercedes, near the resort hotels along Mamaia Beach. Many more Europeans were having their holidays on the Black Sea now that infrastructure-building EU money was coming into Romania. A new highway from Bucharest was nearly completed, which shortened the trip by two hours from the capital's airport to Mamaia.

"I have an idea, but we need time to trace the circuits on these drawings," Bogdan said.

Serif finished his shot glass of Vlad's retribution. "Fine, Bogdan, you have my man's number. May I use your bathroom?"

Bogdan pointed toward the outhouse near a gulley leading out to the bay. Like some of the older houses in that part of the country, there was no indoor plumbing. Bogdan and his temporary girlfriend used the single tap protruding from a concrete slab in the front yard for all their water needs. It provided them with fairly dependable city-supplied water that ran very cold during the winter.

Serif opened the door to the wood and plasterboard outhouse. He saw one seat, consisting of four smooth wooden slats nailed together above a hole in the floor. Beneath the hole, he could see a wooden trough, which led down to a stream of the Black Sea's backwash water – sewage flushing itself only when the tides changed. The smell took his breath away, and he immediately closed the outhouse door and turned away.

"Goodbye, my good friend," Serif called to Bogdan, who didn't seem to notice the quick retreat.

"Bon voyage!" Bogdan yelled.

Serif hurried along the beachfront to his car, his joints aching from the cold. He started the Mondeo's diesel engine and drove to Cernavodă on a narrow two-lane road that he had travelled many times over the last few months. On every occasion, he found road crews working on some patch of the rough thoroughfare, and sometimes the pavement would just turn to red dirt without warning.

Decelerating behind a cloud of dust, Serif came upon a family of gypsies travelling just ahead of him in a sheep-skin-covered wooden wagon, being pulled by a small, thick-haired horse. He could see a man driving the wagon with his wife sitting by his side, and two children behind them, crusted over with days of dirt – the whole family looked filthy.

Serif slowed down and was finally able to pass the old wagon with its passengers looking into his slightly tinted blue window with vacant stares. The eyes of the children looked especially hungry and scared.

The winding road that Serif drove down followed a canal that passed by the nuclear power plant on its way to the Black Sea from the Danube River. Its blackened water tumbled and churned eastward, carrying whatever material had been dumped into it by the local residents. Although the canal was only about 550 yards wide near Cernavodă, it grew in breadth during the rainy season to nearly three-quarters of a mile in some places. A narrow barge carrying machinery parts was floating in a lock that lifted it to the river's swollen height near the power plant as Serif rode past.

At the mouth of the canal, Serif stopped at a little outdoor bar called the Tryst Café, which catered to the locals and infrequent party boats that happened to be cruising the big Danube. Serif sat at one of only four round plastic tables of the Tryst, each with its own weathered green umbrella. A thin woman came over to him and Serif ordered a mineral water and opened his coat pocket to retrieve a Cuban-made cigarillo.

Serif didn't smoke very often, but when he did, he wanted to taste good tobacco, not some trash leaf from Canada. He lit his Cuban cigar with a wooden match and watched the black waters of the Danube, full of Europe's discards and chemicals blended with silt, pass swiftly by the old town of Cernavodă. Barges pushed by tugboats were travelling in both directions that afternoon, and the junction was bustling with traffic, which passed under the King Carol Ibridge, designed by Eiffel's French engineers and built before World War II.

Serif sat at the little café that afternoon, quietly considering some of his advanced assault preparations for Cernavodă's nuclear plant and enjoying the serene atmosphere surrounding him. The Tryst Café was a great place to observe river traffic and escape for a couple of hours before heading back to his house in Mamaia. He expected to see no reminders of the morning's murderous deed.

CHAPTER 4

Carson first met and fell in love with Christy Peterman in Norfolk, Virginia, during his hitch in the Navy. Carson's family history was saturated with naval careers, but he was the only one to go through the nuclear power program after getting his degree in nuclear engineering from Georgia Institute of Technology in Atlanta.

Christy's father, Harold Peterman, watched Carson's career very closely after Christy married him and periodically examined his son-in-law's progress at the nuclear power plant in Georgia. Harold introduced Carson to INWA when he felt that his operating experience had sufficiently matured. Carson and Christy had been married for sixteen years by that time and welcomed the opportunity to live and work in Europe. It would also turn out to be a wonderful education for their young teenage daughter Susan.

Harold Peterman's work at INWA included many highly confidential missions, but it was his unusual ability to solve difficult international problems related to the spread of nuclear weapons technology that got him assigned to a special branch of the Agency. The very small division, which kept offices in the Grand Hotel of Vienna, was unknown to everyone except the Director General and one of his deputies. Harold's position allowed him to recommend one candidate a year to INWA – Carson was his first and only recommendation.

For the first year, Carson monitored, examined, and evaluated non-nuclear weapon states, along with the other Agency inspectors, until Harold introduced him to Todd Sinclair.

Over lunch at a Vienna restaurant, Todd said to Carson, "I want to talk to you about joining an unknown part of INWA. It's a small special investigations section, not included in any UN charter. This program allows you and a few select others to learn the skills necessary to become a covert agent in the body of the inspectorate of INWA. Because of the international agreements that created the Agency's statute after World War II, inspectors were only allowed to enter a country when invited by that country to monitor their peaceful nuclear activities. But after we discovered the clandestine nuclear weapons programs of several countries, it was obvious that in order for the Agency to identify a hidden nuclear weapons program, they would have to become much more human intelligence driven."

"You mean INWA actually has teeth?" Carson asked.

"Yeah, you might say that," Todd replied. "However, we have always kept our extra-curricular activities out of sight and out of mind. If nuclear non-proliferation signers knew of our covert interests, there would be a backlash of protests. And I'm sure some countries would withdraw from the international treaties – for example, North Korea."

Carson smiled enthusiastically, practically chomping at the bit. "I've been waiting for a chance to get involved in a program like this my entire life. Don't get me wrong, safeguarding inspections are very important – we've got to prevent the spread of nuclear weapons – but I realise that it takes more determination in some extreme cases." Carson paused. "Please, sign me up."

Harold came into the restaurant and hurried over to the table where Carson and Todd were sitting. "Sorry I'm late, fellas." He pulled up a chair, sat down, and opened a menu. A waitress hurried over and took Harold's order for a double order of vegetable soup and Trappist beer. As she walked away, Harold turned to Todd. "I assume you've told Carson about the...uh..."

"Yes, I did, and he's on board," Todd replied with a smile.

Harold looked at Carson. "Christy grew up around the Agency's operating methods. I believe she'll understand all the unannounced inspections you'll be travelling to after you've finished your training."

"But here's the catch, Carson," Todd interjected. "You can't tell her about the change in your job."

Carson sat still for a few moments. They were going to train him to be a covert agent, working under the United Nations' umbrella. It sounded somewhat contradictory – the UN was established to be a worldwide organisation of peace, diplomacy, and aid.

"You'll be away from home on six two-week assignments for the field training. In total, you'll spend eighteen months improving your ability to handle some very difficult scenarios," Todd said. "Your tutors are from nuclear weapons states that have a deep interest in stopping the spread of nuclear weapons technology."

Carson took a deep breath. "Okay, I'm still in," he said, convinced that Harold's involvement was proof of Todd's genuineness. "When do I start?"

"Today," Harold replied. "Your schedule will be located at this site."

Harold gave Carson an index card with an Agency website, PIN, and password handwritten in his chicken scratches.

Todd swallowed his last bite of a salami sandwich and said to Carson, "Pick up your new pocket PC from Hilbert Haas in the G tower. It's protected with special codes and encryption sequences that only a very few know. Keep it with you at all times, and don't let it out of your sight. You'll have access to all the INWA resources now that you've become part of our team."

Harold told Carson how he would have to communicate the changes to Christy, giving her enough information to know that he was out on a mission, but not revealing what he was doing or where it was happening.

———

Carson picked up his pocket PC from Haas the next day and logged into its protected database using the PIN and password that Harold had given him. When the hand-held machine came to life, its menu listed training assignments for eighteen months and Carson's normal personal contact information. Its phone list was synchronised with a specific listing of essential contact personnel, but other than that, the pocket PC carried no other Agency identification. It was exactly like all the others issued to regular Agency inspectors.

Before closing the screen, Carson removed the PIN option for login and replaced it with a thumbprint recognition login. He put the pocket PC to sleep with a tap on its screen.

When he arrived home late that afternoon, Christy was in the kitchen preparing dinner. Delicious aromas permeated the house. Their dog, Bingo, a domesticated Australian dingo, stood next to Christy, looking up at her with pleading eyes. He never left the kitchen when Christy was cooking.

"How was work?" Christy asked as Carson came up to her, and she turned to give him a kiss on his cheek.

He leaned down and gave Bingo a few quick pats and some chin scratches.

"Things are going really well these days," Carson replied.

"Oh, I forgot to ask you last night about your lunch with Dad. How did it go?"

Carson finished removing his shoes while sitting on one of their dining room chairs, adjacent to the kitchen. "Good. Your father is still full of life. Looks like I'll be working for a new section head – a guy named Todd Sinclair."

"I know that name," Christy said as she turned the roast over in the oven and added small red potatoes to the roasting pan. She basted them with the succulent juices surrounding the meat. "He's an old friend of my dad."

Carson took off his tie and started upstairs. "I think it's gonna be a nice change working with him."

"Will you still travel to Romania?" Christy called after him. "You've been promising me some great hiking in the Carpathian Mountains."

"Yeah, I know. We'll go soon," Carson replied. "I guess I'll be doing both jobs for a while, until I can turn over the responsibilities to another inspector. I'm afraid the hours may get a little longer for a while, and maybe some extra travel." Christy sighed and nodded to herself.

After changing out of his work clothes into jeans and a sweatshirt, Carson came back downstairs. He put his arms around Christy's waist as she was slicing vegetables to be sautéed. "Wish I could take you along as my personal chef."

"That's all?" Christy turned to face her husband. Before she could say another word, Carson covered her mouth with a passionate kiss.

At that moment, Susan, who had just come home from school, dropped her backpack on a kitchen chair, and said, "Oh boy, they're at it again." She laughed as her parents broke their embrace. "Mmm, smells good in here," Susan said.

"That's what I was just telling your mother," Carson said a bit sheepishly.

"Right," Susan chided. She rubbed Bingo's back. "C'mon, boy, let's take a walk so Mom can finish, uh, cooking."

Bingo, who understood the word "walk," ran into the foyer and pulled his leash from a small hook next to the door.

Training for Carson's new post began with meeting his first tutor in a windowless concrete apartment building. The facade of the training centre resembled all its surrounding buildings, easily missed if a person wasn't led there on their first visit. Harold escorted Carson at 6:30 a.m. one morning, carrying a duffel bag of workout clothes in Carson's size.

The classroom looked much like a small theatre, with highbacked cushioned seats facing a large white screen and podium. When Harold and Carson entered, four other trainees were sitting in the room, quietly facing the podium, waiting for their instructor.

"This is where you'll meet every morning for the next year, before going out into the field," Harold told Carson, handing him the duffel bag. "I'll see you later."

Carson nodded, said thanks, and took a seat. Todd came into the classroom and ordered, "Stand up!"

The class of five stood at attention, beside their chairs.

The instructor came in carrying a laptop and a cup of coffee. "Please take your seats. The name is Major General Briner."

Briner was British and that's about all the class ever knew about him during the twelve months of special training. He carried them through mental, physical, and spiritual training techniques from all over the globe, working ten hours a day, unless travelling. While travelling, they worked sixteen hours a day in whatever country Briner ordered them to train in for those days. The occasional field trials would take the small group of trainees out for a week or two at a time for on-location instruction by American, British, and French Special Forces personnel.

Carson soaked up the covert operative training like a sponge. After the first year of his training, he was separated from the remaining group of trainees and brought into Todd Sinclair's office for a briefing.

"Carson, now that you've finished the basic training, we want you to roll yourself back into the inspectors' ranks of INWA," Todd stated. "We've taken great care to keep the appearance of your schedule close to what it would have been had you been performing normal duties for the Agency. No one knows that you've been out training or what your special assignments will be except me and the Deputy Director General. You've still got six months of field training left in the program, where you'll be playing a dual role – inspector and operative. For this segment, we're going to pair you up with one of our best people in the field."

Todd stepped over to his office door and swiped his key card across a reader. The door popped open. "Come in, Harold."

"So you think you're ready for this, Carson?" Harold asked. Carson hadn't seen his father-in-law for months and was really surprised. "Yes, I feel pretty good about going into this special area."

"I'm glad," Harold replied. "We all have to realise our fate at some point in our lives, otherwise why do we continue? Your assignment is to stay out of trouble until we call on you for a job. Now let's get started on your next segment of training."

During the following six months, Harold put Carson through an intriguing maze of unconventional inspection activities and rules of engagement that he would have to abide by while working under the UN's protection. His training had given Carson a newfound respect for his father-in-law's knowledge and physical endurance. As for Christy and Susan, they didn't notice any changes in Carson's travel; it all seemed to be normal duty as far as they could tell. Until Harold took Carson on his final training mission.

Carson was supposed to follow Harold into a series of warehouses they suspected were stored with thousands of uranium centrifuge parts in Dubai. The Agency needed pictures and at least one small sample of the nuclear material that was being exported from Malaysia to the Dubai port. The A.Q. Kahn network used the massive complex to hold uranium enrichment machinery and six full cylinders of uranium hexafluoride (UF6), ready to be used in a clandestine enrichment facility.

"Hold on to this flask," Harold told Carson, tossing him a small stainless steel UF6 sample bottle.

"Got it," Carson whispered, slipping the bottle behind his Kevlar vest.

Harold had already covered the razor prongs on top of a perimeter fence that went completely around the warehouse complex with a thick blanket and began climbing over. Waving to Harold to go ahead, Carson watched for any movement along the chain-link fence from their position in an unrecognised blind spot of the security surveillance coverage. A few seconds later, both men were inside the complex, standing outside a pale green warehouse with large opaque windows twenty feet above their heads.

Harold motioned to Carson and took his night vision camera inside a corrugated steel building adjacent to a small fluorine gas production skid. Their information sources identified the building on a schematic as the P2 uranium centrifuge storage cache. Carson turned toward a concrete pit where the six cylinders were supposed to be stored. The fairly deep pit was about sixty yards from two fluorine storage tanks, situated by the gas production skid.

Carson returned to where he and Harold had parted with the UF6 gas sample, pausing briefly to catch his breath. "Where's the old man?" he mumbled to himself, as he quickly scanned the area for Harold. Carson noticed that a new camera had been installed near the roof of the centrifuge storage building. Harold must not have seen the surveillance before going inside. Watching in horror, Carson saw the door swing open wildly and Harold came running out of the building with his camera hanging from his shoulder.

Carson saw a muzzle blast against the blackness of the Dubai night coming from the top of the building, immediately followed by a loud crack. A sniper had gotten Harold in his crosshairs, took aim, and fired. Harold was bleeding profusely from a wound in his neck. He stumbled across a short patch of grass to where Carson was crouched with his pistol.

Before the sniper could get off another shot, Carson fired a silenced 9mm into the black image on the roof. The man dropped his rifle and fell backward, out of sight.

Harold reached out his camera with his remaining strength. "Tell Christy...I love her."

"I will, Harold, but you're gonna be fine," Carson said. "Harold? Harold!"

Closing his eyes for the last time, Harold took a deep breath and released it completely without taking another. Carson's eyes welled with tears, but he knew he only had a few minutes to get out of the compound. Carson heaved Harold's limp body across his shoulders using a fireman's carry and ran toward a parked speedboat moored inside a harbour protected by surrounding concrete walls and double-sided gate.

After gently laying Harold's body in the boat, Carson found the keys still in the ignition and started its powerful engine. The craft's bow rose nearly three feet out of the water when he gave it full throttle. Roaring toward the locked gate, Carson fired three shots in an attempt to weaken its latching mechanism. The boat slammed into the gate with its bow high, sliding through a gap in its frame. The two halves of the gate separated beneath him as the boat left the water completely – Carson had crashed through and was on his way home.

Although he was able to escape with Harold's body, Carson had a terrible time coping with the loss of Christy's father. Christy, too, was devastated, but admitted to Carson that she feared her father would one day die on a mission for INWA.

Harold's small funeral was held just outside of Gainesville, Georgia, attended by Christy, Carson, Susan, and his ex-wife Anne. Although Harold and Anne's marriage had become a victim of his work, Anne had never stopped loving him.

Todd met with Carson a few days later at the Grand Hotel. The two men sat down over a cup of espresso in a small conference room.

"Carson, I just wanted to let you know that you can take all the time you need," Todd said.

"I'm okay," Carson replied. "I just want to spend a little more time with Christy before going back to work."

"Whatever you need, buddy," Todd said, approvingly. "By the way, Harold has been replaced. The Director General pulled in Marcel Vanderzee, a Dutchman, from our field office in Monaco. I had a short conversation with Marcel, and he wants you to go back into normal safeguards."

"No! I'll be back in a few weeks," Carson vowed.

"I convinced him that you would be ready soon to rejoin our group, but first spend some time in safeguards," Todd said, trying to persuade Carson to return to the ranks of covert ops slowly. "I need you at one hundred percent, buddy."

Carson sighed with resignation. "Okay, Todd."

The men finished their coffee, and Todd left the room. Carson sat alone for several minutes, contemplating his decision to join INWA and how it had already taken Christy's father. Would she ever accept Carson's new role, and could he continue to work as an INWA covert operative?

CHAPTER 5

Nearly two years after the supercritical experiment of Dr Regina Kny's small but powerful reactor, Reza returned to the mercury mine in Idrija. His constant observation of Kny and the other two scientists, who were separating plutonium from the nuclear pile, was finally coming to an end. It had been twenty-two months since Kny's team destroyed the nuclear reactor deep inside the mountain near Idrija. Reza got into a small hidden elevator that took him five thousand feet down to the bottom of the dark red shaft.

He opened the elevator's cage doors and stepped into the excavated cave where many Slovenian miners had lost their lives to mercury poisoning while digging tunnels through the cinnabar in this huge void. Reza's presence didn't surprise any of the three scientists who were already focused on the day's planned activities. He walked around them, watching the oscilloscopes, frequency modulators, and computer systems blink various parameters at him – few of which he had bothered to understand. Kny was afraid of Reza and kept an eye on him whenever he was close to her desk near the lead shielding.

The scientists' work, concentrated underneath the lead doors covering an enclosed cell, was generally completed. Only cooling of the formed buttons, and machining them into weaponised spheres, remained. They called the room beneath the floor a "hot cell," because radioactivity levels were very high and would cause instant death if the lead doors were opened.

"Can you feel the power underneath us, Kny?" Reza asked, focusing his black eyes down at the two-foot thick viewing glass in the lead door.

Regina Kny was exhausted after eight hours of intense labour. The two older scientists, Broz and Mrak, could only work about four hours a day before having to return to the surface. "I feel it, Reza."

"Serif is returning in one week. We will then assemble both devices with triggers he has acquired from our sources in Ankara," Reza said. "Seems the Black Sea continues to be a hub for the nuclear black market, I'm glad to say."

"I don't want to know anything else about your organisation," Kny said. "Pay me my five million the day we finish assembling the two devices – then I'll be out."

"Yes, of course your team will be fully paid," Reza stated, taken aback by Kny's remark.

Reza limped around the reactor hall, watching as Broz and Mrak put together the final device that would be used to correct the button's geometry inside the hot cell. They easily operated long remote manipulators with "outside the hot cell" handles that resembled motorcycle grips. Arms of both manipulators came through the walls of the hot cell at a ninety-degree angle to prevent any gamma or neutron shine of radioactivity from exiting the hot cell's protective lead and polyethylene shielding – and irradiating the scientists. Built in China, the two sets of manipulators were very advanced and could pick up a one-centimetre specimen using their Teflon-lined steel fingers.

Four hours went by quickly for the two scientists, who loved working on a project as interesting as this one. Kny would often hear them reminiscing about their discoveries using their research reactor near Belgrade and how much better their lab had been equipped compared to Zagreb by the communist leaders. Tito's ministers knew little about his atomic weapons program; it was completely controlled by the military, which was unimportant to the scientists who were working in the labs. But the two men reminisced little about their poor living conditions then, or how they were being treated by Reza now. Promises of working on a lifetime achievement, when Serif first offered them the job, were heavily overshadowed by their growing sense of incarceration.

By three o'clock they were exhausted and ready to call it a day. Kny led her team out of the makeshift reactor hall at four o'clock that afternoon. Dog tired from weeks of constant work, she needed an afternoon to relax, have a glass of wine, and a long, soothing bubble bath. There was plenty of time while the core of plutonium cooled enough to machine into its final shape – critical to a successful atomic bomb. Kny was determined to get her money and live the rest of her life on one of the Virgin Islands. It didn't matter which one; she loved them all.

She drove down from the mountain in her red Jeep Cherokee, a CD of Pink Floyd's *Dark Side of the Moon* playing on her stereo at an ear-splitting decibel level. The Jeep jerked around a little on the small path that led away from the fake sheep barn disguising the mine's elevator shaft but soon smoothed out when she reached the pavement. Slovenia's mountains in the background made her journey back to the hotel along the rushing waters of the Idrijca River a scenic trek – she felt as if she were driving through a landscape painting.

Arriving at her room in a small hotel outside Idrija, Regina Kny got out of her khaki trousers and vest, poured herself a glass of local white wine, and climbed into her warm bath. French oils scented the bathwater and made her feel that she had momentarily escaped the gruelling work in the depths of the mercury mine. Closing her eyes, she drifted away to a time in her childhood when money wasn't the most important thing to her.

Her father bought Regina her first exploratory science kit when they lived in a large home near the Chalk River, in Canada. She remembered when he came into her mother's modern kitchen from his job at the research centre, carrying a package covered in Christmas wrapping paper. She had excitedly opened the large kit of chemicals, small laser, microscope, and dissecting tools on Christmas morning, and happily told her parents she would one day be a famous scientist.

Her reminiscing was suddenly over when Regina Kny opened her eyes, took a sip of the white wine, and heard a voice outside her window shouting orders. Although she had never learned Slovenian fluently, she recognised that whatever language was being spoken, it wasn't local. She jumped to her feet, and opened the curtains enough to see the dirty street beneath her room and Reza with two men holding guns. One man ran toward the back of the hotel, while Reza and the other one ran into the hotel bar and reception area. Quickly drying off and putting on her jeans and flannel shirt, Regina slowly opened her room's heavy wooden door and surveyed the area. She bolted from the room, hoping to escape what she felt was going to be an assassination attempt. She ran quickly to the end of the short hallway, reaching a set of French doors that opened outward, toward the river and her escape. Turning around to see if her attackers had made their way up the stairs, she stepped forward onto a weak floorboard in the wooden balcony.

Termites and water had taken their toll on the wood and it disintegrated underneath Regina's small foot. Her body was fairly light, but her leg broke through the board up to her hip – she was stuck. One leg was dangling beneath the floorboards with the rest of her body exposed to Reza, who was now coming down the hallway. Regina Kny began to panic.

"You have fulfilled your end of our agreement," Reza barked.

She knew that there would be no sense to scream for help – no one would hear her over the sound of the Idrijca's rushing waters pounding the smooth stones as it passed beneath her. She struggled in vain to free her leg from the grip of rotted wood. Reza withdrew a flat razor from his pocket, opened it and held the black handle tightly in the palm of his hand. Reza stepped up to Regina and grabbed a fistful of wet hair. Regina couldn't free her body during the last fifteen seconds of her life, so she tried to free her mind before his knife slit her throat.

Reza's two men arrived at the scene just after the murder.

"Maks, take her body and bury it in the mountains," Reza ordered. "Then come back to my hotel. We have to get ready for the transport of our two packages from the mountain. I know that Mrak and Broz will be disturbed by the loss of Dr Kny, but say nothing. I will explain her sudden departure. Now go!"

Reza left the two men to clean up the bloody balcony, which took them less than twenty minutes after they had carried her body down to their waiting white van. Reza went back to Regina Kny's hotel room to get rid of her belongings while his two henchmen drove to a mountain where they put her body into a shallow grave deep in a forested area. Reza knew that Serif didn't want to kill the other two scientists until he had the two plutonium-core atomic bombs in place, but Kny's work was done when she had announced that they were ready for the machining phase there he had given Reza the order to "get rid of her."

Reza used his laptop to send an email to Serif in Mamaia, this time with an upgraded encryption code. *"Step one is complete, need further instructions."*

He waited for an answer, which came later – again, highly encrypted. *"My mission was successful, hold them until I arrive."*

Reza's respect for his brother's intelligence and cunning was matched only by his fear of retribution from Serif's cold-bloodedness. Reza didn't expect Serif to acquire the bombs' triggering components as promptly as he had from their contact in Ankara. He'd presumed that it would take his brother another couple of months and he would have to keep two remaining scientists alive until their nuclear devices were semi-assembled and ready for transport.

One week after Dr Kny was killed, Serif's helicopter touched down in the field he used sporadically as a landing site near his hotel in Idrija. Reza's two men met him in a green Jeep Cherokee, which they had recently acquired in Croatia. Two medium-sized brushed aluminium boxes were removed from the chopper and placed gently into the boot of the Jeep. The helicopter left the field for refuelling, and Reza's two men brought Serif to the underground reactor hall.

Grabbing his brother by his shoulders, Serif kissed Reza on both cheeks. "Hello, brother!"

He stepped off the elevator into the cave where he saw Mrak standing near a steel worktable. Broz was sitting at a desk with stacks of drawings held together by several large black binders.

On the end of one of his binders was handwritten in black ink:

"Successful test modelling of a nuclear weapon"

Pointing to Mrak's worktable, Serif ordered the two men, "Put those cases over there."

Serif turned to Reza and smiled. Reza acknowledged that Serif had acquired the triggering devices by nodding slowly. The brothers stood together, staring at the aluminium boxes for thirty silent seconds, very proud of how far they had been able to take their dream of producing a functioning nuclear weapon.

"Please, gentlemen, open them," Reza said.

The two scientists in white lab coats popped all six of the clip-down latches on one box. Removing the rubber-gasketed lid from the aluminium box, they could see all the necessary components that they had, up to now, never been able to obtain. Yugoslavia's nuclear weapons program was mostly laboratory scale due to a serious lack of funding. But they had performed many computer-modelling tests in their research program and were very familiar with the Chinese-style triggering device.

Replacing the lid, Broz and Mrak went about organising the parts they had gathered to build the nuclear weapon. They took several weeks to assemble the two nuclear devices, one with a six-kilogram core and one smaller one, which finally weighed only two kilograms. The smaller pit might be honed to fit nicely into the core of a rucksack bomb. A rucksack, or a "suitcase" nuclear weapon, was very difficult to design and build, but once assembled, it could be strapped to a suicide volunteer.

Resources for the various parts were very scarce because of the crackdown on the so-called "dual use" equipment after A.Q. Kahn's nuclear Wal-Mart was nearly put out of business. Kahn's reputation as the father of Pakistan's nuclear weapon allowed him to distribute illicit nuclear weapon components from Dubai, until his operation was finally discovered and he was put under house arrest. Most of the members of his circle of nuclear traffickers were arrested, but some were never brought to justice and were still able to deliver intricate parts of an atomic bomb. The most difficult to find by far was enough beryllium to encase the highly corrosion-susceptible plutonium pit, which came by way of a gift from Serif's mentor in Turkey.

Serif had patiently monitored the evolution as it matured, with little real understanding of the delicate operation that the two former communist scientists were performing. He was acutely aware of the explosive capabilities of the six-kilo nuclear device – it had been explained to him numerous times. But the smaller of the two plutonium pits would be more difficult to predict using the computer modelling programs that Mrak had accumulated on his multiple synchronized laptops. Albeit the geometry of the sphere created the greatest bang for the buck achievable, simultaneous triggering of the surrounding plastic explosives required very advanced circuits.

Feeling confident that everything was ready deep inside the ancient mercury mine, Serif gave Reza instructions to make preparations for the next phase of their operation. Then Serif left to go back to his headquarters in Mamaia.

———

He arrived in his Jet Ranger helicopter at the airport north of Mamaia Beach, where one of his servants picked him up. They drove past the rows of pink and white stucco apartment buildings, and Serif callously noticed the laundry that hung from five stories of balconies and children in dirty hand-me-downs who played with an old basketball on an asphalt court. Through his tinted window, Serif saw a group of girls giggling at some teenage boys in knee-high denim shorts. Browned by the "Mediterranean-like" sunshine around the Black Sea, the girls looked beautiful – their black hair blowing back from an ocean breeze.

Serif made it home in time for his last swim of the long summer in his heated pool. Surrounded by an ornately carved wooden deck, the pool overlooked the poverty of the local area. But Serif had little sympathy for the people he stared down upon. When his swim was done, he sat on the deck inside a small windbreaking gazebo, sipping a glass of Pinot Noir and watching ocean waves dance until darkness fell.

CHAPTER 6

One evening, a few days later, Serif met his cousin Tanya at the Tryst Café on the Danube – the vast river brimming with high waters caused by flooding rains throughout Europe. The two sat at their usual table; Serif ordered a bottle of vodka, and Tanya requested a mineral water. As soon as the waitress walked out of earshot, Serif said, "Tanya, we are ready to begin our final planning."

"We must have your men ready to go by the upcoming Christmas holidays," Tanya said anxiously. "That means in less than two months our plan will be put into motion."

Tanya had spent much of her young life with Serif and Reza's family after her parents were murdered, and she had always been involved in Serif's terrorist interests in one way or another. Serif trusted Tanya almost as much as he trusted his own brother, but because she was a woman, he kept her knowledge of his overall plans to a minimum.

"The upcoming reactor refuelling outage is scheduled for two weeks after the Orthodox Christian Christmas. That would compromise our plans greatly," Serif acknowledged.

"Right, that is why we *must* execute the plan before the power plant is crawling with hundreds of extra workers, not normally on site," Tanya said.

Tanya had no idea how far Serif was willing to take his

hatred for the West at this point. What she knew was that he was going to take the nuclear power plant hostage and melt the core slowly, releasing enough radiation to cause massive evacuations from Romania to the United Kingdom. But she had no idea that he would bring two nuclear devices into their game, which could instantly kill hundreds of thousands of innocent people.

"When will I meet your security man?" Serif asked.

Looking away from Serif, toward a man approaching from the darkness, backlit by distant streetlights, Tanya nodded in the man's direction. Draco was a stout, short, balding man in his late fifties.

Serif stood up at the table. "*Boniazara*, my name is –"

"I know who you are. It is a pleasure to meet you," Draco said.

Serif offered Draco a seat on the one remaining plastic chair.

He and Tanya gave each other a quick nod.

"What news have you?" Serif asked.

"I have arranged for a skeleton security crew to commence at eight o'clock the night before Christmas Day. Do you request something else?" Draco coldly replied.

Draco looked at Serif and waited for a change in his expression. He had just reported the best news Serif could have imagined, but his face showed no reaction.

Tanya took a sip of her mineral water. "Draco is going to find a window of opportunity that will allow your men to enter the plant's site boundary from the south, by the warehouse."

Serif listened quietly as Tanya continued. "There's a large hill adjacent to the west side of the warehouse and accessible from a service road that can't be seen from inside the site. I think you can enter by using a thin cable and pulley device, gliding your men over the fence. They can land in a blind spot of the plant's security cameras. Then they'll be able to approach the plant by way of the turbine building's roll-up door."

When Tanya finished, Serif turned to Draco. "I don't understand why you are willing to allow us to penetrate your facility and create a destruction that will cause the evacuation of Western Europe. Please tell me, what is your motivation, and how do you sleep at night?" Serif stared intently at Draco.

"I'm a man who has lost his country to Christian capitalism. I choose this path out of hate for all European business thieves, who steal our natural resources and ruin our people's lives. Starving the families of our brothers and destroying our ancient heritage," Draco stated. "I will easily give my life for a chance to get back at these bastards."

"Simply put, but I do not accept your reasons," Serif said, and stood up.

"Wait, please tell him," Tanya pleaded to Draco.

"My reasons sound simple to you, my friend. But I am not one to accept people openly. Tanya's dead father was my closest friend. Her confidence in you will be your pass to my story, today." Draco paused. "I am a direct descendant of Turkish monarchs. My family was forced into exile, forced to live like peasants, pleading for an honourable existence after the World War.

"Almost all my family members have been eliminated, but I remain. Although there have been many attempts on my life from the current Turkish underground political muscle, I now pledge my allegiance to JTS. And after this is done, I want my place at the head of the restored Ottoman Empire."

Serif took a second to let Draco's statement sink in. "If what you say is true, you will have your place – that, I promise."

"Thank you, Serif. I didn't know what you would say to

Draco's proposal," Tanya said gratefully.

"Now tell me how my men will enter the control room," Serif demanded.

Draco explained that since he was Cernavodă's Chief of Security, his men would automatically obey his commands, even the ones not in on the plan, until those few were silenced. Draco was very persuasive and, at times, ruthless to his subordinates. He had many guards on his force who pledged complete loyalty to him, but Draco would have to have some non-essential guards taken hostage or shot when the time came for him to take control of security.

Tanya had given them a decent plan of attack – breach the site boundary, then enter through the turbine building and finally reach the main control room. Draco would have to work out the details of how he would take control of the site, using his best men to set up machinegun turrets on top of the highest buildings and his snipers on the cooling tower. Once Draco was in complete control of the security throughout the plant, Bogdan would enter the control room and take over the operating reactor's controls. He would then be able to destroy the plant from the inside – spreading long-term radioactive contamination for thousands of miles.

The plan had a few gaps, but Serif agreed with it in principle. "Draco, I will contact you in one week. Now please, go attend to your plans."

Tanya reached into her black leather briefcase and retrieved an envelope containing thousands of South African dollars as Draco stood up, ready to leave. "Take this now, and we will finish our deal in Johannesburg," Tanya said to a satisfied Draco.

"I am pleased to be in the company of fellow Turks," Draco said. "I will see you in Johannesburg."

Draco walked off into the darkness from which he had appeared – his lighted outline visible long after his face had faded into the black soup of fog and streetlights. One streetlamp flickered a bit after Draco's figure completely vanished, reminding Serif of how dark and cold Europe would be when his plan had become reality. He motioned for the barmaid and ordered a Turkish coffee.

"I have faith that you know what you are doing, Tanya," Serif said. "I am not sure that Draco can be trusted."

Tanya almost looked hurt for a moment, then said confidently, "I watched this man myself for two years before asking for his help. His reputation is flawless. He is willing to do anything to achieve power within our newly reformed State. He will be a great asset to our revolution and final political strategy."

Serif sipped the strong, almost syrupy coffee. "I trust your judgment on this one, cousin." He smiled reassuringly at Tanya, who didn't smile back.

———

The next morning, Serif parked his Humvee at the end of a pier near Mamaia Beach. He could see his new yacht waiting for him, tied up in the last slip. He walked briskly down the pier, looking from side to side at yachts in different stages of construction, all of which were being built by the RYC – the Romanian Yacht Company. Reza's two bodyguards were following close behind Serif, skipping a few steps here and there to keep up with the long-legged Turk.

The RYC was run by two brothers who started their business in 2004, after the Romanian economy became invigorated by extra European Union start-up money. Its clientele were mostly rich Russian criminals looking for a nice boat to spend their afternoons on, while sipping vodka and enjoying the Black Sea ambience. Many of the Russians had invested all the money they could borrow from their Middle East friends into the oil and banking businesses left stranded by Russia's deep economic trough, immediately after the collapse of the Soviet Union.

Serif stepped onto the polished teakwood main deck of his yacht, trimmed in white railing with brass rosettes, and faced the stern. He imagined himself entertaining some stunning and sexy girls he might have brought along for an afternoon of cruising, swimming, and sun tanning. And sex. His boat was also equipped with a fairly large cabin near his stateroom, which could sleep six guests comfortably, if needed.

When he entered the state room, Serif became excited about the prospect of spending time anchored in a quiet harbour somewhere in the Adriatic Sea. Maybe find a Greek island with few inhabitants that he could visit when he needed a break from the boat. Its beautiful red leather-covered furniture and deep padded carpeting throughout gave him a feeling of smug satisfaction – his money well spent.

Removing the six mooring ropes, Reza's two men from Romania, Daniel and Maks, pushed the boat clear of the pier. Serif started the two large gas turbine engines when he pressed a silver-plated button on the captain's console. Serif was very proficient in handling a boat through the traffic of Mamaia – his father had taught him how to handle a yacht when he was a teenager. Serif's father, a captain in the Turkish navy, had been involved in the genocide killing of thousands in Armenia.

Serif admired his father, an unyielding seaman with a quick temper and a willingness to follow the orders of his government. However, a different vein of his father's obeisance to past leadership ran through Serif's dark-skinned body. Serif wanted not only the lands of Armenia returned to the Turks, but all territory once controlled by the Ottoman Empire. This grandiose worship of the Turkish past had been instilled in Serif and Reza by their father.

Serif slowly raised the yacht engine's power, guiding the vessel to the open waters of the Black Sea. Some smaller fishing boats floating near a large oil refinery off his port side could hear a muffled whine of the gas turbines coming from beneath the hull's waterline. Opening up the two engines to full throttle when he cleared the last stacked-rock water break, Serif experienced his boat's awesome power. It made him feel alive. And omnipotent.

Earlier that day, Maks and Daniel had loaded provisions into the hold for their trip south, passing by Istanbul, then into the Mediterranean. Serif's plan was to get back to Mamaia sometime within the next week, in order to prevent Tanya from becoming too suspicious. She thought that Serif needed to go to Istanbul to pick up more guns and had no idea that he was heading to the coast of Slovenia.

Serif manoeuvred his yacht for several hours toward the Bosphorus Strait. Upon entering the Sea of Marmara, he docked at a refuelling station near Istanbul's bustling main harbour. His men filled the fuel tanks while he reported to the Turkish authorities – a requirement for all vessels entering the harbour.

Serif explained to his fellow Turks that he was there to refuel his vessel and convinced them that he was only out for a pleasure cruise in the Mediterranean Sea. Within minutes, Serif started one of his two turbines and pulled away from Istanbul, then once out in the open waters, he ran both engines and travelled through the Dardanelles, then up the Baltic coast to Slovenia.

While Serif was at the helm of his yacht, Tanya met with Draco at her comfortable house in the Romanian vineyard district to discuss the security breaching plans at Cernavodă's nuclear power plant.

Tanya ignored Serif's comings and goings for the most part, because she knew that he was trying to get the manpower and guns together to ensure the success of their terrorist attack. But, occasionally, she needed to ask him specific questions, and she did not fully trust any communication between them except their face to face meetings. Tanya was very paranoid about the possibility of their organisation being penetrated by a wiretap or Internet bird dog looking for software vulnerabilities, which is the reason she had friends in many places watching out for electronic intruders, including Serif's home, cars, and yacht.

CHAPTER 7

INWA inspectors continuously monitored nuclear facilities throughout the world on a routine basis. When Carson became one of these inspectors, on assignment in Romania, he was often paired with the most promising people, fulfilling the role of mentor. On one such occasion he was with another American, Herman Hammerschmidt, for two weeks of complementary access investigations, while verifying the absence of undeclared nuclear activities and material inside Romania.

It was unusual for two inspectors from the same country to travel together, but Carson was helping Herman become Romania's next INWA country officer. Carson gave Herman as much information as he could about the history of Romania's suspected weapons program – Herman would have to learn the rest on his own. It took a tremendous amount of work to become an INWA country officer – the men and women were required to know all the details of the nuclear facilities, research centres, and locations that kept nuclear material in whatever state they were responsible for.

Travelling separately, Carson and Herman met in the mountains of Romania, at an old uranium ore milling plant. Built during the 1970s, the plant used a huge grinding machine to pulverise tons of raw mined ore into a manageable powder.

The uranium ore was then processed by chemical and heat treatment into what is known in the nuclear industry as yellowcake – a required precursor to nuclear fuel.

Carson and Herman each drove up the winding mountain roads in separate cars, after visiting other facilities before finally meeting for their last inspection at the milling plant.

Carson first met Herman in Vienna, when he came into the Agency after 9/11 with a long history of nuclear power plant operations and engineering experience. Graduating from Georgia Tech six years after Carson, Herman was now well respected in the field of root cause analysis. His work with various US utilities in managing their core damage mitigation procedures, along with nuclear accident detection and analysis skills, qualified him as a specialist in nuclear safety and security. He and Carson had similar backgrounds, making communication between them much easier than speaking with inspectors whose mother tongue was something other than "Engineer's English."

After their three days of inspection were completed at the uranium conversion plant, they met in the car park of their hotel, high in the Carpathian Mountains.

"So, where are you headed, Kit Carson?" Herman said with a chuckle. "I never get tired of saying that."

"Yeah, I know," Carson replied. "I'm gonna stop off on the way to the airport and play a little golf in a village outside of Bucharest. They've got a decent hotel on the course, so I'll see you next week sometime. We can go over everything we talked about this week."

"Yeah, that'd be great. Where are you gonna play golf in Romania?" Herman's tone was mocking.

"There's a small nine-hole course between here and the airport. It's a pretty modest course, but you wouldn't believe the difficulty of some of the hills and traps. You're welcome to stay and play, if you want."

"I was never much for playing golf, y'know," Herman said, closing the door of his Renault and starting the car's engine. "Take care. I'll see you back on campus." Herman referred to the Vienna International Centre as a campus – it made him feel young again, when he was a "rambling wreck of Georgia Tech."

Carson finished packing up his car, grateful that the weather was unusually warm for December – at lower altitudes – and afforded him an opportunity to be outdoors and relax a little, away from high technology.

The road leading down the mountain from the hotel was narrow, logging trails taking off from the main road at important positions along the way. Logging hardwood trees was a serious business for the locals. Its rapid execution depended greatly on the weather – snow and ice being detrimental to their limited business success. Carson's drive was overcast and gray; clouds hung so low some even touched a magnificent stone-faced peak to the west. Carson was exhilarated by the view of mountains and valleys as he drove down the blacktop, noticing deer standing in small herds along the way.

Passing through a little village of wooden houses with rusted roofs, Carson pulled into a fur trader's stop next to Bran Castle, better known as Castle Dracula by the tourist trade.

He stepped out of his car, stretching his long muscular legs, stiff from days of constantly walking in and around facilities. Carson strolled toward a small courtyard where the daily open market was being held. Locals and vendors came down from the surrounding mountains to sell colourful handmade tablecloths, delicately carved wooden figurines, hand-painted plates that were fired in local kilns, and luxurious fur coats that hung from three racks, protected from the sunlight and the heavy fog by a cloth tarpaulin draped over long wooden stakes. Located so close to Bran's castle one couldn't help thinking how the stakes looked like something Vlad the Impaler would have used to skewer thousands of his enemies – mounting their still wriggling corpses high above the market's crowd of shoppers.

Carson walked around the makeshift bazaar tents. Men, their wives, and children lived and worked in old wooden shacks in the surrounding mountains, where they crocheted tablecloths or used the natural clay found near some uranium mines to form the hand-painted dishware they were selling. Most of the better craftsmen and their wives made a reasonable living selling to tourists.

Stopping at the best fur trader selling that morning, Carson looked through about forty items ranging from silver fox, full-length coats to raccoon-skin hats. He felt the pelts as he walked further underneath the tarp, coming closer to the Romanian salesman who was talking to another local about the most expensive silver fox coat on his racks.

Although they were speaking in a local dialect, Carson could make out a few words and realised that they were bargaining over the price of the immaculate fox coat. The buyer was speaking rapidly, explaining his position with hand and body gestures – an ordinary measure in the negotiation process for this region. But without purchasing the coat, the potential customer left shortly. The fur vendor shook his head and smiled as he put the silver fox coat back on its hanger.

Noticing that a tourist had entered his sales area, the trader thought he might make a quick sale to the American. He walked over to Carson and held up a beautiful red fox jacket. "Your woman will like this one," the trader said with a gap-toothed smile.

Carson's intention that morning was to only shop for next year's Christmas present for Christy. He browsed the man's merchandise, then said, "I like the silver fox."

"No, that belongs to my friend," the fur trader said. He turned to put away his favourite teaser – the red fox jacket.

"Yeah, he looked happy to know that his wife was gonna get a nice Christmas present this year," Carson said.

"Not his woman, his momma," the fur trader said in broken English. "He wants surprise her."

Carson looked back over his shoulder to see the man who had negotiated for the silver fox coat get into a large white van without markings of any kind. The man sat in his van which was parked on a patch of dirt alongside the road between the furrier's outdoor sales and Carson's Pajero.

Something seemed odd about the van, its driver taking a cell phone call while waiting for the diesel engine to warm up. Carson couldn't put his finger on why he felt emptiness in his gut when he glanced at the driver and his vehicle, until he noticed a gun barrel leaned against the back window of a rear-panel door.

"Where does his momma live?" Carson asked the fur trader.

"His momma is living up there," the trader said, pointing toward a mountain covered in low-hanging fog.

"Yeah," Carson replied, turning his attention back to the business at hand. "How much for this silver fox hat?"

"That one?" the fur trader remarked. Taking a piece of paper and pencil he wrote the number 125,000 – one hundred twenty five thousand Romanian lei, or about fifty US dollars.

Carson wanted to buy a little something extra for Christy this year, so he wrote 100,000 down on the paper. Without a word, the trader wrote 110,000 and waved his hand across the number to indicate that was as good as it was going to get. Carson looked away again to the driver in the white van and then agreed. He gave the trader the money in lei that he had withdrawn from the airport automatic teller in Bucharest. The trader handed him the silver fox hat, and Carson walked away toward his car parked on the other side of the van.

Seemingly upset about what was being said to him over his cell phone, the driver of the van jumped out of the front seat and went quickly to the rear of the vehicle and opened one of its two large doors. Carson walked by slowly, trying to understand why the man was so disturbed and to take a look at the weapon that was leaning against the rear window.

Keeping his distance, Carson caught a quick glimpse inside the van. He could see green military boxes with crossed sickle and hammer embossed along their sides. The man was too busy rifling through video cables and tools to notice that someone was keenly observing him. Carson couldn't read the writing underneath the Soviet Russian symbol, but he could see that there were at least two boxes, before the man covered them with a partially pulled back government-issue army blanket.

Carson continued walking to his car, filing the information away for now. He was interested in anything that looked suspicious while in foreign countries, especially Romania, where he had seen several questionable events when he was the Agency's country officer. His primary job was to ensure there was no proliferation of nuclear materials or know-how to any countries other than the original five nuclear weapons states. But on occasion, Carson uncovered some sinister evidence not related to a nuclear program. Now he wondered why a van with Romanian number plates and no outer markings would be carrying military hardware.

Nearby, a family of gypsies was attempting to put its scavenged truck tire back on the axle of their covered wagon, using what looked like an ancient mallet and some long birch sticks. Carson watched for a moment and shook his head. He glanced at his watch and realised he needed to get to his next hotel by lunchtime. He'd have to log the suspect white van in his memory for now – nothing looked to be nuclear related or worth his urgent investigation. He decided to report it anonymously to the local authorities after arriving at his hotel.

Carson drove cautiously down the winding, treacherous two-lane road, glancing at the concrete stanchions that held up the power lines along the edge of the road. The stanchions looked similar to a concrete ladder leading up to the two power lines that were precariously held in place by glass insulators. Local mountain people had been supplied their electricity by this means for many years and saw no reason why it should be changed, although they lost their power very often during the winters when heavy ice hung on the lines and brought them to the ground.

Driving along the pig-path of a road, Carson thought about how many times he had been in Romania and performed nuclear weapons-related inspections all over the country. Western countries, using Romanian uranium resources, developed a program of mining and milling the ore from the mines in the Carpathian Mountains, to be used as fuel for their own nuclear reactors. But Romania's communist regime, led by the tyrant Ceaușescu, had other ideas for its most popular natural resource. Although Romania was a communist country, during the initial stages of construction of the reactor located in Cernavodă in the 1970s and '80s, Ceaușescu wanted to be independent of all Soviet influence and turned to the West for expertise and support.

Ceauşescu decided to build the two boiling water reactors near a large bend in the Danube, just before it dumped into a delta at the Black Sea. It was an easy place to get supplies shipped in by barge on the Danube River. Forced labour dug a canal linking the Danube to the Black Sea, between Cernavodă and the coast, which was used as a constant cooling water supply for the nuclear power plant. Many men lost their lives digging the deep canal, but it was a small price to pay for Ceauşescu to be able to brag about having the largest nuclear power station in Europe supplying his country with electricity.

Nuclear power reactors generate tons of plutonium that have to be safeguarded from potential proliferators. Carson had turned the responsibility of implementing the international treaty requirements on the operating boiling water reactor and the unit under construction at Cernavodă over to Herman during his last inspection at the site.

Carson had driven the thirty-eight miles to the Black Sea several times during his Cernavodă Nuclear Power Plant inspections. He felt it was necessary in order to get a better feel for the atmosphere surrounding the country's struggles and possible motivation for proliferating nuclear materials for sale to Middle East terrorists who might be trying to make a bomb.

Ports along the Romanian coast were open to traffic from many ex-communist countries, which bordered the sometimes violent Black Sea waters. A lot of smaller ships and barges also ended up in Constanta after travelling down the Danube River from countries in Western Europe. The cargoes of these vessels were often put onto other ships heading across the Black Sea, then reloaded with cargo that could be taken back upriver. Constanta and its neighbour Mamaia were very busy seaports.

Carson knew the area around Mamaia pretty well, but

he knew the nuclear power plant's design at Cernavodă much better. It was a boiling water reactor much like the reactor he qualified on while working for private utilities in the US.

"Finally," Carson muttered under his breath as he saw the first indication of his hotel in the foothills of the Carpathians. He turned onto a small road that led him into a poor town whose main source of income was from a Renault automobile factory that had just been built.

Travelling up the pothole-filled road toward the only golf course in Romania, Carson noticed the people walking around in tattered clothing, some stopping in the little shops to buy staples shipped in by rail or a local Romanian entrepreneur who had figured out the logistics problems for the people.

Surprisingly, the little town was situated in a convenient place for a few Romanian oil field managers from Austria or wealthier factory owners who played golf. Historians said the oil fields were raped by the Soviets during the '70s, but their techniques were so antiquated that they only scraped the surface of a wealth of subterranean black gold. Austrian and German technology was now proving that a lot of money could still be made in the Romanian oil fields.

After checking into the golf club hotel, Carson played his long-awaited round on the course before sitting down to a Tuborg beer and a mixed grill of various meat dishes. The lamb and chicken were tender and moist, but the beef was tough as usual in Romania. He lit a Cuban cigar, a Cohiba that he saved to celebrate his golf game "in country." Carson enjoyed it much more than his ordinary dinner.

Carson ended the night with a local cognac and a quick call home from his room on his cell phone.

"Hey, Susie Q – can you hear me?" Carson said through the faint connection.

"Hey Dad, I can hear you okay," Susan replied.

"How's everything going?" Carson asked. "Wasn't today your last day before winter break?"

"Yeah, I finished everything I was supposed to today," Susan said. "But Mom is on my case again. When are you gonna be home? I need your help on some of this physics homework; it's a killer."

"I'll give it my best shot, honey," Carson said. "Check the itinerary that I gave you before I left; remember we don't talk about travelling times over the phone. Tell your mom that I'm flying out on time, okay?"

Christy was attending her evening art class that night and would take the ten-fifteen train back home, as usual. Although she didn't have a full-time job, Christy stayed very busy organising and participating in numerous activities offered by the United Nations Women's Guild of Vienna.

"Oh yeah, I remember now. I'll see you when you get home, Dad," Susan said.

"Okay S.Q., love ya," Carson ended.

"Love you too, bye," Susan said.

Pausing for a moment after snapping his cell phone shut, Carson looked out of the window into the night and thought about how much he loved Christy and Susan – they were the most important people in his life, and he wanted to keep them safe. Christy was a rock-solid anchor to Carson's life of travel and investigative work in the ever-changing international theatre of nuclear weapons. He relied on Christy's strength and put great faith in Susan's determination to finish school at the top of her class.

He could hear a Romanian newscast playing in the background on his small TV set as he got ready for bed. It was a replay of the Chechen terrorists taking over a grammar school in southern Russia, killing so many of the children with an explosive device. A horrible act compounded by a botched rescue attempt by unprepared Russian special police forces. When the European weather forecast ended, Carson switched off the TV and the red shaded lamp on a tiny night stand.

Lying in the lumpy bed, Carson's thoughts drifted back to the white van parked near Castle Bran. His gut told him not to forget it.

CHAPTER 8

Carson was scheduled to investigate a report of illicit trafficking that had been detected at the Romanian port of Constanta before flying home. He was to visit a port waste storage facility, where fuel pellets were quarantined – he would have to identify the batch of undeclared nuclear material's uranium content.

Carson pulled his report from his case and went over every detail of the incidental finding by the radiation monitors at Constanta's seaport. An INWA technical cooperation project helped the Romanians set up a post that monitored sea-land containers as they arrived from other countries. Constanta was quickly becoming the gateway to Western Europe from the former Soviet Bloc countries, and everyone believed that incoming shipments should be screened for any signs of nuclear material smuggling.

After reviewing the data, Carson put his briefcase and his isotope identifier into his rented Pajero and headed toward the Black Sea and Constanta. As soon as he had passed through a terrible traffic jam surrounding Bucharest, he turned the volume up on his spinning Santana CD and kicked his vehicle into high gear. Carson dodged potholes and people trying to sell things along the way. The same two-lane winding road went right by Cernavodă's nuclear power plant, and he would eventually cross the new red evacuation bridge.

As he drove, he remembered a conversation he had with Christy just before he left for his trip. She had mentioned that he had a class reunion coming up sometime in June and that Bruce was organising the whole event.

"Carson, don't forget to answer Bruce's email when you get back home," Christy had said as she kissed him goodbye.

Bruce and his wife Terri lived in Morven, Georgia, Carson's hometown. He and Bruce had been friends since high school. Carson always made a point to visit him whenever passing through Georgia. Their friendship kept him grounded. He and Christy planned to spend their thirty days of home leave in the US the following summer; the class reunion would give Carson a chance to see all his old friends again.

"I'll do it first thing when I get back," Carson had promised as he gave Christy an extra hug and a kiss.

Carson was jolted out of his thoughts just in time to avoid a horse-drawn cart, travelling down the road in his lane. Passing on the left side, he noticed that the very thin man in rags for clothes was holding the reins, his flowery-scarfed wife sat next to him, and two dirty youngsters in the bottom of the hay-lined bed stared at him through hollow black eyes. Carson could feel their hunger in the pit of his stomach.

Every ten kilometres he saw small concrete road signs, resembling tombstones, announcing the distance from Bucharest and the name of the next small village.

Turning into Dragos Voda, a small hamlet left very poor from the Ceauşescu regime, he slammed on the brakes to avoid a herd of sheep crossing the narrow road. As Carson waited impatiently for the herder to get his animals across the road, he noticed the houses nearby. Each seemed to have two distinct features besides being rundown – they were heated by one fireplace and had a water tank on stilts behind them. He imagined that the external surge volume allowed the water to heat during the day for use by the large families of Romanians living in these areas.

Behind a fence stood a man holding a piece of seasoned oak, ready to lay it on a large fire in a pit that the man's son had just dug. This was the family's barbecue pit. Very soon the boy would stoke the hot coals that were going to be used to grill a lamb that the father had skinned that morning.

Carson let out a short ironic laugh and thought sadly that the difference between the barbecues he fondly remembered from childhood and this Romanian cookout was that this would be the only meat these people would eat for several days. But Carson realised that things were only going to get better in Romania, their way of life would improve now that they had joined the European Union.

A teenage boy came up to Carson's idling car and tapped on the window. "You want buy a CD? Sting, Deep Purple, Bach, I have them all."

Selling pirated CDs along the row of backed-up cars seemed to be profitable for the teenager and his friend who was selling Nikes from the back of his old Dacia. Carson waved the boys along.

Within another hour, Carson arrived at his hotel in Mamaia. Cold winter winds coming down from the mountains caused some of the water rides nearest to the hotel to freeze. But the large water pumps of the water slides were much too expensive to allow them to freeze and bust their casings, so the larger adult rides in the park were drained.

Unloading his overnight gear, Carson walked up to the entrance of the four-star hotel and went inside. "Good day, my friend. Do you have a double room available for tonight?"

he asked the desk clerk, who spoke English and said an instant, "Of course," with a warm smile.

Carson was handed a room key that was attached to a heavy brass plumb. Room keys in many European hotels were supposed to be turned into the front desk when the occupant left for the day, signalling the house staff that the room was ready for cleaning. The heavy plumb was annoying to carry in his pocket, so Carson always removed the key from its ring until he checked out.

Carson opened the curtains on the windows of his room and could see the beach and its low-breaking Black Sea waves. He put his toiletries in the small bathroom and noticed that the shower stall was curtainless and that there was a small drain near the middle of the floor. Carson had managed these open showers in the past and would be able to keep the water focused enough not to wet everything in the bathroom.

Locking his hotel room door with the outer deadbolt, Carson went down the elevator and dropped his key off with the desk clerk. The incoming dense cloud cover caused a temperature drop and Carson was chilled as he crossed the car park to get to his Pajero. He wanted to reach the illicit trafficking nuclear material as soon as possible, in case the heavy clouds decided to release their icy rain. After a traffic battle of about thirty minutes, Carson made his way out to the contraband storage site, where he met Marion, the Romanian Port Authority representative.

"Good afternoon. Carson Griffin from the INWA," Carson said, handing him a card.

"Good day. I want you see our problem," Marion said in his best English.

"I understand from Bucharest that you may have some uranium here," Carson said.

"Yes, Mr. Alexander here also," Marion said.

Carson turned to find Alexander coming from inside the Port Authority headquarters, a plain structure with a rope-surrounded ship and anchor plaque nailed above its steel door. Alexander, a balding, chubby man in his mid-fifties, was the Romanian Nuclear Safety and Security Authority representative at the location.

"Good afternoon, Mr. Alexander," Carson said with a polite smile.

Reaching out his hand and nodding, Alexander said, "Hello, Mr. Griffin. We have problem here."

Trying to get around the small talk and minimise incomprehensible translations, Carson went immediately into his investigating posture. "Okay, let's take a look at the material."

Marion led the group, which was now up to six with the addition of some of his helpers who were along for the show, to a storage building. After opening a corrugated tin door to the tin building, Marion stepped back from the group. He didn't like to be around radioactivity – he had heard from school that it would make him sterile.

Carson went into the holding area with his isotope identifier set in a radiation detection mode. Los Alamos National Laboratory in New Mexico had helped to develop this extraordinary hand-held piece of equipment that could determine a substance's uranium or plutonium content within one to three minutes of identifying a gamma-emitting source. Its alarm beeped slowly at first, but as Carson moved further into the building, the beeps were closer together, which meant that he was getting near the source. This always reminded Carson of getting-hotter-getting-colder games he used to play when he was a kid in Georgia. Carson thought it was the best device that the Agency had given him and nicknamed his detector "The Judge."

Pegging the metre of his device, its alarm now a constant obnoxious tone, Carson found the illicit nuclear material stored in a steel box. The box was locked with a Russian-made padlock that one of Marion's helpers quickly knocked off using a sledgehammer. Inside the box, Carson could see numerous rows of fifteen-centimetre lead pipes, each with their ends crudely crimped. There looked to be at least one hundred of the cigar-shaped shielding tubes, stacked neatly in the gang box. One end of the box was blackened with soot by some kind of high temperature source, which evidently melted the lead from two of the shielding tubes.

Marion explained to Alexander that the gang box had been discovered near the aft bilge of an ocean-worthy trawler, sitting next to a freshwater evaporator that was being used by the boat's crew to make potable water. A fishing boat of that size needed a lot of extra fresh water for washing down the sea urchin-encrusted equipment. Their evaporator ran day and night trying to keep the freshwater holds full, thereby generating a lot of heat near the gang box filled with uranium pellets.

Carson spoke slowly so that he could be clearly understood – handling radioactive material demanded it. "Mr. Alexander, I would like to test the material inside one of those tubes." Carson pointed to a partially melted tube. "Can you open this one?"

Alexander removed the tube from the gang box and put it gently on a nearby table. Carson's detector still registered the presence of some kind of radioactive material. The detector's meter face was reading a safer level now that they had separated the tube from the others, but it was still screaming its solid tone. Carson calibrated his instrument before trying to identify whatever was producing the highly radioactive alarm readings.

Marion's fear of radioactivity was overcome by his need to be in charge of his men's activities. He was losing control of a situation that he actually had lost control over the moment Carson identified a radioactive source – INWA was now in charge of the scene. Rushing to help with the disassembly, Marion took the pair of pliers from one of his two men and opened the soft lead covering. Three pellets rolled out of the very dark grey pipe and onto the table, each about the size of a thimble. Partially hidden in the remaining piece of lead were two more, which Marion thumped out with a quick drop of the tube against the tabletop.

Carson separated one of the five pellets from the others and held the business end of his pistol-shaped detector very close to its surface. After about sixty seconds, The Judge generated a message across its greenish tinted screen – it was uranium. Carson had seen this type of uranium-pelletised fuel before. His detector showed him this was natural uranium, ready for a heavy water reactor that could be used to generate electricity when used correctly or weapons-grade plutonium if used immorally.

Carson immediately called his headquarters in Vienna using his dedicated pocket PC phone with scrambled transmission. He dialled into INWA. "Carson G16-Y9. Line secured."

"Todd Sinclair, please," Carson said anxiously.

A few seconds later, Todd came on the line. "Hello, Sinclair."

"Todd, it's Carson. I've identified the trafficked material as natural uranium pellets. They were probably produced from a CANDU uranium oxide press."

"Okay, Carson. Quarantine it at the research reactor site in Piteşti. I'll get someone to verify its arrival," Todd said.

"Will do," Carson replied.

"Good work, buddy. Have a safe trip home," Todd said.

"Thanks, Todd," Carson said, standing a few yards away from over two million dollars' worth of illicitly trafficked uranium.

Carson snapped his PC phone closed and turned to Alexander. "Please have your men put two pellets in these two vials. I need to take them back to Vienna for further testing and analysis."

Alexander handed the vials to Marion who put the pellets in the small plastic bottles and handed them to Carson. Marion put the three remaining pellets back into the partially opened lead pipe and hammered the ends closed again. He placed the pipe back into the box as Alexander called Bucharest to let them know about INWA's results.

Alexander walked around in circles talking to his director in Romanian before turning to Carson. "Mr. Griffin, we want to take box to Piteşti."

Carson nodded. "Yes, Piteşti would be the best place to quarantine these pellets."

Carson had inspected Piteşti many times and knew the research centre on the other side of Bucharest very well. Other nuclear materials were already declared and under Agency seal at the site.

After counting the remainder of the tubes lying in the box and measuring a randomly selected high percentage of the items, Carson asked Marion's men to drill an array of very small holes through various points around the exterior of the box. He then put special steel sealing wire through the holes, safeguarding the nuclear material under the sealing wire and two special Agency metal seals until its arrival at the research centre.

"Mr. Alexander, someone will meet you in Piteşti on

Monday to verify their receipt of this nuclear material," Carson stated. "They will unseal it there for your police detectives to examine further."

"We will comply with anything that you wish," Alexander said.

Romania's new government had really beefed up the illicit trafficking department of the nation's security infrastructure. Although they were much more focused on drugs coming from across the Black Sea, they supported the installation of radiation detectors at various points of entry at the Constanta port. But the detectors' use was limited by their inability to detect a vessel carrying plutonium or uranium passing the port offshore. The sodium iodide crystals that detected the energy of gamma radiation were very large compared to other laboratory devices, but the crystals were directed at sea-land containers being passed through a portal – not, for instance, a yacht speeding by Constanta's port on its way to Mamaia.

Carson left the port district and nuclear contraband, heading back to his hotel on Mamaia Beach. He couldn't wait to get home and spend Christmas with Christy and Susan. Holiday lights reflecting off the snow in Vienna made this time of year especially beautiful in the parks and surrounding mountains. His memories of their annual visits to the many Christmas markets throughout the city and stopping at favourite cafés for warming coffee drinks or hot chocolate and Viennese pastries made Carson all the more anxious to get back home.

CHAPTER 9

As Carson entered his hotel room, his pocket PC began to ring. An operator said with a heavy Austrian-German accent, "Please hold for Mr. Sinclair."

When Todd came on the line, the two spoke for a few minutes about the nuclear material that would be transferred to Piteşti. Then Todd said, "Carson, I've got some good news from Cernavodă unit number two. Seems they're receiving a shipment of fresh fuel tomorrow and will be ready for someone to verify its receipt, immediately. The Romanians want to start using the fuel a week from now, and we don't have time to send another inspector before Christmas."

"No problem, I'll take care of it," Carson said, then added, "but you know that I'll have to fly home on the red-eye from Bucharest on Christmas Eve if I stay through tomorrow."

"Listen, we'll make all the flight arrangements for you from here," Todd said. "I'll have Ellie call you once the changes have been made. Thanks, Carson."

Carson hung up with a resigned sigh, then pushed his speed dial for home on his unencrypted wireless line. "Hey, it's me."

"We've got everything almost done here, babe," Christy said, her voice cheery and excited.

"Good, hon. I can't wait to get home," Carson said.

"Listen, I've got to take care of another important project tomorrow."

"Oh, no!" Christy exclaimed. "When will you be back?"

"I'll be coming on Santa's sleigh," Carson replied.

"Okay. We'll be waiting up for you. Be careful," Christy said, thinking about how many times she and Susan had to wait for him through past holidays.

Christy always understood the significance of her husband's work – tough as it was to accept. Since their marriage twenty years earlier, there had been many holidays with Carson working, either for the Navy's nuclear program or as an on-shift Senior Reactor Operator at the nuke plant in Georgia. Christy didn't like it, but she had gotten used to it, and she knew he wouldn't be staying in Romania during the Christmas holidays unless it was extremely important.

Carson called the front desk to extend his reservation for another night and requested a wake-up call for the next morning. The hotel room was equipped with its own hot water pot and instant Italian coffee for his first cup of the day.

Mamaia's cold, blustery winds would make a walk on the concrete seaside promenade miserable, so Carson decided to spend the afternoon sitting in the hotel's restaurant/bar, generating his report for the day's activities. He'd have to find a comfortable place for his laptop, flanked by a solid wall that would hide his screen while he worked.

He found a secluded seat at a heavy oak table, and took his time writing up his report, describing the details of his impromptu analysis with the isotope identifier. Connecting The Judge to his laptop with an umbilical cable, he was able to download the gamma energy spectra he had taken of the uranium pellets from its fairly large database. When everything was loaded and his report ready for submission,

Carson called the waiter over and ordered a typical Romanian meal of cabbage rolls, a spicy minced meat dish with a grilled chicken breast, and for dessert a sweet doughnut drenched in cherry syrup. It was at times like these that Carson longed for a plate of southern fried chicken, collard greens, black-eye peas, fresh cornbread, and for dessert a slice of sweet potato pie.

Carson's table, located behind a large bay window, allowed him to see the reflection of a man sitting two tables away from him. Dressed in a woollen pea coat, covering a brown cotton shirt and dungarees, the man was nursing a Tuborg Gold beer. Carson could see that he was trying to watch a television mounted above the bar that was showing the Romanian soccer team losing their game to Italy. Occasionally, the man would look in Carson's direction as if he wanted to say something to him but couldn't for fear of being seen.

After finishing dinner, Carson packed up his laptop and went into the lobby where he pushed the elevator button. Carson felt the man's presence as he approached. Standing next to a large green plant, the man whispered, "Hey, you from the INWA?" Carson smelled an old sea smell coming from the man that reminded him of turbine condenser cleanings – back when he was in the Navy.

"Yeah, I am," Carson said, his suspicions now confirmed.

"I have something that you should know," the seaman said. "But I need money. Two hundred dollars, US."

It wasn't Carson's first informant encounter, but this one seemed somewhat intriguing. He hesitated for a moment when the elevator doors opened and an elderly woman walked by him, slowly making her way toward the restaurant.

"I've got it in Euros," Carson said.

"Okay, show me in here," the seaman pointed toward a

small unused parlour.

Carson followed the man into the small room, a door at each end covered in heavy drapery. The lighting was dim, but he could see a dark wood bar with a large mirror hanging behind it showing their reflection. He smelled a sickening mixture of cat urine and mildew.

"I knew you would be here. That cargo at the harbour was easy to find. Even for those port idiots," the seaman said.

Carson showed the man a 100-Euro bill. "This for now; the rest when I hear what you have to say."

"My cousin said the Turk is going to melt down Cernavodă," the seaman blurted.

"Who is the Turk?" Carson asked. "And who is your cousin?"

"That's all you get for 100 Euros – cheap bastard," the seaman retorted.

"Where did you learn your English, old man?" Carson wanted to know.

"Canada, of course," the seaman stated. "We Romanians learned a lot from the Canadians while Ceauşescu stole their nuclear secrets."

It sounded to Carson as if the man knew something, but it was difficult for him to be absolutely certain that he was telling the truth.

"Show me some proof," Carson demanded.

Reaching into his pea coat inside pocket, the seaman produced a strange-looking key. Carson immediately recognized what it was: a nuclear reactor's mode-switch key. Never seen outside of any control room, including Cernavodă, the six-inch key was used to align a column of circuits mounted in the main control panel. When inserted and turned to a particular position, the key would cause a massive realignment of logic relays underneath its switch surface. These relays manipulated many components in the complicated controls of the reactor, but most important was its command over starting the nuclear reactor or putting it in a "safe-shutdown" condition by initiating a SCRAM.

"I stole this from a boat captain down the boardwalk who used to work at Cernavodă as a senior reactor operator," the seaman said. "He wanted me to help him destroy my family's hometown. He said that everyone would have time to get out, but that's not the point."

Handing the key to Carson, the man looked around as if he thought he was being watched from somewhere outside the dark, foul-smelling room.

Carson frowned. "Where is this captain?"

"His name is Bogdan," the seaman said. "You will find his wooden house near the pier – it's the one closest to the Atlanta Bar."

Carson took another look at the mode-switch key, handed the seaman the other one hundred Euros and watched him limp out of a side exit. The wind whipped in behind the seaman when he opened the glass door. Carson now knew that there had to be some truth to what the seaman said. There were usually only two of these special keys made, and both were kept closely controlled by the management of any nuclear power plant. A copy of one of these keys might have been possible, if an insider with access was able to acquire a proper impression of the original key.

Taking the elevator back to his room to pick up his car keys, Carson grabbed his coat, laptop, and The Judge, then headed out to find Bogdan's house. He didn't trust the security of the hotel enough to leave his laptop, the mode-switch key, or The Judge in the room. But Carson knew that carrying the mode-switch key with him was a bad idea, so he locked it securely in his car's glove compartment and deposited The Judge and his laptop in the trunk. At least the Pajero had a car alarm which, with any luck, would discourage local thieves from breaking into the vehicle.

He knew the neighbourhood that the seaman had mentioned was rough. However, at over six-foot-four-inches tall and a powerful 250 pounds, Carson thought that he would be able to hold his own. The normal INWA inspectors were not formally trained in self-defence, but his special-ops training had prepared him for this kind of situation. Carson didn't carry a gun on normal inspections, like the one he had been assigned this week before Christmas – it was just too hard to get through airport security.

Carson drove down to the waterfront and parked along the main street, two blocks away from the Atlanta Bar. His car and equipment would be safest under a streetlight, in plain sight. He walked along a row of rundown shacks, checking for any sign of life within the dimly lit houses. Most people were in their homes trying to stay warm – only the tourists were moving around the beach city on this night.

Carson noticed through one house's curtainless window a man and his wife watching television. It was a Romanian channel with twenty-four-hour, non-stop folk singing by Romanian singers dressed in authentic costumes – definitely not a show that anyone outside the country would ever want to watch.

Stepping over a broken wooden gate and into Bogdan's yard, Carson crouched as he got closer to the side of the house. He tried to look inside while hiding behind three fifty-five-gallon metal drums whose white paint gave them a reflective illumination caused by a streetlamp. Carson heard barking but knew the dog was too far away to be barking at him. He decided to move forward; straightening up a little, he stepped out of the shadow of the drums and rushed toward the corner of Bogdan's house.

Without warning, he heard a man's deep voice behind him. "May I help you?"

The fact that the man spoke in English startled Carson. Without being able to make out the man's face when he stood up from his crouched position, Carson raised his hands.

"Uh, I seemed to have lost my dog," Carson replied.

Bogdan's man, and Carson's new acquaintance, was Marius Zadra. "Really, maybe we can find him inside?"

Pulling a pistol from his coat pocket, he shoved Carson toward the door of Bogdan's house. It was hard for Carson to see his way through and around the junk strewn all about the small side garden. With his hands still in the air, Carson's feet finally felt the concrete walkway.

In the light of a yellow porch lamp, Carson reached out to turn the brass doorknob. He could hear voices coming from inside speaking Romanian and quick bursts of laughter interrupting a story one of the men was telling. The door opened, and Marius pushed Carson inside.

"Who do we have here?" Bogdan demanded as he stood up. "Check his pockets."

"I found this guy outside, browsing through your garden, Bogdan," Marius said as he patted Carson down for weapons and identification.

Carson kept his United Nations Laissez-Passer with him at all times – the diplomatic grease would ease his way through most situations when travelling to countries all over the world. But Bogdan wasn't impressed by the multi-lingual exemptions printed on the front and back of its ten pages. It was Carson's hotel key and the key to his Pajero that was of much more interest to Bogdan.

"I'm not as impressed by this United Nations passport as you might have hoped, Mr. Griffin," Bogdan sneered. "But maybe you can help find something that has been taken from me. Have you been contacted by any sailors while staying at your hotel?"

"No, I don't like to talk to strangers," Carson replied with plenty of sarcasm in his voice.

Bogdan turned toward Marius. "Check his hotel room and find this Pajero."

"Will do, boss. Oh, here's the pocket PC that was in his coat pocket," Marius said as he left Bogdan's house with another member of Bogdan's operating crew.

Bogdan took the pocket PC and flattened it with a sledgehammer on his doorstep, crushing its locator chip. Carson tried not to wince. "So, you work for the INWA. What are you doing here in Mamaia?" Bogdan asked.

"Taking in some sun, evaluating the tightness of local bikinis," Carson replied as he lowered his hands.

Bogdan pointed to a chair near a handmade book shelf filled with technical manuals from Cernavodă. "Sit."

Carson sat next to the shelf and noticed a roll of drawings that resembled piping and instrument diagrams he had used many times in the United States. Looking a little closer at a wooden box that was placed between the bookshelf and what might have been a closet door, Carson could make out other drawings, each with their own printed legends. Watermarks on the thick rolls of paper looked to be copied, the originals no doubt still in the engineering building in Cernavodă.

Marius soon returned to Bogdan's house and said with a satisfied look on his face, "I found the mode-switch key in his car's locked glove compartment. But there was no sign of our thief anywhere near the car or his hotel room."

"I think that you will want to join us tomorrow, Mr. Griffin," Bogdan said. "A UN hostage might turn out to be just what we need for an additional diversion."

"Sorry, I have plans for the weekend," Carson said sarcastically. "You'll have to carry on without me, I'm afraid."

Marius shoved his fist into the base of Carson's neck with a powerful blow. Carson dropped to his knees and nearly blacked out.

"Put him on the floor, and zip-tie his feet and hands," Bogdan instructed Marius. "We would not want Mr. Griffin to think about leaving before morning. I will send a message to the Hunter and have the thief tracked down."

Carson couldn't believe what he had stumbled into – he recalled what he had learned from an old Master Chief Petty Officer in the Navy about hostages and nuclear reactors. Kill anyone you don't know and some you do – there was no such thing as a hostage, only casualties of friendly fire. Carson wasn't worried about becoming the next casualty, if it meant stopping the terrorists from carrying out some kind of nuclear reactor meltdown and major contamination release. However, he could do little to help in his current position, other than listen very carefully to any planning strategy he could overhear coming from the other room.

Cernavodă's procedures were written by the American contractors from Bechtel Engineering, creating a need for all the reactor operators to understand English clearly. When talking about operating in the control room, they all reverted to English, a fortunate break for Carson. Although he had learned a lot of his Romanian language on the fly, he was fluent enough to carry on a decent conversation. But the technical aspects of the plant were much easier for him to understand when the terms were spoken in his native tongue.

Carson knew that it couldn't have been easy for these men to get the plans for Cernavodă. And obtaining a reactor's mode-switch key was impossible without someone working with them on the inside. He listened to Bogdan's crew discuss their plans to take control of the nuclear power plant while he was lying on a small flat mattress, his hands and feet bound together with a heavy plastic zip-tie designed to hold large electrical cabling together in the plant. Carson tried to ignore his body's cramping and focused his attention on overhearing as much as possible.

"My contact is providing us clear passage into the control room by way of the turbine building," Bogdan was saying. "We will have to take control of the reactor before the on-shift crew can shut down the core. The shift manager will order a reactor operator to turn the mode switch to the shutdown position and remove the mode-switch key. That action will cause a reactor SCRAM, and it will take us over twenty-four hours to restart the unit."

Jacob, a tall, thin man with two days' growth of beard asked, "Will I have to maintain the plant's turbine-generator on line?"

"Yes, if you can," Bogdan replied.

"One more question," Jacob said.

"What is it?" Bogdan looked annoyed.

"When do we get paid?" Jacob asked.

Bogdan's deal was that Serif would pay him and his crew after the job was done and they were safely hiding in Riga, Latvia. "I will meet you at the Steak Roaster, one week after the job," Bogdan replied. "We will split up the money, and then we must all change our identity, as we have discussed. I have arranged for a plastic surgeon to evaluate each of you for facial reconstruction upon our arrival.

"I want you all to think very clearly about what we are about to do with our lives and the amount of money we will make. But most of all, think about where you will spend the rest of your days," Bogdan cautioned. "I can guarantee you that we will be hunted down by the Europeans and probably the Americans, so you must agree to have the surgery that we have all discussed – without it, no one will be safe."

Carson knew he wouldn't be making it out of this situation in one piece. The information was flowing much too easily for Bogdan to let him live. He listened intently for a possible defect in the operator's skills – it was easy for him to understand their technical jargon. However, the surgery that they were talking about having to hide their identity would require bringing in plastic surgeons from somewhere outside of Latvia. Carson had no idea how they would be able to get that done. He contemplated the idea that there must be a wider network of support out there taking care of these guys and some crazy Turk.

"It will take us all working together to pull this thing off," Bogdan said. "The moment we expect containment breach we will SCRAM the reactor. By doing this, we will control the pressure inside the containment, thereby controlling the radiation plume leaving Cernavodă's reactor. We will use the ventilation emergency exhaust valves to release some steam occasionally, then re-close them with an extra hydraulic assistance device that we are going to install." Bogdan looked around at the men to be sure they understood his every word as they listened intently and occasionally nodded.

"Serif will make our demands known to the European Union. We will hold down the radioactive release until we are sure that Serif's demands are met, then shut down the reactor's neutronic chain reaction with a full liquid boron neutron-poison injection. The poison will absorb all the neu-trons that are being used to further the meltdown of the re-actor's uranium core."

Bogdan's instructions from Serif were clear enough. He wanted his collaborators to believe the plan ended with Bog-dan's crew in control over the life-killing plume they were releasing into the air, spreading radioactive contamination for several thousands of miles. The terrorist operators knew that the plant could send its deadly plume high enough for elevated wind currents to create a swirling effect in the ra-dioactive cloud. The swirl would distribute the radioactive contaminates even further, dispersing a catastrophic quan-tity of radioisotopes over a huge area.

"Who is this Serif?" Jacob asked. "And why haven't we met him?"

"You will know when you see him, Jacob," Bogdan said. "He will be bringing our money from the JTS."

Carson knew nothing about this mad Turkish terrorist until his name was just mentioned. He had heard of the JTS from news articles on the Internet, but he was unaware that the terrorist organisation was operating in the realm of nucle-ar reactors. What Carson did realise was that these conspir-ators were just pawns in a monstrous scheme to destroy the lives and livelihoods of millions of Europeans by spreading radioactivity throughout cities and farms located between the Mediterranean and the North Sea.

Carson thought of his wife and daughter, decorating the Christmas tree and preparing dishes for a Christmas Day dinner, and for the first time in his life, wondered if he'd ever see Christy and Susan again.

CHAPTER 10

Serif's yacht arrived at Slovenia's coast in the mid-afternoon two days before Christmas. Daniel and Maks tied off the boat to a pier with four mooring lines in an effort to keep it as stable as possible for the transfer of the precious cargo. Serif was proud of the fact that although the hull was narrow, its size had been no hindrance to the boat's agility while negotiating waters through the Bosphorus. Passing Istanbul and cruising around the Balkan Peninsula to Slovenia in a beautiful new yacht was a dream come true for Serif. He smiled contently as Daniel fastened two nylon rope lines to the pier's iron mooring ears. But Maks' line had too much slack, allowing the boat to bounce off the pier's rubber-wrapped wooden pillars. Although Serif liked Reza's hired men for their ability to carry out murders when ordered, he had serious misgivings about their intelligence. Maks' leadership kept the two barely out of trouble at times, especially after Daniel had sipped a little too much Tuica. But at least both men were cold-blooded and would kill without hesitation.

According to plan, Serif's helicopter was waiting on a small airstrip about a ten-minute drive from the pier. The pilot drove Serif and Maks out to his chopper from the pier, leaving Daniel to watch over the yacht. Less than two hours later,

Serif landed with Maks near Reza's hotel outside of Idrija.

Maks climbed into the backseat of Serif's Hummer while Serif sat in the front passenger seat, letting Reza drive. "Tell me where we are, Reza."

Serif's brother filled him in on the work performed by the two nuclear weapons experts, Mrak and Broz, and told him of the final recovery of the damaged reactor fuel. "The scientists have dissolved and processed enough weapons-grade plutonium for two bombs," Reza said with a satisfied smile. Dr Regina Kny's unusual procedure and specially designed hot cell built into the reactor containment pool had allowed the men to weaponise the gathered plutonium.

Upon entering the restaurant of the small hotel, Reza motioned for Mrak and Broz to come over to Serif's table from their perch at the bar. Both men felt very uncomfortable near Reza – a man they knew had killed Dr Kny, her body fed to deep-running Black Sea fish. They had discovered some more of her ingenious, unpublished scientific papers filed neatly in the underground nuclear reactor hall buried deep in the mercury mine. They thought that they would offer them to the brothers as ransom for their lives, if necessary.

With everyone seated at the round dining table, Serif began. "We have worked very hard to get to this moment in our quest to regain Turkish power in the world. We must move the weapons tonight. I want them on my yacht by tomorrow morning. And I want to have them in place by the day before Christmas, ready for use. Don't disappoint me."

Neither Broz nor Mrak knew up until that moment what the plans would be for their devices. They thought that no one in their right mind would actually use one of the bombs. Serif had told them that he was going to give them to his country as an international negotiating chip, proving to the world that Turkey is advanced enough to have its own nuclear weapons program. The reason seemed logical at the time; besides, they stood to make a lot of money, each man receiving two million Euros. But now, they were feeling more certain than ever that the odds of their continued existence on earth were dismal.

"Yes, they are ready," Broz said. "The triggering devices built by the Russians are tested and functional."

"Wait a minute!" Mrak interrupted and looked with alarm at Serif. "You never said anything about using these devices. We were under the impression that they were only going to be used for show, nothing else!"

"Yes, we told you what you needed to know, Mrak," Serif said in a calm, steely voice. "Now you will continue your work and help us to give the world a new order."

Mrak and Broz felt from the beginning that they had made a horrible mistake in forming an alliance with this psychotic Turk, but they wanted so badly to prove they could actually produce a nuclear weapon, that they ignored the possibility that these terrorists might betray them. Broz sighed in resignation. It was too late to change anything now.

"We will need some time to get things up and running, once we are on station," Mrak said. "It will take us a few hours to make sure the detonators are aligned properly. One miscalculation or a loose wiring connection could prevent the plutonium pit from going super-critical at the time of detonation."

"Without the proper alignment of the timing mechanism, we would get a normal large bang that would do a lot of damage," Broz added. "The kind you'd get with any plastic explosive blast. But what you want is control over the *Big Bang!* An enormous release of atomic energy that will annihilate everything for many kilometres from its epicentre, then spread radioactive contamination into the atmosphere for thousands of kilometres."

Serif looked out of the restaurant's window and saw heavy cumulus clouds moving toward the mountainous region of Idrija. He pondered his choice in silence but would never renege on his decision to use the atomic weapons.

"I will have them moved tonight," Reza stated emphatically.

Serif stood up quickly. "Good evening, gentlemen. I must get some rest before tomorrow."

With no time to spare for dinner that night, Reza and Maks left the restaurant en route to the mercury mine, hoping to avoid a wrathful reaction from Serif should their task not be completed as demanded. Serif wanted everything packed in crates for their aquatic journey from Slovenia to Romania aboard his yacht.

Dusk revealed a full moon looming on the horizon between fast-moving clouds as Serif watched from his hotel room window, his eyes fixed on his brother's car as it drove off. Then Serif turned to the small table where he had placed his laptop, pulled up a chair, and sat down in front of the computer. He began building a new website using the encryption codes that Reza had given him to help disguise his new alias.

Serif continuously changed his website's point of origin, but he named his site the same every time – it always included his latest preliminary declarations for his next carnage campaign. Over the years of planning and executing terrorist acts all over the Middle East, North Africa, and Europe, his sequence of execution evolved into sending a warning through cyberspace and then claiming the act on the same website. They all started with the same three letters J for Jihad, T for terrorist, S for symbol – JTS.

Jihad is upon you who do not adhere to the word of Allah. JTS has begun the countdown to the end of Judeo-Christian world domination.

Typing in the words empowered Serif with an overwhelming sense of entitlement – he wanted his name known as the son who brought Turkey back to its most powerful status. Underlining his heading he continued:

For my brethren of the Ottoman Empire – our lady the Black Sea, will feel the wealth of her greatest nation, Turkey, rise from slumber to regain her original powers and fulfil your destiny as the world's greatest race of man.

Serif loaded two pictures he had taken of Istanbul, one of the Top Kap palace and another of its harbour. Bordering the entire screen with red, orange, and yellow flames, the webpage took on an even more ominous appearance when he added a photo of partially burned bodies found at the Auschwitz concentration camp by American liberating troops in both lower corners. Satisfied with his creation, he logged off and packed the computer away for the night.

Turning on the TV in his Slovenian hotel room, he found that his favourite Al Jazeera news program was just beginning a story of President George W. Bush's problems in trusting the Iraqi government to control their own nation. He smiled a little when he heard that the police station in Baghdad had been blown up again by a suicide bomber. This time they caught a six-year-old child on videotape walking through the front door with enough TNT strapped to his body to destroy the entire first floor of the building.

After taking a shower, Serif slept soundly until the next morning, when he was awakened by a knock on his door. He opened it enough to see his brother standing there.

"We are ready," Reza announced, coming into the room. "The scientists and Maks are near the road leading from the mine. They have prepared everything for transport to your boat."

"I, too, am ready," Serif said.

It took Serif some time to get himself together every morning, as Reza well knew. Serif always lit a candle and prayed to Allah for the strength he needed to defeat the infidels suppressing his country. About an hour later, Reza met his brother in the hotel lobby. Serif had his computer and satellite equipment with him.

"Are you using the new encryption that I gave you on the thumb drive?" Reza asked.

"Yeah," Serif replied. "I constructed a new webpage last night. It took me a few minutes to upgrade my system, but then it was easy to use."

The old man running the hotel came quickly behind Serif and delivered his personal bags to the Hummer. After loading their equipment into the vehicle, Serif and Reza drove down a dusty, half-paved road under construction. Eventually they found their way to two white panel vans sitting at an intersection two miles from the mine entrance.

Both men stepped out of the big Hummer and onto a dirt car park where they met with Mrak, Broz, and Maks, who had been standing there for some time, waiting patiently.

"Are the explosives installed?" Serif asked Reza.

Maks brought out a remote detonating device from his pocket and handed it to Reza, who then handed the gadget to Serif.

"Yes, brother," Reza replied.

Without much ceremony, Serif pushed a small silver button on the remote detonating device labelled "Kny's Lab." The men felt a rumbling underneath their feet when the two metric tons of explosives collapsed the mineshaft above the nuclear reactor, burying all remnants of their underground atomic weapons facility. It was a sweet sound to the two scientists who had been working in that dark cave for nearly two years. Broz even cracked a little smile when he noticed a small cloud of dust coming from the barn where the elevator they had used to reach the underground facility collapsed.

Handing the remote back to Reza, Serif got into the Hummer, started the engine, and waited for Reza and Maks to get into the drivers' seats of the two vans. Mrak and Broz each took their positions, one in each of the two vans with their respective nuclear weapons. As he pulled away, Serif waved, motioning for the others to follow him out onto the road leading away from the mercury mine. Both vans moved in behind Serif's vehicle and began their journey through the mountains to Izola, where Serif's yacht awaited its deadly cargo.

The mountainous terrain was slow going for the short caravan, but once they reached the highway near Ljubljana, they raised their speed to around seventy miles per hour and blended right into the daily traffic. If there were any suspicions of their plot, or even an eyewitness to the loading of the weapons into the two white Mercedes vans, it would have been virtually impossible to track them, even with a helicopter. White vans were scattered up and down the roads leading to the Black Sea coast, carrying all kinds of cargo. But only two had nuclear warheads suspended from their floor with strands of cabling.

Hours later, the group reached the harbour where Serif's yacht was moored and Daniel was still waiting. After taking a coffee break at a small outdoor café for the morning traffic to slow down, they offloaded the larger of the two crates from Reza's van and put it into the boat's cargo hold. The two kilograms of plutonium used in the second bomb needed fewer explosive panels in its detonator, making the crate lighter and easier for the four men to move. Serif and Reza watched their crew closely from the yacht's stern bench seat.

The operation finished when the smaller of the two crates had been lowered into the hold by a small winch temporarily mounted near the yacht's cargo hatch. The scientists went below to secure the two packages in their special suspension rigging, built to help maintain their stability while sailing the rough waters of the open sea. Mrak and Broz had taken drawings of Serif's yacht, which Reza gave them a few weeks earlier, and constructed the suspension apparatus to match the cargo hold's bulkhead tie-down dogs perfectly. Serif slowly stood up from his seat on the stern and looked out toward the setting sun.

Sunset across the Adriatic Sea seemed to be an ominous prelude to what was being planned by the terrorists. Half-buried on the horizon, Serif could see the orange dome of the sun which resembled the shape of a mushroom cloud he'd seen in films of the atomic bomb being dropped on Hiroshima. Serif snapped back to reality when Mrak and Broz came up from the cargo hold, both sweating and tired from their work below.

"Reza, take my helicopter to Mamaia. I'll meet you there tomorrow night," Serif ordered.

"Okay, my brother. See you soon," Reza replied, kissing Serif on both cheeks.

Serif turned and went to the door leading into his yacht's berthing area. Everyone stood on the main deck, waiting for their next orders as Serif went below to inspect the cargo hold. Reza made his way to the pier, looking back to see if the scientists were following him. His scarred leg was aching badly from all the lifting he had been doing that day while moving the bombs. The pain in his leg had put him in a foul mood.

"Mrak and Broz, come with me," Reza ordered.

"We must take our tools with us, Reza," Broz said.

"Fine, meet me at the van in ten minutes," Reza retorted.

Broz went quickly down into the cargo hold to retrieve the tools he and Mrak had left in an army duffel bag and a separate aluminium metal case. The case contained various electronic instruments, each with a specific purpose related to the bombs' timing and successful detonation. He brought the equipment on deck, handed some things to Mrak, and the two followed Reza off the yacht.

From below, Serif yelled up to Maks and Daniel, "Let's cast off! I want to be in Turkish waters by midnight."

The two men moved quickly, equally anxious to get underway.

Reza left both vans in a car park near the pier and drove Mrak and Broz back to Idrija in his brother's Hummer. They arrived at the helicopter's small landing field and within minutes were on their way to the Black Sea coast where they'd meet Serif for the preliminary assembly of the two nuclear weapons. It was much too dangerous to assemble the devices completely until they were actually on station and ready for detonation. The stop in Mamaia on their way to Cernavodă would allow Reza and the scientists time to travel by air to their rendezvous and put more of the bombs' apparatus together before travelling up the Danube River.

Mrak looked out from his side of the helicopter and saw that they were flying over the Carpathian Mountains. Snow covered many of the lower peaks and all of the mountain-tops. Reflecting the clear bright moonlight of that December night, the mountains took on a picturesque ornamentation you might only see on a Christmas postcard.

Reza and the two scientists were met at the airport near Mamaia and driven to Serif's house by his housekeeper. As they rode, Mrak and Broz discussed the technical details of how they would set up the detonation sequence. When they arrived at Serif's house, Reza posted guards by their rooms, locking them in until morning.

———

Serif slowly pulled away from the pier at Izola, Maks and Daniel watching for anyone who might be following them out to sea. Serif had been careful to observe all the port rules in order to minimise attention that might be given to his craft as it glided effortlessly through the water. It was a beautiful boat with streamlining that made many other yacht captains of the Slovenian harbour envious. However, no suspicions were aroused in the port that often saw yachts of the same size and style cruise through their waters.

Once in open waters, Serif revved his engines to full throttle, cruising across the low swells of the Adriatic at maximum speed. A short while later, Serif gave the helm over to Maks and went below to find something to eat. The galley was well equipped with Romanian wine, caviar, breads, cheeses, and fresh fruits. Serif enjoyed his first meal of the voyage, riding the sea with two nuclear weapons suspended in the yacht's cargo hold. After eating and with a glass of red wine beside him, Serif opened his laptop and logged onto his encrypted email site.

> *My cousin,*
> *We are ready for your arrival. You will find your*
> *access open at 2300.*
> *Tanya*

Serif felt himself swell with anticipation as he thought about the approaching execution of his two concurrent plans. Tanya's message informed him that Draco would have his men ready to move the next night – Christmas Eve.

The two teams knew nothing of one another – Bogdan preparing to take over the nuclear power plant's main control room and the scientists who had constructed two nuclear weapons. Mrak and Broz were isolated from the others in the mercury mine under the close guard of Reza, whom Serif entrusted with the scientists' continued wellbeing. Reza was now tasked with having the scientists prepare the smaller warhead for detonation. The two-kilogram nuclear bomb would completely destroy Cernavodă's nuclear power plant and blast tons of highly radioactive spent fuel into the world's atmosphere. Serif sat back in his thickly padded easy chair and closed his eyes for a moment of meditation. His mind was cluttered with thoughts of things that had to be done over the next two days.

Hours later he awoke to Daniel's nudging. "Sir, we have arrived in Turkey."

Surprised that he had slept so long, Serif gradually got himself out of his easy chair. "Aye," he said.

He followed Daniel upstairs and took over the helm; they were about three miles from the Istanbul harbour.

"Looks like home," Serif mumbled.

The city of Istanbul was brightly lit with night lights from balconies and hotel car parks along its coast. The port was a major commercial transitioning point for cargo transported from the West to the Middle East. Loading and unloading activities were carried on throughout the night. The port, overburdened by an enormous and growing shipping industry, allowed Serif's yacht to enter without inspection.

Serif easily manoeuvred into port through calm waters that reflected the moon's ghostly glow. Serif moved between two other yachts moored at a pier near a refuelling depot.

"Tie her off, and wake up that guy in the fuel depot," Serif ordered. "Maks, make sure we have enough fuel to finish our trip. I will return in two hours."

"Aye, captain," Maks replied.

Daniel tied off the boat by himself while Maks hustled along the pier to arouse the sleeping teenager at the fuel depot. Both Daniel and Maks were of Romanian descent and were serving life sentences in an Istanbul prison before Serif bought their freedom. Now they were his well-paid mercenaries. They had followed Serif and Reza for several years, gaining their trust, but Maks' ultimate goal was only to make enough money to live out the rest of his life in South America. Daniel would follow his friend when they both had enough money to leave their current employer. That day would come, once things were settled up after this job, in Riga, Latvia.

Serif walked to an old wooden gatehouse near the end of the pier and found a taxi waiting under a streetlamp to take him to a small hotel. The dry air near the city's centre parched his eyes and made them ache. He was tired and needed rest, but there was not much time for rest- things had to be done.

A man in a turban came to the desk. "May I serve you?"

The hotel was used by the JTS for meetings between high-ranking members of the terrorist organisation who were in hiding around the city. "Give me the rendezvous room," Serif said in his native language.

The man gave him a key and roll of toilet paper. Serif's room was furnished with one narrow bed and some old furniture. Serif threw his rucksack onto a small table and, without even using the washbowl to wash his hands, fell onto the sunken bed and into a shallow sleep just before a knock came at his door.

Serif sat up quickly. "Yeah!"

A voice resounded through the black, tar-covered door. "He wants to see you."

CHAPTER 11

Carson opened his eyes on Christmas Eve morning and found he was still lying on the floor of Bogdan's house, hands bound behind his back with the thick plastic zip-ties. His shoulders ached from being held in the same position all night – face down against the cold tile floor. Alone in the room with a wood-burning stove, still warm from an overnight load of hardwood, Carson rolled onto his back.

The stove's brownish tile was adorned with hand-painted red roses and a green vine that laced its way across the stove's front. Carson stared at it as he wondered anxiously if someone would soon come into the room to give him another beating.

Sitting up as best he could and discovering that his ankles were also tightly tied together, Carson wriggled over to the heater's hearth. Assisted by a wooden chair one of his assailants had left beside the metal door, he managed to stand up and lean against the stove's tiles. Carson moved his body into a position that allowed him to touch the plastic zip-tie, incapacitating the movement of his hands, to the hot metal door of the stove. The heat weakened the plastic just enough for Carson to expand the loop and slip his hands and feet loose. Within seconds, he was completely free.

The room was equipped with a high-speed Internet connection to a laptop that sat on a folding table in the middle of the room. Carson touched the space bar and the screen illuminated itself. Frantically opening the Internet engine, he typed a message to Todd Sinclair.

Todd, JTS active in Cernavodă, suspect someone inside

Excruciating pain shot through Carson as he suddenly realised that he had just been hit across his head and shoulders with something that felt like a baseball bat. Carson fell to the floor. But before Jacob, one of Bogdan's thugs, could connect with his second blow, Carson regained enough of his senses to reach for the brown object coming down toward his face. He intercepted the man's wallop, discovering that he was holding a boat paddle. Suspending the attack for a couple of seconds, Carson blinked his eyes, trying to regain focus.

Jacob had thought he would be able to subdue Carson easily with the boat paddle, thus not calling for help before entering the room. Twisting his body from underneath Jacob's, Carson snatched the paddle away and rendered him unconscious with one fierce thump to his head. Thinking that he had only seen that in movies, Carson grunted, "Huh!"

With all the noise the two were making, Carson figured he only had a couple of seconds before others would come storming into the room. He hit "send" on the laptop and ran out the back door of Bogdan's house as fast as he could.

Running away from the old shack, Carson felt his face stinging from the impact of an icy snowfall that had begun to fall sporadically during the night. Carson moved faster than he could have imagined his legs would carry him, frantically racing down the beach toward the city of Constanta where he thought that he would find better cover from his pursuers.

Jumping over a small seawall, Carson heard the faintest

sound of a gunshot behind him – maybe a small calibre hand-gun, he thought. A moment later, without warning, an eerie noise that sounded like the tail of a long white dress shirt whipping in the summer breezes on his mother's clothes line in Georgia, was heading his way. The sound was coming from a bullet's slowing air drag as the slug came toward him, tearing a hole in the atmosphere, flipping end over end through space.

Carson dipped his body as he heard the gunshot, prob-ably saving him from getting hit by the slow-moving bullet that had ricocheted off a tree branch between Marius's gun and his broad back. Carson decided his luck wouldn't hold out for another shot. He looked up from his position behind the low seawall and saw a jeep filled with three raucous young Romanians, home for the Christmas holidays, riding along the waterfront. Carson didn't want to put anyone else in danger that morning, but he sensed his death was imminent.

He ran for their jeep, which paused momentarily after the group heard the gunshot and climbed into the back seat as quickly as he could.

"Go! Go!" Carson shouted to the driver, who immedi-ately recognised Carson's American accent.

The young man looked toward where the gunman was standing and stomped on the accelerator before another shot was fired. The jeep's rear wheels spun a bit in the hard sand, then they took off, toward the lagoon between Mamaia and a new housing subdivision being built by wealthy Germans. Carson had no idea where he was going and didn't really care as long as they weren't being shot at.

The driver of the old military jeep was a college student named Ben Nicolescu.

"What you are doing?" Ben asked in broken English.

Carson turned around to see that no one was following them down the sandy beach. "Thanks for picking me up. Believe me, you don't want to know anything about what is going on here."

"Okay, if you say so. My name Ben," Ben said. "This my girlfriend, Athena, and brother Sylesty."

Ben felt obligated to help Carson. The Americans had done a lot for his village after the revolution in Romania, and he would do whatever he could to return the favour. Ben's father had been killed while working as a builder at the Palace of the Parliament in Bucharest, leaving his unemployed mother without the means to care for seven children. All but two of his siblings were placed in an orphanage, becoming unwilling members of Nicolae Ceauşescu's legacy of orphaned children.

"Ceauşescu's children" were a result of his efforts to expand communism, forcing Romanians to bear children by banning contraceptives and passing a law that every family must have at least five children. But because of the desperate economic situation, as many as 150,000 children ended up in orphanages throughout Romania. Some endured physical, emotional, and sexual abuse. Ben had seen it all in his seven years of orphanage life, some of which occurred after the 1989 revolution. If not for the support of American missionaries, who came to the country soon after Ceauşescu's execution, Ben would still be living in the filth of the state-run home.

"Are you American?" Athena asked Carson.

"Yes, your English is very good," he replied. "Do you watch a lot of American movies?"

"Yes, we do," Athena smiled. "Our government believes that knowing English will help us when we are fully in the European Union, so they force the TV stations to use Romanian subtitles."

The jeep turned off the beach and onto a paved road that led into a main street. Carson pointed to the next curb. "Let me off here, thanks."

Athena turned to Ben and whispered something into his ear. Ben looked at his girlfriend for a moment, then back to Carson. "Can we take you somewhere, away from here?"

"No, you have done more than enough. I don't want to get you guys involved in this – it's too dangerous," Carson replied.

"My father has a fishing boat tied up at the harbour," Athena said, trying to coax Carson. "I know he would agree to take you to Bulgaria if you want. My father would do it for one hundred Euros – he has done it before."

Carson thought about Athena's offer for a minute. "I have a car parked on the main road, near where you found me, but I'm sure they're watching it now. Hey, do you guys have a mobile phone?"

"Yes, but all of our phones are buy-as-you-go and our time has been used up for several days now," Ben said, his English getting better the more he spoke. "We are on a student's pay and don't have enough money to add any more minutes. But it does not matter – the police are being paid by these men to stay out of their business. You should not call them to help you."

Carson nodded. "Okay, take me to my car. I know they've already gotten my laptop, but they won't understand anything about an isotope identifier and will probably leave it in the car."

Ben now understood the danger of their situation. "You should stay here, out of sight. I will find your device."

Reluctantly, Carson nodded. "You've got a good point. Can you get into my car without being seen?"

"I know how to steal cars," Ben said with confidence. "A little extra training I got at the orphanage."

Carson gave Ben his car's last known location, but by the time they arrived, the car had already been moved from where he had parked it the night before near Bogdan's house. Ben drove around until Carson finally spotted his Pajero. Parking the jeep several streets away, Ben made his way to Carson's car and found it open. He returned within minutes with The Judge and gave it to Carson.

"Great job, Ben!" Carson said. "I have some important mission information stored on this device. Don't know what I'd do without my little friend; thanks again."

"My pleasure," Ben said breathlessly from his run through a grove of trees.

They started for the pier where Athena and Sylesty's father, Jack, was cleaning the morning catch. Athena went alone to talk to her father. She wanted to negotiate the price for Carson's passage to Bulgaria by herself – it would be less expensive that way. She told him that Carson was a friend of Ben's and that he would pay in Euros.

Athena's father knew everyone working on the waters of Mamaia and Constanta, including Bogdan. Bogdan's men had stolen Jack's catch twice in open waters, so Jack had good reason to hate him. Bogdan's boat was just a little faster than Jack's, and it carried many more guns – illegal NATO arms that Bogdan acquired from his Turkish friends over the last two years. Jack's livelihood depended on his fishing and his occasional extra money-making enterprises, known only to his family.

Jack was partial to smuggling things like imitation Levi's and Marlboros into Romania from Chinese sweatshops, when times were more difficult for his fishing business. The capitalist now in charge of Romania frowned upon this abuse of the new system. Bucharest wanted a cleaned-up market, something outside investors would put money into. Still, the seaside was involved in many types and levels of organised crime.

Athena waved her arms like a scarecrow, motioning for Ben to bring Carson down to the pier. Although thin and bony, Athena had a natural beauty which was very obvious to Carson. He could also tell that she was in love with Ben, as he watched her take his hand while walking down the gangway. Her brother Sylesty looked undernourished too, yet his body was strong from hard manual labour aboard Jack's schooner.

The old boat was rust laden from bow to stern, with a thick black exhaust stack jutting from its wheelhouse. Its windows were soot covered, and from the port side, it looked as if Jack had recently extinguished an onboard fire.

"I'll take the one hundred Euros now," Jack said, reaching up from his fish-scale-covered bench.

Carson had lost everything the night before – wallet, identification and his money were all gone. "I'll make a phone call as soon as we hit port in Bulgaria, and you'll get your money, plus another fifty."

Jack looked at Athena. "Do you think he is worth the risk, my trusting daughter?"

"Anyone who is an enemy of Bogdan is a friend of ours, Papa," Athena said.

Jack paused for a moment, then motioned to his youngest son. "Sylesty, get off those lines and start the engine."

Within an hour, Jack was steering his schooner to the narrow mouth of the lagoon, then down the coast of Romania to the first port in Bulgaria. While Ben and Sylesty tied off the boat, Carson checked his isotope identifier to ensure he still had the spectra he had taken of the illicit uranium fuel pellets the day before.

erif was at the helm of his yacht in Istanbul right after his mysterious meeting near the city's centre. He piloted the vessel through the night and until dawn, easily navigating the familiar Black Sea waters as they drew near Mamaia. Approaching the main lagoon's mouth, Serif slowed the boat and brought her through the channel, hugging the shoreline close to the fishermen's pier to avoid a collision with a large clipper making its way out to open waters. Serif could see the fuel depot where Jack's schooner was briefly moored for refuelling, but Carson was camouflaged by netting hanging along the winch arm of the old rusty tub. Unconcerned with the goings-on of Mamaia's modest fishing industry, Serif and his men focused on looking for possible undercover police from Bucharest that might not be on his remuneration list.

Carson had almost finished examining The Judge's last recorded gamma spectra when he looked up from his perch on a stack of nets and saw a fantastic yacht approaching from their starboard side, his view somewhat blocked by the hanging nets. Carson admired the yacht's beauty and thought how wonderful it would be to escape down the coast on something as fast as that.

Carson's attention was suddenly diverted to The Judge. The detector's recalibration had completed itself, sending it into the "Find" mode, and it now, unexpectedly, had started to alarm. Instinctively, Carson began a slow sweep of the area by pointing the sodium iodide crystal in the protected end of the device away from his body. Moving it from left to right in a half-moon arc he tried to zero in on the source of the radiation. The Judge's alarm sounded a constant warble, and Carson stopped his sweep. It was now pointed directly at the passing yacht. Carson had just enough time to take a forty-second scan through the hanging nets, between his detector and the oncoming boat, before it passed by their position.

Carson pressed one of the four buttons on the Judge, commanding it to tell him what isotope the yacht was carrying in her fiberglass hull. In a couple of seconds, the screen beamed a green LED banner:

Plutonium Pu-239

Serif's yacht continued to creep through the lagoon's murky waters, carrying her two weapons of mass destruction. Its crew passed by Carson and his new friends without any idea that they were being monitored by a radioactive isotope finder. Serif was careful to avoid getting too close to Constanta's harbour. But the radiation detectors that the port authority had used to detect the illicitly trafficked uranium Carson investigated the day before in Constanta were far to the south of Mamaia. The cargo monitoring detectors located there were only sensitive enough to detect nuclear materials inside sea-land containers that passed directly underneath their towers, not offshore.

Carson leapt from his crouched position and said to Athena's father, "I have to go."

"What about my money?" Jack asked with irritation.

Ignoring Jack's sudden rant, Carson turned and glanced back at them when his feet hit the pier's thick wooden boards. "Don't wait on me. They will be looking for the jeep and then your children."

But Jack wasn't concerned about Bogdan's bandits this morning and continued to load his fishing boat with supplies.

He felt they would be safe enough once his boat was refueled, and he had his daughter, her boyfriend, and his son out to sea.

Carson ran down the harbour road to an intersection at the main road and grabbed a bicycle that was unlocked in a row of beachside racks. Riding the bike as fast as he could, Carson followed Serif's yacht to its slip and hurriedly went into an old seaside restaurant located on a small canal and surrounded by warehouses. Dim illumination from an overhead wooden, steering wheel chandelier reflected an occasional flicker of light across the mirrored, multi-faceted disco ball, still hanging there from the 1970s.

Carson watched from a window as two men tied off the beautiful yacht. Serif's driver was waiting at the pier, his Humvee idling. Serif disembarked, leaving Maks and Daniel to watch over the boat and its cargo. Carson wasn't sure how many men were actually down in the hold – he had only seen two as he continued to sit at a table and watch their activities. After a few minutes, the men sat on the main deck where Carson could see them playing a game of dominos. It looked as if they were waiting for something or someone, maybe the return of the man who had just departed. Carson thought about leaving and trying to make a phone call back to headquarters but was afraid the men would offload the radioactive material before he could see what was causing The Judge to register plutonium.

CHAPTER 12

Pulling up to his seaside mansion, Serif parked his Humvee on the concrete roundabout that encircled part of his front garden. The garden was well kept with evergreens groomed by inexpensive local labour, who also kept Serif's enormous property-bordering rhododendrons trimmed. He opened the vehicle's huge door and grabbed his sea bag. Unobserved by anyone who might have been trying to watch him from outside his garden, Serif went indoors.

He found Reza standing in the kitchen with Mrak and Broz, making lamb kebab sandwiches. "Good to see you, brother," Reza said with a smile.

Serif threw his sea bag on a chair. "It was a beautiful voyage."

"Bogdan has been by today already and is making his final preparations," Reza said.

"Good," Serif said. "We will begin the operation at twenty-two hundred."

Mrak, who was sitting at the breakfast table in the centre of a flower mosaic tiled floor, looked to Serif for his next orders, sensing that his hours may be numbered if he and Broz weren't ready to assemble the bombs. "Shall we prepare our tools?"

Reza stared at Mrak and Broz before motioning for both of them to leave the room. Broz felt a sharp back pain as he got up – old age and the hard work was catching up to both scientists.

"Get your equipment, and meet us in front in one hour," Reza ordered.

"Yes, of course," Mrak said.

Massaging his back with one hand, Broz led the way into the garage where they loaded tools into a van, along with all the required instruments to bring together the components of their two working nuclear weapons. Many of their testing instruments were older generation oscilloscopes, frequency modulators, and laptops from the 2002 generation of mono-processors. But the two old researchers had worked with much more antiquated equipment during the Yugoslavian nuclear weapon programme years and achieved adequate results with their explosion models.

Readying the triggering device was the most delicate of their tasks by far. It would be maintained in a mechanical safing state until set into its final resting place. The trigger of a nuclear device could be inadvertently fired by any transmitter on the right wavelength. Hand-held radio keyed in the area by one of the power plant's operators might do the trick if they were still freely walking around the plant when the bomb was armed. Mrak knew exactly when to remove this mechanical device, allowing Broz to introduce the sequencing codes to provide the weapon's timed response.

Only Serif and Reza knew exactly where they wanted to place the smaller of the two plutonium warheads – directly under nearly one hundred metric tons of reactor spent fuel. Serif studied the radioactive fallout patterns of a combination low-yield nuclear explosion pooled with spent nuclear fuel for hours with Tanya, his chief engineer for the team. He imagined the fallout containing massive amounts of enriched uranium fuel, depleted uranium, and plutonium. Depending on the changing winds, he expected the bulk of Western Europe to receive the toxic results.

Serif sat down at the kitchen table where Mrak had just been. "Tanya will meet us at the Tryst Café tonight."

Reza's bad leg ached from the cold weather as he sat down at the table across from his brother. "Herman, ready?"

Serif nodded. "He has reduced the shift to a skeleton crew." Serif sipped a cup of ginger tea. "You will enter with Bogdan. And make sure that you keep your eye on him."

"I will."

Serif climbed the winding staircase to the largest of his five bedrooms, all luxuriously and immaculately decorated. From some of Europe's finest art galleries, Serif had amassed an expensive collection of fine paintings. An elaborate Persian rug covered most of his bedroom's white tile floor. The master bath was of a size and décor that deserved to be featured in *Architectural Digest*. Outside the bathroom was a three-way split walk-in closet that held Serif's extensive wardrobe of silk shirts, cashmere sweaters, English suits, Italian leather shoes, and jackets.

But on this day, Serif wore a black jumpsuit, the same as Reza and the two scientists were wearing. They had all agreed that the Turkish-made jumpsuits would be more comfortable and, being one piece, would be easier to get rid of later. Black gloves, watch cap, and high-top Special Forces boots made their ensembles complete.

"Let's go, brother," Serif commanded.

Reza put the two pistols he had just finished cleaning into a duffel bag and followed Serif to where Mrak and Broz were waiting in their own van. Climbing into the Humvee,

Reza motioned for Mrak to follow them as they left, en route to Serif's waiting yacht.

——————

The sun set across the bay from where Carson was sitting, and streetlamps came on along the pier as he continued to watch Maks and Daniel play dominos. They still hadn't moved anything off the yacht. Carson began to think about getting closer under cover of darkness, without any backup from the local corrupted police or from INWA in Vienna. In and out – just take a quick look around, he reasoned.

Carson found an old pea coat in the restaurant's cloak room, gloves still in the pocket and an old Atlanta Braves baseball cap some sailor had brought over from the States. Leaving the restaurant through a rear door, Carson walked down to the pier. He came close enough to the yacht to see that the two men were still sitting on the main deck, bundled up in khaki foul-weather coats, protecting themselves from a chilling wind now blowing across the bay.

Approaching from a blind side, Carson unlaced his climbing boots and slipped them off. He stepped silently onto the boat, its size thwarting any pitch or roll caused by the addition of his weight. Stealing his way around toward the bow, he found a hatch leading down into the cargo hold that was open and out of sight from the two guards. He opened it quietly, dropped his boots inside, and climbed down an aluminium ladder, allowing the hatch to close gently behind him.

A small, red light was enough to allow Carson to see his way past several wooden crates and two suspended metal gang boxes.

He found a wall-mounted flashlight near a door that led to the boat's living quarters and turned it toward one of the two gang boxes. It was about the size of a child's coffin. In the flashlight's beam, its reflection was dulled by some kind of little designs that looked like they had been brushed over, causing miniature swirls on the gang box's surface.

Carson popped the two latches on the lid of one of the gang boxes. The black rubber gasket that ran around the edge of the metal box let loose a tight vacuum noise as Carson lifted the lid and looked inside. He had seen a sphere, or "pit," of weapons grade plutonium like this while attending one of his INWA secret training assignments. But the sight of this thing, poorly guarded and inside a yacht's cargo hold, prompted a heart-stopping chill that ran along Carson's spine. *How did these guys get this much plutonium without being discovered?* Especially since it had already been cast and formed into the correct geometry for use. Not an easy task for experts, but nearly impossible for anyone not intimately experienced with the process.

Carson estimated there were around six kilograms suspended in the box lined with hard rubber. Slowly lowering the top back down and closing it, Carson shone his flashlight on a wooden crate with Chinese markings and several large black Pelican boxes. He saw that each crate had a mushroom cloud spray-painted on its side using a cheap stencil. Carson was now certain they were loaded with arming and fusing components for some kind of makeshift atomic weapon. Adjacent to the gang box that he had just closed was the identical second box.

Avoiding a very high threshold for any panic sensation, Carson took a deep breath, using a technique taught to him by a Swedish psychologist during his special training, to calm himself: he focused only on solving the problem, ignoring the consequences he might receive at the hands of the terrorists because of his actions. Slowly releasing the air in his lungs, Carson concentrated and regained his self-control. He opened the second box and saw the smaller pit also suspended within its box, hard rubber protecting its surface from being damaged while the boat was moving across the water.

Carson briefly considered the guards upstairs. They would surely kill him if they found him, but he had to get rid of these two plutonium pits, no matter the consequences. Taking a moment to focus on the size and shape of the largest pit, he assured himself that this was truly the centre of a spherical implosion device. Opening one of the wooden crates, his suspicions were confirmed. They intended to use the rest of the packed equipment in the cargo hold for their plot. Eventually, the many components would become two live nuclear weapons. But the question arose again: how did these men, who were obviously terrorists from some radical organisation, manage to become proprietors of this technology?

Carson's only explanation was that they had found a way to reprocess a cache of spent reactor fuel somewhere, somehow. With little time to think about it, Carson returned to the problem of how he was going to get rid of the plutonium pits and survive long enough to warn INWA about the imminent attack on Cernavodă. He looked around the cargo hold with his flashlight for something with which to demolish the black spheres in place. But there were only a few special tools and some scientific instrumentation that could not possibly be used to destroy the extremely hard black balls of plutonium. Carson looked around for another way.

Suddenly, his flashlight illuminated a lead-shielded bucket sitting under a workbench. Carson opened the first gang box again, propping the lid open with an old folding chair seat. He used both his hands to pick up the six-kilo plutonium sphere and put it into the bucket. Then, holding the bucket, he walked slowly over to the ladder leading out of the cargo hold and onto the deck. Carson carried the plutonium pit as far away from his body as he could, believing that his detector had seen some more dangerous, impure plutonium isotopes still present. Using one hand, he opened the hatch and stepped onto the cold main deck in his socks.

He glanced around the harbour to see if anyone noticed that he was standing on the boat's walkway, near its bow. The area around the yacht was deserted, except for the two guys still playing dominos on their bolted-down card table. They were still sitting in the same positions, but with an almost depleted bottle of Russian vodka between them now.

Carson hesitated to see if the two might have heard him come up to the rail with the six-kilo pit, but apparently they hadn't heard any noise that Carson was making. He slowly crept over to the chrome handrail and, while holding his breath, emptied the bucket's contents into the water. The ball made a small plop! noise when it entered the black water. Neither Maks nor Daniel heard anything. Just as Carson turned to go back down through the open hatch to the cargo hold, car lights swept across the bow of the yacht from the end of the pier. Ducking behind a life jacket he could see that it was the same Humvee that had carried away one of the crewmen earlier that evening.

Maks and Daniel jumped up from their game, quickly hid the vodka bottle, and went over to the yacht's gangway. Watching them, Carson was certain that the man in the Humvee was in charge. He couldn't see the man's face from his perch behind the preserver, but he knew that someone important had arrived.

As the men greeted each other on the gangway, Carson

quickly crept back over to the hatch and jumped through. Wanting to hide any evidence of what he had been doing, Carson latched everything back and replaced the tools to the same position as he had found them, then promptly slipped on his boots and left the cargo hold. Carson made his way to the propulsion room just as Serif and the others came on board. Carson thought that he might be able to find another exit, once everything had settled down, that would allow him to sneak off the boat unnoticed.

The engine was pristine, cleaner than any diesel he had ever seen in the Navy. Carson couldn't hear anything coming from topside because of the sound-damping panels mounted on all the bulkheads of the engine room. But within minutes, the engine started and he could feel the yacht begin to move away from the pier. The engine ran as smooth as silk, beautifully painted a shiny candy apple red that was superimposed on both sides with chrome manifolds and a flexible chrome exhaust pipe that exited below the waterline.

The terrorists were in a hurry, not checking anything in the cargo hold or engine room before readying the boat for open waters. Once the bull gear was engaged in the yacht's differential, Carson felt it lunge forward and pick up speed. He swallowed hard and cursed under his breath. He was trapped now and knew that he would have to ride out his voyage to wherever the terrorists were going. It had been a hell of a day for the INWA nuclear safeguards inspector, but it was just beginning to get really interesting.

CHAPTER 13

Hours earlier, Bogdan's men had come back to his house after their failure to catch or terminate Carson during his morning escape. Marius and Jacob had searched Mamaia's beachfront and local neighbourhoods in vain.

They had spent all of the previous night going over their plans to take over Cernavodă's boiling water reactor with two equipment operators that Bogdan had hired, Ciprian and Franco. It was a good plan and would probably work if they were able to get into the main control room before the on-shift crew put in a manual shutdown sequence.

Sitting at Bogdan's kitchen table, the group had discussed Carson's escape for more than an hour, trying to figure out how he could have got away so fast. Previous INWA inspectors had left the impression that they were more like diplomats or scientists than covert agents. Ciprian and Franco had met many inspectors from different countries who visited their site and performed routine inspections. Carson Griffin was not a regular inspector by any stretch of the imagination. He resisted their questioning for several hours before finally passing out from their beatings.

Bogdan finally stood up and with annoyed resignation and said, "Okay, let us forget about this INWA inspector for now. I have contacted Hunter to remove him."

"We have another problem, chief," Franco said. "We are each going to have to carry our own self-contained breathing apparatus with us into the plant."

Bogdan's nerves began to show. He glared at Franco. "SCBAs are supposed to be available inside the plant when we arrive. What happened?"

"I discovered that the fire station where they are normally kept has been cleaned out," Franco said. "Whatever the reason, it is not important today. We must find new SCBAs if we want to enter the control room and take over the reactor controls while the unit is still operating at one hundred percent power."

Bogdan nodded. "Yes, and delaying our crossing over the control room envelope threshold could allow the operators time to insert a SCRAM." He thought for a moment. "Okay, here is what we must do. Franco, take Ciprian and go to the fire station in Constanta and get the SCBAs that we need," Bogdan said. "Then meet us at the rendezvous location."

"Okay, chief," Franco replied.

Ciprian grabbed their coats, tossing Franco his as they left for the fire station.

Jacob opened the overview schematic of the site's layout, looking for an alternative way to get the bulky equipment over the security fence. Jacob had been through annual re-qualification classes for many years, before leaving his job two months earlier. The classes given at their new nuclear training centre built for Cernavodă's newest nuclear reactor – Unit II Cernavodă – taught him how to read the complicated drawings.

Bogdan had promised Jacob a one-time payout that would equal ten years of his normal salary, thus making it impossible for Jacob to resist the offer from his previous shift manager and mentor. The other operators Bogdan had approached in the last six months were given the same bargain – all were now looking to their huge payment when they arrived in Riga, Latvia.

"Chief, why don't we just cut through the fence?" Jacob asked.

Bogdan took another look in his pocket-sized notebook at the timing that Draco had laid out for his five-man crew. "Yes, I think you are right. There is no need to rig up a rope from the hill near the warehouse and try to go over the fence. We will enter from the warehouse side of the plant as planned, but through the fence instead of over the top."

The perimeter fence around the boundary of the nuclear facility consisted of two interlocking fences separated by a seashell walkway that was constantly monitored with motion detectors and cameras. Draco had given them a ten-minute window to breach the fence and enter the protected area of the plant, plenty of time for two men to burn and snip through the fencing with a few extra tools and a miniature torch. Draco would have to silence the alarms while they made their way into the turbine building, which shouldn't be a problem for the head of plant security.

Bogdan called Serif on his satellite phone to confirm the change in plans. Serif resisted at first, but after speaking to Tanya, who convinced him everything would go smoothly, finally agreed to the new arrangement. Confirmation of Bogdan's amendment for their entry into Cernavodă gave the chief a viable excuse if they failed to get inside on time.

"Okay, that's it," Bogdan said. "We're going through the fence. Jacob, it's your responsibility to make it happen. You have about five hours to get your shit together."

Jacob had hurriedly left Bogdan's house, leaving Bogdan

and Marius alone to work out the final details of how they would incapacitate the control room staff. "Marius, you'll have to release the gas inside the control building's ventilation system at the proper time for it to knock out the on-shift operating crew quickly. After you rejoin us in the turbine building, we'll go inside and tie up anyone still struggling."

"Yeah, the night shift will be having their usual Christmas dinner beginning at ten o'clock," Marius said. "The equipment operators will have returned to the kitchen area by then, which as you know is fed by the same ventilation system as the main control room. We will be able to gas everyone working on the operations skeleton crew within minutes."

"Good, now let me see the Russian gas bombs," Bogdan said.

Marius opened a wooden crate that he had brought through the Ukraine, then travelled across the Transylvanian Alps after entering Romania. Opening its "hazardous materials" marked lid with a crowbar, he pulled back a flame-retardant cover. Lying in a bed of wood shavings, Bogdan gazed at the four fentanyl gas canisters. It was the same gas used by the Russian's OSNAZ (Special Forces) team in the Dubrovka Theatre in Moscow to debilitate the Chechen terrorists who were holding eight hundred and fifty people hostage at gunpoint, with explosives strapped to several of their women. Many of the hostages died from the gas's use. Bogdan felt he needed that kind of quick knockout power to stop the operators before they could take preventive actions.

Bogdan had found the unused canisters on the Chechen black market, which was the best source of illicit trafficking for his mission. He still had connections with the jihad group in Chechnya known as the Special Purpose Islamic Regiment, which gave Bogdan a way to acquire weapons not easily found on any ordinary black market. Bogdan had even met Movsar Barayev, the leader of the Dubrovka Theatre siege on October 23rd, 2002, during Barayev's rise to power in the jihad organisation.

However, it was Serif's connections to Chechen Shamil Barayev, Movsar's cousin, that kept the plan moving ahead over the last two years. Shamil was reportedly assassinated by an improvised explosive device stuffed with barbed wire, a signature weapon of Shariat, a rival Chechen separatist group. Before his death, Shamil gave Serif a million Euros which came by way of Turkey – its origins were from OPEC. Now that both Shamil and Movsar were dead, Serif's group was being funded directly from a political anarchist based somewhere in Turkey. Serif kept his supplier very secret. Even Reza was unsure how his brother was getting the funding for this nuclear weapons project.

Marius removed the canisters from the wooden crate and put them into his rucksack after carefully wrapping each in its own foam sheeting. The military-designed gaseous drug would cause everyone to go completely unconscious for several hours or kill them if they were unable to fight off its poisonous effects.

What's more, the odourless gas would never be detected by the control room's automatic isolation logic, which shut all ventilation dampers normally, allowing fresh air in from outside the control room boundary. Control isolation logic only put the ventilation system into a recirculation mode when a radiological event occurred on site, in order to protect the operating crew. Sensors connected to this logic were designed to find unwanted radioactive nuclides in the air, not the incapacitating fentanyl gas.

The two men began to gather the equipment and documents they were going to need in a few hours to breach the security fence at Cernavodă and gain full control of the nuclear power plant's control room. Bogdan had paid particular attention to making sure that he would have absolute control over the plant documents by putting them into a pilot's case with his own personal combination.

"Marius, start putting everything into our van," Bogdan said. "I have to call Hunter. He has been out of touch for much too long."

"Okay, chief," Marius said as he picked up his gear.

———

The Hunter found Athena, Sylesty, and their father shortly after Serif's yacht had left the pier in Mamaia – Ben was off Jack's boat when Hunter arrived. The Hunter, an ex-military sniper once enlisted in Ceauşescu's Special Forces, also happened to be Bogdan's cousin. He had had many kills in the revolution, especially during the Christmas uprising in 1989. A man without friends who lived by a railway yard in a small communist-built apartment complex, the Hunter was able to kill people in many ways. But his favourite was with his rifle, which he spent many hours cleaning and talking to when he felt the need.

The Hunter brought Athena, Sylesty, and Jack to Bogdan's empty house where he tied them up in separate rooms – Jack in one room and his children in another. Jack was tortured first, allowing Athena and Sylesty to hear him scream as he told Hunter everything that he knew about Carson. The Hunter continued to extract information from Sylesty after Jack had finally died. Listening to hours of the torturing of her father and brother drove Athena into an extreme state of emotional exhaustion – she finally blacked out.

When Ben returned to Jack's boat after dark and found that they were all missing, he asked the attendant at the re-fueling depot if he had seen his girlfriend or her family. The attendant said he had seen them leaving with a man, whom he described rather well. Ben didn't recognise the description of the man as being someone from Bogdan's crew and imme-diately became apprehensive. Not trusting any of the police in Mamaia enough to call them, Ben started Jack's boat and steered it up the coastline to Bogdan's house, hoping to find a clue to Athena and her family's whereabouts.

Turning off all his lights when reaching Bogdan's pier, Ben tied up Jack's boat and crept up to Bogdan's shack. Step-ping onto an upside-down foot tub, Ben looked through the back window into Bogdan's bedroom and saw Jack with his throat slashed. Blood covered one side of his blue overalls and puddled beneath the wooden chair that he was tied to. It was a horrifying sight even for Ben, who had seen many murders during Ceauşescu's reign but none quite as brutal as this one.

Moving the foot tub around to the living room window, Ben again quietly stepped on top of the tub. Further horror engulfed him as he saw Sylesty's bare body slumped over a sofa, with a bloody hammer lying next to his feet.

Ben jumped down and ran around to Bogdan's rear en-trance. Questing between the house and the end of the pier, Ben found a broken pole he could use like a fisherman's pike and, point first, burst through the door. He stopped for a second to listen for Athena's voice. "Athena, where are you?" he called desperately.

An interrupted scream, so shrill it penetrated the hall-way and the closed door of a room, made Ben realise who it was. He broke down the thick wooden door and found Athena tied to a bedpost, gasping, as the Hunter stood next to her.

Ben plunged forward, ramming the sharp broken end of the pole through the Hunter's ribcage. Eyes wide open from intense pain and his ultimate surprise, the Hunter dropped the knife he had used to cut Athena's throat and ran across the room. He took flight at full speed and went head first into the decorated tiles of the room's wood heater.

Reaching down to Athena, Ben tried to stop the blood gushing from her neck.

"Athena!" Ben cried. "Hold on, I can get you help."

Trying to see Ben through her unfocused eyes, Athena gasped, "Ben, please don't leave me."

"Hold on, Athena," Ben pleaded.

Holding his hand against Athena's neck as tightly as he could, Ben felt her pulse falter, then stop as the warm blood slowed to a trickle. Athena was dead. Ben held her tightly in his arms, rocking her and crying, saying her name over and over in huge, wracking sobs. Her sinuous body remained limp in his arms until Ben finally rested her head against a pillow from the bed, then left her and walked over to Hunter's body. He rolled the killer over.

Hunter's eyes were still wide open and the pike pole jutted from his left side, his jacket pinned to him by the wooden object. Ben reached under Hunter's denim jacket and trousers, trying to find some identification. But instead of finding an ID, Ben found his cell phone and flipped it open.

Surfing the menu for calls made, Ben found that the assassin had just finished a call to a Romanian number. Switching over to the calls received, he discovered that the same number had called him several times over the last couple of days. He resisted dialling the displayed number for now. Ben's friend at the Orange telephone company of Romania would be able to find out whose phone was called.

For now, he was simply overwhelmed by grief and horror. Ben was also certain that the death of Athena, her father, and brother, were linked to the American and that Bogdan was the most likely suspect – and currently number one on Ben's shit list.

———

Bogdan and Marius arrived at the cave Serif had arranged for them, near the Tryst Café at the mouth of the Cernavodă canal. They were the first to arrive, but the rest of the crew would be coming soon to their agreed upon meeting place. They parked their van behind a fence Serif had built to hide the entrance of the cave. It was still daylight as they walked through the pitch black opening.

Bogdan was using his US Army-issue flashlight that he picked up from one of the GI's he met during the Gulf War. Bogdan had once found part-time work at the landing strip just above Mamaia Beach when it was being used as a temporary base and enemy combatant holding area. Turkey alienated the United States just before the invasion of Iraq and wouldn't allow any missions to be flown from their soil or even through their airspace. But Romania was very happy to assist the troops, creating an opportunity for Bogdan to gather information about US forces' movements for his Chechen friends.

As the two made their way into the cave, Marius veered right and found their American-made electrical generator sitting in a small alcove. Serif knew that his crew needed a reliable power supply inside the cave they planned to use as a temporary headquarters, so he had purchased the best Kohler generator he could find. Bogdan reached behind the generator and turned on a series of lights with a circuit breaker. Offloading their equipment from the van, Marius and Bogdan set up the cave for their team's meeting.

Ciprian and Franco arrived with the SCBAs, followed shortly after by Jacob with a miniature cutting torch and bolt cutters that would get them through the perimeter fence. Jacob knew how to handle himself around equipment like this – he'd worked in his father's garage repairing Dacias his whole life, even while working at the power plant. There was little that Jacob didn't know about the French knock-off engine of the Romanian-built cars or their chassis that were thinly wrapped in cheaply manufactured steel panels.

The plant operating crew normally finished their final meeting at about eight o'clock on Christmas Eve, so the men worked while they waited for Serif to give them their go-ahead orders. Once everything was ready, Franco and Ciprian kicked back around a small folding table and checked out their SCBA gear one more time. Marius and Jacob plugged in and turned on their surveillance equipment. Within minutes of energising the first of the closed-circuit surveillance monitors that came online, they saw Tanya arrive at the Tryst Café. Cameras were mounted around the mouth of the cave, approaching roads, car parks, and the small dock below the Tryst. Using the four-way split screens, they could monitor activity in and around the little harbour.

Tanya stepped out of her red Dacia and made her way over to a table and ordered a cup of green tea as Marius monitored her movements. Her silhouette was clear in the full moon, shining down on her from behind the tattered umbrella. Marius recognised her from when he worked in the main control room as a reactor operator for Bogdan. She would analyse data on one of the installed engineering computers.

Tanya sipped the tea that she liked to drink on cold nights, outside by the waters of the Danube River. The weather, although colder than she liked it, was excellent for the night's machinations. She also wanted the Western world to realise that they would no longer control the world's wealth – her cousin's plan would more than demonstrate that fact.

Marius pointed another one of the cameras upriver and maximised its zoom, allowing him to clearly observe objects over a mile away. He could see a glowing fire on the far side of the Cernavodă Canal. Anchored near the bank of the canal was a beautiful riverboat. He knew how wonderful it was going to be able to afford a boat like that, after the night was over and they were safely in Riga.

"Hey, Ciprian," Marius called. "What are you gonna do with your share of the money?"

Ciprian had already finished putting Vaseline on the rubber seals around the masks of the SCBAs and was now busy arranging the gear into its respective rucksack. "I don't know, guess I'll buy a boat."

"Yeah, me too, but first I'm gonna buy my momma a silver fox-fur coat," Marius said. "I found the perfect one at a peddler's stand near Vlad's castle. I'm sure she's gonna love it."

Panning his camera to the left, Marius's line of sight was cluttered by power lines crossing between the camera and the downstream view of Cernavodă's canal, which passed by the nuclear power plant. Between trying to look through the power lines and the darkness of the eerie night, Marius gave up trying to locate one of the two reactor buildings on the nuclear site.

One building contained a finished and operating boiling water reactor, the other a work in progress. The second reactor at Cernavodă would be coming online in eighteen months if everything went as scheduled. However, there were still no reactor fuel bundles inside the second reactor's containment or anywhere within the structure.

Marius knew this nuclear facility very well and had seen the reactor at full power many times. He thought back to how the reactors were built, using extremely cheap labour from the surrounding villages. Hate swelled inside him when he remembered how his father and two uncles had died while trapped inside a made-up water tank, which had suddenly filled with water. He was just a youngster then, but the emotional scars left a lifelong distrust of all governmental oversight.

Lack of supervision and poor communication ran rampant throughout the construction phase of the first unit, creating a black hole for desperately needed social welfare funds. Marius could remember his father saying that the project needed supervision from the West during the reactor's construction, but that they were greedy and only wanted Romania's money.

Marius continued to survey the area with his cameras and saw Tanya waiting patiently at the Tryst as she hummed along with an old song playing on the beat-up stereo inside the café. It was a Turkish tune, cymbals and flutes accompanied by a stringed instrument that sounded a little like a banjo. The music reminded her of time spent with her cousin's family and their lack of intimacy. Hatred for the West ran very deep within the Rezaabak clan, no matter how much aid their nation had received from the Europeans.

Tanya longed for this night to be over and for the journey to Riga with Serif to finally be underway. She couldn't wait for them to have time alone together, relaxed, the master plan carried out, and a new life about to begin for both of them.

Above all, Tanya wanted Serif to know that she was in love with him. And how, despite the fact that they were first cousins and could never marry, she would always be whatever he wanted – lover, friend, partner in any way that he desired.

It had all begun fairly innocently when they were children and would steal away from family gatherings to play together. Tanya especially liked it when her handsome cousin, two years older than her, would kiss her, or playfully fondle her prepubescent body. Tanya always believed that as they grew into adults, Serif still lusted for her. She had no idea that whatever sexual feelings he may have for her, they did not preclude his killing her without a second's hesitation if that ever became necessary.

CHAPTER 14

Carson had now become a stowaway on Serif's boat and had found himself sitting between a diesel engine and wooden crates stacked three high in places. The boat rolled a little as it slowed and turned sharply to her port side.

He listened intently for any sounds that would lead him to believe the terrorists might have discovered that they were missing a six-kilogram plutonium pit. Carson knew there would be an inevitable undesired outcome – he might even meet the business end of a brain-spattering implementor, in his imagination's worst-case scenario, a bullet.

Carson could hear the muffled sound of voices but was unable to make out the words. The voices seemed to be coming from somewhere far from his position near the smooth-running diesel engine, but his intuition was now telling him that the voices were beginning to get closer.

Carson heard a man yelling something in what sounded like a Yugoslavian language. Nearly intelligible, the voice seemed extremely upset.

Mrak stood in the doorway leading into the cargo hold, where he and Broz had mounted the two devices in their stainless steel boxes hours earlier in Slovenia. Although the boxes were suspended as Mrak remembered them being, before taking a nap in one of Serif's well-furnished guest bedrooms, something was now odd about their appearance. Broz and Mrak had made an agreement that from the time the two spheres were ready for introduction into a plastic explosive cocoon, they would always work together on the bombs, trusting only each other to remind themselves of their personal safety.

Slowly making his way over to where he could look into the box, Mrak gawked inside for fifteen seconds before yelling at the top of his lungs in Serbian and then again in English, "Come quick! The pit has been stolen!"

A rumbling of foot traffic came closer and closer to Carson until the other six men aboard the boat were standing either inside the small space or looking through the doorway.

Reza was standing by the empty box, between Mrak and Broz. "Open the other one! See if we have lost them both!"

Broz quickly unlatched the second stainless steel box, revealing the two-kilo plutonium pit still sitting ominously inside. Carson didn't have the opportunity to remove the smaller sphere of fissionable material, leaving the crew with at least one nuclear option. The heavy metal sphere that Carson had released over the side was resting comfortably on the ancient sea bed. Surrounded by discarded nautical debris – an old dinghy, broken pier piles, lost anchors, and a few other rotting items – the black pit had settled into the loose mud, safely hidden.

Without a word, Serif left the group and went topside to reengage the yacht's engine. He needed a moment alone to rethink his plans and decide what he wanted to do about losing the largest of his weapons arsenal. He wanted to give Turkey's opposition group the bigger of the two atomic bombs that his scientists had constructed, after his demonstration in Romania. Exploding the two-kilo bomb would convince the world that the Jihad Terrorist Symbol had nuclear material and the technology to build such a device, leaving no doubt to what extent they were willing to go to gain respect. But losing the six-kilo plutonium sphere created a great void in Serif's plan to hold other countries at bay.

Steering the large craft into the mouth of the Danube River, Serif could hear Reza organising a search of the yacht. Narrowing his suspects, Reza quickly eliminated the scientists because they had been with him since leaving the boat in Slovenia. They could not have taken the sphere from its cradle without his knowing it. Albeit, Maks and Daniel were supposed to be the only ones on board Serif's yacht when it was parked, Reza was confident that his men were loyal to him – until death.

"Start looking for someone who might still be onboard!" Reza shouted toward Maks and Daniel.

The two men quickly obeyed. Maks went down the small hallway to begin scouring the staterooms, while Daniel entered the engine room to see if someone might be in the immediate vicinity of the cargo hold. The two scientists stayed in the cargo hold, examining the smaller pit for any damage that might have been done to its practically flawless smooth surface.

As the door to the engine room swung open, Daniel looked around the stacked wooden crates trying to see behind the running diesel engine. He stepped forward with a Russian-made pistol in one hand, struggling to find the footpath of least resistance through the stored provisions and empty boxes. Fortunately for Carson, Daniel wasn't familiar with the vessel's layout and didn't realise that a yacht this size would have a bilge large enough for a man to hide in below its shiny aluminium deck plates.

Not noticing Carson lying beneath him, Daniel walked all the way around the diesel engine. Observation skills not as honed as they could have been prevented Serif's bodyguard from seeing Carson's unshaven face peering from underneath his feet while Daniel performed a cursory look through the engine room. Accidentally banging his knuckles on a piece of sheet metal protruding from one of the wooden crates started his hand trickling blood and abruptly ended Daniel's search. He left through the doorway leading into the small hall.

Carson slipped out from under the deck plates and listened intently through the door for a chance to make his escape. Not being able to hear anyone moving around outside the engine room's door, Carson opened it ever so slightly. He put his ear up to the crack, again trying to hear anyone speaking near his position. Finally, he heard two men talking almost in whispered tones.

"I can't find anyone onboard," Maks said to Daniel.

Daniel shook his head in disbelief. "I don't understand how someone could have gotten onto this yacht and into the cargo hold. He must have slipped through the front hatch somehow. Well, whoever it was has gone, with Serif's biggest ball of plutonium."

"We have to search again," Maks insisted.

"Yes, look around again, if you want," Daniel retorted. "But I can assure you that the thief is gone."

"Okay, Daniel," Maks agreed. "Let's ask Reza what we should do now."

Daniel gave Maks a frightened look. He knew Reza would be furious.

"If he didn't need us to offload the heavy explosives cradle, you know what he'd do?" Daniel asked Maks.

Maks nodded. "He'd have us killed. Probably do it himself."

"He'll think we double-crossed him," Daniel added.

The heavy cradle they were going to offload was designed to create a hypercritical implosion, which would generate neutrons at such an extremely high rate that the fissionable mass would expel megawatts of energy in all directions when detonated. The expected concussion of the explosion would be equivalent to five and a half megatons of TNT.

Carson continued to listen to the two guards discuss having to explain to Reza how someone was able to board the yacht and remove one of the atomic weapon cores. Neither guard knew how or why they were carrying two atomic bombs into Romania yet, nor did it make any difference to them at this point – all they cared about was their own survival. Maks and Daniel made their way to the main deck, where Reza and Serif were discussing all their possible options.

After the bodyguards' departure, Carson quietly closed the door. He started to formulate a plan of escape from the engine room and get a message back to headquarters about the nukes. But he would have to wait until the yacht was tied up and everyone had disembarked. And if he was lucky, he could get the smaller plutonium pit before leaving.

Maks and Daniel faced Serif and Reza, who were both standing on the main deck with a vague look of disbelief on their faces.

"You idiots!" Reza said, his eyes blazing. "You should have been watching more closely. We have lost a treasure that took years of planning to ripen – our great black olive of destruction." Reza spat the words out. "There is no excuse for your bungling. You allowed an intruder onboard. How could you have missed someone *stealing* one of the pits?"

Both men stood by Serif, hoping he would remember how much they were needed to complete the mission. While everyone else was searching the yacht, Serif had been considering the consequences of losing Turkey's planned bargaining chip for world stage political power. He wanted to continue with the attack.

Although very upset, Serif displayed an outward facade of calm determination. "Reza, we have to keep our heads about this. Let's continue upriver and decide what we shall do when we arrive at the Tryst Café."

Reza walked over to the starboard railing and gazed out at the rolling waters of the Danube. In a few minutes, Reza had calmed himself, grasping the concept of how hard it was going to be to unload all the equipment that had to be transported to Cernavodă's nuclear power plant. Maks and Daniel were needed once the yacht was docked and everything was brought into the cave. Even then they would need the extra muscle to put the bomb underneath the spent fuel pool located next to the reactor's containment building.

Reza could hear Serif's voice behind him. "You men go down and help the doctors prepare things."

"Aye, sir," Maks replied.

Reza moved away from the railing and sat on a bench that ran the length of the pilot house where Serif was manoeuvring the yacht. "Why are you not upset, Serif?"

Serif, looking over the bow of his magnificent boat, shook his head slowly. "I believe that we must prepare ourselves to do whatever is necessary to get the remaining bomb into the exact location that Tanya has indicated for us."

"But the larger of the two bombs has been lost," Reza complained. "No one will believe that Turkey has the knowledge necessary to build a nuclear weapon without evidence."

"Maybe you are right, my brother," Serif said, still looking toward the Danube's upstream pathway.

Serif remained at the helm, his expertise needed to steer the large yacht safely through some of the narrows of the delta. Several fishing parties were visible along the way, and occasionally a few would wave to them as they passed. Serif and Reza ignored them. The scientists and bodyguards continued to stay busy below, trying desperately to minimise their contact with Reza.

Carson heard the two guards bump into the bulkheads as they passed by the door leading to the diesel engine room where he was still hiding. He thought to himself how hard it would be to find the plutonium sphere that he'd dropped into the water back at Mamaia's wharf. Carson knew water was a fantastic neutron moderator and would also shield any gamma rays escaping that might otherwise be detected using a scintillation-type detector on the water's surface. In other words, Carson would have to remember where he had dropped it; otherwise, no one would ever recover the pit.

Next door to Carson's hiding place, Mrak and Broz checked the triggering device for the two-kilo nuclear bomb, which was still packed in black foam inside its Pelican carrying case. Mrak had experimented with warhead miniaturisation when he worked for President Tito. The Yugoslavian leader had great ambitions to become a leading world power – a "nuclear power." Tito wanted to sit on the United Nations Security Council as a permanent member like the Americans, Soviets, Chinese, British, and French – the original five nuclear weapons States.

Mrak prepared the specially designed implosion outer casing, lined with thirty-two flat plastic explosive pentagons that would be connected to the triggering device once the bomb was in its final resting place. It was vitally important that each panel be placed at the exact distance essential to a successful hyperfissionable device. Broz worked busily nearby, lashing together the smaller boxes of instruments so that they could be carried more easily when the time came for them to be moved into Serif's waiting Humvee.

Carson sat behind some empty supply crates located at the rear of the diesel engine, trying to figure out how he was going to get out of there. He would never be able to slip through the yacht's crowded hallways and staterooms full of guards, scientists, and terrorists.

He thought of ways they might seek to use the remaining bomb. Would they take it into a crowded city somewhere along the Danube, which wound its way past many major European cities? Maybe it would be stored in another country until it could be used for leverage in gaining an economical edge, quietly displayed to heads of state as a show of secret strength. And where did they get the plutonium? This was an even bigger mystery to Carson.

He felt the boat beginning to slow; its engine became less burdened as it approached the mouth of the Cernavodă canal. Carson thought it strange that the journey up the Danube had ended so quickly. He remembered that the river flowed north through Romania before it turned into the Black Sea. He felt certain they were still in Romanian territory, but where exactly were they decking, he anxiously wondered?

———

arius took another look at the two couples sitting by a fire down on the canal bank as he surveyed the area. He finally positioned the camera so that he could monitor the Danube traffic. Glancing over to another screen displaying a scene from one of the other two surveillance cameras, he noticed the yacht coming up to the small dock, behind where Tanya was sitting at the Tryst Café. It looked very large next to the short floating wooden pier.

"Hey chief, looks like our ship has come in," Marius said.

Bogdan put away his clipboard containing check-off items for the night's exercise and stepped over to the monitor. "Let's see."

Immediately recognising Serif's yacht, Bogdan ordered a cleanup of all the plant documents that were laid out over several drafting tables. It was time for them to put away the planning and begin the execution phase. His crew worked well together, stowing away much of the gear into duffel bags, leaving the surveillance equipment running for the time being. The crew's ambitions were to be the first terrorist group in the world ever to take over a nuclear reactor's controls and demand ransom for return of those controls. They didn't know of Serif's additional plans for nuclear terrorism.

Serif's two bodyguards tied off his yacht to the small dock at the base of a steep concrete shelf with stairs leading up to the Tryst. An overcast sky created a deeper darkness in the already sinister atmosphere of the small Romanian dock. Serif couldn't see his cousin sitting at their usual table until a cloud uncovered the full moon, which shone down through the other floating lakes of ice and water in the sky.

"Reza, have everyone ready to move when I return," Serif said, stopping the yacht's diesel engine.

Reza gave a short wave as he climbed down into the hull

of the boat. Serif disembarked onto the dock's landing and climbed the concrete stairway toward Tanya. Marius's surveillance view of the two cousins coming together for a kiss on each cheek was well focused and was now being watched by Bogdan as well. The terrorist crew anxiously waited inside the cave for Serif's arrival.

"Hello, my dear," Serif said.

Tanya received his kisses and offered him a chair. "How was your voyage?"

"I put my new yacht through her sea trials, and she did extremely well. And how are things here? Has everything been prepared?" Serif whispered even though the café was empty.

"Preparations here are complete, and we are ready," she replied. "Did you get the guns that we needed?"

"Yes, and I have another surprise for you. Scientists, onboard my yacht, have been working in Slovenia for the last couple of years. With their help, Reza and I fabricated something that you would not believe – you must see it for yourself," Serif said.

"What kind of scientists?" Tanya asked.

"Nuclear specialists – nuclear weapons experts, I should say. My cousin, we have a nuclear bomb onboard," Serif stated.

"What? That's unbelievable!" Tanya exclaimed.

The plans to take over the nuclear facility that Tanya had invested so much of her time and effort in were going to take a back seat to Serif's newest announcement. But that didn't matter, she was thrilled to have such an enormously powerful bargaining chip.

"I want to see it!" she practically shrieked.

Serif now knew that his conditioning of Tanya had made her ready to agree with his plans to detonate a weapon of mass destruction in Romania. But he remained prepared to eliminate her, should Tanya resist his ultimate objective.

"Yes, of course," Serif replied. "But first tell me how are things here? Have you spoken to Bogdan?"

Tanya pointed toward the fence hiding the cave where Bogdan and his crew were waiting. "They are over there. Bogdan contacted me a short time ago to tell me that they were in place."

Serif paused for a moment to take a deep breath. "I have some unusually bad news for you, however. We have lost the larger of our plutonium spheres," Serif said. "We wanted to hold the second bomb in Turkey. Now, one will have to do."

Shocked, Tanya's darker side erupted. "How could that happen?" she asked fiercely. Serif said he had no idea, but he continued to assuage Tanya until she became resigned to his admission.

Serif explained how he had left the two atomic bomb pits on the yacht with his guards. "There was no trace of a saboteur onboard, we searched the boat completely."

"Who would take one plutonium sphere and leave the other?" Tanya asked, still visibly upset. "The thief must have been interrupted, maybe jumped into the water when you returned with the scientists. Do you think it was someone from the Romanian government?" She glared at her beloved cousin. "What about those two idiots you call your bodyguards? Do you trust them?"

"Anything is possible at this point, but I don't believe Maks or Daniel have betrayed me," Serif replied. "It may have been someone from the Romanian Mafia; they are everywhere and have a deep-rooted illicit trafficking business in this country. I believe that whoever stole the sphere is still in hiding – we must continue with our mission tonight. If we stop now, I am certain we will never be able to regroup."

"Yes, if it were a government spy, they would have already found us by now," Tanya said, washing down her second amphetamine with a gulp of bottled water. "We can recover the second pit after tonight."

"Yes, I suppose you're right," Serif said half-heartedly.

CHAPTER 15

The night shift of plant operators arrived on time, with facial expressions that looked like their best milk cow had just died. It was Chrismas Eve – one of Cernavodă's biggest holidays, except for the elections now held during July every four years since the Christmas revolution of 1989.

Theodor Zahara walked up to a steel gate leading into Cernavodă's main control room and requested permission from the shift manager to cross the threshold. He entered the operating area of the main control room and reviewed the reactor operator's logbook. Theodor went up two steps to where Samuel, the off-going shift manager, was sitting.

"How's your day so far, Theo?" Samuel asked.

Theodor opened Samuel's logbook. "Things were going great until I woke up from my midday nap and realised that I still had one more night left on my four-night run."

Samuel smiled. "Well, you'll be happy to know that upper management appreciates you. The site vice president sent your crew a full Christmas dinner – it's sitting in the refrigerators in the kitchen."

Thumbing through the night orders left from the day before by the operations department manager, Theodor chuckled. "Yeah, I was thinking about how lucky I was to be on shift tonight instead of tomorrow. Irene and I were having a bubble bath in our new antique bathtub talking about that very thing before I came into work tonight."

"Did you get that thing installed?"

"Yeah, and it was a hard job for a simple senior reactor operator. We filled her up with water for the first time this afternoon. It's just perfect for two," Theodor said with a big grin. "How's business?"

The two sat together overlooking the main control room as the other crew members came in for their night shift. One by one they received their turnover and began their nightly routine. Theodor finished his briefing with Samuel over the next forty-five minutes, then announced that he had assumed the control room command function. Samuel left the control room, and Theodor read over his crew briefing material for a few moments before turning his command temporarily over to his plant supervisor, then went into the kitchen for a cup of coffee.

In the kitchen three off-going operators were talking about everything that had occurred that day and signing out of their logs. The equipment operators looked a little tired, but because they would be down to a skeleton crew that night, everyone would have to work a little harder to maintain the reactor stable. Cernavodă's nuclear power plant – the largest electricity-generating facility in Europe – pretty much took care of itself; engineered by Americans meant that safety was foremost in every one of the multiple systems that were laid out on the plant's ten acres.

Theodor put a filter and plenty of ground African beans together for a fresh pot of coffee, one of many he and his crew would make that night during the tiring twelve-hour shift.

After pushing the coffeemaker's start button, Theodor

said to the three operators, "How you guys doing tonight?"

Isabella was one of only two females who made it through the tough screening process to get this job at Cernavodă. "I think we are going to make it," she said and headed to the locker room next door.

"Samuel told me that management left us a great Christmas dinner in the refrigerator," Theodor said.

"Thanks, Theo, tell them we appreciate the food," Jake said, putting down his logbook.

Jake and Henri were two of the best equipment operators and had been selected for the next control room reactor operator's qualification class.

"Yeah, thank them for us," Henri said. "We need to continue this tradition of having special food on our holidays."

Theodor poured a cup of strong coffee into his prized Donald Duck coffee mug from Disney World. "You bet."

Isabella looked angry as she came out from the locker room. "Oh, my God! Jake, you gotta get that Vaseline jar out of the toilet stall! I can't stand that nasty thing in there!"

A roar of laughter went through the small group. Everyone knew that one of the operators on the day shift had a hemorrhoid problem and was very non-hygienic when it came to taking care of his medication. Isabella found his small plastic container of lubricant more than once in the bathroom that men and women shared.

Jake started toward the locker room, suppressing his laughter.

Henri chuckled. "Well, at least he didn't leave it on the kitchen sink, like he did the last time we relieved those guys."

Theodor finished his coffee and put the mug in the sink. "I think you guys need a little social guidance." He swiped his identity card at the control room door. The thick steel door's latch released, and Theodor left the kitchen.

Walking by the emergency systems panel that he had operated for five years before being selected for a senior operator's licence, Theodor stepped back up to his desk overlooking the control room and prepared himself for the beginning of shift briefing. As the acting senior manager, he would observe and critique the briefing as Jay Kokoc performed the crew's nightly brief.

Jay was the plant supervisor for the night, coordinating all the operators during their assigned tasks while operating the huge reactor and all its supporting equipment. Jay and Heber Tasnadi, the shift supervisor, took turns performing plant and shift supervisor duties. Heber was the on-shift technical advisor, a position that required a degree in nuclear engineering and was responsible for mitigating core damage during an emergency situation.

"Okay, ladies and gentlemen," Jay announced mockingly to the crew as they mustered together in the main control room. "Let's begin by saying welcome to Cernavodă."

A chuckle rippled through the operators, which consisted of the two supervisors, two reactor operators, three equipment operators, and Theodor. Draco, the security chief for the night, also made an unusual appearance at the briefing that night. The two reactor operators, sitting inside the area between Theodor's desk and the reactor's main controls mounted on a horseshoe-shaped panel, were long-time veterans of on-shift operations. Lothar was in his late thirties and Mario liked to think of himself as a very young forty-seven.

Jay finished his briefing and then asked all the operators to explain what plant information had been communicated to them by the previous shift during their turnover. Once everyone had spoken, Jay asked Draco to describe what the security section wanted to do during their shift.

Theodor noticed how odd it was that Draco was wearing his dress security uniform, medals pinned to his chest and shoes spit shone to perfection. He seemed to be focusing his attention on the crew more than usual, as if he was trying to memorise the faces of the shift's personnel. Normally stationed at a desk during the day, Draco had not met all the operators, especially those recently hired.

"We will be running a security drill tonight between ten and eleven o'clock," Draco stated. "We ask that you please return to the main control room envelope during that time, so that we can account for everyone. We are simulating a terrorist attack, and we would hate to place anyone in a position of being hurt."

"I imagine that your men appreciate your Christmas Eve gift," Isabella said, shaking her head.

"We must stay ready at all times," Draco responded with a harsh look of determination, which he tried to mask with a smile in Isabella's direction.

Theodor knew how important security was at a nuclear power station and had seen the scheduled drill on the "Plan of the Day" during his last day shift planning meeting. He objected to the hassle of having a security drill on Christmas Eve, but he was overruled by management who wanted to do everything possible to ensure they were abiding by the latest security rules. Draco convinced upper management at the meeting that drills were to be held exactly four weeks apart, in order to keep everyone on a firm re-qualification rotation.

"Let's wrap this thing up, Jay," Theodor said.

The crew briefing ended on that note, and Draco returned to his security chief's office in the main security island building. He had reduced his staff that night to seven men –

three who were reliably loyal to him, plus another four who were not. Draco had worked very hard over the past two years, getting ready for this night. He believed that he was fully prepared for what was about to happen. His desk was clean except for a banker's lamp, a deck of tarot cards, and his laptop computer.

Turning on his computer, the screen instantly lit up his office. Draco logged into the terrorist group's special server and began writing an encrypted email to Tanya's Blackberry:

The program is set. Awaiting your friends... Allah is great.

CHAPTER 16

Carson's special training helped settle his nerves and evaluate his situation. "Okay, time's up, Kit Carson! You've got to get out of here," he muttered to himself.

He again surveyed the yacht's engine room for an exit, other than through the door that led him right by the two scientists in the next compartment who were still putting together the pieces of the smaller nuclear bomb. Carson noticed an object hidden behind several of the boxes and crates. It was a short steel ladder with teakwood steps.

Carson quietly made his way over to the bulkhead where the ladder was stowed, but no other exits were immediately visible in the dim lighting. Until Carson looked up. He could make out a thin rubber seam just behind two empty boxes. It was a maintenance hatch, normally used by mechanics that might be making repairs on the engine while the boat was in dry dock, not wanting to walk through the yacht in their dirty, greasy clothes. The handle to the hatch could only be reached by moving things around. Carson carefully and silently moved each wooden box blocking his path.

Loosening the two wing nuts that held the ladder down, Carson was able to lift it to its mounting position. It was heavier than he anticipated, and Carson almost lost his grip as the boat pitched from a swell caused by a passing barge, even though the boat was tied to the dock of the Tryst Café. Carson placed the end hooks of the ladder into two slots that kept it moored to the boat.

Creeping up the ladder's narrow rungs, Carson grew more confident. Although he was unarmed and dressed in a pair of Levi's, black polo shirt, and climbing boots, Carson thought he'd survive if he could make contact with Vienna for some support. But he still had no idea how many terrorists were on the yacht or who they were meeting at the landing.

Tapping the metallic handles of the watertight hatch cover with the palm of one hand, Carson loosened it with great care, in anticipation of what was just outside. Carson pushed up very slowly on its metal-plated surface. The top of the cover was maple wood, stained and shellacked, making its weight much more than he had expected.

Carson grunted softly and lifted the cover slightly while trying to take a look around the main deck before opening the hatch completely. The cover popped up about two inches, unpredictably exposing him to anyone that might have been sitting at the table where Maks and Daniel had been playing dominoes. But there was no one around. Serif had already left the vessel, and the others were down in the cargo hold with Mrak and Broz.

Holding the cover high enough, Carson climbed onto the main-deck and quickly ducked behind the sturdy table's bolted-down legs.

Still squatting, Carson moved to the boat's side to see if he could identify anything in the area surrounding the yacht that would help determine his location. Through the darkness surrounding the yacht, which was now moored about seventy-five yards from where Serif and Tanya were sitting at the Tryst Café, Carson could see the open waters of the Danube. A glistening full moon reflected off the surface of the water like a million tiny mirrors. Carson realised that he was no longer on the Black Sea, but didn't know where he was exactly until he looked to the starboard side of the boat and saw a huge blue neon sign shining through the night: CNE-P Cernavodă.

"What in the Sam Hill?" Carson muttered to himself. He paused for a second to try to understand exactly why these men had brought the two-kilo plutonium sphere to Cernavodă. He knew the small town very well from his assigned inspection duties. Carson would often stay for up to two weeks in a hotel near the nuclear plant. He would come down to the little port when he was bored and have a drink at the Tryst Café – it seemed all too familiar.

He scanned the countryside from his crouched position and saw Romania's only nuclear site, where up to ten projected nuclear power plants were to be built by the previous communist nation. Only one of the power plants was actually built – after the fall of communism, two of the others were in various stages of construction, and the rest of Ceaușescu's grand plan would probably never materialise.

Carson could see that unit number one looked to be operating and unit number two was nearly complete now – its containment identical to unit one. But only the containment structure could be seen in the moonlight for the remaining project – a huge concrete barrel, rising about two hundred feet from the hillside. Carson looked up the embankment leading to the Tryst Café and saw what looked like a man and a woman seated at a small table and having an intense conversation.

Carson was certain that the guards were due to come back topside very soon, so he slowly climbed off the stern of the yacht's wooden deck onto a dive platform and then slid into the chilly water. There had been heavy snowfalls for several months, and the Danube was carrying much of the resulting cold water to the Black Sea. His clothing did little to protect Carson from the immediate feeling of the onset of hypothermia as he entered the mixed waters of the Danube and Cernavodă's canal. Carson experienced a flashback to his North Sea commando training, a stark familiarity with ice-cold water that he would never forget.

Swimming close to the boat's hull, Carson made his way to a floating bait shop at one end of the dock. He climbed out of the water and waited. His body was now vibrating vigorously – trying to warm itself while being cooled by the frigid breeze blowing across his wet clothing. The wind came through the Cernavodă canal pass, down from the Carpathian Mountains, gaining momentum as it travelled.

Carson knew he had to do something to stop the men on the yacht or at least delay them long enough to allow him to call INWA headquarters. But first he had to find a telephone. There were none in sight and the harbour looked deserted. The only structure that Carson could see was the Tryst Café.

Hesitating momentarily to evaluate the situation, Carson heard someone coming up from below-decks on the yacht. Just then Reza and Maks came into view, walked the gangway, and went toward the concrete stairs, then up the embankment to where Serif and Tanya were sitting. The two men had a brief conversation with the couple, then headed toward the mountainside.

Carson remembered seeing entrances to old caves dotted along the base of the mountain during his inspection visits to Cernavodă's nuclear power plant. He couldn't be sure where the two were going – he'd have to move closer to the café to find that out.

It occurred to him that the terrorists may have selected

this location because Cernavodă was very close to the Black Sea, making their escape to the East easier after they deposited the nuclear weapon somewhere in the area. *That's it!* Carson knew he was right. The terrorists were going to destroy the nuclear power plant at Cernavodă. The spent nuclear fuel in the storage pool would compound the dispersal of radioactive contaminants many times over, creating a plume that could be spread by the winds for thousands of miles to the west.

Carson crept forward toward the bait shop. Slipping quietly around to a hidden spot behind the shop where he could leap to the shore, he vaulted a wooden fishing tackle box and planted both his boots on solid ground. Using large stones laid in place during the construction of Cernavodă's canal in the early 1980s, Carson was able to climb up the steep embankment below the café.

Carson jumped over a short handrail and onto the car park. He hunkered down behind Tanya's parked Dacia, which didn't provide him with the concealment that he needed. But his temporary position behind her car allowed him to get a look at the two sitting together at their plastic table. Carson couldn't hear what they were discussing, but he felt sure it involved a plan to use the nuclear weapon that was still on the yacht.

Not realising that the terrorists were monitoring the whole area from inside a cave along the adjacent hillside, Carson's athletic silhouette was now in range of Marius's surveillance cameras.

"Hey, chief," Marius said. "Take a look at this. There's a guy hiding behind Tanya's car."

"Yeah, I see him," Bogdan said. "But I can't see his face. See if you can clean up that image."

Marius tried desperately to improve the blended pixels

being displayed on his monitor to allow him to identify the man's face, but the equipment wasn't as powerful as he hoped. He unboxed another video amplifier and spent a few minutes connecting the device to his computerised display module.

Carson situated himself so that he could see Serif stand and motion to Tanya that it was time for them to go. The two terrorists turned so that their faces were illuminated by a dim streetlight, together with one of the café's bar lights. Carson finally saw the faces of Serif and his cousin Tanya; both looked to be of Arabic descent. Their demeanor didn't give Carson any indication of the couple's horrific intentions – they looked like ordinary people. But he knew that to plan an attack of this magnitude, spreading radioactive contamination throughout Southeastern Europe and possibly into Western Europe, these two would be have to be cold-blooded and evil – "brain-damaged thinkers," his mother would say.

"Reza, you need to see this," Bogdan said.

Reza had been in the cave now for about half an hour, going over every detail of the power plant's takeover with Bogdan. Stepping over to the surveillance monitor, Reza saw Carson moving toward an old observation tower, once used by the Romanian government to monitor Danube traffic.

"Hey, isn't that the guy from INWA?" Jacob asked. He looked again at the monitor and added, "Yeah, that's the same guy we tied up in your house, chief. His name is Griffin."

"What do you mean tied up at Bogdan's house?" Reza turned angrily to Bogdan for an immediate explanation.

"We picked him up snooping around my house last night," Bogdan said.

Bogdan explained how they had caught Carson, beat him unconscious, and tied his hands and feet with zip-ties.

"But somehow he escaped," Bogdan said apologetically.

Reza seethed with fury. "I'm gonna kill that bastard!"

Reza came to the stark realisation that an INWA operative, like Carson Griffin, could have detected a plutonium signature coming from their boat in the harbour and was probably responsible for the missing six-kilogram plutonium pit. Bogdan told Reza that they had found Carson's HM-5 gamma detector in his vehicle, but that when they went back to retrieve the device a few hours later, it was gone. Reza didn't want Bogdan or his crew to know what he and Serif were planning to do with the nuclear weapon – the fewer people that knew of their ultimate plan, the better. He would have to eventually tell them, but it was still too early.

Grabbing one of the many AK-47s that were stacked near Bogdan's computers, Reza left the cave, heading for the observation tower.

Reza called back through the darkness of their hideout, "Get your men ready, Bogdan! This won't take very long."

Serif and Tanya, still not aware of what was transpiring around them, went down to the yacht. Tanya was going to see the bomb for the first time.

———

Carson stumbled over an old broken wooden door half in and half out of the observation tower. The lighting coming from the old tower was almost non-existent, but he could tell that someone had been up the concrete staircase recently. Probably some teenagers looking for a romantic getaway spot or a traveller looking for refuge from a powerful storm; either scenario would have been plausible. The tower was large enough to house several rooms at its base but quickly narrowed to something akin to the small airport tower back in Carson's hometown.

Riverboat crews pushing barges up and down the Danube once needed the tower's guidance through the narrow passages between Cernavodă's King Carol I Bridge. Upkeep of the old tower had fallen off dramatically after the Romanian revolution; however, its concrete walls and metallic roof still made it a substantial structure.

Carson ran up the spiral staircase into the tower's upper observation room. It was only one story tall but would have been impressive when first built. Its walls were covered in full-length windows, enabling a radioman to see in almost every direction when calling out navigation coordinates to a passing riverboat captain.

The room was completely dark inside, but Carson could see the harbour and the car park from his perch. The smell of a dead rat was reeking from somewhere very close by and was beginning to nauseate Carson as he looked around the perimeter of the port area. He could see that the Tryst was empty now that Serif and Tanya had gone onboard the yacht.

Out of the corner of his eye, Carson saw a dark figure, carrying what looked to be a machine gun, round the two-storey abandoned office building next to the observation tower. Watching the running figure temporarily disappear out of sight, Carson could tell that the man was limping. But as he came back into view, he moved very quickly toward the observation tower. Carson knew that somehow he'd been spotted and that the man who had just entered the tower's ground floor was on his way to kill him.

Hurriedly looking for something he could use to defend himself, Carson found a broom with only a few strands of straw on the floor. He grabbed its wooden handle as quietly as he could, taking care not to hit a broken swivel chair sitting nearby.

Carson could hear the man coming up the spiral staircase. Reza's gait – a single thud of a slow stride, followed by a quick shuffle – was distinctly reminiscent of an American veteran of the Gulf War, someone Carson still knew. Carson realised that he'd have one chance to take the man down in this semi-dark room, moonlight dimly shining through the surrounding dirty windows.

Reza stopped momentarily, his eyes still adjusting to the change in illumination. His anger had manifested into uncontrollable rage when he became certain that this INWA operative had taken one of the precious plutonium spheres from Serif's yacht. Reza ran up the last five steps, thinking he could shoot before Carson would know what had hit him.

But Carson was ready when Reza climbed his last step and landed on the wet, mucky floor of the observation tower. The thick broom handle felt like Carson's old Louisville Slugger baseball bat in his hands. Tightly gripped with his left hand and guided by his right, he swung the lumber with all his strength. He kept his swing high and level, just like he had been taught back in high school by his baseball coach.

In the faint moonlight, Carson could see Reza's head snap to the left from the impact of the broom handle's swift momentum, sounding much like the thump of a ripe watermelon. The fully automatic AK-47 dropped to the floor and Reza to his knees.

Switch hitting was something that Carson learned in his freshman year at college, after long hours of playing co-ed softball with girls in his physical education classes. Carson came down across the side of Reza's head with a second blow, then another bone-crushing upward blow that drove the cartilage in

Reza's nose straight into his brain. Blood quickly trickled out of Reza's mouth, ears, and nose. His eyes stared without seeing.

Reza's body dropped to the floor in the poorly lit room with a horrible thud, its limp silenced forever. Carson picked up the AK-47 and started carefully down the stairway. He imagined that there would be someone coming very soon to look for this guy, and he needed to escape as shrewdly as possible. Not as concerned with being discovered, Carson focused on getting out of the tower, where he knew he was a target for anyone who would follow the first assassin.

Carson's extensive experience with surveillance systems made him realise just how easy it would be to set up a few cameras around the port, if these terrorists were serious about their security. He felt absolutely certain that his movements were under someone's watchful eye and who was close enough to send a hired gun to kill Carson.

Slowly stepping out of the tower's concrete doorway, Carson scanned the area for a camera or another terrorist. None were visible from where he was standing, so Carson walked along the side of the office building and stopped at the corner. He looked up at the only electrical device around – a streetlamp. Carson immediately located one of Marius's cameras mounted on top of the light's casing, sweeping the building and surrounding area. Timing his exit between the camera's movements, Carson ran for the cover of an old building.

Marius didn't see him leave the tower or hear a gunshot from Reza's weapon. He imagined that Reza might be taking his time in killing the intruder, torturing his employer's intentions out of him. Marius directed his cameras up and down the Cernavodă canal trying to see more of the nuclear plant and Serif's yacht.

Carson hid in the small building and waited. He kept

watching in all directions for any vehicle or personnel movements. Carson wanted to see what the terrorists were planning to do next before making his way to the town of Cernavodă – still three miles away. Carson's attention was soon caught by moving lights and a small group of figures near the hill across a small field of hibernating tall grasses. He watched as characters of the unfolding drama exited a cave with several boxes and rucksacks.

Looking closely at the men as they loaded the Mercedes vans with gear, he began to recognise some of the faces – this was the same group of men that held him hostage in Bogdan's house. But how were they connected to the crew of the yacht? That connection, Carson concluded, must be Cernavodă's nuclear power plant.

His brain fully engaged and running on nitro, Carson remembered Bogdan and his men discussing their strategy during his short night of captivity. But the crew Bogdan had meticulously groomed for the takeover of the plant never spoke of a nuclear bomb. Carson realised that the operators had no idea that Serif was going to use his two-kilogram nuke to destroy the spent fuel stored adjacent to the reactor. Carson found the two plans to be in awful disharmony with each other.

Icy rain drizzled down around him, superseded by large snowflakes. The dense mixture of water and ice had some effect on Marius's surveillance cameras. But Carson's view of the movements of Bogdan's crew was unimpaired by the sleet, the knee-high grass, or the wooden fence, which exposed their movements through a driveway gap.

The weather reminded him of a day out hiking with Christy and Susan near Schneeberg, one of Austria's famous mountains south of Vienna. Their dog, Bingo, had run away from them and was chasing an enormous jackrabbit through dried grass much like what he saw on the other side of the car park. Christy had waited by an old wooden bench hoping for Bingo's return, while Susan and Carson searched the hillside. He finally emerged from the rugged hill terrain, proudly sporting the jackrabbit in his mouth. Christy just rolled her eyes and grimaced. Susan laughed and told Bingo to "drop it." Bingo always listened to Susan.

Carson remembered seeing Christy's face through a light snowfall from a distance, arriving at their agreed upon rendezvous spot before Susan. He thought how beautiful his wife was that afternoon and how wonderful their life had been together since moving to Vienna.

Carson's euphoric daydream abruptly ended when he saw someone emerging from the cave.

CHAPTER 17

Inside the nuclear power plant, the night shift had their "beginning of shift" briefing, performing their equipment log-taking on the individual rounds sheets. By 8:15 p.m., Jake and Isabella had returned from their respective buildings to the operations kitchen. The kitchen and locker room areas, like the main control room, were all within what engineers called the "control room envelope."

Ventilation systems were in a normal line-up, supplying filtered outside fresh air to the operators as the crew began to prepare their Christmas dinner. No windows were installed on any of the exterior walls leading into or out of the main areas. In case of a nuclear accident, the operators were required to stay within the envelope for their own protection. Inappropriate weaknesses in the envelope that might allow uncontrolled outside air into the occupied space during a reactor's inadvertent release of radioactive gases would have serious consequences to the crew.

Theodor's on-crew felt comfortable working on Christmas Eve – their complacency was deeply rooted. They had never felt threatened by a meltdown of one of the largest boiling water reactor cores in the world. The reactor was incredibly reliable, operating with a yearly full power capacity of around eighty-five percent. The Americans designed it with multiple backup systems to the normal safety pumps and pipes, all of which were required by the US Nuclear Regulatory Commission and now the Romanian State Authorities.

Henri was working in the reactor building, trying to get another heat exchanger in service to cool the spent fuel pool down some. The recent reshuffling of the spent fuel in the pool created a great deal of extra heat when the fuel was temporarily removed from its existing storage channels and placed into others. The water of the pool passed through a separate cooling loop, which normally kept the spent nuclear fuel cooled down and the water from evaporating too quickly.

Henri was standing near the pump control panel, trying to hear Mario's two-way radio communication.

"Henri, come back," Mario repeated for the third time.

The thickness of the surrounding room's concrete, near where Henri was working, prevented radio repeaters from relaying Mario's transmission clearly.

"I read you, control room," Henri replied.

"Good, over," Mario squawked. "Henri, I need you to raise your cooling water flow through the bravo fuel pool heat exchanger, over."

"Roger that control room, I understand that you want me to raise flow through the bravo fuel pool heat exchanger, over," Henri said.

Operators were required to repeat back any orders coming from the main control room to ensure they got their directions correct. Henri hated repeating directions back at first, but in situations like he was in this day, it made sense.

"That is correct," Mario acknowledged.

Henri bumped up flow using a small hand switch on the fuel pool control panel and waited for Mario to contact him when the temperature indication for the spent fuel water began to drop. The temperature of the water was kept as low as possible to prevent unnecessary neutron production or the temperature of the fuel from exceeding a safe condition. Should the operators lose cooling altogether to the spent fuel water, they would have about twenty-four hours to recover it before all the water began to boil, when the huge pool was completely full. No one had any idea how long it would take at a lower water level. But one thing was certain – at a lower level it would take much less time.

Henri knew from his reactor physics training that spent nuclear fuel, when not shielded properly by boron, hafnium, or some other neutron absorber, would feed on itself until the long thin zircaloy tube holding the small pellets in place began a meltdown. Normally, over time, the spent fuel would cool enough to be moved to a dry storage area, but Cernavodă wouldn't have that luxury for several years to come. Although dry storage was an inexpensive solution compared to physically expanding the spent fuel pool, the Romanians would have to ask for the funding from outside their country.

"Henri, this is the control room," Mario said.

"Go ahead, control room," Henri replied.

"You can come on home, the spent fuel pool cooling water temperature looks good, over," Mario said.

"Roger that, control room," Henri replied.

Locking the controlling switches in place with his key, Henri left the area and made his way to the turbine building elevator. A few moments later, he arrived at the rear door to the main control room and after frisking himself with a personnel radiation detector, he entered the envelope.

"How does it look?" Henri asked from the controlled area gate.

"Looks good," Mario replied. "Grab some dinner and I'll watch it for a while."

Turning away to walk back to the operations kitchen, Henri gave Mario a thumbs up. "Okay, man. I'm starving."

———

Positioned near the front gate was Draco's security supervisor's office. It was about two hundred yards from the power block of the plant and situated inside the site's security island. His volunteering for Christmas Eve duty didn't seem odd to the plant's higher management – he explained it as a morale-building exercise for the men who were burdened with the yearly task.

Draco had already called each of his three loyal guards on a scrambled two-way radio, now stationed at their appointed positions, to check if they were prepared to take control of the power plant's vital areas. Under cover of a phony security drill, one man mounted a fifty-calibre Browning M2 machine gun on the roof of the control building that faced the main gate. Another guard put the same kind of weapon on the back side of the turbine building. It would be needed to protect the main generator output transformers from any attack by outsiders trying to trip off the main turbine, ultimately causing the plant to shut down.

Everyone was in place and prepared to take control of Cernavodă's nuclear power station's corporate security force at 9:30 p.m., as per Draco's skillfully designed security breach strategy. His mock security drill ended with his final order for the other four security guards to muster in the security island at the front gate entrance of the protected area.

By 9:45 p.m., the men finished their debriefing and were sitting in the break room joking with each other and feeling like they were finally getting into a Christmas mood. Each of them told of their plans for Christmas morning surprises for their kids and spouses. Draco walked into the room with one of his three guards, who was carrying his 9mm pistol drawn in the direction of the group of men sitting around a metal picnic table. The guard also had a German-made Heckler & Koch G.36 fitted with a NSA 80 II night-sight strapped to his back, with one of those World War II green canvas straps across his broad chest.

"Okay, you men stand up and put your hands behind your back," Draco ordered.

A roar of laughter came from the small group that was just beginning to enjoy their Christmas Eve. With a wry sneer on his face, Draco's man hit the nearest guard with the butt of his rifle and the room went silent. Shock and confusion registered on the men's faces.

"What are you doing?" a guard said, getting to his feet. "Are you serious? Is this part of the drill?"

Draco waved his gun at them as all but one stood in their positions around the small steel table. "Put your hands behind your back and your face on the table," Draco demanded.

The three men put their faces on the cold metal surface while Draco held his pistol on them, and his man zip-tied their hands together. The fourth lay unconscious on the floor as the zip-ties were cinched tightly around his wrists.

"Okay, now sit next to that wall and put out your legs," Draco ordered.

After tying their feet together with the strong black plastic, Draco and his man went into the island surveillance room and prepared to disable all external lines to local and state law enforcement. Draco's other two men rounded up two warehouse workers and three technicians who were located in their shops, tied them up, and put them together in a bathroom. Once the extraneous personnel were bound, the fifty-calibre Browning M2 turrets were re-manned and made ready for what everyone knew would be an extraordinary military push to regain control of the nuclear facility by the Romanian government.

It was now 10:00 p.m. Christmas Eve celebrations would soon be starting throughout the Western world. Just three miles from the nuclear power plant, Bogdan and his crew were preparing to begin their takeover of the plant's control room.

———

At the cave, Bogdan's crew was loaded into two vans, along with their equipment, as he paced around inside the cavern. He wanted to make sure that any evidence of his participation or that of his crew could not be easily traced back to them. Bogdan had already sold his fishing boat, house, and equipment to a local young fisherman. The others in his crew had also relinquished everything they owned, ready to start their new lives as millionaires. None were married or had children, and their desire to leave Romania was overwhelming. A new identity for these men meant a life they had all desperately wanted.

Before leaving, Bogdan opened the breaker supplying all the electrical power to their surveillance system and all other lights in the cavern, then shutdown the small generator. Using only the light of his high-intensity flashlight, he set the dynamite charges that would blow off the roof of the cave the next morning at 10:00 a.m. They would be well into their escape from the facility by then. Walking outside of the cavern, he saw the two vans ready for their short trip to the power plant.

"Chief," Marius called out from the window of the second van. "Where is Reza? I thought that he was coming with us."

"We have run out of time," Bogdan replied. "We've got to leave without him to make our scheduled window. He must be with Serif on the yacht and will come later."

Jumping into the first van, Bogdan called Serif on his new satellite telephone, encrypted and fully protected from anyone who might be trying to identify them or their intentions. Serif acquired the two additional telephones from his Turkish supporters, one for himself and one for Reza.

"Ciao," Bogdan said. "This is Bogdan."

Tanya and Serif were on the yacht with the two scientists, waiting for Reza's call. Tanya was amazed at the technology that Serif had accumulated over the last two years. She had never seen nor knew about his nuclear weapon until that evening, and she felt a little slighted by that fact. But now, Serif depended on Tanya's expertise in knowing exactly where they should place the smaller two-kilo bomb in order for it to do the most damage.

"Where is Reza?" Serif asked Bogdan. "I need to talk to him." Serif sounded a bit upset.

Bogdan hid his surprise and realised he would have to cover for himself – he certainly didn't want to get into the whole INWA inspector fiasco with Serif. Bogdan knew that it was his fault that Carson Griffin was free and that he knew about their plan to take over Cernavodă. Although Bogdan was stunned to learn that his hunter had not killed Carson yet, there wasn't time to think about that – he had to move on.

"Reza thought he saw someone watching you and Tanya,"

Bogdan said. "He wanted to take a closer look, and now I believe he will meet you at the yacht."

Serif was still confused by Reza's leaving the cave without calling him. "*Bine*," he said, meaning okay. "We will call you at midnight from the front gate."

Bogdan worried about where Reza could be, or for that matter, Griffin. But there was no time to stop and look for them. The assault was now engaged, and their timing was critical. Both vans travelled through the park that was in the middle of the little river town. Bogdan and his crew could see the Snow White and the Seven Dwarfs knee-high statues in the kids' section of the park as they rode silently down the narrow street, dodging moon-crater-sized potholes.

Cernavodă's schoolteachers wanted to give the small children an escape from their impoverished lives. The children played in this park on the statues built to eye level of most five-year-olds – fantastic characters in a fairy tale. Dreams of travelling to America and visiting Disneyland were a fantasy for the adults. But children of one of the Danube's most deprived cities could easily imagine themselves living the tale, having fun with their friends in a magical world.

CHAPTER 18

Carson noticed that when the white vans left the cave each carried five men and a lot of equipment, which was contained inside black Pelican cases. He couldn't tell what was being transported in the cases, but he was able to recognise that several SCBAs were being carried by two men during the loading. Carson remembered the style very well from his experience as a fire brigade leader, in the days when he was an operator at Georgia's nuclear power station.

Moonlight reflected off the dark windows of the vans as they drove close enough for Carson to possibly see a face, but the blackness from within wouldn't allow it.

He knew that the terrorists were heading to the Cernavodă nuclear power plant. It looked to him as if all the planning was finally complete, and they were ready to execute their monstrous plan. More than ever, Carson was desperate to find a reliable telephone. If he could notify INWA, they would make all the international notifications to address the potential release of nuclear radiation.

The sheet-metal building that Carson was standing in was empty. There wasn't a house or person nearby to ask for use of their telephone. The Tryst had already closed for Christmas Eve. The town was asleep; there was almost no movement on the streets of Cernavodă, except for Bogdan's vans speeding toward their destination.

Carson knew the way to the nuclear facility from the Tryst, so he started jogging the three miles to the plant. The icy rain continued to fall as he made his way down a deserted road in the same direction that Bogdan had taken. Within ten minutes, he found himself by the park, the knee-high Snow White watching him with her wide eyes as he passed. Carson started up the hill toward the main road where he saw Cernavodă's closed movie theatre, which had been put out of business by the introduction of satellite TV. Miniature space-station-provided signals were being pumped into the area via a local entrepreneur – wise beyond his teenage years. The kid's battery of large white satellite dishes, sitting atop a five-storey communist-built apartment building, could be seen from the park. But more interesting to Carson was an orange wall-mounted telephone sitting next to the entrance of the dilapidated theatre's ticket booth. It was the answer to his prayers.

Carson ran over to the phone and realised that it had not been updated to the European standard. He remembered what a pain in the rear it was trying to get through on one of these old communist-designed telephones. "Okay, you can do this, Carson," he whispered under his breath as he picked up the phone.

He was just able to make out the numbers to get to an operator. "Hello."

"*Allo*," a female said in a distant voice, probably coming from a can on a string, Carson thought.

"I need to make a collect call," Carson yelled. "To Wien, Austria."

"Yah, I speak English," the operator said.

Carson began to speak very slowly. "Please connect me to the International Nuclear Weapons Agency in Wien."

Listening for the answer to his request, Carson asked for a confirmation. "Okay, *bine*?"

Suddenly a click, then he could hear a faint ringing from what sounded like a phone call to the moon.

"*Guten Abend*," a man's voice said. "This is the Vienna International Centre, Sergeant Kohl speaking."

Carson could not believe his ears – he'd gotten through to the security desk at the VIC. "Hello, this is Carson Griffin. I am an inspector, and I have an emergency situation."

Sergeant Kohl was very formal – he had to be as head of the watch for the United Nations building in Vienna. "What is your location?"

"Okay, I can only say this one time, so please be ready," Carson said. "There's a terrorist attack taking place in Cernavodă, Romania, at the nuclear power station."

The telephone connection was silent for a moment. "Please repeat your last statement."

"I need for you to contact emergency preparedness and tell them to commence an international alert for an imminent terrorist attack at the Cernavodă nuclear power plant," Carson said.

Carson wasn't sure what Serif was going to do with the nuclear bomb that he was stowing aboard his yacht, but Bogdan was already on the way to execute the plan that Carson had overheard the night before. Carson thought that it would be too much for the security department at the Agency to grasp if he tried to fully explain his sensationalist claims. However, after finding Carson's picture on the *Who's Who* webpage of the Agency, Kohl had to accept his declaration until he could prove otherwise.

Sergeant Kohl wrote down every word that Carson had said, and then asked the inspector for some kind of traceable information. "I will contact the duty commander about your request, Mr. Griffin, but I need a person of contact or a telephone number to call."

"Call my section head," Carson said. "Todd Sinclair."

"Yessir, Mr. Griffin," Kohl said.

Carson hung up and made his second call. "Hello, is this the operator?"

The voice was very faint again, but it sounded like the same operator that he had just spoken to. "Allo," she said.

"I need to make another collect call to Wien," Carson shouted over the handset.

"*Bine*," the operator said in her best German, "*Was ist diese Rufnummer?*"

Carson knew this one by heart. "+43-1-520-6901."

Again, a hard click echoed across the telephone lines, sounding as if his request was being broadcast all across Romania, passing through the Carpathian Alps somewhere near Dracula's Castle, on its way to Vienna.

Todd's voice came on the line. "Hello?" He was at home with his family on Christmas Eve and had not received Carson's hurried email from Bogdan's laptop. He listened to Carson tell him of the bomb and the planned takeover of the nuclear power plant in Cernavodă.

"You've got to call the emergency preparedness group and tell them everything," Carson said with intense urgency.

"All right, Carson, I'll call the duty officer at once. I felt something was wrong when you didn't show up for the fuel inspection today at Unit II, or call in."

"Tell them that–" Carson heard a click on the line again and his call was over. Not completely disconnected, but the line was silent, like it had been left open somewhere out there in a great fibre-optic mesh that no one could track without a lot of time and effort. Carson could feel heat coming from the telephone, along with a faint buzzing noise. It would have to cool down again before its circuits would allow another call.

Dropping the receiver, Carson continued his jog toward the power plant – still nearly two miles away. He wanted to at least warn their on-site security force that there were terrorists in and around their facility. Carson could only think about what his capturers had talked about the night before in Bogdan's place. How they were going to use the reactor's power to destroy itself and its containment, which would allow huge amounts of radioactive gasses into the stratosphere above the nuclear power plant. However, during their discussions they never mentioned the head of security's cooperation or his security force takeover. Carson had never heard them say anything about Draco's communications with Bogdan or his willingness to kill anyone who might stop their plan from its full implementation.

———

Todd immediately called Anthony Zabaar, the Emergency Director, from his encrypted mobile phone. Zabaar was at his home in Vienna.

"Hello, this is Todd Sinclair – head of nuclear safeguarding section T9."

"Hello, Mr. Sinclair," Zabaar said. "Happy holidays to you and your family."

"Very sorry to interrupt your holidays, sir, but I have some alarming news from one of my inspectors in Romania, near the Cernavodă nuclear power plant," Todd hurriedly explained. "A terrorist group is trying to take control of the nuclear power plant and will hold it hostage, maybe even try to destroy it."

"Do you have any confirmation from the site? Or Romania?" Zabaar quickly asked. "I cannot do anything without confirmation from the Romanian state authority or Cernavodă itself."

"I understand your concern, but you will need to exercise your authority in order to start an investigation into my inspector's report," Todd stated.

There was a long pause as both men thought about their responsibilities. It was Christmas Eve, and neither of them wanted to make a mistake in calling out resources and performing major evacuations of the population of Cernavodă, unless there was absolutely no other choice.

Zabaar spoke in the stalemate of indecision. "I will contact the Romanians."

"You do that, now!" Todd exclaimed and ended his call.

Turning to his wife and two kids, Todd took a deep breath before telling them that he had to dash down to his office for a little while. He couldn't tell them what was going on, but he promised to call them once he knew more and could explain what was happening.

Todd was well aware that Zabaar would have to have confirmation before he would act, unless he could convince him otherwise with some kind of overwhelming evidence. As Todd drove through the deserted streets of Vienna, he wondered if Carson was being held captive and forced to call him with the scare of an attack. Or was his family in danger of being killed if he didn't make the call that might change the world's view of nuclear reactor safety? The accident at Chernobyl had left a lasting impression on everyone and strongly reinforced the Green Party's position in Europe against nuclear power. Another significant accident might deliver an unrecoverable blow to the nuclear industry in the West.

Todd dialled INWA headquarters while he was stopped at a traffic light.

"I am confirming that my inspector called you," Todd said to Sergeant Kohl. "His name is Carson Griffin, and his notification has been recognised."

"Thank you, Mr. Sinclair," Kohl replied. "I will make the call to Mr. Zabaar."

"Thank you, Mr. Kohl," Todd said. "And please send an officer to check on Mr. Griffin's family. I feel they may be in danger."

"Right away, sir," Kohl replied.

———

Todd Sinclair arrived at the Vienna International Centre within five minutes of Carson's call and picked up a cup of coffee on his way to the emergency response centre. Zabaar was waiting for him. "Did you call the Romanian state authorities?" Todd asked anxiously.

"Yes, they have heard nothing from Cernavodă," Zabaar said. "But they are contacting their resident inspector at the power plant. We should hear something very soon."

Just then the phone rang, and Zabaar picked up one of the many international emergency dedicated telephones in the centre. The Agency had set up these lines and posted its one emergency number on their website after notifying every country in the world by official letter that assistance was available to them in case of a major nuclear accident or other significant nuclear event. This particular problem would be handled very differently to a lost radioactive source, earthquake at a nuclear site, or nuclear-powered satellite crashing into the planet.

Zabaar hung up the line and looked up from his cup of coffee. "We may have a problem. The telephone lines from the nuclear plant are dead." Todd looked horrified.

The lines to the power plant had been cut at the hub by one of the security guards working the night shift – a result of Draco's efficiency in isolating the plant from the outside world.

"You must activate the emergency on-call list and get some help in here," Todd ordered. "We've no choice in the matter!"

"I agree," Zabaar stated. His own fear was now palpable.

Zabaar immediately typed his personal identification code into one of many computers in the main controlling centre, and a fingerprint identification screen immediately popped up. He put his thumb on the screen, and his access was granted to the entire listing of on-call personnel for that day. With a touch of his finger, he activated the international emergency call-out listing, sending a message to everyone within three hours of the VIC carrying one of the specially designated mobile phones issued to them while on duty.

Within the hour, personnel from all over Vienna and the surrounding area made their way to the Vienna International Centre to man the various stations of the emergency control centre. There were two international hotlines manned by British communicators. Three other people were put in charge of determining the weather conditions of Cernavodă's surrounding stratosphere and water current charts of the Black Sea. The nuclear installation specialist (NIS) post was second in command to the Emergency Director but had not yet been filled. The person carrying this responsibility was supposed to have a really good idea of how different nuclear reactors actually operated. Since all reactor designs are different in their equipment or fuel load, the NIS had to be able to adapt his knowledge as best he or she could. And they needed to call in a qualified expert for a particular reactor design when the time came.

Zabaar couldn't declare the emergency centre operational until the NIS post was filled and he had the Agency's press office online and on site. While the public slept, their safety was increasingly going to depend on mitigating a disaster greater than any dirty bomb, with contamination spreading to many surrounding countries if the stored fuel was damaged too. Evacuation existed to minimise panic and loss of life though stampedes and traffic accidents, but this?

People continued to come in for their posts as Zabaar waited to hear from his on-call nuclear installation specialist. Todd sat alongside Zabaar as they waited for some information from Carson Griffin, who was still trying to make his way to the nuclear power plant.

Time was running out for all of them.

CHAPTER 19

Serif paced back and forth on his yacht's main deck, waiting for a call or some sign that Reza was on his way to the power plant. After Bogdan told Serif that Reza had left him and his operating crew, Serif began to worry. Reza never arrived late for an agreed meeting, not without good reason. Serif stared into the black waters. What if whoever had taken the six-kilo plutonium pit from his boat was on board when they landed at the Tryst Café and had now captured or killed his brother?

Serif became visibly distraught. He turned to Tanya. "Reza has disappeared!"

Tanya looked shocked at the possibility that an outsider was onto their plan. "What do you mean? Who saw him last?" Her voice was shaking.

"Bogdan said Reza left the cave to investigate someone watching us, but hadn't seen him since," Serif said. "He was going to meet us after checking it out. It has been too long – he should be here by now." Serif kept looking around frantically as he spoke.

"Do you think Reza may have discovered who took the bomb?" Tanya asked.

Serif nodded slowly – the intruder scenario would answer a lot of unanswered questions. The person who had taken his most valuable possession was still on his boat when they left Mamaia; otherwise, international officials would have been all over him. If there had been more than one operative, they could have split, one to notify the officials, the other to follow the remaining plutonium pit – no, there was only one person out there somewhere.

"We cannot wait on Reza. Serif, we must move forward with the plan," Tanya beseeched her cousin.

"Yes, of course," Serif said. "I will send one of my men back once everything is in place."

Calling down to Maks and Daniel, Serif ordered them to get the equipment and nuclear device loaded into their vehicles. He and Tanya would carry the bomb in his Hummer while Mrak and Broz followed in their van with the two guards. Within an hour, they had everything from the cargo hold loaded into the vans.

Furious at the idea that some intruder was still on the loose, Serif searched the yacht one more time, trying desperately to find any evidence of who the culprit was working for. He opened the door to the engine room to see cargo boxes strewn around from when Carson uncovered the ladder he used for his escape. Serif, his dark eyes blazing, his teeth clenched, slowly looked up to the hatch that led out of the engine room, the ladder still hanging from its clip-on position. Oily footprints marked the wooden rungs.

"Of course," Serif hissed under his breath.

He moved closer to the back of the diesel engine and shone his flashlight around the bilge. As the light reflected back to him from some small oil spills underneath the aluminium grating, he noticed that one of the oil spills had been smeared in the shape of someone's upper body. It was now obvious to Serif that the man had been hiding under the grating, though his guards had not discovered him during their search.

Serif went topside, and when he looked at the engine room's hatch cover, he quickly realised this was where his intruder had exited the compartment just beneath his feet.

"He must have jumped from the yacht while I was at the café with Tanya," Serif grumbled to himself.

His eyes followed along a possible path of escape, one that would take him up the fairly high embankment. In order for the operative to swiftly climb the steep, concrete stairs, he would have to have had a lot of strength in his legs. Serif tried to imagine the intruder's size and build, factoring in the possibility that he might have even been carrying a six-kilo plutonium pit when he left the boat, which would have made that ascent extremely difficult.

A few minutes passed before Serif was finally able to put his fierce anger aside for the moment. He knew he had to focus on the task at hand and, with great determination, put his situation into a winning prospective. Reza would make it to the plant in time, maybe even killing the party crasher along the way.

Serif also thought of the worst-case scenario – Reza was dead, and the operative was on his way to inform authorities of their impending activities. Serif took a deep breath and climbed up the concrete stairs to meet his fellow terrorists. He saw Tanya in the car park standing alongside the Hummer and the others waiting inside their white vans. Everything was ready, Serif decided. He was not about to disappoint his mentor by cancelling their plans.

"Let us go, my cousin," Serif said to Tanya.

Together they climbed into the Hummer and drove toward Cernavodă's centre square and then on to the nuclear power plant.

CHAPTER 20

Herman Hammerschmidt arrived back in Vienna after a two-week mission in Romania on the morning before Carson was taken hostage. The last time Herman had seen his colleague was in the car park of their hotel near Brasov, when Carson was heading off to investigate some illegal trafficking in Romania.

Herman was unaware of Carson's situation, and the events surrounding it, when the telephone in his office rang. "Hello, this is Hammerschmidt."

"Mr. Hammerschmidt?" Jorge Rodriguez asked.

"Yes," Herman replied.

"I am so relieved that I caught you in your office. Would you be available to take the emergency preparedness duty from me? My mother passed away, and I must fly to Brazil tomorrow for the funeral," Jorge said.

Herman filled in as a nuclear installation specialist (NIS) for the emergency preparedness section, usually once every three months. He had only been called out for one incident in Hungary over his years of standing the duty.

"Sure, I'll be happy to take over for you," Herman replied. "I'm sorry about your mother. Please accept my condolences."

Forty-five minutes later, Jorge arrived at Herman's office, gave him the on-call mobile telephone, along with his secret codes for access into the databases used during an emergency response, and said a grateful goodbye to Herman. As soon as Jorge left, Herman went back to typing up his inspection reports from his two-week trip to Romania, where everything appeared to be on the level with the country's energetic nuclear activities – nothing newly discovered.

Herman logged out of his computer at five o'clock that afternoon. He hurriedly put everything in a lockable steel safe and took off for his comfortable, well-furnished apartment in the first district. Herman loved the hustle and bustle of midtown, especially on Christmas Eve – it made him feel alive.

Parking his Mercedes 560SL in the apartment building's underground lot, Herman checked his mailbox and found another alimony notice from his ex-wife's lawyer. Postmarked from Atlanta, Georgia, the legal-size envelope brought back painful memories of a stormy breakup and nasty divorce. Herman dropped the letter beside an answering machine, where he noticed he had four messages from three different girlfriends. He decided to eat dinner before returning the calls.

Popping a leftover container of schnitzel and couscous in the microwave, Herman clicked on his big-screen TV and listened to CNN as he poured himself a glass of Beaujolais. A story was in progress about Saddam Hussein's death sentence, showing one of his many outbursts in court. Herman sat in his leather Eames lounge chair and kicked his feet up on the matching ottoman. Rolling subtitles gave updates of a catastrophic earthquake in China, interrupted by an occasional misspelled word. The subject of the subtitles suddenly changed.

"...Terrorist group known only as JTS post new Website, "Countdown to the End"... "Claims massive deaths on Western soil are imminent..."

Herman recognised the group – he had heard something at the VIC about another splinter group of radicals in Romania. He would try to find out who they were when he returned to work on Monday.

As Herman took a sip of the velvety French wine, his emergency preparedness NIS telephone rang. Surprised by the call, he jumped up from his chair and grabbed the phone from his jacket pocket. The recording demanded he immediately respond to a request for emergency support from some country not yet identified.

Herman listened to the entire message, which repeated itself and gave him a callback number in case he needed to contact the on-call emergency director. Receiving the call out was extremely unusual, and Herman knew he needed to hurry. He quickly ate a few bites of food, put on his warm jacket and scarf, his leather gloves, and headed out of his apartment. His return calls to the three women he was dating would have to wait. Fortunately, one of them worked at the VIC and would be very understanding.

———

The VIC was bustling with activity when Herman arrived. He retrieved his login passwords from Anthony Zabaar. Herman knew his responsibility as nuclear installation specialist very well. He was also experienced enough to communicate to the rest of the world, through news releases, what a facility in trouble was trying to communicate to the rest of the world. He used all available resources, including TV reports coming from international news agencies. But his most reliable resource was the international emergency response website, used by any country that wanted to report a nuclear emergency. It was a direct link to the state's nuclear authority, an organisation communicating with the prime minister or president of the country.

"Herman, I need for you to get as much information about what's going on at Cernavodă as you can," Zabaar said, the stress obvious in his voice. "We have an INWA inspector there who has called in an Alert emergency condition from the nuclear power plant – it's a BWR, I think. He says that terrorists are planning an all-out attack on the facility."

"What's the guy's name?" Herman asked anxiously.

"Carson, Carson Griffin."

"Jesus..." Herman said, remembering how gung-ho Carson was about every possible proliferation lead that he pursued. Because Carson had to keep his special training and capabilities secret from even his closest colleagues, Herman had no idea how well Carson could handle himself in a life-threatening situation.

"I'll look into Cernavodă's announcement and try to find out what's going on there," Herman replied.

"Take the PR liaison with you to your station," Zabaar said.

An attractive young woman stepped forward. "Allo, I'll help you translate your write-ups to something the general public can hopefully understand. My name is Stella Chvoja."

"Herman Hammerschmidt. It's nice to meet you," he said and shook her hand.

Herman and Stella logged into the emergency response website, which had been constructed after the 1986 Chernobyl nuclear disaster in the Ukraine. The international community demanded all states sign an emergency response treaty, ensuring immediate worldwide notifications. Had people been properly warned of the oncoming radioactivity from Chernobyl, mass evacuations could have been organised and high-risk areas for radiation exposure could have been quarantined.

Herman and Stella attempted to put together a coherent news release that wouldn't cause undue panic, but would give the general public an idea of what was going on at Cernavodă. The details were still unclear, but Stella had a knack for impact with minimal verbiage and used Herman's expertise to craft a fine news release.

The headline was simple enough: "Alert Declared at Cernavodă Nuclear Power Station in Romania." But there was no need for a massive evacuation of people from the area, so Stella toned down the following paragraph with simple facts and figures about the plant. For the general public, the story was as fuzzy as the actual situation. However, those in the nuclear industry understood that there was a serious problem brewing.

When their first message hit the Internet, calls from all over the world began to pour into the response centre. Liaison officers covering the affected critical zones answered calls from countries immediately surrounding Romania, which included Bulgaria, Hungary, and the Ukraine. But more amazingly calls quickly began coming in from China, Western Europe, and North America. The news release was broadcast on radio and television news channels within minutes of its issuance from Vienna.

Although no one at the emergency centre really knew for sure *what* was going on at the site, the liaison officers repeated what had already been released to the general public and assured the interested states that they would be informed of any changes via the INWA website.

The emergency response assemblage waited for a confirmation call from the Romanians, who were also waiting for more information from their resident inspector. All anyone in the VIC knew right now was that the Agency had an inspector near a site in Romania that could possibly be under some kind of terrorist attack.

CHAPTER 21

Bogdan and his crew parked their vans just past the warehouse rear entrance, behind a grove of trees that completely hid their vehicles. The men of Bogdan's terrorist cell unloaded their equipment and moved to the perimeter fence. Draco had already taken care of the guards on perimeter watch and rounded up most of the extra personnel assigned to work on Christmas Eve. He planned for the operations crew to be the only people still inside the power block.

Jacob, carrying his miniature cutting torch, ran around to the perimeter fence. Igniting the blue hot acetylene, he quickly cut through the chain links, opening a gaping hole that two men could easily pass through. When he set foot onto the seashell flooring between the outer and inner fences, alarms went off in the security island where Draco's man quickly silenced them with a silver toggle switch. Jacob continued to cut through the inner fence until the terrorists had full access to the protected area of the nuclear site.

Filing through the two openings, Bogdan and his men moved their gear toward the turbine building and found their mustering position by its largest roll-up door, designed for off-loading carriages full of steel beams used during construction.

"Okay. Marius, you and Ciprian know what to do," Bogdan said.

"Yeah," Marius replied. "See you soon, boss."

The two men grabbed their duffel bags and ran toward the front door of the power plant.

———

Out of breath, Carson made it to the site car park about the same time that Bogdan and his crew reached the turbine building roll-up doors. Slowly making his way along a wall that concealed his approach to the front gate, Carson got close enough to see Draco standing in the security island through a slightly tinted window. He looked a little familiar to Carson; maybe he had seen him around the plant during one of his inspections, but his guise was quite different in his dress uniform.

He couldn't see any other guards walking around or in their watchtowers, located at four different places along the perimeter fence. The whole situation looked strange to Carson. He might have been able to overlook no one being in the towers, as long as there was a roving perimeter watch. But the guy dressed in his best pass-and-review uniform on a Christmas Eve – well, that was definitely unusual. Carson tried to get a little closer to the security island when he noticed a vehicle coming down the road toward the front gate. It was Serif's Humvee, followed closely behind by the two scientists and bodyguards in their white van.

Both vehicles paused briefly as the gate's hydraulics swung open two heavy chain-linked gates. Chrome-plated pistons on either side of the Humvee opened their arms wide enough for the vehicles, welcoming six more terrorists inside the protected area. With a light wave, Serif drove through the gates opening.

Carson watched in amazement from his position behind a concrete pillar that held a suspension bridge over the power plant's circulating water supply. River water supplied by the canal passed underneath the bridge to the cooling tower, which was normally used to transfer the unused heat energy from the main condenser out into the environment. Although the ominous cooling tower was known as "the reactor's companion," there should never be anything but ultra-pure steam discharged from its hyperbolic design. Carson decided that he would have to enter through the breached fence behind Bogdan if he was to slip into the plant without being seen. The group of operators would probably be too engaged to notice him coming in after them, and Draco's guards were too busy to keep an eye on a pathway they knew to be clear.

———

Marius and Ciprian broke away from the crouching group of men who were near the roll-up door. Bogdan and the rest of his crew would manage their way into the plant through the turbine building. Their access to the main control room would be via a locked back door, accessed only by a card reader. But to get to that position, the four men would have to traverse an internal staircase from the ground up to the main deck of the building.

Marius led the way as he and Ciprian passed a couple of large transformers sitting in the yard of the protected area. Ciprian moved a little slower than his partner, but the two worked well together as they went across the gravel of the yard to the front door of the plant. Diagonally to the front door was the control room's dedicated ventilation room.

"You gonna make it, big man?" Marius asked.

"Yeah," Ciprian said, gasping for air. He was a two-pack-a-day smoker and had the cough to prove it. Ciprian held onto a lighting panel's electrical supply conduit to catch his breath.

"Let's go, Marius," Ciprian whispered. "I'm with ya, man."

Opening the door with a passkey that Marius had reported lost during his days as an operator in Cernavodă's control room, he and Ciprian went into the large room. The two saw supply fans providing fresh air to the main control room envelope from outside ducts.

Inside Marius's rucksack were two sealed, hazardous materials containers which held the fentanyl gas that Bogdan had acquired from his Eastern contacts. Marius thought about stopping in Brasov on his way out of country to pick up the silver fox fur coat he had promised his mother after this job was done.

"Okay, Ciprian. Open that duct cover right there," Marius said, pointing to a tin plate held in place by four swing-lock handles.

Ciprian opened the cover while Marius released the gas into the air stream that was feeding fresh air to the main control room and immediately adjacent rooms, including the kitchen where the operators were eating their Christmas dinners.

"I think this will make everyone a little more relaxed," Marius said.

"Christmas cheer!" Ciprian exclaimed. "Hope you all have a long sleep."

After depositing the two canisters into the ventilation

system, Marius and Ciprian closed the cover and waited for an announcement over the plant's public address system. Bogdan's orders were for them to stay in place until they could be sure that all the gasses had done the job. They'd then use the system's exhaust fans to evacuate the gas from the control room envelope.

———

Theodor was sitting at his desk on the riser that allowed him to overlook the control room – much better than he could if he were situated at eye level with the reactor operators in the horseshoe. Observing all the activities surrounding him in the main control room, Theodor was diligent about performing his duties. His focus was to ensure the safety of the public by maintaining the nuclear reactor in a safe condition, which meant knowing how every major piece of equipment worked in the multitude of integrated components. What he didn't know this night was that the security supervisor, who was supposed to protect him from all types of terrorist threats, was actually a terrorist himself.

Theodor had become the victim of an attack that was well underway by the time the odourless gas began to permeate the atmosphere surrounding him and his operators.

Isabella was sitting in the kitchen on the other side of a heavy steel door that separated her from Theodor and the other operators. She had just begun to eat her turkey, cornbread stuffing, green beans, and cranberry sauce when she started to blink her eyes over and over, sensing something was very wrong. She was now breathing the poisonous gas and gradually slipped underneath the table, suddenly falling to the floor with a thump.

"Isabella! Are you okay?" Henri called out, dropping his cup of coffee and lunging toward her.

Without speaking another word, Henri's body began to jerk spastically. In a matter of seconds he, too, fell to the floor, gasping for breath. Jake fell next to him, without ever uttering a word or knowing what was happening. The gas was extremely fast acting, leaving no chance for the operators to make a break for the exit. The three equipment operators were unconscious and dying within seconds.

The gas, used by the Russian Special Forces to subdue terrorists in Moscow in 2002, was now beginning to take its toll on Cernavodă's operators in the main control room. They began falling like soldiers on a killing field. The two reactor operators sitting at the horseshoe panel that controlled the reactor's neutron flux and primary coolant system were now slumped over in their chairs, their eyes closed, possibly for the last time.

Theodor, holding his chest, tried to motion to his plant supervisor to order the reactor's mode switch placed in shutdown. He watched helplessly as Jay fell out of his swivel chair.

Theodor was the last to go down, his voice suppressed by an enemy that he could not see, smell, or fight against. Theodor's body went limp. He was draped over his huge desk that separated him from the mode switch, which would have shut down the reactor and placed it into a safe condition.

A red telephone frantically rang on the shift supervisor's desk where Heber lay near death, his body now concealing a plant drawing he was studying. Calling into the main control room from the other end of the red phone was the Romanian state authority, now trying desperately to find out what was going on there. The telephone continued its incessant ringing, no automated answering system to take a message.

When no one answered after ten minutes, the Romanian state authority initiated a message to the Vienna Emergency Centre to formally confirm that they needed help in making the notifications. Immediately after alerting Vienna, the Romanians called out their civil defence and alerted NATO to the situation. Within minutes, the minister of Romania's civil defence made a series of calls that ended in a dispatch of nearly one hundred soldiers and their trucks to surround the nuclear site.

Although the soldiers were ill-equipped to perform an all-out assault on the site, they would use small arms fire to contain the situation until NATO was able to send a special tactical force trained for these emergencies.

————

Bogdan and his two remaining crew members entered the turbine building, their plan of attack still viable. Bogdan knew that they would have to wait until Marius put the ventilation for the main control room envelope into an "isolation mode," which would clean up the poisonous gas.

Picking up a wall-mounted public address system handset, Bogdan pressed the announcement pushbutton. "In position – isolate the envelope."

Ciprian turned excitedly to Marius. "There it is! The announcement we have been waiting for."

Marius opened the control panel and turned on a black switch labelled "isolate." Without delay, the running fans stopped, and two charcoal filter trains with their own fans began to run at full speed. Seconds later, the two men could hear dampers re-align themselves to create a recirculating current of air flow that forced the poisonous gases from the control room envelope through charcoal and 0.1 micron-fibre filters.

Within a mere fifteen minutes, the filters had removed just about all the poisonous gases – it was again safe to breathe the air that had, only minutes earlier, left most of the operating crew dead; the others were in a comatose state.

Marius and Ciprian donned their SCBA air packs, left the ventilation room, and took an elevator to the kitchen area just off the main control room. Marius produced a key card that Draco had given to Bogdan for entry into the control room. They heard a loud click resonate through the three-inch steel door, then pulled it open.

Marius could see the three equipment operators through the thick yellowish viewing window of his facemask. His laboured breathing occasionally fogged his plastic viewing pane, but he was still able to make out two men and a woman lying on the floor. Ciprian noticed their Christmas dinners spread out on the table. He felt no emotion other than to laugh derisively.

Marius took a Dräger tube from his jacket pocket and broke its seal in order to test the quality of the kitchen air. After pumping air through the small device for sixty seconds, Marius let the tube saturate itself before examining it for a possible colour change to red. The tube remained clear, indicating that the air was clean enough to breathe safely. But before removing their SCBA's, they wanted to check the main control room which was behind another three-inch steel door.

Draco had given them a key card that would allow them into any plant area they would need to go to during their takeover. Ciprian swiped the card through a narrow slot in the reader.

Click. The door opened, and they stepped inside the control room with their SCBA's still on. Both still had plenty of air in their packs.

Operators once monitoring the huge boiling water nuclear reactor were now sprawled on the floor underneath the apron of the most important panel of the operating power plant: its horseshoe-shaped reactor core control panel. Marius checked the pulse of two of the men – they were both dead, along with their plant supervisor. Only the shift manager and shift supervisor were still barely alive.

Marius opened another Dräger tube to check the air quality and found that it was cleared of all poisonous gases. Removing his mask, Marius motioned to Ciprian that the air was acceptable, and he, too, could remove his mask. Ciprian went into the back panels to verify that everyone was accounted for according to a computerised front gate check-in list Draco had provided.

Marius walked over to the back door of the main control room and pushed down a crash bar, opening the door to allow Bogdan and the other men to enter. Bogdan walked in slowly as the others moved quickly to relocate the bodies behind a glass wall that separated the control room's copy of master drawings for the power plant and control panels. Believing that all were dead, they piled the bodies on top of one another, like life-size rag dolls.

Bogdan stood behind the shift manager's desk. "Home at last, eh boys!"

"You said it, chief," Marius replied.

"Marius, you and Jacob take a few minutes to look over your control room panels," Bogdan barked. "Ciprian, take Franco with you to the back, and you guys look at the operator's logs in the kitchen. Let me know what equipment is operating in the plant when you get a handle on things. We'll meet back in here in fifteen minutes."

———

Carson had already made his way through the opening in the perimeter fence, trying to avoid cameras that overlooked the yard as he ran to the power block's main entrance. He followed the same path that Marius and Ciprian had taken to get into the ventilation space just minutes earlier, ducking behind some smaller outlying buildings and equipment. Carson had overheard their plans to gas the operators while he was tied up on Bogdan's floor the night before and remembered to be very cautious when opening the door to the fan area. He wanted to see what they had done to the ventilation system for himself – maybe he could change the system's air flow direction before it was too late. The notion that Marius and Ciprian might still be in the room crossed Carson's mind, and he realised that he would have to take them out before they would have a chance to stop him.

But what Carson saw when he opened the door to the ventilation space was a cruel shock. It was painfully obvious to Carson that Bogdan and his men had already put the gas into the control room atmosphere and the kitchen and were now cleaning up the air in preparation for their occupation.

Lying on the floor near a supply duct, Carson saw two canisters with markings exactly like the ones he had seen in the white van near Vlad's Castle. Rolling one of the canisters over with his boot, he saw the Russian military symbols and hazardous materials stickers very clearly. But Carson could only read one word on the can's face – fentanyl.

Instead of going up three flights of stairs to the control room, Carson decided to make his way down to the office of radiation protection to see if he could find a working telephone. If he could call back to headquarters, he'd be able to tell them that Bogdan and his men had taken control of the nuclear power plant. Carson needed to let Todd know the worst: terrorists were in control of a huge nuclear reactor, and another group was on their way inside the building with a plutonium-fuelled nuclear bomb.

Running down two flights of stairs to the lowest level of the plant, Carson opened the door to the laboratory used by radiation protection personnel during a normal working day. Overhead lights in the lab were all on, but Carson couldn't see anyone sitting inside any of the four cubicles that were built as workstations for lab technicians. Continuing his search in another room, he heard a clipboard fall to the floor behind him.

He spun around to see a lab tech standing there in her white lab coat, chewing gum and looking a little confused. "Can I help ya?"

She looked to be about twenty-two years old, with copper-red straight hair and obviously smart enough to be the on-shift lab technician. Maybe she had recently graduated from one of Romania's colleges or a technical school near Bucharest. Carson's presence didn't take her by surprise – she was used to processing people through radiation protection procedures for their entry into the power plant.

But Carson was surprised that anyone was still alive and walking around. "What are you doing? Don't you know there's an emergency situation going on here? Terrorists are in the control room!"

She stopped chewing her gum, her mouth gaping, her

eyes wide. "No!" she cried.

"Have you been here all night?" Carson asked, incredulous to even be asking this.

"Well, I was trying to stay out of everyone's way tonight," she said defensively. "Working on Christmas Eve makes me feel anti-social."

"Okay, we'll cover that later. I gotta use your telephone!" Carson exclaimed. "What's your name?"

"Sure, it's over there. My name's Rachel Bucolescu."

Carson went directly over to a landline telephone behind a long counter used to check people into the radiation protection system computers. He picked up the receiver, but the line was dead. Carson dashed in and out of several cubicles, checking their landlines, praying for a dial tone. None were working. All the phones were routed through Security Island at the main gate, where Draco made sure there would be no unmonitored communications from the site. The security supervisor had disabled all the phones except the direct line to the state authority so that Serif could explain their demands.

"All the lines are dead," Carson said with desperation. "They must be blocked at the main switching board. Even the Internet has been disabled. Do you have a cell phone?"

"Yes, but the walls are too thick inside the plant for cell phone transmission," Rachel said. "I've got one question for you, besides who are you? I want to know how come you haven't been taken prisoner or something by these terrorists."

"My name is Carson Griffin, and I work for the INWA. I'm trying to stop a catastrophic release of radioactivity directly from the reactor's core. I was captured by these men last night, but I escaped this morning."

"What are you planning to do?" Rachel asked, now clearly frightened.

"Come on, let's go. They must know that you're here from your entry at the gate tonight," Carson said.

"Where are we going?" Rachel asked, even more frightened.

"Into the plant," Carson replied, taking her by the hand. "They'll never find us out there."

CHAPTER 22

erman sat down at his computer terminal and brought up the Agency's emergency preparedness website. He read out loud the message coming from the state authority of Romania:

"Date of Event: 2006/12/24
Time of Event: 23:00 UTC
Classification: Site Area Emergency

Event Description: Terrorist Intrusion"

"Oh my God," Herman said under his breath.

The state authority released the information only after hearing from the resident inspector and Carson's eyewitness account to Todd from the payphone near Cernavodă's city park. They had tried to contact the main control room many times on their dedicated telephone line without success.

Herman now thought that Carson was somehow involved in all that was going on in Cernavodă. Any good inspector from INWA would do whatever they could to intervene in a crisis dealing with nuclear materials or nuclear power.

Herman looked away from his computer monitor and over to Stella. He let out a long exhale. "Okay, our first message should be a worldwide notification to all public broadcasting agencies that a Site Area Emergency was declared by the state authorities of Romania at the boiling water reactor in Cernavodă. We're only going to talk about the event for now; hopefully, our first hourly update will give us more information about Romania's plans for population evacuations."

Stella typed up the message and showed it to Herman, who approved it, and it was immediately posted on INWA's Nuclear Safety and Security website for everyone to read. A news release followed the Web posting, and, within minutes, the media section began getting calls from all over Europe.

Herman and Stella sat back at their adjacent desks and filed their documents away.

"What do you think?" Stella asked Herman, her voice registering fear.

Stella knew the public relations part of her job very well and understood that many Romanians did not even own a television set. Most information was passed by word of mouth from the few families fortunate enough to have a TV and could send their children around the neighbourhoods to distribute the news. However, it was very late at night, and most people in Cernavodă would be asleep.

"I don't know," Herman replied honestly. "I do know it's gonna be a long night."

The emergency centre at the VIC was completely manned by half past midnight, Vienna time. Romania was one hour ahead of Vienna.

Everyone, including the emergency director, was at their posts and working like mad to get a handle on what was happening at the facility. Anthony Zabaar's desk was in the middle of the room, surrounded by all the supporting stations that he needed to make informed decisions. He faced a wall-mounted giant split-video screen that spanned the area from floor to ceiling. Zabaar's desk was very neat and organised with bins labelled clearly for those needing to communicate with him by document – verbal communication was limited to critical information only.

Zabaar stood up to make his first announcement. "Attention everyone, please be ready for a briefing in fifteen minutes."

Before he could say anything else, his first assistant handed him another piece of paper. It contained confirmation of the Romanian militia moving into Cernavodă and surrounding the power plant. Without a word, he sat back down to fill out a briefing form designed to prevent him from missing any support information. News of the Romanian militia surrounding the nuclear facility would have to wait until the next hourly update on INWA's website.

Zabaar asked Herman and Stella to put out an update during the briefing so that everyone in the emergency centre knew what they had received and announced to the general public. Fifteen minutes later, Zabaar made his way to the wall-mounted screen where six different news broadcasts from various countries were being aired. CNN was given priority by an electronic switcher for the audio signal. Those that wanted to listen could hear the broadcast using a set of headphones at their station. Both CNN and the BBC were carrying specials on giving in the holiday spirit of Christmas. Al Jazeera, emanating from Qatar on the Persian Gulf, and major stations from France, Germany, and Italy, were on their individual screens, none of which had picked up the story.

Zabaar began his briefing. "First, I'd like to thank everyone for responding to the message that was sent out tonight. The state authority for the Cernavodă Nuclear Power Station in Romania has declared a Site Area Emergency." Zabaar spoke quickly. "A group of terrorists from a currently un-known faction has taken control of the nuclear facility, and we have initiated all necessary actions to protect the public. Now, please update me on information that you have, begin-ning with public relations."

A man from INWA nuclear safety stood up. "My name is Clifton Blacken. I am the on-duty psychologist, in charge of crowd control."

"Thank you for coming," Zabaar said.

"The panic that we experienced after Chernobyl was generally caused by a lack of clear communications from the Ukraine and the former Soviet Union," Blacken said with an Irish accent.

"Yes, we are well aware of that fact," Zabaar said, trying to limit an upcoming speech. "What can we expect to see in surrounding states?"

"Right," Blacken replied. "We are fortunate that this event has occurred in the middle of the night, for panic's sake – the news will be slow in coming. But when the news is posted of a terrorist attack of this magnitude, we must make sure that everyone understands enough to decide for them-selves a course of action."

"Thank you for your opinion, Mr. Blacken," Zabaar said. "Everyone must remember that this event, currently de-clared as a Site Area Emergency, could quickly be upgraded to a General Emergency. Our goal at that moment will be to ensure we have negotiated evacuation plans for the civilian population of Romania through the surrounding states. The current emergency planning zone is ten miles in all direc-tions, unless we are given reason to believe that a release is actually occurring."

The room was quiet for a few moments, then Zabaar

said, "Okay, ladies and gentlemen, please give me your reports as briefly as possible."

Zabaar asked for information from everyone in the emergency response centre, including someone who was watching plant data on one of two stations set up to download computer remotely monitored statistics. Then he asked for an update from a meteorological specialist, followed by international radiation protection and communications experts.

"Okay, that's the end of this briefing," Zabaar said. "We will reconvene for the next update on the hour."

Everyone immediately went back to work.

Herman and Stella returned to their stations, where Herman called for the design information for the plant, brought to the emergency centre from a security vault. Herman spread out the drawings on his work table. It was difficult to get a true picture of what was going on at the site, but reviewing the drawings gave Herman a chance to jog his memory about the facility. If something were to go down that he could readily recognise, he might be able to feed Carson some helpful information – that is, if Carson would call in.

———

Serif rolled their vehicles just inside the main gate while Draco's men were finishing their walk-down of the entire site, trying to find a straggler who had carded in earlier for work that night.

"Draco is taking too long," Tanya said. "I had better find out what is going on there."

Serif shook his head and put his arm on Tanya to stop her from getting out of his vehicle. "No, just give him time to sweep the plant for other people who may be wandering around," Serif said. "We have to make sure the site is clear prior to entering the building."

The engine continued to purr for two more minutes before a bright flashlight was pointed at his windshield from the security island guard house. The light blinked on and off three times from where Draco was holding the security guards not involved in the operation.

"Finally!" Tanya said.

Rolling his vehicle forward, Serif turned to Tanya with a smile. "Here we go, my dear."

Mrak and Broz followed the black Humvee through the gate, its shock absorbers loaded with the weight of the explosives inside and the small plutonium pit. Their van was packed full of electronics, detonators, tools, and four men to move everything into place once inside the power block. The transport of equipment and personnel from the trucks would be quick enough when they were parked near the roll-up door because they had installed casters on the largest cases. Broz turned around in his seat and watched the gate swing slowly closed.

Leading the team over an asphalt and concrete path surrounding the power block, Serif wondered where Reza may have encountered the man responsible for stealing his largest bomb pit.

He drove around to the rear of the reactor building, which was used to house all the supporting equipment needed to run the reactor in its normal mode of operation. The reactor building also housed large emergency pumps that would inject water into the core should it begin a spontaneous meltdown. Serif backed up to a train-bay door. When he brought the powerful vehicle to a stop, it was in a perfect position to offload their cargo onto a rolling trolley.

Maks and Daniel left their van and hurried over to Serif and Tanya. Serif had already opened the rear door of the Humvee and uncovered a DC power outlet located on one side of an installed gun rack. Everyone moved quickly, feeling the pressure of an impending response from the Romanian state authorities.

"Daniel, plug this cable into the socket," Maks ordered as he pointed to the outlet.

"Got it," Daniel replied.

The electric lifting platform moved the heavy bomb and its implosion device, loaded with plastic explosives, from inside the vehicle out and over the rolling trolley. It was still disabled and being maintained in a perfectly safe condition, for now. While lowering the bomb onto the trolley, Mrak opened a shiny metal cover and connected his oscilloscope to the umbilical cable coming from the bomb's multitude of small, hair-like wires. The rudimentary mass of wires and explosives looked like a plate of spaghetti with a giant grayish-black meatball sitting in its centre.

Serif's men rolled the cart into the deserted reactor building, then down a long hallway to an equipment elevator. While waiting for the elevator to arrive, Mrak put down the two small black Pelican cases that he was carrying.

"Broz, are you sure you checked the detonator? Is its timing circuit working properly?" Mrak asked.

"Yes, of course," Broz answered. "I even put new batteries in the remote control."

They smiled at each other, knowing that they had both made some minor mistakes over the years. Fortunately, none of their mistakes were catastrophic because the two men thought so much alike and knew each other's faults very well. The elevator arrived, and the two bodyguards pushed the heavy cart onto it. Mrak and Broz followed, each carrying their own Pelican cases.

Serif and Tanya drove the Humvee near the front entrance and parked. Both terrorists walked inside the plant and rode the elevator up two decks to the main control room. Standing outside the kitchen's metal door, they called Bogdan on the public address system. Within seconds, they heard a loud click and the door begin to move.

Ciprian pushed the heavy door open, wide enough to let his employer and his cousin into the kitchen area. Serif quickly glanced around the area, then walked directly over to the control room door. Ciprian swiped a key card through the reader and let the two inside the main control room. Serif couldn't help but be amazed at the size and complexity of the panels and components surrounding him as he walked toward a low gate. Bogdan hit the release button that opened the gate and stepped down from the shift manager's platform.

Bogdan came up to Serif as he entered the strictly controlled operator's zone. "Good evening, Serif," he said with deference.

"Hello, my friend," Serif said. "How are things here?"

"Very well. We have checked all on-line systems. We are ready for the first stage of our program," Bogdan said. "We have had several unanswered calls on the dedicated line from Bucharest."

"They must have been alerted to our plan," Serif said.

Serif felt sure there was someone watching his every move. Maybe the guy on his yacht had even made some telephone calls alerting the Romanian authorities.

Serif gave Bogdan a troubled look. "I have not found Reza. I fear that..."

Bogdan, still hiding the fact that he had lost Carson earlier that morning, replied, "Yes, Serif, I think Reza might be dead." He took a deep breath. "Whoever called the state authority in Bucharest is still out there."

"Bogdan," Serif demanded, "I want to know who this guy is and how he is familiar with the details of our plans."

Bogdan was backed into a corner, but he knew that Serif needed him more than ever now and would have to allow him to continue with their diabolical plot. Operating the boiling water reactor took a lot of expertise and experience – Serif would have to let him live in order to control the reactor's release of contamination into the atmosphere. Tanya was a good engineer, but with no real operational experience, she could never carry out the things that Bogdan's training made possible.

"I had this man in my house last night –" Bogdan started.

"What?!" Serif exclaimed. "Why didn't you tell me about this before now?"

"I thought that my hunter would kill him before he created a problem for us," Bogdan said. "His name is Carson Griffin, and he works for INWA as an inspector – a nuclear safeguards inspector."

"How much does he know about our plans?" Serif asked.

"Well he was tied up in my house most of last night while we discussed the takeover," Bogdan said. "We planned to kill him in the afternoon and dump him in the sea, but somehow he escaped. We found the teenage kids that helped him, but they were of no use in finding where Griffin had gone, even after some painful persuasion from my hunter friend."

Silence fell between them as they stood looking at each other – Serif disgusted and Bogdan sweating bullets. Finally, Serif walked toward the centre of the control room behind the two reactor operators who were preparing for their plan's implementation.

"Call Draco and tell him to find Griffin – he may be somewhere on this site," Serif ordered. "And Bogdan, tell Draco to bring him to me – I want his confession before I kill him!" Serif spat the words out.

Bogdan climbed back up the three steps to the riser and picked up a telephone. As Bogdan contacted the security chief, Serif walked around the control room, gazing at the multitude of instruments. The displays were foreign to him, except one digital LED with large red numbers:

Reactor Power 3,830.009 Mwth

Impressed by the number, Serif temporarily released his anxiety. He was standing in the middle of one of the most powerful machines man had ever made. Harnessing the awesome power of the atom for peaceful application was the dream first explored by free scientists before World War II. But by ultimately employing the first atomic weapon for mass destruction, the original and noble vision was tarnished forever.

Underneath the reactor power display, sitting on a small table, was the ceramic coffee cup of one of the dead operators. Glazed to its side, below a lip mark of coffee, Serif noticed that the cup bore an emblem of a bright sun being crushed by Thor's hammer. Below a painting of the god of thunder's upper torso were printed the words, "We Run the Sun." *How true*, Serif thought.

Bogdan spoke to Draco on the phone and quickly passed

along Serif's orders. He was now more concerned about the lumbering giant that his crew was controlling from the huge room full of blue and grey panels. He glanced up at ten full-length windows high above the shift manager's desk – they overlooked the space where the main panels were located. It was an observation room for the many visitors to Cernavodă, some Romanian delegates, and others from international organisations.

After talking to Bogdan, Draco directed one of his men to continue searching for the only person left on their list of checked-in workers: a health physics technician named Rachel Bucolescu. Draco told his men that there might be another unknown intruder inside the protected area, and they were to bring him to the main control room. Draco arrogantly ignored the information Bogdan had given him about someone entering his fortress – his men would have seen this Carson Griffin on their multitude of cameras.

CHAPTER 23

Carson hurriedly followed Rachel into the turbine building, which was connected directly to the radiation protection laboratory by thick steel doors designed to maintain an atmospheric barrier between the two buildings. After leaping over a turnstile, they were at the door that demanded in a stern woman's voice that they both log into a radiation monitoring system. Rachel swiped her personal key card, and her authorisation was quick. But as soon as Rachel carded into the system, one of Draco's guards picked up her login on his computer screen and called his boss.

Carson prayed his plan to circumvent Bogdan's efforts to take the reactor to the point of meltdown would work. "We need to get into the reactor building," he said frantically to Rachel.

"Why?" she asked.

"I think we may be able to SCRAM the reactor from inside, using some of the locally installed components," Carson said. "But I need to talk to my colleague in Vienna; schematics for every nuclear reactor in the world are in the INWA vaults."

Rachel nodded. "Okay, I know where we can find a place to transmit with my cell phone," Rachel said as they walked past two gigantic heat exchangers. "It's outside the concrete walls of the power block. It's only covered by a corrugated steel roof – I know that it'll work."

"Let's get going," Carson said. "We'll need to take the stairs up to that elevation once we're inside the reactor building."

Rachel led the way down a hall, then through another key-card-protected doorway. The door slammed behind them with great force due to the high pressure difference between building atmospheres. The reactor building was at the lowest pressure compared to other buildings in order to contain any release of airborne radioactive materials from a small coolant leak, so that they could be cleaned up by charcoal filter trains.

Carson and Rachel moved swiftly to the end of a passageway that encircled the outside of the containment building. They passed equipment on both sides and a steel-grating deck that they could see through as they ran. Sounds of high-pressure fluids all around them and the roar of positive displacement pumps created a deafening noise that was transmitted through the chilly air they were heaving into their lungs.

Arriving at the reactor building's stairwell door, they hesitated for a second to catch their breath. Rachel was startled by the sound of a loud door slamming shut.

"Someone's coming!" Rachel whispered.

Carson also heard the noise behind them. "Let's keep moving."

Still unsure how many men were roaming around the power block, Carson wasn't ready to do battle with an unknown foe. Rachel led the way as they quietly entered the stairwell and started their climb to the eighth deck. Each stairwell door they passed had a circular portal at eye level, which Carson looked through as they moved upward. He had to make sure no one saw them ascending the concrete steps toward a transmitting area for Rachel's cell phone.

Gazing through the third deck door's portal, Carson could see one of two containment airlocks still closed, its green operational lights brightly burning. Airlock doors could not be opened simultaneously in order to prevent the release of a contaminated atmosphere, should a significant nuclear accident occur inside the containment. The second airlock was five decks higher, where the spent fuel was loaded into the cooling pool on the eighth deck.

They climbed up two more flights of stairs to the same deck where Mrak and Broz were beginning to mount Serif's nuclear weapon underneath Cernavodă's spent fuel pool.

"Did you hear that?" Rachel anxiously whispered as another door below them slammed shut.

Without a word, Carson opened the fifth deck's door and motioned for Rachel to follow him out into the open hallway. Exiting the stairwell, Carson eased the door closed behind them, and they rushed toward the other end of the passageway. Without knowing the location of Serif's bomb team, Carson and Rachel passed a closed hatch where the scientists were arming the bomb. The door's wheel-like releasing mechanism was turned fully counter clockwise. The two didn't notice as they continued down the passageway that someone had entered the void space underneath the spent fuel pool.

"In here," Carson whispered, opening a door that led into a switchgear room.

Rachel stood behind Carson, who held the door open just far enough to see back down the well-lit passageway.

"I'm scared," Rachel said in a shaky voice.

"I'm nervous too," Carson assured her. "Try to stay calm, we'll be okay."

Just then Carson heard a door slam down the hall.

Carson opened the switchgear room door a little wider to try to look around the curve of the containment building, when he saw Serif's bodyguards coming out of the room where they had left Mrak and Broz. Quickly closing the door a little more, Carson looked around the room for some kind of weapon.

"I know those guys," Carson said. "They were on that boat in the harbour."

"What harbour?" Rachel asked.

"It's a long story, but believe me, they're very dangerous," Carson replied.

A man in a security uniform stepped out of the stairwell and walked over to Maks and Daniel. He was one of Draco's men – a radio in one hand and submachine gun in the other. Carson couldn't hear what they were saying because some nearby ventilation fans were running on high speed.

After lighting a cigarette, the guard with the submachine gun walked down the passageway toward the switchgear room, checking another room along the way. When the guard entered the other room and was out of sight, Maks and Daniel went back into the room where Mrak and Broz were working. Carson let the door close slowly and turned to Rachel.

Electricians routing a cabling arrangement in the plant's 440-volt system had left a one-gallon can of cable-pulling lubricant sitting behind one of the panels. Taking her by the arm, Carson moved Rachel back away from the doorway and picked up the can of Aqua-Gel.

Opening the can, Carson said, "I've got an idea."

Rachel stood watching as Carson spread the slippery translucent jelly in front of the switchgear room with his hand. The lubricant spread quickly, forming an invisible, thin layer of extremely slick gel on the floor in a three-by-two-foot rectangle. He was very careful not to step in the solution as he backed away from the room's only entrance.

Carson opened the glass covering on a panel that was used to observe a voltmeter mounted inside the supply panel. The tall panel housed six breakers and one transformer. The voltmeter was only one of three gauges that were monitoring the distribution panel's parameters. After tying the glass covering back with a zip-tie he found near the room's wall-mounted fire extinguisher, Carson pulled Rachel behind an opposing panel where they'd be out of sight when the security guard came into the room.

Slowly opening the door to the switchgear room, the man crept inside, wearing a pair of paratrooper jump boots. Boots that were very good for trekking around in mud and rough terrain, but inside a nuclear power plant they were hazardous – primarily because floors and walls of most nuke plants are coated with a high-gloss paint that can easily be decontaminated should radioactive water spill on its surface. Looking from side to side for Rachel, whose key card had led him into the building, the guard moved forward.

Carson and Rachel heard the security guard slip, his boots losing traction on the well-greased floor. Carson jumped from behind the panel and pushed the guard off his feet, making sure that he broke all contact with the man after he shoved him. Dropping his gun and reaching out for something to hold onto, the guard fell into the open glass observation port, where the 440 volts were awaiting a fresh electrical conduit. A bolt of lightning ran through the man's body, leaving a black hole from his left shoulder down through his trunk and out an exit wound at his left ankle. The smell of burning flesh was sickening. Rachel turned away and fought back the nausea as Carson went over to the body.

Carson knew it would be safe to approach the man now

that he was clear of the panel, but he waited for the smoke to subside before picking up the guard's radio. He held it close to his ear, listening for any clues about what might be going on in the main control room. Carson pointed at the guard's submachine gun as Rachel emerged from behind the panel.

Gingerly walking over to the body, Rachel bent over while holding her smock collar over her mouth and nose as she peeled the gun from the man's hand. Flicking off a piece of index finger, she checked the gun's condition – more to get her mind off the body than to determine the status of the weapon.

"Are you okay?" Carson asked while switching the radio through its five channels, searching for an ongoing transmission.

Rachel looked over at Carson and then back down at the body. "Well, let's just say I'm a lot better off than he is." The smock dropped from her face – she was coming through the moment on her own. Having seen death many times during the revolution as a child, Rachel remembered seeing dozens of people lying dead in the streets. The painful memories gave Rachel renewed strength – terrorists inside the power block and an imminent threat to the reactor were now her concerns, not anything personal.

Slinging the submachine gun over her shoulder, Rachel quickly rifled through the security guard's black hunting vest. In a front pocket, she found a master key card. Flashing the card at Carson, Rachel wiped the soot from its hard plastic surface.

Slowly opening the door a crack so that he could see into the passageway, Carson realised that Serif's bodyguards were gone. Carson led the way as he and Rachel slipped by the loud ventilation fans and toward the doorway leading to where the two-kilo nuclear device was being armed by Mrak and Broz.

"Come on, we've got to get up to the spent fuel pool deck and make that phone call," Carson said.

"*Bine*, let's go," Rachel said, this time with fearlessness in her voice.

CHAPTER 24

The Cernavodă main control room was exceptionally quiet after Bogdan's earlier briefing of his crew, who now had taken command of the reactor's control rods and its neutron flux distribution. Two previously banned reactor operators sat together in the bounds of the horseshoe panel labelled as the P525, which was controlling the reactor and most of its on-line support operating systems. To their right was another long rectangular panel covered in switches and lights, labelled the P730 panel. Directly in front of them was the P220.

Serif and Bogdan stood on top of the riser to observe the control room manipulations being performed by the licenced reactor operators.

"It is time," Serif said.

"Yes, I agree," Bogdan nodded. "Marius, monitor the P525 panel for any changes to the reactor's water level, pressure, or core power."

Marius repeated back what he had been told.

"Jacob," Bogdan ordered. "Open one reactor main relief valve."

Jacob walked over to the P730 panel, its apron covered with twenty-five safety relief valve switches. These valves were normally used only in case of an unanticipated over-pressurisation of the reactor vessel due to some unexpected surge of steam inside its thick, zircaloy-clad steel walls. It would certainly create havoc inside the reactor's containment building when the safety relief valve was opened at standard operating pressures. Steam that normally fed the main turbine generator would be dumped into a practically airtight space. Steam that spun the gigantic turbine at an appreciably high speed would then be deposited into the containment building. A tremendous surge of nuclear reactor-generated heat energy would rapidly flow into the space.

Inside the containment, which was built around the reactor drywell compartment to prevent any major release of radioactivity, was a suppression pool, expected to absorb short bursts of steam discharged from the safety relief valves. Designed as a circular tank to hold a million gallons of water, the suppression pool was between the containment outer wall and the reactor compartment.

Jacob reached toward the top row and turned the first key lock switch from automatic relief to the open position. A very small red light above the switch came on. A sudden chatter of various alarms sounded off from all three major panels of the control room. Marius silenced the P525 with a pushbutton and watched as water level in the reactor recovered itself from a sudden swell. Feed water pumps that kept the reactor at its desired water level whined a little from the extra load of trying to keep up with the additional draw on the reactor's steam production.

Bogdan watched as the plant stabilised itself, and the suppression pool temperature began to rise slowly from seventy-seven to seventy-eight point eight degrees Fahrenheit – one reactor safety relief valve discharging pressurized steam below its surface. The pool's water quenched the hot exhausting steam as it was being discharged from the nozzle end of a long pipe that went from near the top of the reactor through the drywell's thick steel wall and then down into the pool, absorbing the first relief valve's discharging energy. But the increasing temperature of the water had to be addressed quickly or trouble would soon follow.

"We will hold here until the water temperature in the suppression pool reaches eighty-six degrees, then open the next relief valve," Bogdan said.

Serif and Tanya stood watching a computer screen displaying the pool's temperature as the massive boiling water reactor began to heat the water in the containment. Designed to suppress some of the heat released from an emergency depressurisation, the pool was usually closely monitored by the operators. It was the only thing preventing the release of steam from the reactor into the atmosphere of the containment which would, over time, pressurise it above its maximum stress limit. The rupture of the containment would allow a radioactive release that Bogdan imagined they could control for as long as needed.

Serif took Tanya by the arm, out of hearing range from Bogdan, Marius, and Jacob. "I don't understand why we just don't try to melt the core. Why control these relief valves like this?" he asked nervously.

Tanya's engineering experience helped her ability to explain. "These reactors are designed by American engineers who make it harder to keep them running than to trip them offline with an automatic shutdown. It's called a SCRAM." Serif listened intently as she continued.

"When the water level inside the reactor drops below a predetermined level, the reactor control rods are automatically inserted very rapidly, and the core's nuclear reaction will cease and will then cool down. And if they try to drain all the water from the vessel, those huge pumps on that panel over there will inject enough water to flood it completely," Tanya said, pointing to the P730 panel.

Serif nodded and repeated something Bogdan had told him. "The containment building will keep any release from the reactor from escaping into the environment and getting caught in trade winds that would spread it for thousands of miles."

"Exactly," Tanya said. "Our best option is to try to slowly boil off the water in the suppression pool until it has completely vaporised. The steam will eventually rupture the containment building, and we can discharge as much radioactive material as we desire. Controlling the heat in the reactor is the key to our success."

Tanya smiled approvingly as she continued. "Bogdan's plan is fantastic, Serif – he's thought of everything. The blueprints that you provided to him were just what he needed to construct this scenario."

Serif added, "Once we've decided that he's exhausted enough of the steam into the world's atmosphere, we will make our escape." Tanya smiled at Serif and nodded.

The red telephone on the shift manager's desk rang again – it was Romania's state authority in Bucharest. The caller no doubt wanted to know what demands the terrorists sought to release the nuke plant. Serif stepped back up on the platform and lifted the receiver. His voice was loud and menacing.

"This is Serif Muhammad Rezaabak, citizen of Turkey and vindicator of the Ottoman Empire," Serif said. "My demands from the Western world's governments are the following: lift the sanctions on my country and all those of my brethren in the Middle East, release the Chechen prisoners of war Russia has captured and tortured with the aid of the

West, and finally, give Turkey back its wealth that you have stolen over decades of corrupt world domination. Twenty billion Euros is my demand."

Serif slammed the receiver back onto its cradle, his heavy dark brow furled with anger. On the other end of the telephone, the highest ranking official of the state authority, who realised that he would not be able to grant any of those demands, immediately called his superior. He told the president of Romania the demands of the terrorists. Together, over the telephone, the men made the decision to inform INWA that what they had already suspected was indeed true. The Agency's emergency response was already activated based on two known facts: Carson's phone call to Todd and the Romanian state authority losing all contact with the nuclear facility's main control room.

Although the state authority's representative was near the main gate and could see that something was very wrong with the security coverage for a night shift, Serif sealed their suspicions with his impossible demands. The only demand that might be negotiated was the return of wealth. But Serif's demand for twenty billion Euros was basically just a deplorable proviso for his insanely unrealistic ransom.

———

On the computer screen behind where Tanya was standing, images were displayed from four areas of the perimeter surrounding the site and fed by the security surveillance system Draco was controlling. Three display panels switched every thirty seconds to a new camera view, but one was locked on the front gate. That camera was now showing military vehicles pulling into position, waiting for their orders to move in and retake the power plant from the terrorists.

"Bogdan," Tanya said. "The Romanians are here."

Bogdan picked up the radio handset mounted on the P525 panel. "Franco, start the emergency diesel generator and energise the fence."

Franco and Ciprian were already in place at one of the three backup diesel generators. The generator was large and could supply enough electricity to run several large electrical pumps, fans, and other supporting equipment. But the two building operators had taken a couple of hefty cables and connected them from the generators outside transformer to the chain-link perimeter fence – a powerful electric barrier now encircled the nuclear power plant.

From the front gate, the small Romanian civil defence force heard a loud, locomotive-sized engine start up when Franco pushed a button. Black soot blew from the top of the diesel generator building as the engine stabilised itself. Ciprian was standing by the output breaker that they had connected via the makeshift jumper cables to the security fence. Although the high-pressure emergency pump was now disabled, the security fence would be impenetrable.

"Close in the breaker, Ciprian," Franco ordered.

A sudden drain on the diesel generator caused it to moan a little as the current exited the supply breaker and travelled down the fifty metres of high voltage cabling connected to the perimeter fence. The generator came back up to full speed as the fence began to glow red hot at the location where the cables were bolted.

"Tanya, call Draco and tell him the fence is energised," Serif said.

Draco sounded relieved when he heard Tanya's voice on the phone. "Have you control of the reactor?" he asked.

"Yes. Bogdan is beginning to pressurise the containment building now," Tanya replied. "I am calling to let you know that the perimeter fence is energised."

"I know. We are monitoring the scrambled radio channel of your operators – I heard everything," Draco said.

"Good," Tanya said. "I see that you have friends at the gate, maybe looking for an invitation?"

"We are ready to resist them for as long as you will need, my lovely friend," Draco said. "And now that the fence is electrified, we will have the edge."

At that moment, Tanya looked over at one of the four displays on the security monitor and saw three black-uniformed Romanians rush toward the front gate. Sparks flew from the lead man's helmet, and his clothing seemed to spontaneously combust. Engulfed in flames, the man immediately fell lifeless onto the asphalt as the others scurried back to their temporary command station.

"Very nice," Tanya coldly muttered into the phone.

"We are standing by for a more vigorous attempt to enter the perimeter by the militia," Draco said.

Draco informed Tanya that three turrets were set up on top of the power plant, positioned to rebuff any entry attempt by the forces now surrounding the perimeter fence. The turrets were also equipped with anti-aircraft, shoulder-launched missiles, courtesy of the Chechens and their Chinese supplier.

"May Allah be with us in our jihad," Draco finally said.

"Praise, Allah. Until later, Draco," Tanya said.

Draco spread the word to his men not to go near the site's boundary and then poured himself some Turkish coffee from an antique pot. The long handle of the brass pot allowed him to pour the thick black liquid into a fine Turkish cup. Draco took a satisfied sip as he watched the monitors.

———

Marius stepped away from the P525 panel to get a better overall look at what the plant was doing, now that a portion of the reactor's heat energy was being discharged into the suppression pool at about six percent of the total reactor power being generated. Bogdan was clever enough to keep the largest amount of steam supplied to the main turbine generator, enabling him to run the reactor at one hundred percent power. The high-quality steam carried with it a significant amount of water that was now being lost from the normal heat cycle of the boiling water reactor.

Picking up the scrambled radio handset, Marius gave another order to the building operators. "Ciprian, cross-tie the secondary water storage tank to the condensate storage tank – we're gonna need more make-up water."

Squeaking through the loudspeaker, they all heard the reply. "Aye, Jacob, will do. Franco is going to the radioactive waste water recovery station to redirect water into the make-up tank."

"I understand," Jacob replied.

Bogdan kept close watch over the plant's parameter display console. "Jacob, the suppression pool is at eight-six degrees Fahrenheit. Open the second safety relief valve."

Jacob repeated back Bogdan's orders and stepped over to the P730 panel, again facing the array of relief valve switches. Above the top row of switches, a mimic board showed that the relief valve would discharge into the suppression pool on the other side of the containment – directly opposite the first valves discharge header. Jacob opened the valve with a quick turn of the key lock switch, then took a step back to monitor the plant's reaction.

Several alarms went off on multiple panels mounted around the main control room. Marius watched the P525 panel parameters as he let the automatic feed water system adjust to a new steam demand being put on the reactor. The turbine generator electrical power output was diminished by another six percent, due to the loss of steam supply now being routed into the suppression pool.

The boiling water near the spider-shaped discharge piping under the waterline of the suppression pool created a vibration that could be felt everywhere inside the containment building. The engineering and construction of the suppression pool was complex – rebar and concrete interlaced throughout its base, connecting it to the reactor building deep underground.

The entire lead-impregnated concrete base of the power plant experienced the vibration of the collapsing steam. Serif could even feel a little rumbling underneath his feet while standing in the main control room.

A sudden flurry of red and amber lights cascaded across the panel Jacob was using to discharge steam into the containment building. Jacob looked up from the apron of the panel and identified two red annunciators that appeared to be the most important of the twelve flashing lights.

"Suppression pool high level," Jacob shouted over the warbling noise of the audible alarm.

The steam was condensing and raising the water level in the containment to an abnormal level; any higher would cause the pressure in the building to rise. Dumping steam into the containment with the reactor's safety relief valves was similar to forcing pressurised beer into an airtight half full keg – after a while the level would begin to rise. But, eventually, you'd have to patch the ceiling when its plug blew out. In the scheme of the terrorist's planned containment rupture, it was an added bonus.

"I understand, suppression pool high," Bogdan repeated back.

The power plant was responding as it was designed to and informing the operators that there was a serious problem occurring in the containment building. The red annunciator alarms meant that a manual operation to lower the level in the pool should be performed, but these operators had no intention of mitigating the ensuing over-pressurisation.

Containment pressure began to rise slowly as the terrorists watched the gauges and indicators providing them all the information that they needed to stop the event.

"Jacob, I want you to announce the containment pressure rise at half-pound increments," Bogdan ordered.

"Aye, half-pound changes," Jacob replied.

They watched the plant as steam continued to discharge below the waterline of the suppression pool. Once its average temperature increased enough to allow boiling, the pressure would ramp up at an uncontrollable rate, rupturing the containment.

The vibration from the steam collapsing under the water's surface continued to shake the foundation of the power plant and knocked dust from the ceiling panels of the switchgear rooms in the plant. Jacob shouted out containment temperature and pressure parameters as Marius worked furiously to manipulate the feed water controls. Marius had to act fast to keep up with the demand now being put on the huge pumps and their controls. The giant motors surged as millions of gallons of water were forced into the high-pressure reactor vessel.

CHAPTER 25

Carson and Rachel finally made their way to the spent fuel pool deck on the building's eighth floor. Carson had been monitoring the terrorists' radio transmissions on the handset he had taken from the dead security guard.

A strange sound suddenly startled both of them.

"What's that noise?" Rachel asked.

"I don't know," Carson replied. "Feels like some kind of vibration coming from inside the containment."

He walked toward the second containment airlock, still closed and its pressurised rubber seal fully inflated with air. Carson looked through the thick glass portal in the heavy steel door, but it was too small to see what was going on inside the containment. "They're doing something in the main control room – they could be opening a reactor relief valve."

"Oh, Carson –"

"Rachel," Carson interrupted, "give me your cell phone."

Carson dialled Herman's cell phone number. He noticed that Rachel's complexion was very pale and her features drawn – the poor young woman looked dehydrated. Carson knew that to prevent anyone from ingesting contamination there was a no eating or drinking policy implemented inside the power block. There were only a couple of places they could find a drink of water: one was in the health physics lab, the other was the operator's kitchen by the main control room. A voice came on the telephone. "Hello?"

"Herman, is that you?" Carson asked.

Herman was sitting in the emergency centre working on the next media release with Stella. He got up from his chair and walked out into the hallway.

"Yeah, Carson. What's happening?" Herman asked. "I heard you might be inside the plant."

"I am. Bogdan and the terrorists are going to melt down the reactor. At this rate, they are going to destroy the containment building very soon," Carson said. "I believe they've opened at least one of the main relief valves and are discharging steam to the suppression pool."

The telephone lost its signal briefly, but then Carson broke through again. "They'll either rupture the concrete or blow out one of the exhaust panels near the steel roof. They want to release pressurised, contaminated steam into the atmosphere and –"

Herman interrupted. "Did you say Bogdan? Did you hear any other names?"

"Bogdan was the leader of the group of operators, but I did hear the name Serif at least once," Carson replied. "Look, I must get those valves closed. Tell me where I need to go to override the signal coming from the control room."

"Give me ten minutes, Carson," Herman said. "I have an idea, but I need to make sure. Call me back in ten."

"Good," Carson said as he hit the *end* button.

Rachel was standing by Carson's side as he spoke to Herman. She had gained psychological strength in the past half hour but was clueless as to what was going on behind the thick outer door. The rumbling noise was now becoming much louder. The vibration underneath Carson and Rachel's feet was the result of nucleate boiling as two more relief valves were opened underneath the suppression pool's surface.

Although Carson and Rachel were unable to see anything going on inside the containment, they could see the spent fuel pool right in front of them. The surface of the deep clear pool was rippling from end to end, with some of the larger waves beginning to crest over the sides of the pool. Rachel jumped on top of a gang box housing underwater tools used to manipulate the spent fuel twenty-five feet below its surface.

Rachel could only see the tops of the spent fuel bundles stored vertically in a matrix of hundreds of rows and columns, which looked menacing – black and uninviting. Carson jumped on top of the gang box with her to check out what she thought was so interesting at the bottom of the spent fuel pool. The radiation from it was minimal because of the water's ability to attenuate most of the high energy particles. But Carson knew that the radioactive effects would be lethal if anyone were to get too close to the fuel bundles currently in wet storage. If a bundle removed from the reactor was positioned at the end of a football field, a man running at full speed toward it would die from radiation exposure before ever touching its cladding.

"What's causing the vibration?" Rachel asked, worriedly.

"It's caused by steam being released from the reactor into the suppression pool, inside the containment," Carson replied. "That steam is five-hundred degrees Fahrenheit. When it hits the eighty or eighty-five degree water it creates bubbles that collapse in waves. That's the vibration we feel. We can't get inside the containment now – it's a death trap. The steam that's being generated would suffocate us."

"What's gonna happen if we can't stop it?" Rachel's voice was panicky.

"Eventually the suppression water will turn to steam," Carson said. "We don't want to be around here when that happens."

"Call your friend back," Rachel demanded. "Tell him to send someone to get us outta here!"

"Doing my best, Rachel. Please don't panic."

Jumping down from the gang box, they stood together looking up at the roof of the reactor building. It was nothing more than corrugated steel, but it was about sixty-five feet high. Huge supply and exhaust fans were available to keep the great room at a sensible temperature and fresh air moving around in the closed space. The exhaust fans were also equipped with a filter train that could remove some radioactive contaminates should the spent fuel begin to overheat during a loss of water accident.

Carson redialled Herman. "What did you find out, buddy? We've got to get out of the plant, very soon."

"Do you remember isolating the main control room during simulator training?" Herman asked. "You're going to have to make your way to the remote shutdown panel four decks below the main control room. Then you have to find the two electric circuit breakers that separate the control room from the plant itself."

"Of course!" Carson exclaimed. "That panel can put the plant in a cold shutdown mode."

"Yeah, that's right," Herman said. "Carson, hurry! The suppression pool is at one hundred and forty degrees, and the containment pressure is starting to creep up. We're viewing all the parameters from the plant on a fibre-optic connection that's still working, for the moment."

Romanian state authorities had installed the line during an early construction phase of the plant. Ceauşescu's communist cronies in Bucharest wanted to make sure they could always see what was going on at their only nuclear facility. The line was not on any drawings that Serif had stolen, but it was feeding information directly into the Romanian emergency centre in Bucharest. The state authorities were relaying that information directly to INWA via a broadband cable installed after an international drill two years earlier.

"They've got to run out of water soon," Carson said.

"These guys are pretty smart, Carson," Herman warned. "Don't count on them forgetting to fill the make-up tanks," he said. "I imagine they'll add river water to the reactor through the firewater cross-tie system if need be."

"Okay," Carson said. "I'm on my way to the shutdown panel. Our cell phone probably won't work there – too much concrete and steel. I'll call you when I can."

"Good luck, Kit," Herman said.

The moment Carson ended the call, Rachel said, "I know where the panel is. We have to go back down to the health physics lab, then up the stairs one deck."

"Let's go!" Carson said, ushering her out. They quickly made their way down the stairwell of the reactor building. On one of the floors, Carson remembered seeing armed men going into a room under the spent fuel pool. He wondered aloud about the room.

"That's where we store some of our equipment," Rachel told him.

They reached the bottom floor, and Rachel led the way to the turbine building door. She hit the card reader and unlocked the hatch-like door that swung open with great force. Carson followed Rachel into the health physics lab.

"I've got to get a drink of water," Rachel said as she put down the Heckler & Koch on the long counter of the lab.

Running by her cubicle, Rachel grabbed a bottle of swamp water, locally sold by the 'mom and pop' store near the plant. She took several long swigs of water. "I'm ready," she said.

Carson picked up her gun, and the two started toward the stairwell. As they began to climb, it occurred to Carson they had left a path of card readers all the way to the health physics lab. He prayed he'd get to the shutdown panel before Draco's guards were on top of them, but what he didn't know was that Draco's men were already stretched to the limit trying to fight off the Romanian militia reinforcements. The only man who was supposed to be looking for Carson and Rachel was dead in the reactor building, killed by a bolt of 440-volt lightning.

––––––

Romania's civil defence force commandos were bewildered by the electrified perimeter fence. Their initial advance should have gained them access to the protected area and then been followed by a search and rescue team, but instead one man lay dead on the road, killed by the high current being conducted through the chain links of the fence. The band of soldiers didn't know what to do next, since they were limited to shoulder-fired weapons and a few grenades.

A sergeant fired a short burst from a machine gun into the gate's locking mechanism, but the small-calibre weapon failed to break the hydraulic security device. The sparks and noise, however, did get Draco's attention. He turned to the guard who was watching several monitors. "Contact our men on the roof and have them kill a few of the militia."

Within seconds, shots from two sniper rifles held by South African-trained mercenaries lit up the night sky six times, and six soldiers fell dead in the car park. The sergeant ducked behind one of the jungle camouflage-painted trucks, as did everyone else standing near enough to see the killings. A flurry of bullets from the militia ineffectively bounced around the power plant's roof.

"Come over here with that radio," the sergeant yelled to his radioman.

Taking the radio handset, the sergeant began shouting into its mouthpiece. "Headquarters, this is Sergeant Isarescu. Have met significant resistance at the perimeter fence of the plant, over."

A static-filled voice on the other end repeated back what the sergeant had just said.

The sergeant started again, "Seven men killed, perimeter fence electrified, and snipers on roof of the building. Need course of action, over."

"Hold your position, Sergeant. Return fire as needed," the voice replied. "Do not advance. NATO forces are on their way to the site, over."

"Roger," the sergeant replied and turned to his radioman. "Tell everyone to hold their position."

Then the static broke again and the voice said, "Clarify, Sergeant. Did you say that the perimeter fence was electrified?"

"Affirmative, headquarters. It has been turned into a high-voltage electric fence, over," the sergeant yelled.

"Roger that," the voice said. "Headquarters, out."

"Well, that was a lot of help," the sergeant said angrily.

Opening the door to one of the logic relay rooms, Carson began searching for the remote shutdown panel room.

"Look, here's the doorway leading –" Carson stopped as the lights suddenly went out.

Carson froze in his tracks.

"What was that?" Rachel asked, grabbing his arm.

"I'm not sure," Carson replied.

Relays and contacts began to clatter throughout the switchgear room where they were standing. A moment later, a few emergency lights came back on, just enough to illuminate their path between the high-voltage panels and to avoid coming too close to the 440 volts of electricity behind each of the panel doors.

"The main turbine supplying electricity has tripped offline," Carson said. "These lights are running off the emergency diesel generators."

Rachel looked very distraught as Carson continued. "It's getting much too dangerous for us to be here." Rachel looked at him helplessly. "Follow me," Carson said, leading her further into the switchgear room.

CHAPTER 26

Herman left his desk for another briefing by Anthony Zabaar. Todd Sinclair was waiting outside the centre in an unoccupied office, hoping to find out Carson's whereabouts.

Zabaar started the briefing with an update. "Over the last five hours, we've been carrying out our procedures for the declared Site Area Emergency at Cernavodă's nuclear power plant in Romania. The terrorists have taken over the main control room and are attempting to destroy the reactor containment building by using reactor steam discharged through the safety relief valves. If heating the suppression pool continues, there will be a release of radioactive contamination into the atmosphere. This plume could spread over several hundred, or even thousands, of miles. Consequently, we have upgraded the classification of this event to a General Emergency."

The room's silence was deafening for those who did not understand what a real General Emergency meant to the overall scope of the situation. Some public relations executives of the INWA, who had been monitoring the news being broadcast on screens facing the crowd of emergency response members, were visibly shaken by the upgrade. One woman sitting at the meteorological desk ran outside to call home and warn her family. Others held fast to their assigned posts, awaiting the remainder of the briefing and their orders from the emergency director.

Zabaar continued. "We suggested that the Romanians attempt to shut off electrical power to the nuclear plant by opening switching breakers feeding some of the non-essential equipment. Although we know that the reactor control rods should have been automatically inserted into the core by a reactor SCRAM when the electrical power was stopped, that has not happened. The safety relief valves are still open, and the state authority reports reactor power still at thirty-five percent.

"We believe that some of the reactor's control rods were partially inserted by the SCRAM, but a hydraulic malfunction has prevented the entire neutron-absorbing poison from being introduced into the reactor's core."

Zabaar turned to Herman and asked for his update.

Herman adjusted his glasses and looked at his clipboard. "Carson Griffin called me from inside the plant during the past hour. His report was grim, but with some divine intervention, we hope that he's able to help. We gave him an alternative plan to close the reactor's main relief valves and, with extremely good luck, shut down the reactor."

Herman looked down at his notes. "Suppression pool temperature is still climbing, but an automatic cooling system started when we cut power to the plant and seems to be holding the pool temperature at about one hundred eighty-five degrees Fahrenheit."

Zabaar interrupted. "The site boundary perimeter fence is charged with high voltage that must be supplied from one of the diesel generators. We're unable to advise the Romanian state authorities on how to go about turning this power off."

"We're waiting for another phone call from Carson Griffin," Herman said. "He needs a few more minutes." Zabaar nodded.

The on-duty meteorologist updated the team with bad news. Weather conditions were stable, better than expected for a Christmas morning in Cernavodă. However, winds at higher altitudes were very strong and swirling, the worst conditions possible should a radioactive plume exit the dome of the containment building.

Zabaar ended the meeting, and Herman stepped outside for a much needed cup of coffee. Todd Sinclair was sitting with Christy Griffin in the office just outside the centre. Christy looked tired and extremely worried. Christy usually didn't want to know too much about what Carson was doing on his missions for INWA. She had also agreed with her husband that it would be safer for them if he kept his work separate from his home life. Up until now, they were well practiced at doing just that.

It was about four in the morning when Todd had phoned Christy to tell her that Carson was in the middle of the Cernavodă terrorist attack. Christy decided to let Susan sleep, not wanting to worry her teenage daughter on Christmas Day. Susan's cell phone was on her nightstand cluttered with University of Georgia paraphernalia. Christy would call her daughter the moment she knew anything.

"Have you heard anything else, Herman?" Todd asked.

"Carson seems to be making a difference," Herman replied. "I never knew he was so well equipped to handle a mission like this."

"But is he all right, Herman?" Christy pleaded. "How many times have you spoken to him?"

Herman took a sip of his coffee. "Christy, I don't think he's been hurt, but... we know he's in a very dangerous place,"

Herman replied.

"Can you call him?" Christy asked, tears beginning to creep down her cheeks. "I want to talk to him."

Herman shook his head. "No, he's down in the depths of the power plant. There's just too much concrete and steel to get a signal on a cell phone. All the phones, except one dedicated line, were knocked out when the terrorists took control of the plant. We believe that their group includes some of the plant's security force – they're watching over the perimeter."

Todd put his arm around Christy. "He's gonna be fine, Christy. I trust his judgment and his experience."

"I've got to get back to my post. I'll let you know when I hear any news," Herman promised.

Christy sat down in a swivel chair next to one of the windows of the small office and stared out over the city of Vienna. She could see the lights flickering on the other side of the Danube River, now beginning to get busy with barge traffic. The view was partially blocked by a tower adjacent to the large park behind the INWA building, sparsely lit with red and blue lights attached to a rotating restaurant that turned slowly atop the tall structure.

Christy let out a small ironic laugh. Todd looked at her, puzzled.

"What?" he said.

Christy kept staring out the window. "I can see the restaurant where Carson and I had our last wedding anniversary dinner. Very fancy place that rotates at the top of the building. We hated it there."

"Why?" Todd asked. "Because it rotates?"

"No. Because the food was so lousy."

Todd chuckled. Christy turned to him, and tears again welled up in her eyes.

arson reached the emergency shutdown panel room's door.

"Let me see that security guard's key card," Carson said.

"*Bine*, here let me," Rachel said. She slid the dead guard's card through the narrow slot. The door had a large sign on it that read:

NO ENTRY WITHOUT PERMISSION OF SHIFT MANAGER

Carson pushed open the heavy steel door and let Rachel step in. He followed, releasing the door carefully so that it would close completely and not set off an alarm in the security island. Inside, they saw the remote shutdown panel mounted to the steel and concrete floor. The panel was designed to control the necessary equipment to take the huge boiling water reactor down to cold shutdown mode.

"Now let's see," Carson mumbled. "Here are the reactor's main relief valve override switches."

"Just close them," Rachel said. "Won't that stop everything?"

"It'll definitely slow things down," Carson replied. "But first we need to electrically separate this panel from the main control room."

Examining the ten-foot-tall panel from top to bottom, Carson found the control separation switch on its top right quadrant. "Here we go." He turned the switch to "separate" and removed its key. The remote shutdown panel came to life, lights began to glow, and a faint alarm sounded – synchronised with the flashing amber light above the separation switch. Gauges responded, showing the reactor's primary parameters, along with the suppression pool temperature.

Rachel watched Carson intently, saying nothing, but praying for a miracle.

"Okay, the reactor is still limping along at about thirty-five percent of full power," Carson stated. "Suppression pool temperature is at one hundred and eighty-five degrees Fahrenheit. We've got to start the liquid shutdown system; it'll inject sodium pentaborate into the core, stopping the nuclear chain reaction."

Carson pushed a red button on the panel's left side and watched as a dial indicator began to show the level in a neutron poison tank begin to lower. "Great, at least that's working. And look! Reactor power is falling."

Rachel had little more than a basic working knowledge of what was going on, but she was relieved to see Carson excited about the power reduction. "Sounds like a good thing?"

Within a minute, reactor power was down to around five percent, a promising sign. Reaching for the first safety relief valve, Carson hesitated.

"If we're lucky, when I close this valve we won't cause others to open automatically. Here goes," Carson said.

As the switch was rotated, Carson saw pressure inside the reactor vessel spike up a little, but all the other valves that could have put extra steam into the suppression pool remained closed. He continued to rotate the hand switches for the safety relief valves until they were all closed.

Suddenly they heard a loud slam of the outer door leading into the switchgear room. Bogdan had sent Jacob down from the main control room to investigate why they had lost control of the reactor. With only a few seconds to spare before Jacob entered the panel room, Carson and Rachel immediately looked around for an escape route. A sealed sliding door at the back of the room was designed to allow access to what was going to be unit number two's remote shutdown panel. The other reactor unit wasn't completed yet, but most of the walls were in place.

"Help me!" Carson whispered, as he hurriedly began removing all the keys from the individual locking switches of the shutdown panel controls. Rachel pulled as many as she could and gave them to Carson.

Carson broke the seal with a swift jerk on the sliding door's handle and burst through the opening, Rachel in tow. He turned around hurriedly to shut the door when he heard the click of the latch release of the other panel room door. Fast enough not to be seen, Carson shut the sliding door and flipped its handle into a permanently locked position. Rachel was already heading down a corridor that led into the dark bowels of unit two's turbine building.

"Come this way," Rachel said. "We can hide in unit two until someone comes for us."

"No, I've got to get back up to the main control room," Carson said. "But you'll need to stay in unit two. They're too busy to look for you now."

In the quiet of the unit two turbine building, they could hear gunshots outside.

CHAPTER 27

Mrak secured the final wiring in place with translucent, colour-coded zip-ties – purple would be carrying the primary timing circuit's pulse. He and Broz had been in the room under the spent fuel pool for several hours, exhausted from the work they were doing. Mounting the two-kilogram nuclear bomb into its suspension system and arming the device took a great deal of mental energy.

Serif's two body guards were observing every move made by the two nuclear scientists. Maks continuously walked between where they were working underneath the spent fuel pool and out into the passageway – he hated the cramped space. Daniel stood behind one of the tripod-based stands used to hold the bright temporary lamps they had set up; normal illumination was too dim for their work. Mrak and Broz were careful with the placement of the hot lamps – not too near the triggering device.

"Time to go," Maks said. "Finish quickly."

Mrak stood up from his position. "We are finished. The timing circuit is now armed."

Both men stepped back to observe their work with a mutual sense of pride. Broz moved toward Mrak from behind a small panel. He had pretended to work on the panel, in order to distract Daniel from the hidden tool in his right hand. Broz was carrying a long, thin screwdriver pointed down and away from his body. The old man comfortably moved around the area where Mrak was cutting zip-ties with a pair of miniature pliers and put himself between the bright temporary lights and a nearby bulkhead.

Maks and Daniel now agreed it was time to notify Serif that they were about to leave the area and that the bomb was set.

Broz and Mrak felt sure that this would be their last chance to get out of their deadly predicament. Serif would surely give Maks the order to kill them once the timer was set to detonate the small atomic bomb.

Mrak put his pliers into the tool box at his feet and waved at Daniel to come over to him.

"Give me a hand with this. It's too heavy for me. You know that I'm sixty-seven years old?" Mrak said.

Daniel stepped into the bright light and reached down to move the box. "You're an old bastard."

Just then Broz stepped in behind Daniel and drove the screwdriver between his shoulder blade and his spine, its shaft penetrating his heart and left lung. The look of surprise was welded on Daniel's face in death, as the two older men watched him slowly fall to the floor.

Mrak spat on Daniel's body. "Your momma's an old bastard!"

Grabbing Daniel's pistol, Mrak stepped back out of the bright lights and into a crevice behind the door. Silenced from the outside world by thick concrete walls, Maks was unemotionally shot through his left temple when he entered the room. Serif's bodyguards had murdered many people throughout their days as terrorists, but this day, Hell called them home.

"Let's get the prize and get out of here before Serif realises his men are dead," Mrak said.

Without pause, Broz opened a thick, small, black Pelican case. Its interior had once carried the plutonium pit that was now inside the plastic explosive device. The two scientists hurriedly removed the plutonium pit from its cradle inside the bomb. Broz carefully took out one of the plastic explosive panels, as Mrak held the panel's thin electrical leads clear of any metal that might cause an unplanned arc of current. When the panel was moved far enough away, Mrak reached in and pulled the pit from its resting place and put it into the Pelican case.

"What about the triggering device?" Broz asked.

"Reset the timer for four hours from now," Mrak said. "We will need the diversion for our escape. The blast will take them by surprise, and two old men can limp off this site with quite a nice prize." Broz gave Mrak a nervous smile.

"May God go with us," Broz said.

Broz climbed up onto a stainless steel slat being used for easier access to the timer panel. Unbolting and removing a small panel with a battery-operated screw gun, Broz reached inside the timer's box-like covering and put a flat screwdriver into a slotted screw and rotated it clockwise four clicks. After replacing the small panel, he attached a tamper-resistant tripwire through the bolt heads and energised it, preventing anyone from opening the panel without breaking the circuit and setting off the bomb.

"I don't believe that the Romanians will know what has happened for a while," Broz stated. "Serif and his cousin will be the only ones who suspect that the explosion was supposed to be from a nuclear weapon."

"Yes, and everyone else will believe that this explosion

was part of his power plant meltdown – a continuation of another stratagem," Mrak added.

Broz nodded. "It is a good plan," Broz said. "Let's go."

The two men took only the small Pelican case with them as they slowly exited the room. Mrak and Broz never gave a second thought to the amount of spent nuclear fuel in the pool just above the plastic explosives. Going into a stairwell, they descended to the ground level they had entered several hours earlier. But instead of heading back to their van, they went toward the turbine building interface door.

———

In the beginning of the battle for control of Cernavodă's nuclear power plant, the Romanian militia was unquestionably ill-equipped to deal with the machine guns mounted on top of the turbine and control buildings. The two guards who were firing over the perimeter fence alternated with a third guard while reloading. The three men kept a constant volley of bullets flying, never allowing a shot from the parked vehicles to go unanswered.

One large truck with ten men arrived simultaneously with Draco's order to begin launching shoulder-mounted rockets at the Romanian forces that were mustering near the front gate. The men in the truck never got a chance to dismount before a fire-breathing projectile entered their vehicle. Penetrating the rear seat, just prior to the missile's detonation, a spark flew from its tail. The hot ember went into the driver's right eye as his left eye saw fire boil out from underneath him. A microsecond later, the truck was blown to bits – body parts and machine smelted together by the heat.

After another ineffective charge of a few gung-ho Romanian militiamen who arrived late on the scene, the poorly armed young men settled back to wait for additional help.

NATO forces were contacted from Vienna about the ensuing attack on the nuclear power plant only forty miles from their Black Sea base. Around 1:00 a.m., NATO sent out one hundred and twenty soldiers armed to the teeth with weapons and ammunition. But it wasn't until the Abrams tank arrived around daybreak, along with a large assignment of US-trained Special Forces, that the tide began to turn. Rolling over the security island at the front gate, the highly manoeuverable tank rolled closer to the power block to take out the rooftop machine guns. Unfortunately, all the security guards that Draco had tied up in the security island were killed during the NATO tank's sprint through the building – casualties of friendly fire.

Just as the tank crew aligned their laser sighting system, an Apache helicopter flew over their position. Within a few seconds, the weaponry that had killed so many of the Romanian militia was silenced by the tank's machine gun cannons. After the high voltage supplied to the fence had been knocked out by a shoulder-launched missile, Draco's men could no longer hold off the military onslaught.

Draco was shot during the final attack of green- and khaki-clad soldiers overrunning his stronghold in one of the security towers. Without pause, they continued their assault until the Special Forces eventually made their way up to the main control room. Dead mercenaries were lying all around the site by the time the eight men and two women entered the control building.

Daybreak broke sluggishly over Romania on that Christmas morning. Rapid blasting gunfire from the power plant roof had been completely halted, replaced by an occasional single fire from a NATO sniper. Serif's men, who had been listening to the horrendous noises from the attack while trying to destroy the plant from the inside, thought that Draco had obviously lost the battle.

The two old scientists had just reached the circulating water system pump house on the ground floor of the plant. Two gigantic pumps stood at least twenty feet high on either side of the large room. The pumps normally supplied cooling water to the main turbine condenser from the colossal tepee-shaped cooling tower at a combined flow rate of over a hundred million gallons per minute. Both pumps were now at a standstill because of the power loss experienced during the night's ensuing battle.

Beneath the pumps, under the concrete floor that the two old scientists were standing on, was a man-made cavern, which was normally full of water and used as a suction source for the pumps. The pump caisson had connecting underground water pipes from Cernavodă's canal dumped into the cavern through a large opening beneath the water's surface. The cavern was normally completely full when the Danube River was high enough to supply Cernavodă's canal with murky river water. But during the winter months, the circulating water pump allowed for an air pocket to form, an air pocket from the plant's underbelly to the canal.

Exhausted from their ordeal and knowing all was not well with their situation, Mrak turned to Broz. "We're gonna have to give ourselves up to whoever is out there trying to take control of the plant back from Serif. I'm very tired."

"I agree, my good friend," Broz consoled him. "The military will be inside the plant very soon, and we have no chance of swimming out of here through this water."

They heard a door slam shut behind them as they stood looking at each other, trying to catch their breath.

CHAPTER 28

Jacob had returned to the control room where Serif and Bogdan were standing – surprised that the reactor was going sub-critical and the safety relief valves were closing.

"Someone has separated the controls from the main control room, Bogdan," Jacob said, exhausted from running.

Bogdan shook his head in disbelief. "Serif, we have lost control of the reactor. There is no way to drive enough steam into the containment to rupture it from the inside, now."

Serif was devastated by the news. Nevertheless, he knew that he had one more surreptitious solution. He might not be able to get the twenty billion Euros that he was demanding before releasing the plant, but he could still detonate a nuclear weapon that would destroy the spent fuel pool and spread contamination for hundreds of square miles.

"Bogdan, have your men execute our plan of escape," Serif barked. "We have to leave this place, immediately!"

Radioing Ciprian and Franco to meet them at the circulating water pump room, Jacob and Marius left the control room through its rear door.

Serif made one more telephone call to the Romanian authorities. He picked up the red phone and waited less than thirty seconds before a high-ranking official came on the line.

Serif began his sermon. "Listen to me closely, you lovers of the Western world. I, and many like me, will never rest until your beliefs are extinguished, your children are submissive to our rule, and your desecration of the Ottoman Empire avenged."

Slamming the phone back down, Serif motioned to Tanya to get moving. They followed Bogdan out into the turbine building and met the reactor operators who were already standing at the elevator, waiting for Bogdan to catch up. Together, the group of terrorists began their trek down to the circulating water pump room, arriving at the door of the room – a key card reader between them and freedom from the military surge.

———

Rachel had convinced Carson that she couldn't stay in Cernavodă's unit two power block without waving around an INWA identity card. The military would never believe that she wasn't part of the terrorists' plot. Besides, it was easier to guide Carson to the main control room than to try to describe the path of least resistance for him from the unit two side.

Re-entering unit one through another sealed doorway, the two climbed a narrow stairwell and found themselves standing outside the door leading into the kitchen area.

"Wait," Rachel said. "We can look down on the main control room from upstairs. There's a viewing gallery up there. It was installed as part of a retrofit idea from Three Mile Island's political backers."

The idea was that anyone with proper clearance could

stand above the main control room and observe the operators performing their duties. Carson remembered hearing about some of the plants built in the late 70s and early 80s that had this public display feature. The current operators didn't like people coming into the viewing gallery to watch them perform their normal duties, but the decision to build it was made many years before their time.

Climbing stairs to the next elevation, Carson and Rachel slowly entered the viewing gallery room. Thinking that they would be seen if someone glanced their way, they slid behind a metal filing cabinet.

"What can you see down there?" Rachel asked.

Carson was still carrying the gun that they had picked up from the guard, so he put it down on the floor and peeked over the filing cabinet, using both hands to stabilise himself.

"I can't see anyone down there," Carson answered.

He moved to the opposite side of the cabinet and took a more aggressive look over the balcony through one of the tall, thick, slightly tinted plate glass windows. The gallery itself ran for thirty feet, above the long part of one wall of the control room. Not wanting to risk being seen, Carson watched very carefully for any movement around the control panels for several minutes.

Carson moved away from the gallery windows and crouched down beside Rachel. "I don't see anyone moving around down there. They must have left already," he whispered. "I'm gonna have to enter the control room to verify it's empty. You stay here and watch my back."

"*Bine*, I'll tap on the glass with one of these if I see anything," Rachel said, eagerly holding up a metal ruler she found lying on a drawing table. "Be careful."

Carson picked up the Heckler & Koch and went back

down to the kitchen door. He hesitated a moment before opening it with the guard's key card. He brandished his gun around in the open spaces of a foyer, then Carson crept through an open door leading into the kitchen, where the shift operators had been poisoned by the deadly gas. Scanning the area, checking behind every hiding place available, Carson was unable to find a living soul. Confused by what he saw, Carson shook his head and mumbled, "What the devil –"

Stepping into the control room, careful not to let the door slam behind him, Carson walked behind the P730 panel until he could steal a look around the massive piece of human ingenuity. The open spaces of the main control room, where the on-shift operators and Bogdan's crew once stood, were now empty. Audible alarms were sounding on all the panels, creating a deafening ensemble of sirens and warbles. Red, yellow, white, and blue lights were blinking wildly above every panel, trying to grab the attention of a plant operator. Each annunciator window carried a printed message for an operator to take a corrective action in order to mitigate some contributing malfunction to the reactor's problems. Some of the lights continued to flash, even though their message windows were announcing that their controlling circuits had already carried out an automatic function.

Carson could see that his work of separating the remote controls from the main controls ended the terrorists' attempt to pressurise the reactor's containment to the point of rupture – and then meltdown – of the nuclear core. Whoever had entered the remote shutdown panel room after Carson was unable to reinstate the controls to the panels in the main control room. But where were the terrorists now?

Carson stepped up two short steps into the shift manager's riser and looked up at the viewing gallery, where he could see Rachel standing, ruler in hand. He waved for her to come down to the control room. Within minutes, she was standing beside him, observing the same situation. Silencing some of the panel's alarms, Carson began to hear the NATO troops coming through the main control room door. One man, who was shouting orders over a loud radio transmitter, seemed to be in charge. Within seconds, the entire company had entered the control room.

"Whoa! Whoa!" Carson shouted. "I'm with INWA."

Holding their hands in the air to signal that they were not armed, Rachel and Carson stood very still.

"Hold your fire!" Major Sykes shouted to his men. He was a British officer and a long time expeditionary force leader. His previous combat experience included the initial British assault in Iraq's lower provinces and two other classified offensives that he survived unscathed.

Following closely behind the NATO barrage was a small team of nuclear power plant operators from Cernavodă's operations department and two experts from the INWA emergency preparedness organisation.

"You are a very lucky man, Carson Griffin," Sykes said. "Your photograph is not very flattering, but I can tell that it's you."

"Yes, I know," Carson nodded. "If not for luck, I would have been dead some time ago."

"I'm Major Sykes, NATO's first strike force of the Black Sea. Did you happen to see where these bloody terrorists went to?"

"No," Carson replied. "I've spent the whole night avoiding those bastards. I don't know where they might have gone."

"Well, we have the entire plant surrounded. There's no route for them to escape," Sykes said.

As the operations crew worked cautiously to recover control of the reactor, more NATO forces continued to penetrate the outer perimeter of the site boundary, using the path created by the Abrams tank.

Major Sykes ordered his troops to search the area for anyone who might still be near the control room, but it was too late to catch Bogdan's crew – they were already in the circulating pump room. Carson watched as the Cernavodă operators began the long process of putting the main control room in command of the reactor. Reversing his earlier reactor controls separation from the remote shutdown panel was a daunting task for the crew, but their off-normal procedures were more than adequate to complete the undertaking.

Rachel was about to be escorted back down to her workstation, where a cluster of health physics and chemistry personnel were already mustered to support the plant's recovery.

"Thanks for the good times, Carson," Rachel said.

Carson smiled. "Not a problem."

Rachel impulsively hugged him. "I can't believe that we survived! If I ever hear of another terrorist trying to meltdown a nuclear reactor, I know who to call. Take care of yourself, my friend."

"I'll keep my phone charged," Carson replied.

Rachel looked at her military escort. "Let's go, bambino. I need to take a long nap!"

Carson watched her leave, then turned to Major Sykes. He explained how he had defended himself near Cernavodă's river port. Describing the canisters of empty gas near the ventilation fans supplying the main control room, Carson pointed to the isolation logic recovery panel. "I was lucky to escape capture in the reactor building. By the way, you'll find a body in one of the switchgear rooms."

Then suddenly, Carson remembered seeing men at a room near the stairwell that he and Rachel used to get to the eighth floor to make their cell phone call. The men were entering and exiting a room that should have had nothing to do with the control of the reactor itself.

"Major Sykes," Carson said. "There may be something important that we've forgotten, out in the plant. There's a room on the fifth floor we should investigate – below the spent fuel pool. The terrorists may have been using it as a weapons cache."

Sykes nodded. "I'll send a man down with you, but be very careful. Those guys are still out there in the power plant somewhere. We're currently doing a building by building search for the operators who seem to be very experienced at running this reactor."

"Thanks, Major," Carson said.

Leaving the control room, Carson made his way back to the room on the fifth floor. The door was locked after Mrak and Broz made their escape with the two-kilo plutonium pit. Riveted to the door of the room was a small silver sign that read "Spent Fuel Pool Piping Space."

Major Sykes's man opened the door with a master key obtained from Draco's locker in the ruins of the security island. Carson walked inside the dimly lit room with an intense feeling of trepidation. High-powered temporary lights on metal stands illuminated an object behind a separating wall, initially out of Carson's line of sight.

He could see two figures lying on the floor, both very much unable to rise to the occasion.

"You got a torch or a flashlight?" Carson asked the escort.

The soldier handed Carson a camouflaged flashlight, which helped light the darker corners of the foyer. Carson saw

Maks and Daniel's bodies lying near the entrance. One of them he recognised from his brief glimpse while in the switchgear room down the hall. Then it occurred to Carson that these were the two he'd seen on Serif's yacht. It was hard to understand why their bodies were left in the room without regard to the possibility that they would be found rather quickly.

Carson couldn't believe his eyes when he stepped around the wall that blocked his view of the partially dismantled atomic bomb. He saw a semi-spherical implosion device loaded with plastic explosives sitting in the middle of the inner room of the nuclear power plant. Suspended from many small web-like steel wires tied to several stanchions around the sphere, Carson remembered seeing this rig on Serif's boat.

"What the hell is that?" Carson's stunned escort muttered.

Shinning his flashlight into the open cavity of the semi-sphere, Carson could see that the pit he'd seen on Serif's yacht was no longer inside the implosion device. However, the implosion device itself was still connected to a control panel, which seemed to be energised.

"I believe that it was meant to be a nuclear weapon," Carson said. "But some of its essential panels are missing, along with the most critical component – its plutonium core."

He tilted the flashlight away from the bomb and toward the concrete ceiling. The smooth surface seemed so safe beneath the tons of spent nuclear fuel, until his light returned to the huge ball of plastic explosives sitting just below the pool. Carson immediately came to the horrifying conclusion that there were enough explosives sitting underneath the spent fuel pool to blow a huge hole in its bottom – maybe even through some of the spent fuel stored under less than sixteen feet of clear water.

Located on the front of the bomb's detonation control panel, Carson spotted an electronic triggering circuit with its timer displayed through a small glass window counting backwards in milliseconds. The whirling digital clock read in minutes:

49:01:42

"Call Major Sykes on your radio and have him evacuate the site," Carson ordered the soldier. "Tell him that when this bomb goes off, it's gonna create an opening in the spent fuel pool large enough to drain the pool's entire volume of cooling water within an hour from right now."

The soldier nodded and immediately exited with his radio in hand. Carson stayed behind to see if there might be a way to disable the device, but all he could see were many overlapping circuits. Even if he disassembled the tripwire that Mrak had put through the cover of the timer device, he knew there wasn't going to be time to disable the bomb. The two scientists planned to allow this part of their bomb to explode without interruption.

Within five minutes of the soldier leaving the room, three standby bomb experts arrived to assess its damage capabilities. The device was a suspended collection of explosive panes, each with its own circuit emanating from the complicated triggering mechanism. It was obvious to the team that the suspension mechanism holding things in place had been laced with at least three booby traps. Any one of these traps would probably cause the bomb to detonate if an attempt was made to circumvent their purpose. The timer was now down to 38:33:11 minutes and still whirling backwards by the millisecond.

Carson and the experts wanted to minimise the explosion as much as possible by trying to render some of the panels inoperative. The lead bomb expert immediately began to gently remove individual detonators from the explosive panels. Ten minutes later, he motioned for everyone to walk toward the doorway. "Let's go, gentlemen. We're not going to be able to safely disable the bomb any further before she blows this place to kingdom come."

The experts had removed four of the detonators, but it was hardly enough to stop a devastating explosion from taking place. Its massive size and the detonator's instability would not allow them to remove it from the power plant in enough time to prevent it from going off, possibly in the middle of the move.

Once in the hallway, the lead bomb expert gave Major Sykes the bad news over a military walkie-talkie. Sykes ordered another site evacuation. Control room operators were given directions to stay on-station – their controlling of the reactor was essential to maintaining it in a safe shutdown condition. They would be protected by many feet of concrete and steel reinforcements that lay between the control room and the spent fuel pool area of the reactor building.

The leader of the bomb squad grabbed Carson's arm. "We should all get out of here, right now!"

"I couldn't agree more," Carson said.

One of the bomb squad experts closed and dogged down the thick metal door. It might hold the blast if the separation wall between it and the bomb was well built. But the room's ceiling, which was actually the bottom of the spent fuel pool, would be breached by the upsurge of energy since the focus of the blast had always been in that direction. The digital indicator on the timer device now read 02:42:01.

The men ran down to ground level and found the nearest escape route – a railway bay at the front of the power block, facing the main gate. During construction, much of the primary system piping and supporting equipment had been delivered by a flatbed carriage. Next to the train bay's roll-up door was an emergency exit with a crash bar that the men ran through as they tried to get as far away from the massive plastic explosive as possible. Carson was the last to leave, still trying to think of a way to stop the detonation, but there was no other way.

CHAPTER 29

Ciprian and Franco had quickly made their way to a manhole near the circulating water pump room, which was actually a separate building. Using a crowbar, they wrestled with the cover, trying to get it off as fast as possible. Bogdan and his crew were preparing to drop through the manhole.

Mrak stood looking outside at the morning sun, his back to the door. "Broz, I believe that we are not going to find a better way out of this situation."

"I am afraid you're right, my good friend," Broz said, standing beside Mrak.

The two scientists turned around to see six men and one woman staring at them from between the two gigantic circulating water pumps – both machines deadly silent and at a standstill. Power was lost to the pumps long before Mrak and Broz entered the pump house. It would take several days to recover the power grid from the NATO assault it had taken over the past six hours. The remaining diesel generators were supplying emergency power to all the reactor support systems until normal power could be restored.

Bogdan turned to Serif. "What is this?"

Serif was not ready to explain himself to Bogdan, who only two days earlier had been a boat captain on a piece of shit tin can. "I will handle these two."

Tanya stepped toward the two scientists alongside Serif.

"Did you finish your staging of the nuclear weapon?" Serif demanded.

"We had a change of heart," Mrak stated. "We decided that you are an evil fool of the grandest magnitude."

Broz was stunned that Mrak had decided to make this his final stand, but he went along with his colleague and friend. He knew that they should have been killed as soon as their work was completed anyway.

"I would have to agree with my old friend," Broz said.

Mrak shook with rage. "You and your sick brother can go to hell! I will never answer to you again," he bellowed.

"Why do you talk to me this way, Mrak?" Serif asked, shocked at the man's fury. "You know that your life hangs in the balance of my grace."

"Your grace is a pit of darkness. Only sin and destruction wait in its heart," Broz snarled.

Tanya noticed that Broz was carrying a Pelican case and pointed to it. "What do you have there, scientist? It looks very heavy."

Broz ignored her. "I will not be part of your crazy plans any longer," he said, glaring at Serif. "Do what you wish with us! We are through."

Not hesitating, Tanya raised her silenced 9mm pistol and shot Broz in the face. Blood, skin, and tissue flew everywhere. Tanya calmly walked over to the Pelican case and opened it. She found the two-kilo plutonium pit. "So, Serif, now what do you think of your great scientists?"

"Mrak, you disappoint me," Serif said, genuinely hurt. "I would not have killed you."

"You are a liar and a terrorist," Mrak sneered.

Serif put his hand on the old man's shoulder and stepped

behind him. "I can no longer trust you, my disloyal servant."

Serif's blade coldly penetrated Mrak's back, stabbing him through the heart. The white lab coat he was wearing instantly absorbed the warm red blood. His body fell in a heap onto the concrete floor of the pump room.

"Come, Tanya," Serif motioned. "Bring the case with you."

Bogdan, Marius, and the others had already dropped through the manhole into the cold water and were breathing the air left in the top of the tunnel leading out to Cernavodă's canal. Each man started swimming to the mouth of the concrete intake structure, where they would pick up their scuba tanks positioned there by Bogdan's fishing boat two days earlier. Reza had also provided them with eight sets of underwater jet boots that would give them an extra thrust while swimming downstream in the deep canal.

Tanya stepped off the edge of the manhole and fell nearly twelve feet before hitting the blackish water. The water's stench was overwhelming and Tanya fought the urge to throw up when her head came back to the surface. Bumping against something hard floating beside her, Tanya quickly realised that Serif had already lowered the Pelican case with the two-kilos of plutonium into the water. Watertight, the case's buoyancy kept it afloat as Tanya disconnected the nylon cord from its handle. Serif would need to admit a little water into the case when they reached the end of the tunnel, in order to swim below the surface of the canal with the plutonium in tow.

Serif took another look around the room, then stepped off the manhole's edge and plunged into the cold water. He and Tanya swam out to where the others were anxiously waiting for them with their scuba gear already donned and their jet boots strapped onto their calves. Serif and Tanya quickly put on their underwater gear. Marius, being their best swimmer, led the group of seven out into Cernavodă canal. They used a nylon cord to help keep them together and swimming in the same direction.

Once in the canal itself, the currents toward the Black Sea helped them with their escape swim, sweeping them along. Thirty minutes later, they emerged near a small village where Bogdan's boat waited outside the evacuation zone. He had spared no expense in stealing a fast, sleek speedboat. The operating crew of terrorists sat quietly near the vessel's stern while Serif again opened Mrak's pelican case. The sphere glared back at him as he viewed the potentially powerful lump of heavy metal. Power that he had almost been able to use to reinstate his country's medieval reign once again over much of Europe.

The Christmas morning sun shone brightly over the wake they were leaving as the crew and passengers navigated to the Black Sea in the speedboat, undetected. Evacuated waterways, within the ten mile EPZ around the site, created a water traffic problem that veiled their getaway. Tanya watched the passing landscape along the narrow channel as she contemplated why they had failed to execute at least one of their two strategies to spread radioactive contamination over Western Europe. She and Serif now knew that Carson Griffin had stopped the meltdown of the reactor's nuclear core and the breaching of the containment building by using the remote shutdown panel controls. His actions had prevented the terrorists from contaminating targeted European countries to the point of inhabitability. The loss of control of the reactor so early into their plan was catastrophic. Once the controls had been separated from the main control room by Carson, their long awaited ballroom dance with the powerful nuclear reactor abruptly ended.

"I will find this Carson Griffin," Serif said, his dark eyes staring fiercely at the churning black waters.

Tanya snapped back to reality and turned to Serif. "It will be easy to find him and his family. You must have revenge for Reza."

"Yes, I know he killed my brother," Serif said. "And it was Griffin on my yacht. Here's a picture that Bogdan took of this INWA operative."

Serif closed the case as Marius steered the speedboat towards the last port along the canal before reaching the Black Sea at Constanta. They would have to find a good place to hide their boat for a few minutes, so that Serif and Tanya could get out. Marius positioned it near a pier jutting from a grassy hill at the end of long row of ships. Bogdan's crew tied off the boat, and Tanya leapt across a low wall along the pier's edge.

Handing the Pelican case to his cousin, Serif stepped off the boat and called back to Bogdan, "You take your men to the rendezvous. I will meet you there with your money in seven days."

"Aye," Bogdan replied.

Serif took the case from Tanya, and the two walked toward town, while Bogdan and his men headed out into the Black Sea. Bogdan, Ciprian, and Franco would continue along the coastline until they reached Istanbul where they were to board a commercial ocean liner. Their pleasure cruise would take several days, travelling from Istanbul through the Mediterranean to Amsterdam, where they were planning to change to a Scandinavian line that would take them on to Riga, Latvia. Each man had a new passport, identifying them as Latvian citizens.

Although an international manhunt was now underway for the architect and perpetrators of the attack on Cernavodă's nuclear facility, Serif and Reza had planned their escape routes very carefully, using sea travel as much as possible to minimise their being tracked.

———

Marius and Jacob broke off from the group and would cruise along the Romanian coast near Constanta, using the only planned land route to Riga. Marius had made this arrangement with Reza while they were in the cave outside the Tryst Café. He had even saved enough money from his advance to buy the silver fox coat for his mother before going underground for a few years.

Marius and Jacob bought a slightly used Dacia in Constanta and began their drive to Latvia, via Bran's Castle.

"Can you believe what has happened?" Marius asked Jacob as they drove.

Jacob was saddened and disappointed by the way things had turned out. "No, I can't believe it. Reza and Serif have always been so careful to follow through with their promises."

The Dacia's steering felt sloppy to Jacob as he drove toward the Carpathian Mountains. The two nuclear power plant operators turned terrorists veered onto a back road to avoid the police and militia who may have established roadblocks around the larger cities and major highways.

"Jacob, I've got something important to tell you – it concerns our future," Marius said. "Truth be told, I've been contacted by the Turkish underground."

Jacob had resigned himself to withdrawing from society after the Cernavodă attack, but Marius had been his friend for a long time, and he worried about his safety. "What do you mean, Turkish underground? We are finished with this business!" Jacob retorted.

"These guys are very serious about their work, believe me," Marius continued as he steered the Dacia around the many potholes in the road. "I met one of them about two weeks ago. He said he was keeping an eye on things in Cernavodă and wanted me to tell him if anything went wrong."

"What was the guy's name?" Jacob asked, stunned by Marius's connection with Turkish terrorists.

Marius and Jacob had always gotten their directions from Bogdan and had never actually spoken to any of the Turkish underground themselves. Marius hesitated, trying to decide whether to tell Jacob about the money he had been offered or to let him make his own deal with the Turks.

Finally, Marius said, "He didn't actually give me his name, just a phone number."

"Just a phone number?" Jacob fired back.

"Yes. Anyway, I told them that you may be interested in making some extra money working for them," Marius said, withholding further information concerning his contact. "Face it, we are never going to return to Romania, and we could make a lot of money working for these guys. They are backed by the big oil cartels of the Middle East."

Jacob knew that everyone would be getting plastic surgery in a few days, and he would have to start a new life. Knowing that he wouldn't be getting everything that they had been promised because of the botched job at Cernavodă, Jacob wanted to walk away from this deal – it smelled of betrayal.

"I am going to have to pass," Jacob replied. "I want to find a nice warm place to relax for a few years."

Marius stared down the road as the two sat in silence for a few minutes. "I am supposed to meet to my contact in

Buzău and introduce you to him," Marius said. "Let me tell him that you are in, Jacob."

"No, I am out of this business!" Jacob replied emphatically. "After we meet in Riga with Serif and get our money, I want to leave everything behind me and move on."

Marius was disappointed – he knew that one day he might have to kill his good friend because of telling him his secret, but he was willing to do anything for the kind of money the Turks were offering him. Marius's military background and his ability to get things done gave them confidence in his competency – he would make a fine Europe-based assassin.

Two hours later, they entered Buzău and drove to Dacia Square in the heart of the city. Parking their car near the mosaic of white, red, and grey Măgura marble that covered hundreds of square yards in front of the Communal Palace, the men walked to a marble obelisk in Crâng Park. Within moments, a man wearing a thick black overcoat and black boots came over to them.

"Jacob, I would like for you to meet a Chechen hero," Marius said.

"Hello," the man said, looking into Jacob's eyes with great intensity. "You can call me Adriana."

Jacob felt intimidated, but stood up to the man. "I appreciate your offer, Adriana. But I do not wish to join you."

"That's a shame, Jacob. Marius had spoken so highly of you," Adriana sighed faintly. "If you change your mind, just call this number and ask for Adriana."

"That's an easy name to remember," Jacob said, taking a business card with a phone number printed across its surface.

"Yes, it's your sister's name. That's why I chose it – to remind you that I know where your family lives," Adriana said.

Looking over at Marius, Adriana tipped his black hat,

smiled and left as abruptly as he had arrived.

Marius walked Jacob back to their Dacia, and the two drove away from Crâng Park without saying a word to each other. Marius contemplated the thought of killing his friend during their journey but decided to wait until after the money was split in Riga. Jacob felt a chilling pane of ice form between them, the colour of his peril – red.

CHAPTER 30

arson was out of breath from the long run down the reactor building's staircases as he reached the outside of Cernavodă's nuclear plant. He now stood with the Romanian ambassador to INWA, waiting for an explosion that could not be avoided. Looking around the plant yard, Carson saw hundreds of Romanian and NATO soldiers roaming around the site. What he remembered as gate one's security island was now a pile of rubble, steel protruding from underneath several tons of concrete.

Suddenly, Carson could feel the earth shudder under his feet. Then the sound of a distant rumble came from deep inside the nuke plant. Some onlookers thought they would see the roof blow off of the reactor building, but the thick concrete and steel walls of the power plant held very well against the force of Mrak and Broz's bomb implosion apparatus. Had the device been complete with its plutonium core, there would have been a tragically different story on the international news media.

Channel One of INWA's command station radio, currently monitoring the plant's normal airwave traffic, was jammed with chatter coming in from several of Cernavodă's building operators who were working diligently inside the nuclear plant. The evacuation orders for essential personnel were repealed after the explosion – there was no reason to believe that there would be another bomb.

"Reactor building operator, this is the main control room," a voice said.

"This is the reactor building operator. I am outside the storage room below the spent fuel pool now. It looks like the outer walls held, but I can hear water flowing somewhere in the room."

"Reactor building operator, do not open the hatch to that room," the voice said.

"Aye, I will go one level down to see if there is any damage underneath," the operator replied.

"Affirmative. Reactor building operator, be informed that the spent fuel pool level is lowering rapidly and will uncover spent fuel very soon," the voice said.

A few minutes later, the reactor operator was on the radio. "The room two floors down is filling with water as well. I opened the hatch and could see a big hole in the ceiling above. I think the bomb must have blown a hole in the floor of the room above me and the bottom of the spent fuel pool."

"Dog down that hatch and go to the emergency make-up valve for the spent fuel pool," the plant supervisor urgently ordered. "We are losing the cooling water that's keeping the fuel bundles from overheating."

A NATO radioman was standing alongside the Romanian ambassador and translating the radio traffic to him as the operators explained the situation to the control room. Overhearing the reports, Carson knew that keeping water over the spent fuel was essential to maintaining the fuel's outer metal covering intact. The ten-foot, pencil-sized fuel pins, stored vertically in tubes in the pool, created an enormous residual heat load once removed from the reactor. Some of the 3,750 bundles stored in the holding racks deep underwater were blown to pieces by the bomb.

The uranium pellets from the damaged fuel pins were heavier than water and sank directly into the two rooms below the spent fuel pool, through the explosion openings in the floor and ceiling. Long, thin, shiny tubes that once held the black pellets were spread all over the floors of the two rooms, as well. The copious amount of water flowing through the hole in the bottom of the spent fuel pool soon filled the lower level room and started to fill the upper room just under the pool.

"Looks like the spent fuel level is nearing half its normal level," a reactor operator said to the plant supervisor.

"Get that make-up water going," the shift manager ordered.

"You heard the man," the plant supervisor said. "Get an operator to the make-up panel, right now! We need that valve open!"

The reactor building operator radioed the control room. "I have opened the emergency water supply to the spent fuel pool." The water was helping, but the pool level continued to lower as it filled the room just below. Within a few minutes, the water was barely two feet above the top of the spent fuel; then the level finally stopped going down. The control room indicators were only calibrated to measure the top four feet of water in the pool. No one ever imagined that the operators would need to know the water level when it was so low.

"I have lost indication of any water level in the spent fuel pool," the reactor operator said.

The rooms below had finally filled themselves with water, ultimately stabilising the pool at the extremely low level. The heat energy remaining in the spent fuel that was recently discharged from the reactor into the pool would soon begin to boil the water left behind – evaporating it completely. Once the fuel was exposed, there would be nothing to keep it cool, and its cladding would crack open, releasing fission products into a part of the reactor building. Unlike the reactor located inside a containment structure, the spent fuel was exposed, due to the unfortunate design accepted before terrorism had become so rampant in the world. A corrugated steel roof with little resistance to a rising plume of radioactive contamination was the only thing that stood between potentially damaged fuel and the world's atmosphere.

Operators in the control room were watching intently as the radiation levels in the reactor building began to increase rapidly. Ventilation systems, taking suction from the fuel pool area, realigned themselves to limit the release of contamination through the exhaust piping. Charcoal filter trains began to clean up the atmosphere within the building, but they would soon be depleted. Within a few hours, the situation would become much worse if the operators could not get water on top of the hot nuclear fuel.

The INWA command centre's radio continued to squawk. "Open the emergency make-up water supply all the way!" a voice shouted. "We've got to get water into that pool right now!"

"The make-up valve has been fully open for a long time, control room!" the reactor building operator replied.

Carson remembered seeing two fire hose stations on either side of the spent fuel pool when he and Rachel were trying to make their cell phone call to Herman. He went over to INWA's command centre table where three experienced co-ordinators were examining the plant layout. The off-site coordinator looked up from the diagrams as Carson approached.

"My name is Carson Griffin. I'm with INWA."

"Yeah, I know who you are," the coordinator snapped. "No time to talk." He turned away to order another back-up team of operators from Bucharest.

Carson persisted. "Look, I saw a couple of fire hoses on the pool main floor. And I know the fire pumps are equipped with diesel motors."

The coordinator turned back around to Carson. "I see. Excellent idea, Griffin."

Picking up a direct line into the control room, the coordinator said, "Control room to reactor building operator."

"Go ahead," the operator replied.

"Go to the spent fuel deck, open the nozzle valves for the two fire hoses, and put them directly into the spent fuel pool. Then open their supply valves and leave the area immediately. We are already getting high radiation alarms in that zone."

"Affirmative, I understand that it is in a high radiation zone," the reactor building operator said.

"That's correct," the plant supervisor replied. "The shift manager has requested that you perform this action to save the lives of many others in your country."

Carson listened for the confirmation, knowing it would not be long before the fuel began giving off very high radiation to anyone exposed and unprotected on the spent fuel deck. It was hard to say how much radiation the operator would get, depending on the final water level in the pool and his time spent in the vicinity. The water, acting as a coolant and as a radiation shield, was drained from the spent fuel pool into the two rooms below, and the emergency make-up system was not keeping up with the remaining water's rapid evaporation.

"Reactor building operator, this is the main control room," the plant supervisor said.

Everyone standing around Carson was waiting for the reply, but none came.

"Reactor building operator, control room," the radio squawked.

Everyone around Carson looked worried.

A young voice from a weak, yet determined-sounding, operator was finally heard. "Hoses in pool, valves are open."

"Roger that reactor building operator," the control room voice replied. "Thank you. What's your current location?"

The weak voice replied, "I'm in the stairwell leading down to ground level, control room. I don't feel too good, control room. Please advise."

The INWA coordinator called the shift manager and informed him that he had sent in a rescue team to recover the reactor building operator.

"Make your way down to the ground level. We're sending some people in to get you," the plant supervisor said over the radio. "Looks like you've accomplished your mission. The spent fuel pool level is returning,"

Indications in the main control room showed that both firewater pumps were running. An automatic valve opened and put more water from Cernavodă's canal into the storage tank. The fact that the water quality was incredibly bad was unimportant – it would do the job of cooling and shielding the highly radioactive spent fuel.

With both rooms underneath the spent fuel pool filled with water, the pool stabilised near its original level. It would now protect workers cleaning up the mess, but no one knew how long that would take. The maintenance personnel would need to first repair the damage done by the bomb, using some specialised assistance from INWA.

C'arson opened a bottle of water and drank it all down in large gulps. "Do you guys have a landline that I could use to call my wife?"

An INWA health physics worker pointed to a table of telephones near a wall of the tent. "Sure, use any of those."

Dialling Christy's cell phone, Carson heard the telephone's muffled volume. "Hello, honey."

Christy's voice was shaky but filled with relief. "Carson, are you okay?"

"Yeah, it's been quite a trip to Romania," Carson said. "Is Susan with you?"

"No, she's at home in case you called there first," Christy replied. "When will you get here?"

"I don't know for sure, babe. They want a full report before I leave the country."

Christy exhaled. "Thank God you're okay."

"I'll call again when things get organised," Carson said. "Love you."

"Love you, too," Christy replied. "Hurry home."

Carson started writing notes at a table in the back of the command centre – recording everything that had happened, starting with the first day of his inspection in the Carpathian Alps. He remembered the drive past Bran's Castle and his conversation with the fur trader. It occurred to him that the gas canisters he saw in the back of the white Mercedes van were the same military canisters he had seen in the ventilation room supplying the main control room with poisonous gas.

Carson grabbed a cell phone from a row of six that were

in a multi-charging station and headed out to a helicopter parked near the gate of the power plant. He was grateful to be wearing a warm and comfortable black bomber jacket provided by the staff of the ambassador to INWA.

Carson contacted Herman at the emergency response centre in Vienna. "Herman, I don't have much time to discuss why, but I need a favour."

"Anything, buddy," Herman said.

"I remember seeing a white van near Bran's Castle with Russian gas canisters in it, and a guy who promised to return for his mother's silver fox coat was driving the van. It was the same terrorist that I saw last night running into the power block," Carson stated excitedly. "I know that he's going back up to the castle, probably on his way right now."

"Take it easy, Kit Carson," Herman said. "Todd told me what you've been through."

"I'm not sure who I can trust here, Herman," Carson said. "Get Todd to clear me using INWA's helicopter to get up to that mountain – this guy could be on his way there to see his mother right now."

"I trust you know what you're talking about, Carson," Herman said. "Todd's in with top brass trying to figure out who these guys are. We'll get you what you need."

"Thanks, Herman."

The helicopter was about a half mile walk from the front of the plant, so by the time Carson reached it, the NATO pilot had already been called by his commander. Todd had given instructions to fly Carson north to Bran's Castle, telling NATO command he was needed for an Agency routine task, withholding the true nature of his mission.

"You Carson Griffin?" the pilot shouted over the roar of the chopper blades.

"Yeah," Carson yelled.

"I've gotta make this run quick," the pilot said. "We've got more injured personnel to move to Bucharest once they're stabilised."

Carson swiftly climbed aboard, and the pilot jerked the chopper off the ground, heading northwest at near full speed. Moments later, as the pilot glanced down at one of the huge barges from the Black Sea, Carson's attention was momentarily glued to the cave entrance where he had seen Bogdan and his crew load the white vans with equipment for their attack. Flying in the helicopter had the added advantage of being able to watch Bogdan's timed explosion destroy the cave, closing its entrance with tons of rock. Carson watched as dust flew high in the air after being blown out of the mouth of cave and through an old vent shaft. The explosives did their job very well.

———

The helicopter landed in a large open field south of Brasov near Bran's Castle. Carson could hardly believe that only two days earlier he had seen Marius bargain with the fur trader over the silver fox coat.

Carson yelled his thanks to the pilot, who gave him a quick salute and shut the door of the chopper. He lifted off into the fog that had descended over the mountain.

Carson jumped small bushes as he ran through high grass. Not much of a hurdler, he fell once before reaching the tree line. He knew it would be a short jog to a position near the bazaar. Close to the top of the hill, dense undergrowth hid an old Romanian graveyard – some of its headstones dating back to the thirteenth century. It was cold and the fog blocked any sunlight that was trying to penetrate the forest of evergreen trees. Carson was forced to go through the eerie graveyard.

Stepping onto a weathered tombstone, black and green from mold, he slipped and fell head first into a clump of thistles. His black bomber jacket protected him from the long thorns, but some had cut his hands and the right side of his face. Stunned a bit from the fall, and bleeding, Carson continued out of the graveyard and down the hillside.

A clearing at the bottom of the hill led to a paved road. Carson remembered driving on this road, winding his way narrowly through the mountains before passing near the bazaar. He arrived at an outdoor café where he could watch for Marius's approach to the fur trader's stand. Carson headed straight for the bathroom and washed the blood that was drying on his face and hands. He came back into the café and ordered a coffee as he observed from a safe distance the fur trader discussing the price of coats and hats with potential customers. Carson watched as the man sold two coats and a red fox wrap over the next two hours.

It was beginning to get late when Carson noticed a white Dacia pull into the dirt car park. Two young men stepped out of the car; Carson immediately recognised Marius. He watched him go over to the fur trader, shake his hand, and give the man some money. The fur trader turned around and took Marius's beautiful silver fox coat from a rack behind a canvas tarpaulin. Even from a distance the coat was gorgeous – silver-white with a hint of black deep within the fur.

Carson paid for his coffee and watched closely as the two men got back into their Dacia. Jacob admired the coat for several minutes, the car idling as they spoke. Carson knew he would have to follow them carefully if he wanted to find the plutonium pit that he had been so close to taking from Serif's yacht.

Marius put the fox coat into the back of the Dacia and drove out of the car park. They steered clear of a gypsy's sheepskin-covered wagon and started up the narrow road toward one of the nearby mountains.

Carson quickly scanned the area for transportation when he noticed a man getting out of his gold Satellite Sebring convertible. He left his car running to keep it warm as he ran into the coffee shop for what he thought would be a quick cup of coffee to go. Carson jumped into the car and drove after the Dacia up the side of a fairly steep mountain, dodging pedestrians along the way. When the man returned, holding his Turkish coffee with heavy cream, he stared in speechless surprise at the now empty space where his car had been idling.

The road wound its way through wooded areas separated by occasional openings of green winter grass and waist-high thistles. As they got higher, Carson could see snow at the base of larger trees. The late afternoon sun began to break through the thinner fog of the higher altitude, letting Carson put more distance between his car and the Dacia. A few minutes later, Marius pulled onto a dirt side road that led to an old shack.

Parking the Satellite further up the mountain, Carson watched mother and son reunite through a pair of binoculars he found in a birdwatching kit in the back seat of his host's vehicle. Romania's many species of rare birds in the delta region and in the mountains attracted naturalists from around the world.

Jacob took the silver fox coat out of the car and handed it to Marius, who presented it to his mother. Carson could see her cry and grab Marius's neck with her large, fat arms that nearly covered his entire head. She wore a brightly decorated smock and over it a ragged brown coat that she quickly threw to the ground as she put on her new fur. Together, the three went inside the shack, its windows faintly lit and smoke coming from a stone fireplace flue.

Carson sat in the car in uncomfortable anticipation, hoping they weren't going to be sitting down to a meal, or perhaps an overnight stay. An anxious few minutes went by, then the door opened and the two terrorists came out and got into their Dacia. Carson had already turned the Satellite around by the time they had decided to leave. He pulled out of his wooded hiding place, pacing himself safely behind them as they made their way back down the mountain.

Marius drove to Brasov in the Transylvania region, and they checked into a beautiful ski resort hotel. Carson watched from the car and used his mobile telephone to take four or five pictures of the Dacia and its number plate. Without an electronic tracking device to help him keep up with the car, he removed the left rear hubcap from its wheel, throwing it into a wooded area below the hotel car park. Then he ripped a piece of red plastic from a huge pothole barrier near the entrance of the hotel and tied it to the car's right rear bumper.

Using his encrypted mobile telephone, Carson called Todd. "I'm in Brasov, and I found two of the terrorists, as we hoped," he said.

"Your suspicions were correct," Todd replied. "Good work. Stay with them until you can confirm the location of the pit."

"Todd, do me a favour. Contact Christy and let her know I'm gonna be late," Carson said.

"I'll let her know. And you be careful. Please."

"Giving it my best," Carson said and hung up.

Carson checked into the hotel with a window directly

adjacent to the Dacia and set his alarm to wake him every two hours. He spent the next six hours trying to get some sleep, before getting up the next morning and positioning himself so that he could watch for the two men coming out of the hotel. When the men finally came out of their room, they climbed into their car and drove northward, through a multitude of small villages along the way to their next hotel. The car was easy enough for Carson to spot on the road as they continued their trek the next morning, red flag whipping wildly from its bumper.

After the third day of following the terrorists, Carson called Christy to let her know that he was fine and not to worry. Christy assured him that she understood that he was in the middle of a mission and couldn't come home for a few days. Their conversation lasted for about forty-five minutes before Christy got around to bringing up Cernavodă.

"I was really worried when Todd told me that you were in the middle of the Cernavodă incident," Christy reminded Carson.

Carson brushed back the curtain in his rundown hotel room for one more look at the Dacia. "Yeah, that was a close one."

"You be careful, Carson Griffin," Christy scolded.

"I will," Carson said. "Gotta go, love ya."

A couple of days later, Carson felt completely exhausted. He hadn't had a decent meal in a long time and needed to get a full night's rest without the constant two hour interruptions. While he watched Marius pump forty litres of benzene into their small fuel tank, Carson called Todd to let him know what was happening.

Todd was surprised that the two were now in Belarus and still using small back roads to avoid the police. Not wanting to draw attention to Carson's pursuit, Todd kept the information of where Marius and Jacob were travelling to himself.

Carson followed them for six days through ex-Soviet territories – all the way to Riga, Latvia.

CHAPTER 31

Portentous Tavern was dimly lit, although it was two thirty in the afternoon. Turkish water pipes were positioned in the middle of every table, and each was surrounded by knee-high sheepskin-covered stools. Serif entered and walked briskly through a crowd of men smelling of tobacco and body odour. His mentor would be sitting at a handmade secretary's desk through red leather doors, padded with sheep's wool to muffle any voices coming from the other side. The leather was stained with tobacco tar from smoke that was generated by a band of Turkish gunslingers scattered around – some seated at tables, others walking around in fine Italian shoes and expensive designer jackets.

Many of the men carried automatic weapons and paraded their long black moustaches around as they watched Serif walk past them, audaciously carrying his plastic Pelican box. One man wore the large-brimmed black hat that signified he was a member of the reigning mafia of Istanbul. Smoking a fat Sumatran cigar, the man looked sinister sitting in a hand-carved high back chair against a wall next to the red leather double doors.

Searched from head to toe, Serif now waited to be seen by a man whose face was always hidden from him when he had been summoned for two short audiences prior to that day. Hidden behind a Persian tapestry, the man would speak through a voice distorter – the ultimate secrecy.

The man in the black hat watched Serif's every move until a small blue light mounted in an antique light fixture suddenly illuminated. Leaning forward in his chair, the doorman's face was now fully visible. Serif could see a deep blade scar in the blue light's faint glow. Healed for many years, the crisscrossed furrows on his forehead looked like a warning to anyone who might decide to speak to him without an invitation. Wearing a sarcastic smirk, he waved Serif forward.

Another thug opened the red leather door allowing Serif to enter the room; it was elaborately decorated in Turkish furniture – Persian rugs and gold fixtures at every turn. Serif could see that the tapestry once used to hide the identity of his mentor had been removed on this evening. His gaze quickly focused on a large man sitting behind an ornate secretary in the darkened room – lanterns and candles were burning around the room.

"Come in, Serif," a voice boomed. "Shake the appreciative hand of Shamil Barayev."

As the man stood up in front of him and extended his huge hand, the blood drained from Serif's bewildered face. He was stunned at the sight of Barayev, after so many years of hiding. Barayev's face looked weathered and scarred from years of war, fighting, and living in severe climates where temperatures ranged from below freezing to near brain-boiling heat.

Serif stepped forward. "I thought that you were dead."

Barayev's death had been falsely reported over the international covert operations grapevine, extending from the Kremlin to Langley. He was supposedly killed by a barbed wire improvised explosive device (IED), but in fact he had survived, allowing his best "lookalike" to take the hit for him.

He had become too popular as the resistance's leader and was getting a lot of publicity. The Special Purpose Islamic Regiment of Chechnya needed a new face at the forefront of the resistance to carry on what Barayev had begun. He would serve their cause better by raising money through the Turkish support network.

"Life has a way of surprising us all. I must maintain my identity secret – my enemies are everywhere," Barayev said. "Take a seat; let's talk about your future."

Serif sat in an intricately carved wooden chair once owned by the Sultan of Turkey, Barayev in its larger twin behind his desk.

"I have brought you the remains of our atomic weapon," Serif said apologetically. "I was betrayed by the scientists we agreed to employ."

Although there were two water pipes in the room, Barayev lit a Churchill-sized cigar. "Yes, I have seen the news."

"I ask you for a chance to redeem myself and avenge my brother's death," Serif said, his voice firm but humble.

Silence in the room allowed Serif to hear the faintest sound of shuffling. He shifted his eyes rapidly in the direction of the sound and saw a black panther chained to a column – it momentarily startled him. Immediately returning his gaze to Barayev, Serif waited for his verdict. The panther settled down to finish his half-eaten human femur bone.

"Take this case and make me another bomb, Serif," Barayev said, waving toward the Pelican case. "I will tell you later where we will use it."

"Thank you, General," Serif said. "I have one other request, sir."

Barayev nodded. "Pick up your gold on your way out."

Without a word Serif stood and turned to leave the

room, Pelican case in hand.

"Serif," Barayev added, pulling his thumb across his neck. "If you fail me again – you and your family."

Serif respectfully bowed his head toward Barayev and left the room, taking care to watch the men as he carried the two-kilo plutonium sphere out of the notorious Portentous Tavern. He realised that he would now have to find another scientist who would be capable of building a fully function-ing nuclear weapon. Not an easy thing to do with such a small amount of nuclear material. The scientist would have to be well educated by one of the medium powers of the world; su-perpowers were now a thing of the past. Only the US could afford to construct super carriers, boomers, or stealth weap-ons of inestimable destruction. *Kazakhstan's nuclear scientists might be useful*, Serif thought as he walked through the crowd of Turks to the tavern entrance.

———

Tanya was waiting for Serif at the Istanbul harbour aboard Barayev's newest yacht, the Isis. She was a beautiful vessel, much like the one that Serif left at the Cernavodă port, seaworthy, fast, and built by the Ro-manians. He was disappointed that he had to leave his boat sitting in that dreadful little harbour on the canal. Because Carson Griffin had been all over his yacht and would have surely passed any information he had learned onto Interpol, Serif would now have to take Barayev's yacht through the Mediterranean and north to Riga, where he was planning to meet Bogdan and his crew – he still owed them the balance of their earnings.

"I didn't think you'd come out of the Portentous, Serif," Tanya said. "And you have our money!"

Serif put the leather satchel with the gold on the pier and the Pelican case over the edge of the yacht's port side. "We were given another chance, my cousin," he said with a sigh.

"The money is down payment for building a new nuke!" Tanya exclaimed incredulously.

Tanya was fatigued from lack of sleep over the past few days – she had endured many restless nights prior to their plan finally unfolding. She now found herself further isolated from her country, and, even worse, she had no control of her own destiny, especially now that Serif was back on board with the plutonium pit.

"Do we have a choice, Serif?" Tanya asked.

"No, we are fortunate that we were given a chance to redeem ourselves," Serif replied.

With that said, the two terrorist cousins left port and headed out to sea.

━━━━━

Arriving at the Grand Palace Hotel in Riga on New Year's Eve, Marius and Jacob checked into the rooms that had been reserved by their colleagues the day before. Bogdan, Franco, and Ciprian had arrived by train two days earlier, carrying all their belongings in rucksacks slung across their backs. Carson parked the Satellite near enough to watch the two men he had been tailing for the last week go inside the five-star hotel in the cobblestoned fifteenth century city centre.

Remnants of the Christmas celebration were still scattered around the centre square near the hotel. A huge cider tree log lay at the base of a Christmas tree at one end of the square. Decorated with banners and painted with red and white stripes, the log had been pulled through the city of Riga by a group of young men and women on Christmas Eve, along with many others. They claimed that the logs would pick up bad spirits while being dragged through the entire city; then while chanting *Cal a Dor* (Come out into the Fire) the logs were burned in the middle of Riga's town square. The practice was a medieval pagan worshiper's ritual that was still carried on by the citizens of Riga – now mainly for the tourists.

Carson walked into the hotel lobby wearing clothes he had picked up along the way from Istanbul: jeans, a black shirt, and a rucksack across his right shoulder. He blended in well in the bustling room full of tourists and business people. He overheard many of them talking about the log-burning festivities, but what Carson wanted to know most had nothing to do with pagan celebrations. He wanted to know why two men had travelled the 1,100 miles from Romania all the way to Riga, Latvia. He suspected that there would eventually be a regrouping of the terrorist crew, since their Cernavodă plan had failed. His suspicions quickly evaporated when he saw Bogdan standing near the check-in desk, talking to a squatty Latvian man.

Ducking into a side café off the lobby's main floor, Carson watched Bogdan shake hands with Marius and Jacob, then escort them to the check-in desk. They were soon on their way upstairs via an old four-passenger elevator, with a baggage-toting bellhop following closely behind. Remembering how Bogdan had beaten him for information during his long interrogation brought Carson's blood to a simmer, but he held his temper in hopes of getting closer to Serif.

Carson sat in a black velvet booth and ordered a fruit

punch from a hovering waiter. He sipped on the concoction for an hour, waiting to see if the terrorists would return downstairs. Dinner was being served at eight in the dining room.

Around eight thirty, the elaborately decorated wooden elevator doors opened, and Bogdan, Marius, and Jacob stepped out, walked through the lobby, and entered the dining room. Balloons hung from the ceiling around the room, and long strings of coloured crepe paper flowed from one windowsill to the next. The modest New Year's Eve decorations disguised the kitchen from the rest of the dining room, creating a motif of medieval Latvian celebration.

The place was soon crowded with tourists, and all the tables were taken. Ciprian and Franco had now joined Bogdan, Marius, and Jacob. Bogdan slipped the maître d' some Euros, and within minutes the five men were sitting in a small, semi-private room where they would be able to talk without having to yell over a small string ensemble.

Carson took advantage of the pause in the group's movements and checked into the hotel's one remaining suite, using his specially funded credit card under the name Chase Moseley. An INWA inspector's per diem was much less than what he was going to have to shell out upon departure, but he couldn't afford to leave the hotel and lose track of Bogdan, whom Carson was confident would soon make contact with Serif.

Feeling fortunate not to have been noticed by any of the men so far, Carson would have to change his appearance if he was going to maintain such close proximity to the terrorists. Grabbing a walking cane from the umbrella urn near the elevator he went up to his suite.

Carson called an escort service and then changed into a dark blue suit, white shirt, and a conservative tie. He placed a small tack in his left shoe to remind him to limp when he walked. Carson then molded the six-day hair growth on his face into a goatee and shaved his head with a four blade disposable razor until it was shining. Adding some padding into his shirt's belly gave him the appearance of an older man. His disguise complete, Carson left his suite and headed for the elevator.

The female escort Carson had arranged to meet in the lobby arrived on time. She was pretty and wore an evening dress of lavender satin that attracted all attention away from Carson. Her small, black choker necklace with a single red rose was a call sign from the agency that confirmed this girl was his date for dinner.

"My name is Minnie," she said, smiling at Carson.

"Hello, Minnie," Carson said as she took him by the arm, waiting to be led into the dining room by a tall, paunchy, bald man with a cane.

Carson's appearance attracted no attention – Minnie was a great diversion. Men stared openly as she strutted by. Carson could see that her eyes told a story of pain and disappointment, but her attitude was one of having fun for the moment.

The maître d' led Carson and Minnie to a just vacated table in the crowded, noisy dining room where Carson positioned himself in line with the opening of Bogdan's semi-private room. He could see that the men were enjoying their Argentinian beefsteak dinner and red wine.

Carson and Minnie ordered dinner, and Carson asked for a bottle of good Beaujolais. He kept an eye on Bogdan's party as the men soon moved from wine to vodka shots. Carson pretended to enjoy Minnie's company. She spoke well-informed English and at the appropriate times. At the stroke of midnight, she gave Carson a small kiss on his cheek, but he was distracted with his surveillance and hardly noticed Minnie's gesture.

A New Year's Eve party was now in full swing. There

was a fireworks display over the bay near the hotel, and the string quartet had given way to a jazz band just before midnight. Couples were drinking and dancing to the exhilarating music, some of which Carson remembered from his many trips to New Orleans with his very patient wife, who he now wished was with him more than ever, celebrating the New Year, laughing, and dancing. "I'll see you soon, Christy," he whispered under his breath, as if trying to send her a message telepathically.

Carson snapped out of his brief reverie when he saw Bogdan's men start to leave the party one by one, until only Bogdan and Marius remained at their table. Ciprian and Franco had both found female comfort for the night, and Jacob went into Riga's streets to try to sober up. Carson had no intention of following any of the underlings now that he had Bogdan in his sights – he would just wait and watch. At around two o'clock, Carson began to give up hope that he would see Serif on this night. Maybe there would be no final meeting, and this was all he would see of the crew as the party began to thin out a little. Keeping a close eye in Bogdan's direction, Carson continued to listen to Minnie rambling on about her life in Riga and her holiday trip to St. Petersburg.

Without warning, Serif entered the dining room at 2:15 a.m. with Tanya on his arm. She wore a cobalt blue velvet dress that gracefully clung to her sinuous figure. Serif was wearing an Italian tuxedo that was perfectly tailored. Together they looked stunning, obviously coming from another, more elegant, party. Still stone cold sober, Serif was well aware of his timing and the reason that he was meeting Bogdan at such a late hour at the Grand Palace Hotel.

"Hello, boss," Bogdan said as he stood up. "Please join us." Bogdan was very much aware of why Serif was there with

Tanya – he expected to get his payoff.

When Minnie made another trip to the ladies' room, it allowed Carson to more closely focus on the terrorist leader. Serif and Tanya were seated alongside their associates from Cernavodă, smiling occasionally as Serif motioned for a waiter. Actually seeing Serif up close for the first time made Carson feel even greater anxiety about finding out where the plutonium sphere was hidden. Carson turned away and watched a reflection of the group in a mirror situated near Bogdan's table. In the mirror, he saw Serif hand the metal briefcase to Marius.

Waving to the waiter to bring his check, Carson wanted to move outside before Serif and Tanya finished their business.

"Are you ready to leave?" Minnie asked as she returned to the table.

"Yes," Carson replied. "I must get some rest before dawn."

Minnie had earned her money for the escort service, but now she wanted to make a little extra for herself. She wrapped her arm under Carson's and whispered in his ear, "I will let you rest, after our bedroom business."

"No, my dear. Here's another fifty Euros," Carson said, handing her the money. "Maybe another time."

"You have my number," Minnie said as she released her customer.

Carson paid the check and said goodnight to Minnie in the lobby of the hotel as he helped her into her heavy fur coat. He put Minnie into a waiting taxi and hurried back into the hotel.

Swiftly entering the men's room, Carson changed his appearance again. Removing his coat, shirt, and the tack from his shoe he transformed himself into a normal-looking pedestrian. Grabbing a watch-cap and black, seaman's pea coat that he found hanging in the garment room, Carson was ready.

He stepped out of the main entrance of the hotel and walked slowly to the taxi stand.

Serif soon came out with Tanya on his arm and stood at the entrance as his driver brought his Mercedes around. Carson got into the lead taxi and gave the driver two twenty-Euro notes.

"Follow that Mercedes," Carson instructed.

"My pleasure," the taxi driver said. "My name's Alexander."

"Good to meet you, Alex," Cason replied. "Not too close."

Alex drove the taxi slowly out of its parking place, pacing himself two cars behind the Mercedes in the thick New Year's Eve traffic.

"I used to work for the government, drove many officials around Riga," Alex stated.

Carson watched the Mercedes closely as they drove across a bridge toward the coast. "Really? Sounds interesting."

"Yep, I know this city very well," Alex continued. "I was here for the revolution from those communist bastards in Russia. It was a terrible time."

"I've heard horror stories of their oppression," Carson said.

"You don't know how hard it was for us, my friend," Alex said. "Where are you from?"

"I travel around a lot," Carson said.

"You sound American," Alex said. "I learned my English from American movies. I really like Stallone and Pacino, and that guy in *The Bourne Identity*."

As he drove, Alex listened to a new release of Jerry Lee Lewis songs on his car's CD player – a *Johnny B. Goode* riff rattling the door panels. They followed the Mercedes across town and to the railway station, where Serif and Tanya got out of the car and went inside Riga's central station. Passengers were few in the mostly deserted, red-brick station as Carson got out of his taxi.

"Have a good night, sir," Alex said, changing the track on his player to Jerry Lee Lewis's 1958 rendition of *Great Balls of Fire*.

"Good music," Carson said. "I think Jerry's a little nuts, but he used to put on a good show." Carson gave Alex another ten Euros. "Happy New Year, Alex."

"Same to you, Mr. American," Alex said gratefully.

Carson walked into the station, his mind focused on finding the nuclear "ball of fire" he was now searching for in Latvia.

CHAPTER 32

Southern Riga was almost completely covered with train tracks once used by the Soviets to take resources away from Latvia and ship them back to Moscow. Now the railway was used mainly for commercial distribution of commodities coming into communist-free countries from the West and Scandinavia. A few of the smoother ribbon rails were used by a government-subsidised passenger train service owned by several local businessmen.

It was 3:00 a.m. according to the large oval clock hanging from the middle of the train station. Carson walked through the huge lobby, watching Serif and Tanya from a distance. Ticketing counters were empty – anyone riding a train this early in the morning would have to use the electronic ticketing machines peppered throughout the station. But Carson noted that Serif didn't seem interested in buying a ticket – he walked like a man on a mission.

Reaching the next to last track, Serif and Tanya went down the deserted platform to a three-car personal train. The engine was warmed and idling, waiting for its only two passengers. Boarding the second car, Serif and Tanya disappeared into the brightly painted red and silver steel horse that would soon carry them away from Riga and Carson's surveillance.

Taking advantage of a porter's inattention – he was loading a large cart of baggage onto a passenger train – Carson pushed the cart down the platform, hiding behind the baggage. When he reached the end of Serif's last carriage car, Carson jumped aboard and quietly entered it from a narrow rear door.

Inside, Carson could see that the third car was loaded with crates and large cases full of equipment. One-third of the car was designed as a kitchen, with black and silver-faced industrial appliances. A refrigerator, sitting adjacent to the double stacked oven/microwave, looked huge compared to the other appliances.

Carson felt himself jerk as the engine began pulling the two cars from the station. He realised that he could probably ride out the trip in the cargo car and try to get some rest while waiting for the terrorist cousins to reach their final destination.

The train moved out of Riga and into the countryside. Blackened granite ballast under the two rails of the tracks gave way as the heavy diesel/electric engine, mounted aboard its considerable steel carriage, moved across the earth.

Opening one of the crates near the rear of the cargo car, Carson found two cases of Turkish brandy. It was too early in the morning for him to taste the high-proof drink – a nap would suit him better. Carson sat back on a bale of rags, lying over several long pieces of insulation foam, and instantly fell asleep.

The track ran parallel to the Daugava River, past a great reservoir frozen over from its dam to its mouth. Daybreak brought frigid winds that blew across surrounding tundra. The icy river looked beautiful, resting silently – waiting for the spring thaw to open its swift waters. But spring was many months away, and the Latvian people who lived near the lake would know freezing winds for many more nights. Fortunately, they were used to extreme weather and had grown to like it.

Carson awoke to the squealing train's wheels as it slowly pulled into Lielvarde station to switch to a very seldom used rail. This segment of track wasn't equipped with electric cabling, so Serif's engineer started the diesel engine. After twenty minutes, the train began to pull slowly forward until it regained its normal speed. The bumping of the steel wheels over poorly joined track segments put Carson back into a shallow sleep, which soon turned deeper.

He dreamed of the first time he met Christy. She was attending classes at the college next to the naval base in Norfolk, Virginia, where she was studying to be a chemist. One afternoon, Carson visited the college bookstore where Christy worked to pick up some books on metallurgical design techniques. Christy was stocking a new set of World Book encyclopaedias near the back of the store.

"I love those," Carson blurted, without giving much thought to follow-up conversation.

He remembered being dumbstruck by how beautiful Christy looked that day in her blue jeans and yellow sweater. Her brown hair flowed down her back and swayed as she moved toward him.

Dark brown eyes, inherited from her Cherokee grandmother, gave her an exotic appearance.

"You much of a reader?" Christy asked.

Carson couldn't breathe for a moment, trying to think of something intelligent to say that didn't sound pretentious. "Yeah."

"But not much of a talker," Christy said with a smile that revealed very white teeth.

"Well, I've lost all the thoughts in my head – for the moment," Carson replied.

"I hope it wasn't too painful," Christy said, still smiling. "Would you like to get a cup of coffee and maybe they'll come back?"

Carson remembered falling in love with her from the first moment that he saw her. "Yes, I would."

"Good, I need a little break," Christy said as they started to walk toward the coffee shop in front of the store.

They sat at a small round table and talked for about an hour, discovering that they both wanted to get to know each other better. Their romance blossomed throughout that summer. Christy finished college the following winter, and they decided to live together for a while after Christmas. Happily in love, Carson and Christy were married in the Navy chapel the next spring and had been together ever since.

———

At 10:00 a.m., Serif's train pulled up to what seemed to be the end of the track – a sheer stone mountainside. Roughly twice as high as the engine, an opening revealed itself to the three-car train. There had once been an attempt to burrow through the mountain in order to allow train passage by tunnel into Estonia, via a torturous path over frozen tundra. The plan was abandoned when a Latvian miner's strike went into full fury, ignited by poor working conditions and numerous deaths at the hands of the communist government.

Carson was completely awake when the train finally came to rest inside the cavern. He wanted to believe that, very soon, Serif would lead him to the location of the plutonium. Carson found himself inside a hidden sanctuary, a place where Serif felt safest – its whereabouts known only to his engineer and Tanya. He could hear the engine wind down, relieving its brakes with a final hiss of air. Quietly moving closer to a window mounted in the door that he had used to board the car, Carson looked to see if anyone was near enough to observe him leaving the train.

The door suddenly opened and standing right in front of him was Tanya, holding her Heckler & Koch MP5A2 – pointed directly at Carson's chest.

"Did you think we wouldn't have alarms on our doors?" Tanya asked. "You should have been a bit less obvious, Mr. Griffin. Our cameras have been watching you since you boarded our little express in Riga."

"If I'd known that you were this clever, I would have just sent you an email asking for directions to your hideout," Carson sarcastically replied.

Serif came out from behind a wall where he could be seen. "Greetings, Herr Griffin."

"You can call me Mr. Griffin," Carson retorted. "American by birth, y' know."

"Yes, you are," Serif said. "We've come to know you and your family very well over the last few hours. Satellite phones and the Internet are very powerful tools for us, thanks to our Chinese friends. But I don't think you know who I am, Mr. Griffin. My name is Serif Muhammad Rezaabak, war emissary from the Turkish Empire to the west."

Holding his hands out from his side, Carson observed his surroundings. "I think I know who you are – you're a madman."

"Madman? I think not. You see, Mr. Griffin, our future is inevitable. Turkey will regain her power and glory. Our party is gaining strength with every bomb you drop on our Islamic brothers in the Middle East. My mentor will soon return to his home country to raise the Chechen armies against the

Russian invaders, and I will create a wasteland to the west."

The train's engineer, who was also carrying a submachine gun, searched Carson from head to toe. He removed Carson's pistol and mobile telephone and threw them back inside the carriage.

"I believe you've got all the intelligence you need, Serif," Carson bristled. "Your plan has worked brilliantly so far."

"Let's just shoot him," Tanya said to her cousin.

"No, I want to find out how he knew we had a nuclear weapon," Serif said, glaring at Carson. "Bogdan was well aware of how to destroy the nuclear power plant and turn it into a radioactive, contamination-spewing volcano, but he knew nothing of our alternative plans. You must have found another leak in our organisation."

"Of course, I did," Carson said. "Isn't it obvious? It was you. But I did have to kill a guy in the observation tower at the Cernavodă port before I understood just how serious you were about this insane plot to destroy the nuclear reactor."

Serif's face registered a fierce fury. Vengeance for Reza's death churned inside him. "That was my brother!"

"Oh, I see. Well, he was going to kill me, so he left me no choice but to kill him first," Carson said coolly.

Silence separated the two men for a brief moment as they stood staring at each other. "Take him to the storage tank," Serif finally said.

The engineer shoved Carson toward an opening behind a stone wall, which led them out of the train's cavern and into what had once been an underground station. Its walls, floor, and ceiling were covered in large white tiles grouted together with a dark grey material, giving the hallway the appearance of some kind of maniac's laboratory. Carson followed Tanya, who was leading their way down the long corridor to a hatch at its end.

Opening the steel door using a push button, Tanya stood aside as a pneumatic mechanism rotated a large wheel in the door's centre. Serif entered first, followed by Tanya, and then the engineer shoved Carson through the doorway. Ducking his head, Carson stepped over the knee-knocker at the door's bottom and looked up when his feet landed inside Serif's subterranean residence.

An elegant chandelier hung from the middle of the living room's twenty-foot-high ceiling. Persian rugs were under every piece of mahogany furniture that adorned the spacious room. A huge flat-screen television was mounted on one wall, above an impressively small Bose surround-sound system. But what interested Carson most was the thick glass wall to his left. Behind it was an aquarium full of water, and at its centre was the two-kilo plutonium pit.

"So you still have your plutonium," Carson acknowledged.

Serif turned slowly from pouring himself a drink. "Ah, yes. My most prized possession to date. And in a few hours, I will know where my six-kilo pit is, Mr. Griffin."

Carson knew that the de-ionized water in the steel tank thermalised the neutrons coming from the plutonium sphere, and the mountain's dense rock shielded any gamma radiation coming from the pit. It would be nearly impossible to find the pit from outside the cavern.

Tanya came to Serif's side, wrapping her arms around his waist. "It has become our power, our reason for continuing to fight. We will make another bomb for the West."

"And you, my unlucky INWA inspector," Serif said with malevolent glee, "will no longer be around to see our plans unfold. But I don't want to kill you too quickly; I owe you a slow, painful death."

With that, the burly engineer punched Carson in the abdomen, doubling him over in pain as he gasped for breath. The second blow, across Carson's face, drove him to the floor.

Carson looked up at Serif through the blood dripping from a cut above his left eye. "I'll be here, when you're ready," Carson uttered.

"Oh, this won't be the most fun," Serif said. "Torturing your wife and daughter will give me much more satisfaction. Your killing of my brother will be avenged once I have destroyed everyone you treasure."

"Leave them out of this, you bastard!" Carson said, his voice choking. "They have nothing to do with what I've done."

Carson had given Christy strict instructions to stay in close contact with Todd Sinclair while he was travelling. He had spoken to both Todd and Christy twice since he'd been tracking Marius and Jacob across the continent; the last time was two days ago. Carson would need to find a phone or a computer to warn her.

"Do you think you can disrupt all our plans to bring back the power and glory of the Turkish Empire without paying a price?" Serif said. "Barayev will give our world a new beginning."

Tanya prepared a hypodermic syringe at a small table in one corner of the room. A clear, syrupy liquid was drawn up from the vial. Carson was still reeling from the engineer's blow when Tanya pumped the drug into his shoulder. He felt the room spinning almost immediately, still holding himself up from the cold floor on his hands and knees.

Carson looked up at Serif, whose face was now blurred and out of focus. "Is this your idea of a fair fight?"

"I don't have to be fair," Serif snapped. "You're going to find that this cocktail will wear off very soon, and you will know exactly what is happening to you. I would not want you to miss one minute of your drowning."

Serif motioned to the engineer. "Take him to the aquarium room upstairs. We will watch him suffocate from our table while having lunch."

The engineer grabbed Carson by the arm and back of his neck, forcing him forward through another hatch located between a wooden bookcase and Turkish antique floor lamp.

Carson's escort roughly pushed him up a spiral staircase. The spiralling confused Carson even more by the time he landed in a dimly-lit room full of manufacturing equipment used to make gas centrifuges for enriching uranium. Computerised lathe machines, precision drill presses, and other heavy duty electric machines were all permanently mounted to the room. Its walls were exposed cave rocks – dark gray plates of shale. The sound of running water and a transformer hum trickled through Carson's drug-induced stupor.

The engineer sat Carson down in a metal chair and turned to pick up three large plastic zip-ties to bind Carson's hands and feet. Passing behind a tall drill press, the engineer was, for a few seconds, unable to see his prisoner, giving Carson a moment in which to pick up a small pair of wire cutters from a nearby table. Sticking the cutters inside his trouser pocket, Carson fell to the metallic floor. He was lying face down when the engineer stepped around the drill press so that he could see his prisoner. Confident that Carson had just fallen out of the chair because of his drugged state, the engineer finished gathering the zip-ties before picking Carson up from the cold floor.

Sitting him back in the chair, the engineer bound Carson's feet together and then tied each arm to its side of the chair. It would be easier for the engineer to attach the chain hoist, mounted on a circular rail above them, to the chair's back, than to try to get Carson in a position to be lowered into the aquarium any other way. But Serif wanted his prisoner to be fully alert when he died, subsequently giving the engineer time to do a little machining while he waited for Carson's head to clear.

CHAPTER 33

Tanya prepared their lunch of goat cheese, bread, olives, mangoes, and other fruits, both fresh and dried. She placed everything on a thick wooden table directly across from the aquarium that held the plutonium pit. The table faced the aquarium's longest side; several underwater lights illuminated the room with a bright bluish glow. After lighting six long, thin candles that sat in an antique Ottoman holder in the middle of the table, the two cousins sat down for lunch. Tanya looked longingly at the man she loved.

"Do you believe Barayev will deliver what he has promised to us, Serif?" Tanya asked.

Serif poured himself a glass of Turkish red wine. "Yes, of course I do. He is the leader of a worldwide movement that will put an end to the Western powers that have subdued us for too long."

Tanya knew her limits and thought it wise to allow Serif to continue the conversation about Barayev's plans only if he wanted to. "The feta from Latvia is a little too dry for me. What do you think?" she asked, trying to change the subject of their conversation.

"We must continue with our goal of obtaining our own nuclear weapon," Serif said, ignoring her trivial question.

"NATO has placed nearly sixty nuclear warheads in our country, and they keep them closely guarded. The technology is too specialised to draw intelligence from scientists that we have produced in our country, so we'll have to go to Kazakhstan. It will be impossible for us to acquire such a weapon without doing what we did in Slovenia. The uranium centrifuge rotors we are building will not be ready for three to five years." Serif smoothed some cheese on a piece of flat bread and bit into it. "You're right, a bit dry."

Before Tanya could respond, Serif continued. "The politics of Turkey will not allow us to achieve our goals through governmental negotiations – we must force Europe to move back," Serif said adamantly. "Soon we will find other scientists from Kazakhstan's former Soviet nuclear weapons program. They will help us put together a 'backpack' bomb like the ones the Soviets designed in the eighties before the revolution, small enough to be carried into a target of our choosing – maybe in the boot of an unsuspecting staff member's auto.

"The repercussions of blowing up the UN building housing the world's nuclear safeguarding institution with a Russian-built atomic bomb will set old rivals against one another again. The quest for control of Middle East oil has already caused many problems between the West and the other two most powerful countries in the world: Russia and China."

Tanya ate quietly, wondering if the first strike Serif was planning would actually motivate the Russian bear to negotiate, combining their forces with a Chinese dragon in order to stop Western alliances. "Our entertainment should begin at any moment," Tanya said, looking toward the aquarium tank.

"Yes, it is time," Serif said, taking Tanya's hand across the table and giving it a playful squeeze. "I'll give our man a call."

Serif looked intently at his beautiful cousin. Tanya could feel the desire in his eyes.

———

arson heard the faint sound of a metal grinder running in the background of a lathe that was using a computer programme to automatically turn out an aluminium centrifuge rotor tube. The sound of the machinery could wake the dead, but Carson's mind was still dazed from the drug injection. He could feel that his hands and feet were tightly tied to the metal chair he was sitting in. It took nearly forty-five minutes of head shaking and deep breathing before Carson had finally begun to recover his wits.

The engineer walked over to Carson and slapped him just to make sure he was awake and aware. With a little chuckle, he pushed a button on a control box hanging down from the hoist that was connected to Carson's chair and began lifting him slowly into the air. Carson's shifting weight brought his hips close to his right side where he could reach the small pair of cutters he had slipped into his pocket. Just then, the radio on the engineer's belt began to vibrate and squawk something garbled over its tinny speaker. He stopped the noisy hoist to listen to the incoming communication.

The conversation was completely muffled by the loud noise of the lathe, but Carson imagined it was Serif, now anxious for Carson's execution. Carson was to be dropped into the aquarium, tied to the heavy steel chair that would take him to the bottom. The engineer turned away from the lathe and put one finger in his opposite ear from the radio so that he could hear Serif. Carson now had an opportunity to cut his hand free.

Once his right hand was cut loose, he quickly cut the ties around his feet and then his other hand. Carson hadn't noticed the nylon belt holding his waist to the chair until he realised that he was still suspended in mid-air, dangling from the chain hoist. Finding the belt's buckle, Carson dropped from the chair with a deadening thump to the floor. His head still swimming, he focused all his energy on the engineer who finished his conversation with Serif and turned around just in time to see Carson begin his charge.

The giant of an engineer reared back to attempt a punch before Carson hit him with a low tackle, but he was too slow and went staggering backward, smashing against a metal workbench. The engineer, who outweighed his opponent by ninety pounds, threw Carson aside like a small child while regaining his balance. His back hurting, the engineer bent over for a couple of seconds, his lungs heaving for air. He finally stood up straight with an angry grunt.

Carson had landed halfway across the room from the engineer's throw and was tangled in a rack of rigging and pieces of cable hanging together. Carson struggled to his feet, his vision still blurred by the drugs.

The engineer came after him with amazing agility for a man his size. He lifted Carson over his head and body-slammed him to the steel floor. Miraculously, Carson's hand landed on one of the cylinder casings that would be used in the lathe to turn out one of the thousands of uranium centrifuge rotors. It was about the size of a baseball bat and nearly as long. Picking himself up to his knees, Carson wheeled around with the aluminium tubing and hit the engineer across his right kneecap, smashing it into a chunk of bone chips and splinters – sending the big man down on his other knee, howling in pain.

Carson staggered to his feet and again swung the long cylinder. His aim to hit the engineer's bowed head was right on target. The engineer was out cold, probably forever, but Carson was not going to hang around to find out. He imagined that Serif and Tanya had realised their drowning of Carson was not going according to plan.

Carson grabbed the engineer's Colt .45, which was stuffed inside the back of his dungarees and stumbled forward. Awkwardly making his way to the top of the spiral stairs, Carson moved to block the hatch, but it was already open, as if someone had just run through it in a hurry. Carson closed it anyway and jammed a mop handle into the centre-mounted hand-wheel, disabling the door from being opened from Serif's living quarters.

Carson first needed to get the plutonium from the aquarium before trying to escape. He climbed back up the stairs, his head clearing enough now to see straight. He turned off the lathe, finally stopping the maddening noise. Carson walked over to the huge, uncovered aquarium, placed the Colt on the side of the tank, and dove head first into the crystal-clear water.

Swimming down to the pedestal that was holding the plutonium pit, Carson glanced through the thick glass and saw a nervous Serif and Tonya still sitting at the table. Seeing Carson, Serif jumped to his feet in disbelief. Carson used the back of his hand to flip Serif off with one stroke under his chin, then picked up the small black sphere and swam up to the surface of the sixteen-foot-deep tank.

Carson now knew the threat was imminent. He quickly climbed out of the aquarium and scanned the machinery for some way to destroy the plutonium sphere. His training at the Agency included courses on weapons' construction, and some were about their dismantling. Carson knew that the sphere's geometry was very important for the nuclear weapon to reach its full yield – he had to crush or disfigure it somehow. But he had very little time; Serif was already making a lot of noise trying to get through the hatch below.

Spotting a sizable hydraulic press sitting near the stairs leading down to where Serif and Tanya were beginning to cut through the door with an acetylene torch, Carson picked up his newly acquired pistol and ran to a breaker that turned on the press's power. Lights on a side panel came on as electricity coursed through the huge machine, its controls and buttons labelled in Chinese.

"Thanks a lot, Chairman Mao," Cason mumbled.

Two red lights above the pushbuttons looked to be the controls Carson needed to make the huge steel jaws of the press come together. He thought that maybe the pushbuttons were separated far apart intentionally, to make the operator of the press use both his hands to press the buttons simultaneously – a smart safety feature. Carson's intention was to put the sphere inside and crush it into powder, but he had to test his theory about the buttons first. He sat the pit on a wooden stool by the machine's control panel, and pushed the two red buttons.

When the two small lights went out, a heavy, slow-moving stainless steel jaw came down from the top of the machine and mated with its bottom jaw, a steel cradle mounted to the floor. Carson, seeing that the power of the machine would be enough to overcome the plutonium pit's binding force and turn it into dust, released the two buttons.

As he placed the plutonium pit into the cradle, a shot suddenly rang out. Originating from the bottom of the stairwell, the bullet bounced off an I-beam directly above his head and buried itself in the ceiling of the cavern. He ducked behind the bulky press and saw Tanya coming up the stairs, her machine gun blazing – bullets were splattering all around Carson. He was pinned down for the moment. When Tanya reached the top of the stairs, she jumped behind a steel workbench for cover. Serif followed, carrying his favourite 9mm pistol. But before Carson could get a shot off, Serif took cover behind the workbench alongside his cousin.

Tanya's fury was suspended for a moment when Carson fired a shot over the metallic table in their general direction with the Colt .45 pistol. It made a huge noise inside the rock cavern, but the shot was wide of his intended target and ricocheted into the blackness of a cave opening.

Serif and Tanya broke in two directions when they heard the last career of the bullet. Rattling some of the steel flooring while they ran across a few plates, they vaulted for cover. Carson saw Tanya crouch behind the lathe situated near another drill press that was made of cast iron and painted military green. The room was crowded with machinery being powered by a loud-humming transformer station. However, Carson could still see Tanya's squatted body from a reflection in the stainless steel panel at the base of the drill press.

Carson heard a shot ring out, and there was a flash on the cave walls from Serif's pistol. He fired again from the other side of the aquarium, missing Carson's head by millimetres as the shot continued travelling through the gun smoke-filled atmosphere of the cavern. The metallic impact echoed around the cave's walls.

"You have no escape, Griffin!" Serif yelled.

Tanya fired another round, each bullet bouncing near Carson's position. The machine gun jumped in Tanya's hands as she blasted away. Carson's gut told him that she was not going to take the time to try and aim long enough to kill him with one shot. She was hoping to eventually hit him as she sprayed ammunition in his general direction.

"Maybe we can arrange an agreement?" Carson asked Serif, adrenaline clearing his head. "You let me destroy the pit, and I'll take you to prison. Along with your girlfriend, of course."

"I don't think that you have a choice here, Griffin," Serif shouted as he fired a shot into a barrel of oil next to where Carson was crouching.

The oil burst into flames, forcing Carson to lunge backward. Catching himself on a stool, he regained his footing and ducked behind a half wall across the room from the huge metal press. The plutonium pit was still in the lower jaw of the machine, waiting for Carson to push the two red release buttons that would allow the press to crush the sphere into dust.

Tanya moved closer to the drilling machine but still behind the lathe. Carson took aim at the base of the drilling machine's iron stand and fired a .45 calibre bullet into the heavy metal.

It ricocheted into Tanya's torso, bursting her abdominal organs, blood vessels, and bones.

"Serif –!" Tanya screamed.

She fell to the floor, a look of surprise and pain on her lovely face as blood pooled all around her lifeless body.

"Tanya!" Serif called out.

"Your girlfriend is quite dead, Serif!" Carson yelled back.

Serif spoke in his most convincing voice, deep and menacing. "I will kill you, Griffin."

Two successive shots came from Serif's direction as he

moved around the aquarium for a better angle.

"What was the deal with her anyway, Serif?" Carson shouted. "She looked too hot for you."

Carson didn't look up from behind the press before firing one shot in Serif's general direction and then ducking behind the panel he had used earlier to turn on power to the press.

"She was my cousin, you camel's ass," Serif replied, firing back and creeping his way into a position to take the plutonium pit from its lower jaw. Quietly turning around, Serif was now facing an opening in the platform's railing and the black hole in the back of the cave. He descended a metal stairway welded to the platforms under girders, pinned to the rocky floor of the cave, and near the transformers that fed all the power to the equipment above.

At the bottom of the stairs, Serif hastily released two hasps on either side of a metal gang box sitting at the dark opening leading out of the machinery room. Still inside the box where he had left them were ropes, flashlights, rock climber picks, and harnesses – spelunking gear.

Carson couldn't hear Serif leave the platform and go down the stairs leading away from their gun battle because the machinery around him was still running. "Tell me something, Serif."

No answer came from the other side of the room, only the idling hum of the computerised lathe, now finished with its turning at the last centrifuge rotor.

"What?" Carson yelled. "Are you out of witty names for me?"

Carson squatted down and took a quick look from behind the power panel. He ducked his head behind the panel, waiting for another close range shot from Serif's pistol.

But there was no sound coming from Serif's position over that of the running machinery, waiting for someone to take over its controls.

Carson picked up a small piece of metal from the floor and threw it to the other side of the aquarium's opening, then came out from behind the panel – arms extended with the .45 Colt cocked. Walking forward as he scanned the room for Serif, Carson moved around to a spot where he could see the huge metal press. He saw that it was now empty – Serif had taken the pit!

Slowly moving around the machinery with his gun cocked, Carson realised that Serif had escaped without him seeing which direction he might have gone until·he reached the rear of the platform. Examining the opening in the platform's railing, Carson saw the metal stairs leading down into the darkness of another cave passageway.

The black hole was nearly thirty feet in diameter, with a jagged stone entrance that looked extremely uninviting. Carson knew something about mountain climbing from his adventures with Christy and felt fairly comfortable going in after Serif. Losing the plutonium pit back to the terrorist was not an option – he had to retrieve it, with or without the proper gear.

Climbing down the metal stairs, holding onto the railing with one hand and his pistol with the other, Carson made his way to the cave's floor. Glancing toward the humming transformer, he noticed the open gang box sitting just underneath the machinery platform. "Amen!" he muttered.

Inside the box, Carson found a coil of flat rope, a light on a headband with battery pack, a climbing harness, and climber's pick. It wasn't everything he needed to make the descent into the black hole, but it would have to do. Knowing that Serif had more experience spelunking, Carson donned the harness, turned on his head-mounted light, said a very quick silent prayer, took a deep breath, and started going down into the darkness.

CHAPTER 34

Christy came into their apartment after walking Bingo around the stable just down the road. She was exhausted from entertaining her daughter's friends during her New Year's Eve party the night before. Stomping off the snow covering her brown leather boots, Christy grabbed a towel and wiped Bingo's paws before releasing his leash.

Susan was still asleep, but Christy was going to have to wake her soon – it was now nearly one in the afternoon and her essay, due when she returned to high school in three days, was still unwritten.

The apartment smelled of roast chicken and vegetable soup, one of Carson's favourite meals. Christy wanted to have it ready when he flew home that evening. He'd called her two nights before, letting her know that he would be home on the first day of the year, as they planned. Since he had missed Christmas a week earlier, Christy had made him promise to be home on January 1st. Those years of working unpredictable schedules and trading off holidays had produced many odd traditions around Christmas and New Year's Eve, as well as the Fourth of July, Thanksgiving, and Easter.

Bingo stood next to Christy in the kitchen as she stirred the soup, hoping to experience its flavour as well as the tantalising smell.

"Not right now, Bingo," Christy said. "Go wake up Susan. Go on!"

Bingo seemed almost human at times, listening to Christy's commands and running up the stairs to Susan's bedroom. Pushing the slightly ajar door open with his nose, he jumped onto the bed. Bingo barked a little, then immediately ran back downstairs to get his reward for a job well done.

"Bingo!" Susan yelled, rolling over in her bed.

Reaching the bottom of the stairs, without warning, Bingo went into an alarming tirade of barking and growling as he stood near the apartment's rear glass doors.

"What is it, boy?" Christy asked as she came through the open doorway between the kitchen and living room.

Christy saw a man standing behind the glass door with some kind of pistol pointed directly at Bingo. Screaming, Christy ran upstairs where Susan was now standing beside her bed, eyes wide open, petrified with fear.

The silenced gunshot sounded like a loud pop over Bingo's last yelp before he was killed. Within seconds, the man had broken the glass and was inside the apartment, wearing a black ski mask and dressed in black clothes. He moved slowly through the living room, then headed upstairs, checking two vacant bedrooms and a bath before arriving at Susan's closed and locked bedroom door.

The masked man was a Chechnyan assassin arranged for when Serif made a call for help on his satellite phone to Barayev's headquarters as he travelled along the icy Daugava River.

Kicking the door open with one swift blow from his hiking boot, the killer took a half step back, then lunged forward into the room. Watching helplessly as the head end of Susan's chrome-plated putter travelled toward him in animated slow motion, the assassin blinked his eyes closed. He felt the club hit him squarely between the eye holes in his stocking mask, originating from behind a seven-foot-high white wardrobe. Susan stepped forward as the man's automatic pistol shot wildly into the walls and ceiling of her bedroom. Christy stood very still at the end of her daughter's bed, while Susan reared back for another swing at the killer's head with the steel-shafted golf club.

"Hit him again!" Christy yelled.

But before Susan could get the club up for another blow, Christy fell over into a pile of clothes lying on Susan's floor, hitting her head on the dresser on her way down. She lay unconscious in a heap.

"Mom!" Susan cried out.

The killer began shaking his head from side to side trying to regain his composure. Susan turned back around and raised the putter above her head quicker than the Chechnyan could react. She hit him across the top of his mask-covered head, striking his skull with all her might. It made a sickening thumping sound, like the splitting of a watermelon on a paved road during a hot summer afternoon.

The gunman fell down the stairs, and was sprawled out on the bottom steps, a death rattle emanating from his throat. Susan dropped the golf club and ran to her mother. She turned Christy over into her lap, shocked at the blood drenching on the front and back of her blouse. A small tear in her white blouse looked to be only a small puncture near her left breast, but the blood poured out profusely.

"Mom?" Susan urged. "Speak to me, Mom!"

Rocking back and forth, Susan's body heaved as she tried to catch her breath and finally release a high-pitched shriek. She blocked out everything going on around her for several minutes, which gave another intruder time to make his way inside the apartment.

When the sound of someone standing behind her startled Susan, she jerked her body around and reached for the golf club to try to defend herself. But without warning, she felt a sharp pain in the right side of her neck, and then it shot through the left side of her face, rendering her unconscious.

Standing over Susan's limp body was Marius, also dressed in black, wearing a black ski mask and holding an empty injection ampoule of animal tranquiliser. Marius looked at the unconscious bodies of mother and daughter, somewhat bewildered about what he should do next.

The plan was supposed to include Carson being inside the house when they broke in. The Chechnyan had instructed Marius to stay in the garden until he called for him to come inside. He would then show Marius the proper method for murdering an enemy of the JTS and his family. The Chechnyan planned to take Carson's family hostage and murder his wife and daughter when instructed. Serif would have to personally give them the go-ahead after they reported Carson was dead, before they took out the two women.

Marius put his mask and gun in his jacket pockets and lifted Susan from the floor, carrying her down the stairs, past the dead Chechnyan, whose blood and brain matter were leaking all over the beige carpeting.

Dropping Susan onto an overstuffed sofa in the living room, Marius bound her arms and legs with black zip-ties. He noticed Bingo lying in the hallway between the kitchen and living room. Grabbing one of his limp hind legs, Marius put the dog into a large green garbage bag and threw it into a broom closet. He then went back into the kitchen and made himself a sandwich. Smelling the delicious aroma of the soup on the stove, Marius ladled some into a large cup.

Marius was determined to carry out his first assignment

for Barayev, even if his task was handed down through three levels of hierarchy before reaching him personally. He was to wait for a call from Serif before killing Carson's family, and that was what he was going to do. If no call came from Serif by two o'clock, he was to wait for Carson to return home, holding his daughter hostage in case he needed some leverage. Once Carson was dead, the girl wouldn't be needed and could be disposed of immediately.

"So, you are awake?" Marius said to Susan, walking back to the living room after finishing his soup. Her eyes were now open, but Marius had covered her mouth with masking tape. "Let me take that tape off," he said. "Make sure that you don't scream. I would hate to kill you, but I will."

Marius pulled Susan's mouth gag off with a quick jerk.

"My father is gonna kill you," Susan blurted.

Marius sat down in the sofa's matching chair. "I am not worried about your father. He is only one man."

"Where is my mother?" Susan demanded.

"She is still upstairs," Marius replied. "Now I have a few questions for you, Susan."

"Don't speak to me," Susan said.

"What time will your father get home?" Marius asked.

"None ya," Susan answered.

"Clever," Marius said. "Okay, you don't have to tell me when he's gonna be coming through that door. But just so you know, you are on the clock until Daddy is dead. Then you are definitely next."

Marius turned on the TV and surfed until he found the New Year's Day Rose Bowl parade from the US. He turned the sound up as a marching band from Valdosta, Georgia, performed *Hey Jude* as they marched down the wide avenues of Pasadena, California. Hundreds of high school kids from all over the country played their hearts out, basking in their moment on national and international television.

Marius was so engrossed in the program that he didn't notice that his duffel bag had popped open slightly when it landed on the floor next to the television set. Susan could see two black round disks protruding from the zippered opening.

"I have to go to the bathroom," Susan said.

"Okay," Marius said as he rose. "Don't try anything stupid and keep the door open."

"I'm not gonna keep the door open, you pervert," Susan snapped.

Marius cut her ties with a Swiss army knife, and Susan stood slowly, her muscles still feeling the effects of being drugged. She went into the half bathroom and closed the door. Susan looked around desperately for an escape, but the small window behind the toilet was too high and narrow for her to climb out before Marius would come in and catch her.

Flushing the toilet, an idea out of the blue popped into Susan's head. She lifted the white ceramic toilet cover and, as the water ran to refill the reservoir, she unscrewed the float's metal arm and then removed the threaded rod. Susan jammed the flapper valve closed and stuck the rod inside her pajama trousers, hoping that she would have an opportunity to stab it into Marius's throat. She walked back into the living room where Marius was still engrossed in watching a favourite American event. He let Susan sit back down on the sofa without her zip-ties for the moment.

Susan sat very still, her arms crossed in front of her, trying to think of a way to get to her cordless phone, which was in her bedroom. Carson had programmed Todd's telephone number into it, in case something happened that she was unable to handle by herself. Susan remembered that her father had given her strict instructions to call INWA headquarters immediately should she become aware of anything suspicious.

"My dad should be here any moment," Susan said to Marius. "I know that his plane landed this morning."

"I believe you are lying, Susie," Marius said. "You don't have any idea where your father is right now. But if I don't hear from my friend by two o'clock, our plans will take a new direction."

"Oh, really?" Susan said sarcastically.

"Yes. Now be quiet. I'm trying to watch the parade," Marius said.

Susan could see that he was aggravated and now seemed to be much more anxious than he had been an hour earlier. She would try a different tack.

"What's your name?" Susan asked.

"Marius."

"Do you have a girlfriend or a wife?" Susan asked. "You don't look much older than me."

"No, only my mother," Marius replied, his Romanian accent beginning to break through. "You should not get to know me too well, Susan. I'm a bad person – I kill people."

"Marius, do you love your mother?" Susan asked, a choke in her voice.

"I love my mother very much. I bought her an expensive fox coat for Christmas," Marius said. "She loved it."

"I'll bet she did," Susan said. "Do you mind if I get a drink of water from the kitchen?"

"No, I will get it. You stay here, and don't move." Marius went into the kitchen.

Susan quickly pulled the metal rod out of her pajamas and pushed it down between the cushions of the sofa. She knew there wasn't time to run upstairs and get to her phone before Marius would return.

The family's landline telephone was sitting on a desk beside the kitchen doorway, where Marius could see her. She heard the water stop running and then a sound coming from the kitchen as if Marius was going through the cupboards looking for something.

He poked his head around the corner of the kitchen doorway. "Would you like some tea?"

Thinking that it would buy her more time, Susan turned to reply. "Yes, please."

Marius went back into the kitchen while Susan looked around frantically for her mother's purse. Maybe she had left her cell phone in it. Susan spotted the tan leather shoulder bag on the seat of a dining room chair. It was a short three steps from where Susan was sitting, but it would feel like three miles.

"If you look in the fridge, you'll find some milk for the tea," Susan shouted.

When she heard the refrigerator door open, she jumped up from her seat and ran over to Christy's purse. Grabbing the cell phone from inside the bag, she dashed back to the couch. Marius looked around the doorway again just a second after she sat back down.

"Would you like sugar?" Marius asked.

"Yes, that would be nice," Susan replied as calmly as possible.

Marius went back to his tea-making as Susan hit her mother's speed dial for Carson. Letting it ring until the voice mail answered, Susan whispered below the volume of the TV, "Dad, help me! I'm home and a man is here with a gun."

Susan ended the call and shoved the phone into the small

drawer of the end table next to the sofa. Startled by Marius's silent reappearance over her shoulder, Susan swiftly recovered as he said, "Here's your tea," and handed her a small mug.

"Thank you," Susan replied.

Out of the corner of her eye Susan noticed that Marius was growing steadily more anxious. He nervously began surfing TV channels, and his hand holding his mug of tea was shaking.

CHAPTER 35

Red flat ropes were pinned to either side of a descending slope that Carson negotiated after entering the cave's rear passageway. Serif had already been through the opening and passed the first landing on his way down into the cavernous bowels of the cave. Carson had to catch up with Serif, who knew the cave's twists and turns much better than he did. But Carson also thought it best to be ready for an ambush, should Serif decide to hide inside one of the numerous cavities and surprise him.

At the bottom of the rope trellis, Carson stood on the first of two landings and surveyed the area using a powerful flashlight and his head-mounted light. He realised that he was standing inside another large cavern at the beginning of a long passageway that projected into the blackness for as far as the light could shine its powerful beam. The walls and flooring were jagged with hefty boulders, and stalactites of calcium hung from the ceiling like elongated cones.

Water dripped onto Carson's head from one of the nearest stalactites. He tilted his head down to shake the water from his light and noticed that there was another assembly of red ropes leading through the passage opening and into the darkness.

Stepping off the landing and onto boulders, Carson

crossed over a void and into the tunnel ahead of him. The ropes ended at the mouth of the next tunnel, which narrowed to a height of only five feet. He crouched over and began moving as fast as he could through the labyrinth, dodging jagged stone edges along the way. Minerals exposed to his flashlight's high beam sparkled, making Carson believe that the cave was rich in a valuable metal – maybe even copper. But the air seemed to be surprisingly fresh compared to what he thought it would be like in a tunnel this deep underground. He suspected that there had to be an air shaft somewhere leading back up to the surface that allowed some amount of ventilation.

Without warning, the floor seemed to drop out from under Carson's feet as rocks shifted, and he slipped into a wide fissure. Carson's sudden loss of footing caused him to tumble once, head over heels. He cringed when he heard his flashlight smash into the sharp edge of a boulder, crushing its lens and knocking out his much needed light source. Regaining his footing, Carson shook the flashlight vigorously, thinking that by some miracle the bashed torch would suddenly give him light. It didn't. Carson now realised he'd better closely guard his only illumination – his miner's headlamp – if he was ever to get back out of the pitch black cave. The yellowish beam was sufficient for the time being to see his way forward into the dark tunnel.

Continuing to walk along the crack, which seemed to be growing wider and deeper as he followed the rocky path, Carson began to smell a reeking stench. "What is that?" he mumbled. The odour inflamed his sinuses, and he concluded it was the smell of urine and feces. Serif had had to relieve himself off the edge of the fissure running along the footpath, leaving Carson a positive sign that he had recently travelled that way. Like tracking an animal in the jungle, Carson thought.

Carson's headlamp was nearly extinguished when the tunnel finally led him to a huge void, created by the crack widening itself until it was no longer a fissure but a bottomless cavern. The space looked to be much larger than the first cavern at the tunnel's opposite end, but it was hard for Carson to see very far into the blackness with his headlight having dimmed.

Standing very still, he listened for any sound that might be coming from Serif's movements. Carson could hear a kind of scratching sound from somewhere out in the blackness and above him but too far away for his light to see. He turned off the headlamp for a moment, hoping to catch a glimpse of Serif's flashlight or maybe see a spark from the scratching of his pick. Surveying the blackness, Carson saw a sudden flash of light shining straight down from above, in the middle of the cavern. It was Serif, dangling from a rope near the ceiling, trying to pick his way through the overhead shell.

Realising that Serif was too busy to pay much attention, Carson turned his light on again and quietly made his way around to where Serif had previously built a one-rope ladder – knots tied at every yard or so for a foothold. The rope was suspended from six pitons embedded into the side of the cavern and leading up to Serif's position near the crest of the space. Serif didn't hear Carson sneak up on him as he continued hammering for all he was worth, trying to break through the ceiling and ignoring everything around him.

Carson started climbing the rope, inching his way to where Serif was chipping away, until he was almost halfway up the side of the cavern. With no warning, the ceiling seemed to explode from above, afternoon daylight beaming through the hole. Serif had broken through a thick plate of ice, formed across the cavern's narrow overhead peak. It was his exit to the outside world. Light constantly grew brighter as snow and ice continued to fall though the opening, revealing the actual depth of the cave below them. The fissure along the tunnel's path opened up into an infinite hole, which seemed to travel to the centre of what could have been an ancient volcano in the crust of the earth thousands of years ago.

Serif was unexpectedly engulfed in the falling snow and ice as he tried to look away from the bright sunlight. Carson was within a few yards of where he was hanging from the same rope, his body being pulled downward by the collapsing snow cap over the cavern's roof opening. The piton holding Serif's weight suddenly popped out of the crevice, and the Turkish terrorist fell abruptly – all his tools and his gun emptying out of the spelunking harness. His body's weight jerked out two more pitons from their anchors, which he had hurriedly driven into the crevices while trying to escape. Carson, too, was now dangling from the first of three remaining pitons.

The plutonium pit swung back and forth from Serif's waist in a small cloth climber's chalk bag hanging from his harness as he tried to grab hold of the rope. Using both hands to hang on, he turned himself face up again and saw that he and Carson were suspended together from the piton that controlled their destinies.

"*You!*" Serif yelled.

"It's too much weight," Carson yelled back while clutching his fists into a crack on the surface of the cavern's wall.

Carson's quick action stopped their fall to certain death, but now that his hands were both wedged into a narrow opening, he was unable to reach the Colt .45 protruding from the back of his trousers. If he could grab it with one of his hands, he might be able to shoot Serif before he scaled the rope between them. Serif started pulling himself up the taut rope hand-over-hand, his legs wrapped around the rope below him.

Carson knew he would have to let go with one hand for a few seconds to get to his gun, but as soon as he pulled it free, his other hand went with it. Both men fell downward, jerking as their weight briefly tested the first piton before it popped loose, and then the second one broke free. While still in motion, Carson pulled the gun from his trousers, took aim at where he thought Serif would be hanging below him, and fired. But Serif had already cut himself loose when the rope swung close to a short stone shelf. Soaring from his end of the rope through the cold updraft of the cavern, Serif grabbed hold of the shelf's edge, his body dangling.

Suspended from the one remaining piton, Carson swung out over the deep expanse below him once before he fired a shot near enough to the piton holding his weight to release it from its crevice. Carson's body fell toward the shelf, tumbling over where Serif was hanging onto the edge with both hands. Carson put down his gun and grabbed Serif's arms at the wrists with both hands, pulling with all his strength. The two men heard the cloth bag, still hanging from Serif's harness, rip open on a sharp rock. Both looked down just in time to see the plutonium fall out.

The two-kilo pit bounced once off Serif's foot before accelerating as it fell down into the great fissure below them. Unconsciously pausing for a few seconds in order to hear the impact of the sphere somewhere on its way through the darkness, the two men listened. But neither of them ever heard the sound of its impact on the walls or floor of the deep cavern, as the pit continued freefalling for as long as they could hold their pose.

Serif turned his sneering face toward Carson. "You think that you can stop us?"

"Actually," Carson said, grunting from Serif's weight, "I can stop you today."

Letting go of both Serif's wrists, the terrorist fell backwards.

"And worry about the rest tomorrow," Carson finished.

The expression of hatred on Serif's face was accentuated by his demonically dark skin and red-rimmed eyes as he slowly disappeared into the obscurity of the black abyss. The visual impression of Serif's final demise would be firmly fixed in Carson's memory for the rest of his life.

Remembering something sinister Serif had said to him earlier, Carson's thoughts flashed to his wife and daughter. He took a moment to think through a possible scenario whereby Serif could send one of his thugs to his home and take out his family. Carson now became frantically worried about Christy and Susan – he hadn't been able to contact them for a couple of days.

Carson picked up his dim but still operating headlamp and strapped it back on. Grabbing up as much rope as he could find, he headed back out of the cave. His lamp completely failed inside the void space just before re-entering Serif's hideout. However, he was able to feel his way to the opening that led into the aquarium room by using the ropes pinned to the cave wall. It was a welcome relief to be back inside a semi-civilised living area, for all that the air smelled of gunpowder and shit.

Climbing up the platform's ladder, he could hear the transformers underneath still buzzing with electric current supplied by the hideout's environmental support systems. Within minutes, Carson was standing at the rear door of the train, where the engineer had taken away his gun and cell phone. He ripped the door open with the last of his waning strength and climbed inside the car where he had hidden during his ride through Latvia. Carson's phone wasn't easy to find in the cluttered rail carriage because it had fallen directly into a tangled mess of old climbing harnesses. When he finally unearthed it, he frantically dialled a code to check its messages.

Carson saw Susan's call from Christy's mobile phone on his missed call list and hit the call back button. He listened intently for an answer as he walked along the railway tracks inside the vestibule of the cave toward the entrance. When he opened the heavy wooden sliding door leading outside, Christy's voicemail answered, and he ended the call. Snow covering the surrounding countryside looked grey as the short winter's day was allowing the sun to go down early that afternoon.

He noticed that a small greenish envelope was glowing on the screen of his phone now. Carson called into his voice mailbox to see if Christy had left him a message. His daughter's voice shocked him at first, and he missed some of what she had said over the television background noise. He played the message again, with the volume turned up to its ear-bleed setting. "Dad, help me!" Susan had cried.

Carson shoved the mobile phone into his pocket and ran out of the railway entrance to the cave, desperately looking for any mode of transportation. Carson heard an engine running from the top of the mountain, near where Serif had been trying to break through the ice with his pick to get out of the cave. Climbing over a ridge, he saw Serif's helicopter pilot sitting in the cockpit of his waiting chopper. Serif had used his satellite phone to call from inside the cave, once he reached the ice-capped opening, to have the pilot pluck him from the top of the mountain. His pilot would wait for Serif to break through the ice – however long that would take.

The sun extinguished itself on the crest of a forest of evergreen trees as Carson made his way up the side of the rocky mountain, using a well-worn goat path. The helicopter pilot sat in his warm cockpit, facing away from where Carson was making his laborious ascent. He never looked around to see Carson bound over the top of a boulder and run up to the chopper with his gun drawn. Jerking the pilot's door open, Carson pointed his pistol at the pilot's head and shouted over the roar of the helicopter's idling engine, "Let's go! Serif won't be coming. He decided to get in another cave dive."

———————

The flight from Latvia's wilderness to the horse pasture near Carson's home in suburban Vienna took five hours. Carson considered calling headquarters and telling Todd what was happening. But for the moment, he didn't want anyone else involved until he knew what the situation was in his family's home – not even Todd Sinclair. Confident that he was doing the right thing, he kept his phone in his pocket while watching the lights of various cities passing underneath him.

Manoeuvring the helicopter to the pasture covered by a light snow from an afternoon flurry, the pilot sat the chopper down about half a mile from Carson's home. Carson wanted to be far enough away not to be heard if his wife and daughter's captors were waiting for him but within a short jogging distance. The pilot, with Carson's gun to his head, shut the engine off. Carson quickly tied the pilot's hands and feet to the seat he was in.

The night air caused Carson to catch his breath when he jumped out of the warm helicopter onto the snow. He turned around, grabbed a green flight jacket from the storage compartment behind the passenger seat, and put it on as he started running toward his house. Carson feared that he might be too late – the message on his phone was now nearly six hours old.

When Carson reached a ground level side window of the house, he pulled out his pistol and peeked inside. The flower box mounted to the windowsill hid his face as he surveyed the living room for any movement. It looked deserted from his position, so he moved around to the back of the apartment and saw where the glass door had been broken, shards of glass scattered on both sides.

Slowly opening the door – examining the area quickly for any kind of obvious booby traps – Carson walked inside. He held his pistol out in front as he stepped toward the sofa where Susan was bound with zip-ties and lying on her right side. Susan's knees were pressed into the back of the sofa, buried in the overstuffed cushions, and her mouth was covered with a piece of tape. Her dark brown eyes were wide open, bursting with an unspoken message. She started shaking her head no and tried to scream something through the tape.

Carson looked over his daughter's twisted posture on the sofa and the area surrounding her very carefully. With her hands pulled behind her back, he could hardly see the detonator of a black landmine sitting underneath Susan's body. Situating herself between two of the three sofa cushions, Susan had wedged some kind of rod down onto the mine's armoured face. Just underneath several pillows, Carson saw the mine's safety cotter key unexpectedly pulled free. The pillows were also partially covering a thin wire that Carson followed along the sofas back until it disappeared underneath a Persian rug. Susan was using the rod to hold down the landmine's firing pin, preventing it from exploding when Carson tripped a spring-loaded device hidden underneath the rug and jerked the cotter key from its safety position.

"Hold on, Susie," Carson whispered, putting his gun away. "Don't let go 'til I tell you it's okay."

Susan held on for all she was worth, pressing the toilet's float arm into the land mine's face as hard as she could. Marius had enjoyed educating Susan about how he was going to kill her father, using her for bait and the landmine as an instrument of execution. But Susan had figured out that keeping the firing pin depressed once the safety cotter key was pulled would prevent it from exploding.

Carson reached underneath his daughter's shivering body to take the toilet bowl rod from her extremely tired fingers – relieving her of her tight grip. Susan rolled over onto her knees and, with all her remaining strength, straightened herself up, moving her body away from the bomb. Susan's movements revealed more of the stainless steel wire, allowing Carson to pull the cotter key from under the pillow and stick it back into its unique place on the bomb's collar.

Lifting the landmine gently with both hands, he walked slowly outside. With supreme care, Carson carried the device to a shallow water cistern that had long been abandoned in the pasture just down the road from their home. He kicked off the well's concrete covering and dropped the landmine down into the water. It sank safely to the bottom of the cistern without a sound. Carson ran back home and quickly cut the zip-ties that bound his daughter's hands and feet.

Susan pulled the tape from her mouth and jumped into her father's arms. "Dad!"

"You're okay, honey, you're okay! Susie, where's your mother?" Carson asked.

Susan screamed. "Upstairs! She was bleeding –"

Carson brushed back Susan's long brown hair and looked directly into her eyes. "It's going to be okay. We'll get through this."

Carson made the climb upstairs, holding his gun in one hand and moving cautiously toward Susan's bedroom. There was no evidence of the terrorists being in the Griffin home, except for the landmine that was under Susan and the bullet holes in her room. Marius had removed the Chechnyan's body, hauling it away in the white Mercedes van hours before, leaving no signs of his having been in the house.

Carson imagined that the assassin might have planted another landmine near or even under Christy's body, whose feet and legs were visible to him now. But when he saw his wife lying in a pool of blood, nothing mattered – he dropped his gun and grabbed her up in his arms. Fortunately, Marius's inexperience led him to believe that the one booby trap would be enough, and Christy was not rigged with another bomb.

Carson cried out, "Christy! Can you hear me?"

Checking her jugular for a pulse, Carson called down to Susan, who was still standing at the base of the stairs. "Call an ambulance, Susie!"

"Okay," Susan cried as she ran toward the phone.

Carson held and rocked Christy in his arms and kept repeating, "You're going to be okay, honey, you're going to be okay." His wife finally responded with a few soft moans as Carson kept rocking.

CHAPTER 36

The Delta flight from Vienna landed at Atlanta's Harts-
field International Airport on a sunny May afternoon. Susan Griffin couldn't wait to get off the plane,
go through Customs and the two security checkpoints, and,
finally, get her luggage.

When she arrived in the baggage claim area, a familiar
female voice called out, "Susie – over here!" It was her grandmother, waving excitedly as she stood there in her tan summer
slacks and sea-green silk blouse.

Susan ran over to her, and the two embraced and kissed.

"Oh, Grandma, it sure is good to see you again."

"And I've missed you so much," her grandmother said,
then pushed Susan at arm's length away from her. "My, my,
you sure are tall... and beautiful."

As the two pulled Susan's suitcases off the moving car-
ousel, her grandmother said, "I've got your room all fixed
up. I think you'll like the colours that Lilly and I picked out.
We're going to have a good time this summer before you go
off to college."

In the airport car park, Susan's grandmother guided
them to her big old Cadillac that was kept in perfect condition. "Gran, who's Lilly?" Susan asked as they put her luggage
in the trunk and then climbed into the car.

"Oh, my Jack Russell terrier... she's a puppy and going through the 'terrible two's', but you'll love her."

"I'll bet I will. And I can't wait to taste your great cooking again. Food in Vienna is okay, but I sure missed your southern fried chicken and cornbread."

"And don't forget the black-eyed peas and collard greens," her grandmother said with a laugh as she manoeuvred the car through the chaotic airport traffic and out onto the interstate.

"And," Susan added, "pecan pie for dessert."

"Of course," her grandmother said with a wink.

They were driving north to Gainesville, where Susan's grandmother had a large but cozy house. Susan would be staying with her until the summer was over and then move into the dormitory at the University of Georgia on the Athens campus. It would be the beginning of Susan's new life in the INWA protection program.

Carson and Christy had decided it would be best if their daughter lived back in the States for a few years and spent school breaks and holiday vacation times with them. They, too, had been moved to another house – this one in the mountains on the outskirts of Vienna and in an area where there were numerous homes belonging to other members of the Agency.

Susan's grandmother glanced over at her as they drove north. "Susie, we'll have plenty of time to talk about your terrible ordeal, but I just want you to know how amazingly brave and clever I know you were to have been able to do what you did.

"When I spoke to your mother while she was in the hospital, the first thing she told me about was how you had – what's the expression – 'saved the day,' by preventing the landmine from going off. She was so proud of you. So was your dad."

Susan's eyes teared up. "I don't know what I would have done if –"

"*If* didn't happen, Susie... you mustn't dwell on it, dear."

"But terrorism seems to have gotten its grip on so many countries these days."

"Yes, I know honey, but they'll be defeated one day – all those evil groups – maybe not in my lifetime, but, hopefully, in yours... evil never triumphs longer than good."

"I hope you're right."

"Be brave, Susie... you come from very good stock, you know. Both your parents are made of strong stuff."

Susan nodded and looked over at her grandmother as she pulled into the driveway of her house. Lilly could be heard barking excitedly. "Now let's see how much terror that little terrier has wrought. Last week she ate her way through two sofa cushions!"

"What did you do, Gran?" Susie asked as the two got out of the car.

"Bought another sofa!" her grandmother said as she popped open the trunk and started taking out Susie's luggage. They both laughed as they headed up the front steps of the wraparound porch of the Victorian-style house.

———

Carson had taken some time off from work to be with Christy. She was recovering sooner than her doctors had expected. Despite the large loss of blood, she had been in excellent health when the horrifying incident occurred, so she was able to get through the gruelling weeks of rehab and heal rather quickly. And she insisted that Carson get back to work sooner than later.

"You're just lolling about the house, complaining that

the weather's too cold to play golf, and since that's all you want to do –"

Carson interrupted her, taking her in his arms. "No, not all I want to do. I can think of a few other things. Well, one really," he said, kissing Christy.

Christy gave him a playful punch, and Carson held her tightly. They started to kiss again as the phone rang. "It's Susie, I know it."

"How do you know?" Carson eyed his wife curiously.

"She has an uncanny knack for interrupting our kissing," Christy said.

Just then Susie's voice, leaving a message, said, "Where are you two? Not in bed, again! It's the middle of the day there..." Christy grabbed the phone.

"Hi, sweetheart, we were just out the door... going off to play golf."

"Sure, right," Susie said with a laugh.

———

A week later, when Carson was back in his INWA office, Todd Sinclair knocked on his door. "Come in," Carson called out.

Todd entered the office, saying, "If you've got a few minutes, I'd like you to meet someone."

Carson said, "Sure," got up quickly from his desk, and followed Todd out of the office. They went to an off-limits area of the Grand Hotel and into a small conference room.

At the head of the conference table sat a tall, thin man dressed in a white silk shirt and pinstripe suit. He smiled as Carson and Todd came toward him and shook Carson's hand, saying, "It's good to finally meet the man from Cernavodă. My name is Marcel. I'm the one who took over when your father-in-law died. Please sit down."

"Good afternoon, sir," Carson said. "I've heard so much about you."

Carson sat at the table with Todd and Marcel across from him. Marcel handed Carson a red folder marked "Top Secret" that contained reconnaissance information. Carson opened the folder and thumbed through the papers and photographs. The first three photos were of Jacob, Franco, and Ciprian, and attached to each was a death certificate from an Interpol file.

"These are the terrorists I left in Riga," Carson acknowledged.

Todd looked over at Marcel and then back at Carson. "We identified them from surveillance data recovered from the nuke plant in Cernavodă. Seems the JTS got to them before we were able to perform a proper interrogation."

Producing another red folder, Marcel pushed the file across the table to Carson. "Remember this guy?"

"Yes, his name is Bogdan Saliba," Carson replied. "But you already know that from the near meltdown he created at Cernavodă."

"We've been tracking Saliba since your call from Riga giving us his location. The other terrorists were already dead by the time Interpol arrived to make the arrests, but we were able to track this guy using one of our in-country operatives. We hoped that he'd lead us to more members of the organisation, but instead he has made himself quite comfortable in the Canary Islands," Marcel stated. "Saliba had a boat waiting for him, an escape craft. He and another terrorist named Marius Zadra left from the port of Riga and headed west."

"Marius was seen the day after your home was attacked

at the Marriott Hotel in Vienna," Todd said.

Carson gazed at the file in front of him. "Do you mean Marius Zadra is still out there?"

Todd stood and walked to Carson's side of the table and put his hand on Carson's shoulder. "We've sent one of our other agents to Turkey to try to pick up Zadra's trail. But he hasn't checked in with us in over a week."

"We need to find out who is funding this group of terrorists," Marcel interjected. "And if they have contrived another plot involving nuclear material. I'm quite sure that Serif Rezaabak was only a pawn in a much larger scheme." Marcel glanced over in Todd's direction, then looked back at Carson. "Are you ready to come back to work in covert ops, Griffin?"

"We've raised your clearance level to eyes only, Carson," Todd said. "Your work in Romania and Latvia has put you in a key position to follow through with this assignment."

"I believe that Saliba's nuclear experience will be called upon again in the future," Marcel said. "Zadra will also be used in the future. He's probably going through plastic surgery right now in a clinic somewhere in the Virgin Islands."

Carson nodded. "You can count me in. Bogdan is a nuclear terrorist – the worst kind. He must be stopped."

———

Hanging up the phone after a long conversation with Susan, Christy walked outside to where Carson was pulling tea weeds from their rose garden. After his meeting with Marcel, Carson was using gardening as a convenient distraction.

"How's our girl?" Carson asked Christy.

"She's doing fine. She said she's looking forward to starting college and eating in the school cafeteria where the food is lousy and she can lose all the pounds she's gained on Grandma's home cooking."

Carson chuckled as he stood up from his crouched position then winced and rubbed his lower back.

Christy chided him, "I think you now qualify for membership in the backacher's garden club. There is one, you know, back home in Georgia." Carson brushed dirt and grass off his old denims as Christy continued, "You better ask Todd Sinclair to hurry up and give you another assignment."

Carson gave his wife a very sober look. *Little does she know*, he thought as he put his arm around her shoulder and the two walked into their house.

———

Ben Nicolescu, the young Romanian who had helped Carson last December, and had lost his girlfriend and her father in the process, now stood on the dredging machine that his father's friend used to clean the bay area near the new homes being built in Mamaia. The vacuuming device was equipped with a flexible sixty-foot trunk that sucked debris and biological growth from designated swimming areas in and around lagoons.

"I know that there is something down there, Rene!" Ben yelled to his friend over the engine's roar and the whine of the hydraulic pump.

Debris that had fallen down beside the pier where Serif's yacht had been anchored poured into the barge's holding tank behind the dredging machine. Ben vividly remembered watching Carson sneak onto Serif's yacht under cover of darkness and drop something very heavy over its side.

Now, staring down from above the holding tank, Ben waited to see anything unusual come through the flexible hose and be deposited on the screens below him. Rene moved the hose using a slow left-to-right brushstroke over the bottom of the bay's sandy floor. Ben felt sure that he knew what he would find on the bottom of the harbour as he watched the muddy debris being pumped. Years of discarded garbage from anchored vessels passed through the device and landed on the screens.

"Hold it!" Ben yelled at the top of his voice.

Rene shutdown the machine's hydraulic pumps and slowed the turbo-driven diesel engine. "Okay, take your time."

Ben's discovery of Athena, Sylesty, and their father dead in Bogdan's house and the media news about the attempted destruction of Cernavodă's nuclear facility confirmed for him that Carson had been instrumental in preventing the nuclear explosion Serif had planned. Ben was also convinced that what dropped into the Black Sea was made of weapons-grade nuclear material.

Ben jumped over into the open tank of the barge, wearing a pair of thigh-high rubber boots and carrying a short-handled flat shovel. He started digging through the stinking Black Sea dregs. Moving strips of metal, machine parts, bits of lumber, and muck, he dug frantically into the muddy mess.

Suddenly, Ben saw what he had been searching for during the past three days of sifting and digging. A black ball of heavy metal stared back at him from the middle of a child's bicycle inner tube.

ABOUT THE AUTHOR

Among the award winners of the 2005 Nobel Peace Prize given to the International Atomic Energy Agency (IAEA), **David H. Hanks** held an International Nuclear Safeguards Inspector post at the IAEA in Vienna, Austria, for several years.

His many years of experience in international nuclear nonproliferation and expertise in the operation of nuclear power plants provides a unique insight into this nuclear thriller.

Now living in Georgia, David has published several technical documents related to nuclear safeguards and wrote *The Disappearance*, a novel based on the disappearance of his mother.

Have a book idea?

Contact us at:

info@mascotbooks.com | www.mascotbooks.com